FOLLOWIN̄

FORREST REID was born in Belfast
His father died when he was still a
ing therefore fell to his rather con
As a youth he felt ill at ease with
family's Presbyterian faith, and tl
local schooling, he was apprentice̖ ... ̣̣ ̣ ̣̣
work was not demanding, and Reid coped with the tedium of commer-
cial life by retreating into a dream world of wonder and beauty, inspired
by his reading of the Greek classics.

Reid later disowned his first two novels, *The Kingdom of Twilight* (1904)
and *The Garden God* (1905). The latter risked controversy with its portrayal of romantic friendship between two boys; Reid dedicated it to his
literary idol Henry James, who was outraged and never spoke to him
again. After the death of Reid's mother, a small legacy enabled him to
devote himself more fully to his writing, and in the 1910s he published a
string of excellent, though not commercially successful novels, including
The Bracknels (1911), *Following Darkness* (1912) (said to have been an influence on Joyce's *A Portrait of the Artist as a Young Man*), *At the Door of the
Gate* (1915), *The Spring Song* (1916), and *Pirates of the Spring* (1919).

The best of Reid's works, though, came later in life, beginning with
Uncle Stephen (1931), which, with *The Retreat* (1936) and *Young Tom* (1944),
made up the *Tom Barber* trilogy, regarded by many as his masterpiece;
the final book in the trilogy won the James Tait Black Memorial Prize as
the best novel published in 1944. Reid's other mature work includes *Brian
Westby* (1934), inspired by his friendship with nineteen-year-old Stephen
Gilbert, who also went on to become a novelist, and *Peter Waring* (1937)
and *Denis Bracknel* (1947), rewritten versions of *Following Darkness* and
The Bracknels, respectively. Forrest Reid died in 1947, well regarded by
critics, but never having achieved the widespread popular recognition he
deserved. When Valancourt Books reprinted *The Garden God* in 2007, all
of Reid's books were out of print. Valancourt is now in the process of
restoring his best works to print.

ANDREW DOYLE is a playwright and stand-up comedian. His plays include
Borderland (national tour for 7:84 Theatre Company, Scotland), *Jimmy
Murphy Makes Amends* (BBC Radio 4) and *The Second Mr Bailey* (BBC
Radio 4). His most recent solo stand-up show was *Whatever It Takes* at the
Soho Theatre, London. He has a doctorate in English Renaissance Litera-
ture from the University of Oxford where he also worked as a lecturer.

By Forrest Reid

FICTION

The Kingdom of Twilight (1904)

The Garden God (1905)*

The Bracknels: A Family Chronicle (1911)

Following Darkness (1912)*

The Gentle Lover (1913)

At the Door of the Gate (1915)*

The Spring Song (1916)*

A Garden by the Sea (1918)

Pirates of the Spring (1919)

Pender Among the Residents (1922)

Demophon: A Traveller's Tale (1927)

Uncle Stephen (1931)*

Brian Westby (1934)*

The Retreat (1936)*

Peter Waring (1937)

Young Tom (1944)*

Denis Bracknel (1947)*

NON-FICTION

W. B. Yeats: A Critical Study (1915)

Apostate (1926)

Illustrators of the Sixties (1928)

Walter de la Mare: A Critical Study (1929)

Private Road (1940)

Retrospective Adventures (1941)

Notes and Impressions (1942)

Poems from the Greek Anthology (1943)

The Milk of Paradise: Some Thoughts on Poetry (1946)

* Available or forthcoming from Valancourt Books
(N.B.—Valancourt has republished Uncle Stephen, The Retreat, and Young Tom in a
single volume under the title The Tom Barber Trilogy.)

FOLLOWING DARKNESS

FORREST REID

"Lost, lost, for ever lost,
In the wide pathless desert of dim sleep,
That beautiful shape!"

SHELLEY.

With a new introduction by
ANDREW DOYLE

VALANCOURT BOOKS

Following Darkness by Forrest Reid
First published London: Edward Arnold, 1912
First Valancourt Books edition 2013

Published by Valancourt Books, Kansas City, Missouri
Publisher & Editor: JAMES D. JENKINS
20th Century Series Editor: SIMON STERN, University of Toronto
http://www.valancourtbooks.com

Library of Congress Cataloging-in-Publication Data

Reid, Forrest, 1875-1947.
  Following darkness / by Forrest Reid ; with a new introduction
by Andrew Doyle. – First Valancourt Books edition.
    pages ; cm. – (20th century series)
  ISBN 978-1-939140-53-1 (alk. pbk.)
  I. Title.
  PR6035.E43F65 2013
  823'.912–dc23

                              2013017953

Set in Dante MT 11/13.5

INTRODUCTION

FORREST REID (1875-1947) was all too well aware of the fickle nature of literary trends. By 1930 he was arguing that forgotten gems such as Richard Jefferies's *Bevis* (1882), F. Anstey's *The Pariah* (1889), and Margaret L. Woods's *A Village Tragedy* (1889) "ought, if out of print, to be reprinted".[1] *Following Darkness* (1912) also falls into this category, a novel once described by E. M. Forster as "a masterpiece", yet now virtually unknown even amongst students of literature.[2] This present edition is the first reissue since it was published a little over a century ago. That such a powerful and important work should have fallen into relative obscurity is proof, if proof were needed, that quality is no guarantee of longevity.

Reid was correct in his assertion that *Following Darkness* was "the first novel of its kind to be written in English".[3] This new, daring form of *bildungsroman* predated both Compton Mackenzie's *Sinister Street* (1913) and James Joyce's *A Portrait of the Artist as a Young Man* (1916). Faced with a work of such startling originality, a number of critics balked. Anne Macdonell of *The Manchester Guardian* decried its lead character, the adolescent Peter Waring, as "a subject for the pathologist rather than the novelist", a figure with "evil tendencies" who "unutterably disgusts".[4] She later wrote to Reid to ask why he should "flatter by elaborate analysis a boy's aping of better sinners than himself".[5]

The extent of this misreading can hardly be overstated. Macdonell's objections are those of the Christian moralist who idealizes youth as a period of prelapsarian innocence. The expectation of sentimentality—what Brian Taylor describes as that "almost universal fatality for those who write about childhood"—means that *Following Darkness* will always be likely to disturb readers of a certain disposition.[6] In this respect, Macdonell has much in common with Peter's father, a man whose puritanical traditionalism precludes any possibility of empathy with his son. "Though he loved me," says Peter, "I felt he did not trust me, or rather that

he believed I had an infinite capacity for yielding to temptation."
The events of the novel prove his father right, and it is Reid's
unflinchingly honest portrayal of adolescence, his refusal to sentimentalize, that makes *Following Darkness* such uncomfortable
reading for the likes of Macdonell. It is also precisely why it is so
successful.

Peter Waring is one of Reid's most fascinating creations; a
deeply flawed, morally ambiguous figure who nonetheless earns
our sympathy. He is capable of the most appalling snobbery, and
his reaction when confronted with a senile but harmless pensioner
in the Botanic Gardens is downright vicious: "His fumbling hands,
his foolish, empty pipe, his bleared and rheumy eyes, depressed
me, and I wondered why he couldn't be put into a lethal chamber."
Such an extreme response, brought about by nothing more than
irritation, nevertheless rings true as an example of the emotional
caprice of the adolescent. As Peter admits: "The spirit of youth is
not merely bright and vivacious; above all, it is not merely thoughtless and noisy. It is melancholy, dreamy, passionate; it is admirable,
and it is base; it is full of curiosity; it is healthy, and it is morbid;
it is animal, and it is spiritual; sensual, yet filled with vague, half-
realized yearnings after an ideal."

Peter's acrimonious relationship with his staunchly religious
father is a deftly drawn study of intergenerational conflict, rem-
iniscent of Edmund Gosse's groundbreaking autobiography
Father and Son (1907). Peter seeks refuge from his father through
his regular visits to Derryaghy House, the home of the wealthy
widow Mrs. Carroll who has promised to fund Peter's education in
Belfast. For Peter, life with his father is a stifling affair, an existence
of "colourless, melancholy monotony", whereas Derryaghy repre-
sents the possibility of creative and intellectual liberty. When Peter
brings home a copy of Shakespeare's *Venus and Adonis*, it is the
poem's erotic content that most displeases his father. "It is full of
all kinds of voluptuous images and thoughts", he complains. "You
have been too much at Derryaghy lately." Mr. Waring's assessment
of the poem is accurate enough, but it is not Shakespeare that he
truly fears; in his world of Christian piety, Peter's incipient sexuality must be curbed at all costs.

This is the backdrop to Peter's desire for Katherine Dale, Mrs. Carroll's niece who, with her brother Gerald, comes to stay at Derryaghy. Reid's friend John Bryson saw *Following Darkness* as essentially "the story of a boy's unrequited first love with all its changing moods of devotion and despair", but the reality is far more complex and intriguing.[7] What sentimentalists might interpret as first love is, as Reid makes clear, nothing more than a romanticized infatuation, one that has become inflated through the temperament of this unique and sensitive youth.

During his sojourns at Derryaghy, Peter is irrepressibly drawn to the portraits of Mrs. Carroll's ancestors.

> There was something almost vulgar in being physically alive among that shadowy company. I longed to pass the threshold of their world and learn its secrets. Perhaps if I were really to love that dark, sweet lady, Prudence Carroll, to declare my love, to kiss her painted lips, I might be admitted to it. Would she be jealous when I left her? To love a dream, a memory, that was very possible; but to be faithful to it? (*Following Darkness*, Chapter XI)

When Katherine appears on the scene, Peter's obsession leads him to detect a resemblance, albeit one that is more spiritual than physical. His longing for Prudence is projected onto Katherine, so that she becomes a kind of avatar of her deceased relative. "She had the same eyes," Peter tells himself, "the same expression . . . perhaps, then, the same spirit . . . A sort of daydream had begun to weave itself into my thoughts". He even goes so far as to suggest to Katherine that she may be the reincarnation of Prudence, a notion she immediately dismisses as nonsense. With this in mind, it becomes clear that when Peter eventually paints his own portrait of Katherine, it is not the symbol of unrequited love that it at first appears to be. Rather, it is Peter's unconscious attempt to recreate the portrait of Prudence Carroll, the idealized object of his desire.

This obsession of Peter's entails a peculiar fusion of *eros* and *thanatos*, not solely in his invocation of the dead Prudence through the living Katherine, but also in his tendency to envisage the latter's death. One example occurs in Chapter XII, when Peter insists on taking her to see an old graveyard. "You are buried here," he says to Katherine, a joke she finds singularly distasteful. Later, as they sit together by the coast, Peter is moved to recite Edgar Allan Poe's poem "Annabel Lee", in which the speaker declares his love for a woman who has died of exposure. "It was written about this place," Peter tells Katherine, knowing full well that this cannot be the case. His intention is to recast Katherine as Annabel, but she is oblivious to his macabre fantasy. On another occasion, he imagines himself dying after an unspecified accident: "suddenly Katherine rode up and springing down from her horse threw her arms round me, kneeling in the blood and dust of the road". That Peter is sexually aroused by images of death and violence reveals an understanding, however latent, that the realization of an ideal entails its destruction. Like Petrarch's Laura, the death of the loved one immortalizes the desire, and so ennobles it.

In Russell Burlingham's invaluable study of Reid, he argues that there is "nothing overtly sexual, little even of sensuality" in Reid's novels, and yet Peter's physical and psychological development is inextricably linked with his libido.[8] As Peter goes through puberty he is aware of new physical sensations: "My voice had altered; my mind was coloured by vague and happy dreams. Sometimes when I turned in bed or stretched myself, the contact of the fine linen sheets against my skin gave me a peculiar thrill, which ran all down my spine." Likewise suggestive is Peter's moonlit walk across the golf-links by the shore after having posted an ill-advised love letter to Katherine. Responding to his instinctive animism, he senses that the earth beneath him is "living and breathing" and kisses the grass.

> I was filled with a passionate sense of life, and lying there . . . I could look out over the sea, and feel myself perfectly alone . . . My head was bare, the salt sharp smell of the sea seemed to have set all my nerves tingling, and I unfastened my shirt that my breast might be bare also. All the past had slipped from me, and I lived in this moment, squeezing out its ecstasy to the last drop, as I might the juice of some ripe fruit. (*Following Darkness*, Chapter X)

There is rather more than a thin bat's squeak of sexuality in such imagery. What is being described here, of course, is Peter's first experience of masturbation. This is presumably the episode to which Reid was referring in a letter to Theodore Bartholomew: "There was only one risky thing in the book, and nobody has grasped it."[9] Notably, the *double entendre* "I could . . . feel myself perfectly alone" was omitted when Reid rewrote the novel as *Peter Waring* (1937).

Moreover, Peter's crippling sense of shame towards the end of the novel is clearly sexual in origin. Having moved to Belfast to attend school, he is compelled to live with his Uncle George and Aunt Margaret in a garret room above their shop. This working-class environment brings out Peter's inherent snobbery, not least because he has to share the room with his cousin George. On his first night in Belfast George shows him a picture of a semi-naked young woman and tries to initiate a discussion about sex. Peter is uncomfortable with George's "Rabelaisian talk"; evidently he prefers his own private idealizations of love. Eventually, George produces some photographs of a more pornographic nature:

> "I don't want to see them," I said, pushing him away; but he may have detected a note of weakness in my voice, for he only laughed.
> "Don't be a fool," he answered brutally. "I'm not going to do you any harm."
> He drew them from the envelope and showed them to me, one by one, while the gas flamed and flared above our heads.
> (*Following Darkness*, Chapter XXVIII)

Subsequently, Peter feels as though his mind "had been gradually submitted to a poisonous influence . . . like a vapour from some fever-breeding marsh", and this realization coincides with his first suicidal thoughts and a desire to confess to a Catholic priest. If the extent of Peter's shame seems conspicuously disproportionate, this is perhaps explained in Reid's rewriting of the passage in *Peter Waring*:

> He drew the photographs from the envelope and showed them to me, one by one, while the gas flamed and flared above our heads.
> I tried to push him away, but he bent closer. Then: "Don't be a

fool," he said suddenly, in a low thick voice. "I'm not going to do you any harm." (*Peter Waring,* Chapter XXVIII)

There the chapter ends. By simply altering the order of the sentences, Reid has created a provocatively inferential lacuna. In this latter version, the likelihood that Peter and George have engaged in sexual activity with each other is far more pronounced.

The exploration of an adolescent's burgeoning self-awareness, both sexual and spiritual, is typical of Reid's *oeuvre*. But *Following Darkness* is unique amongst his fiction in being the only narrative told in the first person, and so the author is able to offer unmediated access to the psychological development of his boy hero. Reading his novels is like stepping back into the lost mindset of youth. The recreation is eerily authentic; Reid somehow manages to convey that wonderfully naive, part idealistic, part solipsistic realm of the imagination that is eventually obliterated through the process of maturity. I can think of no other author who has come close to this accomplishment. The scope may be narrow, but within those limitations Reid is unsurpassed.

Of Reid's sixteen novels, only two—*The Gentle Lover* (1913) and *Demophon* (1927)—are set outside of his native Ulster. For the most part, the story of *Following Darkness* takes place in the rural landscape of Newcastle, County Down, in the shadows of the Mourne Mountains. But for Peter this landscape is a kind of palimpsest upon which two realities compete for prominence. He exists in the penumbra of a dreamscape. He repeatedly refers to his "dreamland", a place of "deep lagoons, and sleepy rivers winding slowly down through green lawns and meadowlands", an idyll that exists beneath the patina of everyday life. He fantasizes that he might one day "find a magic door leading into a strange world that was yet quite close at hand". As far as Peter is concerned, there is no distinction between the oneiric and the mundane, what he terms "a sort of undercurrent of dreaming that ran through my life".

Peter's philosophical outlook is that of the pantheist, and it is his sense of a metaphysical communion with nature that partly accounts for his ultimate apostasy. This is most vividly expressed in Peter's dream in Chapter XXXIII, during which Jesus Christ materializes and demands Peter's submission. Curiously, this Christ figure has a "narrow effeminate face, pointed beard, and a soft treacherous expression in the slanting eyes". Peter refuses to kneel before him and instead pledges his fealty to Satan, at which point the face of Christ becomes distorted with a "horrible look of baffled rage and malice" as he disappears with a "shrill scream". This sinister encounter is then unexpectedly eroticized by the appearance of a naked "dark angel" who undresses Peter, anoints him, and brands him upon his chest before dragging him to Hell.

It is perhaps this aspect of *Following Darkness* that most disturbed Reid's critics. It is telling that when Reid came to rewrite the novel he excised this particular sequence, but the pantheism of his principal character was retained and reinforced. For a Christian reader, such allegiances to ideals rooted in Greek antiquity were bound to be interpreted as Satanic, and it is perhaps this view that explains Peter's dream. It is the Christ figure who is the stuff of nightmares; the demon assumes the role of saviour, alluring and protective, and Hell is redefined as a place where there is "no torture" and no pain. In an article that appeared just after Reid's death in 1947, E. M. Forster wrote of the novel that "some critics sensed Satanism in its title, and became excited. Idiots, they had forgotten Puck's 'Following darkness like a dream.'"[10] Maybe it is true that the Shakespearean allusion had been missed, but it is surely no great stretch of the imagination to see heretical overtones in Reid's imagery.

Heresy, of course, depends upon perspective. Reid's renunciation of his father's Protestantism was not motivated by spite or malevolence or even rationality. It was purely instinctive. His was a creed of life, not death. Christianity, with its emphasis on eschatology and the doctrine of vicarious redemption through the sacrifice of Jesus, had no appeal for him. He saw it as a death-cult, quite opposed to the life-affirming ideologies of Plato and Socrates. That Peter Waring should share the pagan sensibilities of his creator is no great surprise. Reid often allows his characters to discover what he already believes to be true and, in Peter's case, his break from religion is an integral aspect of the formation of his identity.

Peter's ultimate fate remains a mystery. We know that he

becomes an art critic, a career anticipated in his comparisons of Katherine's beauty with the work of Renoir and Whistler. The narrator of the prologue, his Belfast friend Owen Gill, claims that he may have dabbled in the occult, perhaps suggesting that he was forever trying to find ways to resurrect the memory of Prudence Carroll. Owen is convinced that he became a victim of murder, but no further details are forthcoming. Some critics have argued that Reid had intended a sequel, which would explain why these elements were deleted when the novel came to be rewritten. Indeed, there is a tantalizing reference to Peter Waring "the art-critic" in *At the Door of the Gate* (1915), Reid's novel of lower middle-class Belfast. But perhaps it is more fitting that Peter should remain forever young in the mind of the reader.

In a private letter to Reid written after the publication of *Following Darkness*, the psychologist G. Stanley Hall called it "the best presentation of the psychical phenomena of the adolescent ferment that I have ever seen".[11] But it is the novel's poeticism and essential humanity that should guarantee its survival. It is a paean to Reid's unconditional love for his homeland, a Hellenized Ulster in which dreamscape and reality can co-exist. In this sense, it is a mythopoeic achievement, a genre-defying work of astonishing subtlety and poise. In his review of Reid's novel *Pirates of the Spring* (1919), E. M. Forster envisioned a day when Reid's genius would finally gain "the recognition that has so strangely been withheld from it".[12] Reid himself had predicted the fate of *Following Darkness*. "I have an idea," he wrote, "that the book is going to fall dead into the limbo of failures".[13] He was aware that his disinclination to sentimentalize in his depiction of youth might limit the novel's appeal, and yet he steadfastly refused to write "with an eye to the public and what it wants".[14] For that, we can be eternally grateful.

ANDREW DOYLE

April 29, 2013

NOTES

1   Forrest Reid, *Retrospective Adventures* (London: Faber & Faber, 1940), p. 74.

2   E. M. Forster, "The Work of Forrest Reid", *Nation* (10 April 1920).

3   Forrest Reid, *Private Road* (London: Faber & Faber, 1940), p. 117.

4   Anne Macdonell, review, *Manchester Guardian* (4 December 1912).

5   *Private Road*, op. cit., p. 120.

6   Brian Taylor, *The Green Avenue: The Life and Writings of Forrest Reid, 1875-1947* (Cambridge: Cambridge University Press, 1980), p. 185.

7   John Bryson, "Forrest Reid and the Early Novels", *Threshold* 28 (Spring 1977), pp. 16-26. See p. 23.

8   Russell Burlingham, *Forrest Reid: A Portrait and Study* (London: Faber and Faber, 1953), p. 56.

9   Quoted in Michael Matthew Kaylor, *Arch-Priest of a Minor Cult: A Study of Forrest Reid*, published as vol. II of *The Tom Barber Trilogy* (Kansas City: Valancourt Books, 2011), p. 60.

10 E. M. Forster, "Forrest Reid 1876-1947", *The Listener* (16 January 1947).

11 *Private Road*, op. cit., p. 120.

12 Forster (1920), op. cit., p. 77.

13 Taylor, op. cit., p. 70.

14 Ibid.

NOTE ON THE TEXT

Following Darkness was published by Edward Arnold of London in 1912, in crown octavo format at a price of six shillings. Although Forrest Reid published a rewritten version of the book in 1937 under the title *Peter Waring*, the present edition is the first-ever reprint of the original text of *Following Darkness*. The text of the first edition has been reprinted here verbatim and without any change in spelling or punctuation.

FOLLOWING DARKNESS

TO E.M.F.

FOLLOWING DARKNESS

It is not without some hesitation that I offer to the public the following fragment of an autobiography, even though in doing so I am but obeying the obvious intention of its author. When the papers of Mr. Peter Waring came into my possession I had indeed no idea of its existence, and I have now no means of telling when it was written. The fact that he left it unfinished proves nothing. He may have begun it and abandoned it years ago: he may have been working at it shortly before his death. That he intended to carry it to completion, there is, I think, abundant evidence in a mass of detached notes and impressions bearing on a later period of his life. These, rightly or wrongly, I have not printed, partly because the earlier portion has in itself a certain unity and completeness, which would be marred were I to add anything to it, and partly because they never received his personal revision. Moreover, many of them are in the highest degree fantastic and exotic, so that it is at times difficult to take them literally, especially if the simplicity and directness of the earlier pages be borne in mind.

Those who are familiar with Mr. Waring's writings published during his lifetime—writings in which the personal element is so slight—will hardly be prepared for anything so intimate as this journal. His critical methods were entirely scientific. Of their value I am not the proper person to speak, having neither the necessary knowledge, nor, to tell the whole truth, the necessary sympathy. Our paths, if they seemed to run parallel for a moment, diverged very early in life, and I could never take much interest in the work to which he devoted his real, though, I venture to think, somewhat narrow gifts. He was still a young man—barely thirty-six—when he died, but he had already become eminent in his own particular line, that of the newer art criticism, invented, I believe, by the Italian, Morelli. It was scarcely a career to bring him much under the public eye, but his "Study of the Drawings of the Early Italian

Masters" gained him, I understand, the recognition of a small
number of persons, of various nationalities, occupied in making
similar researches. He was busy with the proofs of the second and
larger edition of this work when, on the 10th of September, 1911,
he died under tragic circumstances. The mystery of his death,
about which there was some noise in the papers at the time, will,
I think, never now be cleared up, though, to my own mind, it is
perfectly clear that he was murdered.

In relation to the autobiography, a word or two of comment
and explanation is possibly due to the reader. To begin with, I have
altered all the proper names save two—my own, and that of Mrs.
Carroll, of Derryaghy, Newcastle, County Down, his oldest friend,
which I have allowed to remain. I feel this, myself, to be unsatisfactory, but I cannot see how at present it is to be avoided. Again,
though I have added nothing, I have left out a few pages—only a
few—and none, I believe, of importance, so far as the understanding of the whole is concerned. For this I have no excuse to offer,
except that it seemed to me that he himself should have omitted
them.

In the main the portrait he has given of himself coincides with
my own impression of him in early life. I can remember very well
when I first came to know him at school. I was more struck by his
gifts then, perhaps, than I was later, though even at that time he
seemed to me to be intensely one-sided. He was very intelligent,
but from the beginning his whole manner of looking upon life was,
in my opinion, unfortunate. It may sound harsh to say so, but as
the years passed I do not think he improved. Latterly, he appeared
to me to have little but his fine taste. It was as if everything had
become subservient to an æsthetic sense, which was extraordinarily, morbidly acute. Yet even while I write this I have a suspicion
that I am not doing him justice. If he had been nothing but what I
say he was, I should not be able to look back with tenderness upon
the friendship of those early days, whereas the recollection of that
friendship will always remain one of the pleasantest memories
of my life. I regret that it should have been broken, but that was
almost inevitable. It came about slowly and naturally, though no

doubt the actual break was hastened by a mutual friend of ours, who informed me that Waring had described me as borné and tedious. That is the kind of thing which rankles. You may say to yourself it is of no consequence, but to have an uneasy feeling that your friend finds your company dull quickly becomes unendurable. A man would rather be thought almost anything than a bore; hence it was that for a long time I entirely ceased to see him. I regret it now, for he may never have made the fatal remark, and even if he did, judging from his journal, it need not have been inconsistent with affection.

The last time I saw him was at Mrs. Carroll's house, about a year before his death. She had asked me down, I suppose by Waring's request, and I went, though I stayed only one night. I had not seen him for years until this occasion, and I was struck, and even shocked, by his altered appearance, and still more by his manner, which was that, I imagined, of a man haunted by some secret thought that has come between him and everything about him. This impression, though I do not desire to lay stress upon it, may throw a light on certain of the later notes I have not printed, and these, in turn, may afford some clue as to the mystery surrounding his death, for it is evident that he had come under the influence of strange and disreputable persons, who professed to experiment in occult sciences—spiritualism, and even magic. His hair had turned quite white at the temples. He seemed restless and dissatisfied; and, whatever else he may have found in his long wanderings, I could not believe he had found peace.

Late in the evening we sat together. He was so silent that I looked at him to see if he had fallen asleep. The room we were sitting in—the morning-room—gave on to a garden at the side of the house, into which one could easily pass through tall French windows. The night was warm, and one of these windows stood wide open, letting in the scent of flowers, but with a curtain drawn across it to keep out moths and other winged creatures attracted by lamplight. I did not speak, but waited for him to talk or to keep silent as he chose. After a while I got up to examine a few black-framed etchings that hung upon the walls. These, with some pieces of china, formed the only decorations. I drew back the curtain and looked out into the night. The moon was high above the trees, and I could hear the low sound of waves breaking on the shore. When I turned round he was watching me, and I was struck by his expression, which was that of a man on the point of making some very private communication. But perhaps my sudden movement disconcerted him, for he said nothing, and in a little I could see the impulse had left him. I began to talk, not of my own work, which I thought would have no interest for him, but of his, which I was surprised to find he seemed to regard as equally unimportant. I asked him what had first led him to take it up.

"There was nothing else," he answered.

Seeing that I waited for him to go on, he made an effort to shake off his abstraction. "If I hadn't found it I should have bored myself to death. What is there for a boy of eighteen, with no taste for society, and left to wander about Europe alone, to do? Fortunately, I had always cared for pictures, and early Italian art appealed to me particularly."

"Of course, you had your writing."

"I never wrote a line except to take notes. I was nearly thirty before it occurred to me to publish anything. Even then, it was only for a few pedants more or less like myself that I wrote. My writings are of no account. The only people I can imagine it pleasant to write for are quite young people. They might lend your work a sort of charm by reading their own youth and enthusiasm into it. But it is not easy to arouse enthusiasm by describing how Bernardino de' Conti paints ears, or how Pontormo models hands. For one thing, nobody wants to know. All that it leads to is that presently you find yourself approaching the most innocent work of art with the mind of a detective, revelling in clues and the æsthetically unimportant. Nine-tenths of your enjoyment comes from the gratified sense of your own ingenuity. Of course it is wrong. When I was a boy I fell in love with one of Giotto's frescoes in the Upper Church at Assisi, a thing half-peeled from the wall, and representing Saint Francis preaching to the birds. But why I liked it had nothing in the world to do either with Giotto or Saint Francis. I simply saw a bit of decoration, a Japanese print in gray and blue. . . . . That is the proper spirit. One day, however, a year or so later, I was in the Louvre, in the Salle des Primitifs, and before me was a beautiful little picture which hangs on the side wall, near the door. Below it was printed an artist's name, Gentile da Fabriano. I looked at the picture again, and I said to myself, 'Why Gentile, when it is obviously by Jacopo Bellini?' That was the beginning."

"You don't think, then, it matters very much?"

"About Gentile? Not in the least. I haven't even persuaded them to make the alteration in the catalogue."

But I could see he was talking merely not to be silent, so I got up and we lit our candles. At the top of the staircase I said good-night, for our bedrooms were on opposite sides of the house, but he pushed open a door. "There is a picture here," he said.

I followed him into the big, dark room, black shadows that seemed almost solid gliding away before us. He took my candle and held both up so that their light flickered across a small canvas that hung just above the level of our eyes. The painting represented the head of a quite young girl, and I recognised it at once as a portrait of Katherine Dale. I am no judge of pictures, so I will only say that this picture gave me pleasure. Yet I should have hesitated to call the face beautiful, and it certainly was not pretty. It reminded me rather of an early Millais—that is to say, the subject reminded me of a Millais type. There was the same breadth of forehead, the same rich colouring and steadfast, serious eyes that were more like the eyes of a boy than of a girl. I wondered why he had brought me in to look at it just now, and thought it had perhaps been painted by a celebrated artist.

"Whose is it?" I asked, and was greatly surprised when he told me he had done it himself, from memory. I had never seen any of his work before, and I congratulated him on his success, which seemed to me to be really a genuine one. I asked another question, but he did not reply. He merely returned me my candle, which I held up for another look. The small, wavering, uncertain flame lent a curious air of life to the portrait, and I continued to regard it, for the frankness and simplicity of the young face gave me great pleasure. When I glanced round I discovered I was alone. My companion had disappeared without my noticing it, and evidently he

had gone out, not by the way we had entered, but by another door
at the farther end of the room. That this was the case I had more
positive proof next moment, for a sudden draught extinguished
my candle so swiftly and unexpectedly that I had an odd feeling
that somebody had stolen up behind me and blown it out.

OWEN GILL.

CHAPTER I

WHAT is there in this house, in these surroundings, so utterly different from those I was born amongst, that revives a swarm of
memories of my childhood and youth? My notes are piled up on
the table before me, they have been there for several days, and
I have not touched them, though I came here to work. A warm
Italian sun floods the stiff and formal garden stretching from my
window, with its pale paved walks, its fountain, and dark cypress-
trees; but when I shut my eyes, it is quite another garden that I see,
and now, when I have at last taken up my pen to write, it is not
to fulfil the task I had set myself, but to chatter idly of a boyhood
passed under other skies, grayer, softer, and colder. The odd fact is
that ever since my arrival here, in spite of my being upon "classic
soil," in a district rich in historical suggestion, and full, too, of
the colour and odour of the south, I have been communing daily,
hourly almost, with my own youth. I should like to set down
simply what that youth was, without embroidery, without sup-
pression, though, on the other hand, a mere bald enumeration of
the outward facts will be little to my purpose. The facts in themselves are nothing. Unless I can recapture the spirit that hovered
behind them, my task will have been fruitless, and even though
in my effort to do so I shall probably accentuate it, alter it, clip its
wings and make it heavy, yet that must be my aim if I am to write
at all. I have little eloquence, and perhaps no power of evocation,
but the whole great, soft, time-toned picture is before me at this
moment, and I cannot resist the temptation to linger over it. If I
linger over it pen in hand, what matter?

In the foreground there must be the portrait of a boy, but painted in the manner of Rembrandt rather than Bronzino. By this I mean there will be less of firm, clear outline, than of light and shadow. The danger is that in the end there may be too much shadow; but at least I shall not, in the manner of a writer of fiction, have sacrificed my subject for the sake of gaining an additional brightness and vivacity. The spirit of youth is not merely bright and vivacious; above all, it is not merely thoughtless and noisy. It is melancholy, dreamy, passionate; it is admirable, and it is base; it is full of curiosity; it is healthy, and it is morbid; it is animal, and it is spiritual; sensual, yet filled with vague half-realised yearnings after an ideal—that is to say, it is the spirit of life itself, which can never be adequately indicated by the description of a fight or of a football match.

CHAPTER II

OF my earliest childhood I can form no consecutive picture; I shall therefore pass over it quickly. Certain incidents stand out with extraordinary vividness, but the chain uniting them is wanting, and it is even impossible for me to be quite sure as to the order in which they occurred. Some are so trivial that I do not know why I should remember them; others, at the time, doubtless, more important, have now lost their significance; and countless others, again, I must have completely forgotten. But it occurs to me, on looking back deliberately, that I have changed very little from what I was in those first years. I have developed, but what I was then I am now, what I cared for then I care for now. In other words, like everybody else, I came into this world a mere bundle of inherited instincts, for the activity of which I was no more responsible than for the falling of last night's rain.

Of the dawning of consciousness I have no recollection whatever. Back farther than anything else there reach two impressions—one, of being set to dance naked on a table, amid the laughter of women, and the rhythmic clapping of their hands; the other, probably later in date, of what must have been a housecleaning, stamped on my mind by an inexplicable fear of those flakey collections of dust which gather under furniture that has not been moved for a long time. By then I had certainly learned to talk, for those flakes of dust I called "quacks." I do not know where the name came from, nor why I should have disliked "quacks," but they affected me with a strange dread, and here was a whole army of them where I had never seen but one or two. Some stupid person running after me with a broom pretended to sweep them over me, and I started bawling at the top of my voice. Then, for consolation, I was lifted up to bury my nose in a bowl of violets, and the colour and sweetness of the flowers took away my trouble. Probably it was later than this that I first became aware of a peculiar sensibility to dress—not to underclothing, but to my outer garments. To be dressed in a new suit of clothes gave me a curious physical pleasure—a feeling purely sensual, and that must, I imagine, have been connected with the dawn of obscure sex instincts. Such things can be of little interest save to the student of psychology, and it would be tedious to catalogue them in full, but I have no doubt myself that if they, and others, had been intelligently observed, the whole of my future could have been cast from them. To me, I confess, they throw a disquieting light upon all human affairs, reviving that sombre figure of destiny which overshadowed the antique world.

Another and happier instinct which I brought with me from the unknown was an intense sympathy with animals. There was not a cat or dog or goat or donkey in the village that I had not struck up a friendship with. I even carried this sympathy so far as to insist on feeding daily the ridiculous stone lions which flanked the doorsteps at Derryaghy House. I don't think I ever actually believed that their morning meal of stale bread gave much pleasure to these patient beasts, and I had with my own eyes seen sparrows and thrushes—who very soon came to look out for me—snatch it from them before my back was turned; still, I persevered, stroking their smooth backs, kissing their cold muzzles, just as I lavished depths of affection on a stuffed, dilapidated, velvet elephant who for many years was my nightly bed-fellow.

My only impressions of my mother go back to those days or, possibly, earlier—a voice singing gay songs to the piano, while I dropped asleep in my bed upstairs—and then, again, somebody lifting me out of this bed to kiss me, the close contact of a face wet with tears, the pressure of arms that held me clasped tightly, that even hurt a little. That is all. I cannot remember how she looked, or anything else. On the evening when she said good-bye to me and left our house, I knew she was crying, but, though it called up in me a sort of solemn wonder, I did not understand it, and went to sleep almost as soon as she put me back into my bed. It was not till next day that my own tears came, with the first real sorrow I had known.

There follows now a sort of blank in my recollections, which continues on to my ninth or tenth year. I do not know why this period should have been so unproductive of lasting impressions. It is like a tranquil water over which I bend in the hope of seeing some face or vision ripple to the surface, but my hope is disappointed. Nothing emerges—not even a memory of any of those ailments, measles and what not, from which, in common with other children, I suppose I must have suffered. Nor can I recollect learning to read. I can remember quite well when I couldn't read, for I have a very distinct recollection of lying on my stomach, on the parlour floor, a book open in front of me, along whose printed, meaningless lines I drew my finger, turning page after page till the last was reached, though what solemn pleasure I could have got from so dull a game—surely the most tedious ever invented—I now utterly fail to comprehend.

I was always very fond of being read to, except when the story had a moral, or was about pious children, when I hated it. The last of these moral tales I listened to was called "Cassy." I particularly disliked it, but I can remember now only one scene, where Cassy comes into an empty house at night, and discovers a corpse there. This had an effect on my mind which for several days made me extremely reluctant to go upstairs by myself after dark. "Jessica's First Prayer," "Vinegar Hill," "The Golden Ladder"—how I loathed them all! Every Sunday, after dinner, my father would take some such volume from the shelf, open it, and put on his spectacles. Holding the book at a long distance from his eyes, he would read aloud in a monotonous, unanimated voice, while I sat on a high-backed chair and listened, for I was not allowed to play the most innocent game, nor even to go out for a walk. These miserable tales were full of the conversions of priggish children; of harrowing scenes in public-houses or squalid city dens. Some of them were written to illustrate the Ten Commandments; others to illustrate the petitions in the Lord's Prayer. They contained not the faintest glimmer of imagination or life: from cover to cover they were ugly, dull, unintelligent, full of death, poverty and calamity. On the afternoon when "Cassy's" successor was produced—I forget its name—in a state of exasperation, brought about by mingled boredom and depression, I snatched the book out of my father's hands and flung it on the fire. I was whipped and sent to bed, but anything was better than "Vinegar Hill," and next Sunday, also, I refused to listen. Again, with tingling buttocks, I was banished to the upper regions, but really I had triumphed, for when the fateful day came round once more, the book-case was not opened, and I had never again to listen to one of those sanctimonious tales.

Fairy stories and animal stories were what I liked best, while some of the old nursery rhymes and jingles had a fascination for me.

> "How many miles to Babylon?
>   Three score and ten.
> Can I get there by candlelight?—
>   Yes, and back again."

Was it some magical suggestion in the word "candlelight" that invariably evoked in a small child's mind a definite picture of an old fantastic town of towers and turrets, lit by waving candles, and with windows all ablaze in dark old houses? Many of these rhymes had this quality of picture making:

> "Hey, diddle diddle,
>   The cat and the fiddle,
> The cow jumped over the moon:
>   The little dog laughed
>   To see such sport
> When the dish ran away with the spoon."

That, I suppose, is pure nonsense, yet the magic was there. Before and after the cow made her amazing leap the stuff was a mere jingle: it was the word "Moon" that brought up the picture: and I saw the white, docile beast, suddenly transformed, pricked by the sting of midsummer madness, with lowered head and curling horns, poised for flight, for the wonderful upward leap, while a monstrous, glowing moon hung like a great scarlet Chinese lantern in the clouds, low against a black night.

At this time I had few books I cared for, but as I grew older, and my powers of understanding increased, I found more, for up at Derryaghy House was a whole library in which I might rummage without any other interference than that my father could exercise from a distance. Sometimes when I brought a book home which he did not approve of, he would send me back with it; but if I had begun it I always finished it. I had made this a rule; though, on the other hand, if I had not begun it, I let my father have his way.

Everything connected with the East had a deep attraction for me—or, shall I say, what I imagined the East to be—a country of magicians and mysterious talismans, of crouching Sphinxes and wonderful gardens. I delighted in the more marvellous stories in the "Arabian Nights," and I regretted infinitely that life was really not like that. To go for a walk and fall straightway on some wonderful adventure, that was what I should have loved. I remember poring over a big folio of photographs of Eastern monuments. Those mystical, winged beasts with human heads, in their attitude of eternal waiting and listening, touched some chord in my imagination: they had that strangeness which I adored, and at the same time they had an odd familiarity. I appeared to remember—but, oh, so dimly!—having seen them before, not in pictures, but under a hot, heavy, languid sun, long, long ago. The luxuriousness, the softness and sleepy charm of the Asiatic temper—I had something in common with it, I could understand it. The melodious singing of a voice through the cool twilight; the notes of a lute dying slowly into silence; another voice, low and clear and musical, reading from the "Koran"—where had I heard all that? I pictured great coloured bazaars, where grave merchants with long white beards sat cross-legged and silent, where beautiful, naked, golden-skinned slaves stood waiting for a purchaser, where you could buy silken carpets that would carry you over the world, and black, ebony horses, swifter than light.

Mrs. Carroll had given me one of the upstairs rooms at Derryaghy to be my very own, and had let me furnish it myself from a store of old, out-moded furniture, which, for I know not how long, had been gathering dust and cobwebs in a kind of immense, low attic called the lumber-room. Everything was more or less threadbare and worn, but I had plenty to choose from, and the actual rummaging was as exciting as an adventure on a desert island. I had discovered a quaint little piano, with but two or three octaves of notes, and most of those silent, save for a twangling of wires. This I thought must be Prudence Carroll's spinet, for it looked exactly like the one in her portrait; indeed, that had been my principal reason for bringing it downstairs. With Prudence Carroll I had been in love all my life, and sometimes, in the dusk, when I struck very softly one of the cracked treble notes of the spinet, I would imagine her spirit stealing on tip-toe up behind me to listen. Another discovery, and perhaps the most exciting, was of an old davenport, with a secret drawer at the back of it—not so very secret, perhaps, since I had found it without looking for it, owing to the weakness of the spring, and my own energetic dusting. Inside was nothing more interesting than some old accounts, written on discoloured paper, but anybody who opened it to-day would, I fancy, find more appropriate documents. . . . .

There was a cushioned window-seat, low and deep, and from it I could look out over the sea. In summer, with the window wide open, I could listen to it also, and to all kinds of lovely songs coming through it, dreamy and happy and sad. For there was a sort of undercurrent of dreaming that ran through my life. The romance surrounding the picture of Prudence Carroll, that peculiar, brooding quality of mind by which I could give to such things a kind of spiritual life that had for me an absolute reality, was, perhaps, only too characteristic of a mental condition which might unsympathetically be called that of perpetual wool-gathering.

Though I played cricket and football, and bathed and knocked about generally with the other boys in the village, I had no close friend, and I dreamed of an imaginary playmate. For this playmate and myself I invented appropriate adventures. He had a name, which I shall not write here, and I still think he was an extraordinarily nice boy, but he dropped out of my existence about my fifteenth year. I had my secret world, too, where such adventures took place. Behind this inner, imaginative life must have lurked a vague dissatisfaction with life as I actually found it. Now and then I read something which appeared to me to describe my other world, and, as I chanced on such suggestions more frequently in verse than in prose, I became a great reader of poetry. The passages that echoed so familiarly, though so faintly, from my mysterious, lovely land, brought it up before me very much as the scent of a flower may call up a vision of a high-walled summer garden. Whether any reality lay behind it, I don't know that I even asked myself; but, on drowsy summer afternoons, dream and reality would float and mingle together, and I would feel intensely happy.

As I write I would give much to be able to live over again one of those summer afternoons, when the air hung heavy with the scent of mignonette and roses, and Mrs. Carroll sat reading or working, while I lay in the grass on my back at her feet, and the low sound of the sea splashed through the silence of my sleepy thoughts, and the booming of a bee was the slumberous soul of June or July heat turned to music. In those hours my other world was very, very near.

Afterwards I sometimes wondered if there were a place where those lived days were laid away, or if their beauty, happiness and peace, must be quite lost. They had a quality of peacefulness that for me no later days have had: I seemed to dip deep into their cleansing dreamy quiet, as into a clear sea.

Other dreams I had, that were not so pleasant, but they came only at night. One I still remember vividly was unfortunately typical of many. I seemed to be walking down a street with another boy, when our attention was attracted by the high, bare wall of a house. There was something, I know not what, about this house, which made it different from its neighbours and aroused our curiosity. We noticed in the wall, almost on the street level, a small window. This window was open, and a fatal fascination drew us to it at once. I watched my friend crawl through, for we knew the house was empty; then I followed him, the opening being just wide enough to admit me. Inside, we found ourselves on a gigantic marble staircase, spiral in form, and winding up and down as far as we could follow it with our eyes. There were no windows except the one we had entered by, and it, somehow, was invisible from inside, yet the place was perfectly lighted. There were no landings, no doors, nothing but this staircase, absolutely uniform in its construction, with low, broad, marble steps which wound down and down, and up and up. The place resembled a vast, still well, and we could not hear the slightest sound as we stood listening. The steps were very shallow, and we ran lightly down. The other boy went more quickly than I did, and in a little while I lost sight of him, though I still heard his footsteps, growing ever fainter, till at last they died away, and the stillness closed in about me with a strange heaviness. I continued to follow him, but all at once I noticed that the stairs I trod were darker and stained with damp. A faint chill odour and feeling of damp and decay rose, too, into my face, and the light was growing dimmer. I knew I was going down into a great vault or tomb far below the ground, a charnel-house, an unknown place of death. I caught sight far below me of a light as of a lamp burning, and I had an intuition, a consciousness that came to me in a flash, that my companion had awakened something. This knowledge brought with it a memory of mysterious horror, a memory that I had been here before. Then, with an ever increasing terror, I began to run up the steps I had just run down, but my feet had grown heavy and my limbs weak. Up and up I hurried, seeing nothing before me but an endless stretch of winding marble stairs. I did not know where my window was, I might even now have passed it. I heard nothing, but I knew I was being followed, and that whatever it was that followed me was gaining on me rapidly. I could hardly breathe: an agony of fear shook me. Then I heard close to my ear the bark of a dog. It was the window. I dropped on my knees and squeezed my head and shoulders through; I was almost free when I felt myself grasped from behind and with a scream I woke, shaking, panting, bathed in sweat.

There came a time when these nightmares occurred so frequently that I got to be able to waken myself out of them. While I was actually dreaming—when I would have run a few steps down the stair, for example—a sudden foresight of what was coming would dawn upon me, and by a violent struggle I would break through the net of sleep and sit up in bed. Many of these dreams were connected with a dark, mahogany wardrobe which stood in my father's bedroom. When I had begun to dream and found myself in that room I knew something evil was going to happen, and I would watch the wardrobe door and struggle violently to wake myself before it should open. Even when I was wide awake, and in broad daylight, this so ordinary piece of furniture came to have, for me, a sinister aspect. It was odd that I should have suffered so from these grisly nocturnal terrors, for in ordinary life I was not in any way a coward. A feeling of shame made me keep them a profound secret, and as I grew older they diminished, till by the time I was fifteen they had practically ceased.

Perhaps I should here attempt some slight description of my father, whom I have already mentioned, and of my home. My father was the National schoolmaster at Newcastle, County Down, and our house was next door to the school. My bedroom window looked out over the sea, about a hundred yards away, and behind the house were the Mourne Mountains, and the Derryaghy estate, which took in the lower slopes of Slieve Donard. Our house, when the Virginian creeper that covered it was red, looked pretty enough from the road, but was poorly and even meagrely furnished. The most that could be said for it was that it was clean and tidy. The few attempts at ornamentation would have been better away—the two or three pictures, the hideous vases on the mantelpiece. My father had a strong liking for illuminated texts, and there were several of these, in gilt frames, in every room in the house, including the kitchen and the bath-room. What furniture there was was modern, cheap, and objectionable: it was characteristic of my father that he had never even bought himself a comfortable arm-chair.

He was a tall man, thin and grizzled, pale, and dressed always in an ill-cut, ready-made, black tail-coat and waistcoat, with dark gray trousers. I always disliked his clothes, especially the two shining buttons at the back of his coat. He wore a beard and moustache, both somewhat ragged, and his brown eyes were indescribably melancholy. His hands and feet were very coarse and large. There was power in his face, but there was a depressing lack of anything approaching geniality. He gave me the impression that he did everything from a sense of duty, and nothing because he took a pleasure in it. The seriousness of his expression was truly portentous: it was impossible that anything in the world could matter so much as that. He was not well-off—that is obvious from the position he occupied—but he lived in a way that was unnecessarily economical. He was by no means ungenerous if it were some case of distress that had come to his knowledge, but in ordinary life he was excessively near. The only luxuries he had ever permitted himself were these coloured texts, and they cost little.

When I was with him I never felt quite at my ease, and this made me sulky and perpetually on the defensive. I was not more with him than I could help, and as we lived alone together, with only an old woman who came in every day to look after the house and do the cooking, it must have been easy for him to see that I avoided his society. I never pretended to myself to have any particular affection for him, and I don't even know that it would have mended matters if I had.

One night, when I was about fourteen, I woke up in the dark, with the consciousness that it was very late and that I was not alone in my room. The next moment I knew my father was there, kneeling beside my bed. I lay absolutely quiet: I knew he was praying, and praying for me. Presently I heard him sigh, and then rise noiselessly to his feet, but I gave no sign. I heard him move away, I heard my door being softly closed, the faint click of the latch as it slipped into its place. I lay on with my eyes wide open, wondering why he had come in like this. I did not like it. It made me feel uncomfortable, as all emotions do when we are unable to respond to them. I believed my father cared for me far more than for anything else in the world, yet somehow that did not help matters. It was not the sort of love that begets love in return. Though he loved me, I felt he did not trust me, or rather that he believed I had an infinite capacity for yielding to temptation. By this time I understood that when my mother left home she had gone to somebody else. I knew at any rate that she was living, for she had sent a sum of money for my education, which my father had returned, though some scruple of conscience had made him think it right to tell me he had done so. But he explained nothing and I asked no questions. As I lay awake that night I thought of all this, and it occurred to me that it might have much to do with his extraordinary anxiety about my religious and moral life. He was afraid, and I lay awake for a long time trying to puzzle out what it was he was afraid of.

It was quite impossible for him to make me religious. For one thing, it was not in my nature. It was not so much that I disbelieved what I was taught of religion, as that these instructions aroused in me an implacable antagonism. I did not like the notion of an all-seeing God, for instance. Imperfectly grasped, this conception represented to my mind a kind of tyranny, a kind of espionage, which I strongly resented. Moreover, I detested Sundays and everything connected with them. When I went to church it was with a face like a thunder-cloud, and once there, with an incredible obstinacy, I would shut my ears to all that went on, prayers, hymns, and sermon. This fact, combined with so many others, tended, as time passed, to make my relations with my father more and more strained, for he was religious in the narrowest and severest fashion. I remember his taking me, one Sunday evening, when I was between twelve and thirteen, to hear a preacher who had come from a considerable distance to hold two special services. The occasion stands out from all others, because it was the only one upon which I was startled out of my habitual attitude of sulky defiance. For the first three-quarters of an hour all went as usual, and when the sermon was about to begin I prepared myself to think of other things. But the text, or texts, delivered in a quiet, impressive voice, arrested my attention.

"For nation shall rise against nation, and kingdom against kingdom: and great earthquakes shall be in divers places, and

famines, and pestilences; and fearful sights and great signs shall
there be from heaven. . . . . Your sons and your daughters shall
prophesy, and your young men shall see visions, and your old men
shall dream dreams: and I will show wonders in heaven above,
and signs in the earth beneath; blood and fire, and vapour of
smoke: the sun shall be turned into darkness, and the moon into
blood. . . . . And then shall they see the Son of Man coming in a
cloud, with power and great glory."

In spite of myself the words thrilled me with their vivid, men-
acing suggestiveness, and I listened intently to what followed. It
seemed apparent that the end of the world was at hand. The signs
were taken up one by one, and it was shown, to my growing discomfiture, that all had been fulfilled: nothing remained but the
sounding of the last trumpet, which, according to the preacher—
he seemed even to regard it as highly probable—might take place
that very night. By the time he had reached this point my disquietude had become abject fear, and I joined fervently in the last
prayer. But why had I never been told of this imminent danger?
When we got back from church, it was a very subdued boy who
sat by his father's side, a Bible open on the parlour table in front of
him. I read with a feverish haste to prove my changed way of life,
and, it must be confessed, also to keep off as long as possible the
hour of bed-time. There was a horrible plausibility about what I
had heard. The concluding words kept ringing in my ears. "I see
no reason why it should not be this very night." "Wouldn't it, in
fact, be just the kind of thing that *would* happen at night?" I asked
myself piteously; and I was tormented by a dread of the hideous
trumpet note, by a bloody moon, and by the apparition of dead
and shrouded bodies, rising up with glaring eyeballs and tied jaws
and all the mouldering signs of the grave—dreadful, galvanized
corpses, risen from their wormy beds to meet their Lord in the
air. At length I could put off my bed-time no longer. I could see
my father was not convinced by the open Bible, and, with his
usual suspiciousness, had become curious as to what passages I
was so interested in. Ten minutes later, on my knees in my small,
candle-lit bedroom, I was lying to my God of a tremendous love
I had begun to feel for Him; but in spite of this I passed an abomi-

nable night. In the morning I continued my miserable hypocrisy, grovelling before this frightful Deity for Whom I had developed so sudden and demonstrative an affection, and Whom, at the same time, I begged naïvely not to come. Gradually, but not for several days, these terrors faded, receiving their death-blow when my father told me that all Jews must return to Jerusalem before the last day. Now there was a Jewish family living at Castlewellan, whom I thought I could keep my eye on, and as I had heard nothing of their moving I felt fairly safe.

Very quickly I became more emancipated as I began to think things out for myself, and a year later I could laugh at these early fears. My father told me a crude anecdote which he had read, I think, in Mark Pattison's "Memoirs." A man in a public-house in Leicestershire had used the oath, "God strike me blind," and instantly he had been struck blind by a flash of lightning. On becoming converted he had recovered his sight while taking the Sacrament. This edifying tale was, I believe, vouched for by a friend and disciple of Cardinal Newman's, but to me, I confess, it seemed as stupid and revolting as anything I had ever heard. My father declared it to be true, yet I secretly doubted it, and that afternoon, in my own room, standing by the window, I said aloud, and very deliberately, "God strike me blind! God strike me blind!" I waited with a mingled trepidation and incredulity, as if I had thrown some mysterious bomb into the unknown. A sea-gull flew past the window, white against the dark autumn sky: the leaves of the Virginian creeper trembled and grew still. I said again and in a louder voice, "God strike me blind!" But no flash of lightning followed. Down below, on the beach, the gray waves curled over with a slow musical splash. I looked into the sky, but it was calm and untroubled, and I decided that the story was a myth.

Most of my religious difficulties were, however, metaphysical. The conception of eternity was one I could not grasp. I could, in a vague way, figure myself as living on for ever, but I could not with the same facility move my mind backward. I seemed able to imagine that there might be no end, but I could not imagine that there had been no beginning. "If there had been no begin-

ning, how could we ever have got as far as this?" I asked myself.
"Where I am now—this particular moment—must be at a certain
distance from something, or it cannot be anywhere. But if there
is no beginning, then this moment cannot be any further on than
yesterday was!" My brain grew dizzy with vain efforts to think
impossible thoughts. I would break a stick and say, "God can make
it that I haven't broken it. But if I shut my eyes, and when I open
them the stick is whole, that will only show He has mended it.
Yet He is all-powerful!" And so on, and so on; for whatever point I
took up, sooner or later I was met by an insoluble problem. These
problems were, nevertheless, just what fascinated me. The practi-
cal ethics of religion, that I should simply be good and encourage
in myself a variety of Christian virtues—that kind of thing did not
interest me in the least. As a matter of fact, I possessed singularly
few of these virtues. It is true that I detested any kind of mean-
ness or cruelty, that I was truthful, straightforward, and, in certain
directions, loving and gentle enough; but I was egotistical, proud,
and ludicrously self-conscious, quick tempered, flying into violent
passions for very little, and, above all, I had a stubbornness nothing
could move.

CHAPTER III

It is difficult, as I have said, in looking back over those days, to see
things in any fixed order. It is as if one's memories floated in a kind
of haze, appearing and disappearing, melting into one another. But
there is a definite point from which my story becomes consecutive,
and I can carry it back as far as that cold, clear January morning, the
morning of Mr. Carroll's funeral, when I stood beside my father,
at some distance from the grave, among a group of people I did
not know, and whom I should never see again. I examined them
all with a mild and impartial curiosity, and was struck by the fact
that none of them showed the slightest emotion, though all alike
wore a grave and decorous demeanour. I could not blame them,
for I did not feel sad myself. Mr. Carroll had always been perfectly
amiable to me, but I had seen little of him, and when we did meet

he had looked at me vaguely, as if he were unable to remember
who I was. I had only known him as an invalid, occasionally hob-
bling about with the aid of two black, silver-headed sticks, but for
the most part keeping pretty closely to his own rooms. He seemed
to me to be very old, yet at his death I learned that he was not
old at all, his appearance of decrepitude being simply the result of
an excessively disorderly life, imposed upon a naturally wretched
constitution. I learned, at the same time, the history of Mrs. Carroll's marriage; how, before the first year was out, she had ceased
to see much of her husband, and a little later had ceased to see him
altogether. It was fifteen years afterwards, when he had become
the futile person I knew, that he had returned to her. As the coffin,
bared of its covering of sickly-smelling flowers, was lowered into
the ugly, gaping grave, and the damp red earth rattled heavily on
the lid with a hollow, brutal sound, I recalled the strange, white
face, the watery blue eyes, the fixed smile, the soft, polite manner;
but I was not in the least grieved to know I should never see them
again. And when, a week or so later, I was once more in and out
of the house just as of old, I had already ceased to think of him.
Once or twice, passing the closed door of his room in the dusk, the
thought of meeting his ghost, of hearing the tap, tap of his stick
coming toward me down the long passage, gave me a momentary
thrill; but even these poor tributes to his memory faded swiftly,
passed into a total oblivion.

CHAPTER IV

SCARLATINA broke out in the village in the spring of that year, a
week or two before my sixteenth birthday. There were not many
cases, and all were mild, but there was much talk of closing the
school. My father, for I know not what reason, was against this,
and in the end got his own way, but about a month later he had
the satisfaction of seeing me catch the infection just when everybody else was getting better. I can remember quite distinctly the
day I took ill. I had not been feeling well the day before, but had
said nothing about it, and that morning I went to school as usual.

I might as well have stayed at home for all the work I did. I sat there with a book before me, my head aching, my throat dry and painful. The noise of the classes saying their lessons at the tops of their voices, especially the junior class, to whom Miss McWaters was repeating a stanza of poetry, line by line, while they screamed it after her, irritated, even while it amused, me. Miss McWaters was a thin and angular person, no longer young, endowed by nature with a high-pitched voice, prominent teeth, and a red nose, and by art with a yellow, fuzzy fringe. All these qualities now loomed particularly large in my vision of her, though at other times I knew she was a kind and friendly person. Her red nose and her fringe haunted me, her whole face seemed to undergo extraordinary, kaleidoscopic changes; she became a sort of fantastic witch who was exercising horrible spells on these small children standing in a circle round her chair; her mouth grew larger, her big white teeth seemed thirsting to bury themselves in their soft little throats. This impression grew suddenly so sharp that I had to shake myself and sit back in my seat to get rid of it. Then once more she was only Miss McWaters, to whom years ago I had repeated this same verse of poetry in that same shrill sing-song tone which now was going through and through my head. . . . .

I looked about the room with heavy eyes—at the white walls, the torn, ink-stained maps, the scored desks and forms, the wooden floor—and the whole place seemed to move round and round like a wheel. I saw my father, with a pointer in his hand, indicating differently shaped areas on a large blank map of England, and asking a row of youngsters what counties they represented. That was the kind of lesson I had always detested myself and had never even attempted to learn. I knew from my father's angry, "Next—next—next," that nobody in the class was giving satisfaction. And then they all seemed to shrink and float back, while the room shot out like a telescope, and I watched them from somewhere miles and miles away. And the high, clear voice of Miss McWaters proclaimed:

"Our bugles sang truce, for the night-cloud had lower'd,
And the sentinel stars set their watch in the sky."

And a dozen shrill voices replied:

"Our bugles sang truce, for the night-cloud had lower'd,
   And the sentinel stars set their watch in the sky."

The words seemed mere nonsense in my ears, and I had a sort of
delirious vision of a big star, with a red nose and a fringe and large
white teeth, pointing out the time on a huge clock, while a lot of
little stars stood round in a ring and pulled watches out of their
waistcoat pockets and set them to the time told by the big clock.
This seemed funny to me, and I began to laugh; and then, next
moment, I wanted to lie down somewhere and be quiet. My head
was throbbing like a steamboat with a too powerful engine, and
there was a dull aching at the back of my eyeballs. I got up and tip-
toed across the room, but my foot caught the end of a form, and I
nearly pitched through the door, head first.

I had intended going home, but with my hand on the latch
of the gate I decided to go up to Derryaghy instead. Singularly
enough, the thought that I might be sickening for scarlatina never
occurred to me. The distance to Derryaghy was not more than a
quarter of a mile, yet it seemed to me long, and before I arrived I
regretted having started. The hall-door being open when I reached
the house, I went in without ringing. I knew they would be at
lunch, but I had no appetite, and as I did not want to answer questions or talk, I went straight on up the broad, low stairs, with the
intention of going to my own room. At the head of the staircase,
full in the light, hangs the celebrated portrait people come from
far to admire. I sat down on the wide couch before it, not because
I wanted to look at what I had already seen thousands of times,
but because my head swam. I leaned against the back of the couch
and closed my eyes. When I opened them, the portrait being in
front of me, I could not help staring at it, in a dull way. It repre-
sents a young man standing bare-headed on a hill-side, holding a
gun in his hand, and with an elderly dog seated sedately by him.
The curiously long, oval face, with its high forehead and narrow,
pointed chin, has much distinction, though little beauty, and its
pallor contrasts oddly with the faded red of the full sensuous lips,
completely revealed beneath the light, curled moustache. The eyes

are dark, the hair light brown. The hands are hidden by brown gauntlet gloves, and over the dark brown doublet falls a lace collar. The trousers would look black but for the darker shade of the long boots, and this darker note is carried through to the trees behind, sombre and heavy against a yellow sky. Both man and dog are obviously posing for their portraits—the whole thing is a work of art, that is to say, it is something utterly beyond nature. The highest light is in the face, but there is no white anywhere, and, with the exception of the faint red of the lips, no colour save the browns and blacks, the creamy flesh-tints. Over all, the mellow tone of time has cast a kind of golden softness. I had been told that it was by a great Spanish artist called Velasquez—his name, indeed, was there, in large black letters on the dull gilt frame—and that it was a very valuable painting, worth fabulous sums. I can affirm to-day that it is really a fine work; but it is not by Velasquez. It is by Mazo, and is, in fact, only a slightly modified copy of Velasquez's famous portrait of Philip in the Louvre.

This picture had always had an odd fascination for me, though there was something about the face I did not like, something cold and proud, which I knew I should have detested in actual life. I gazed at it now stupidly enough, and then I had a nervous thrill, for it seemed to me to have come all at once to life. One part of my brain knew this to be nonsense, and that I had been seeing queer things all day, but the other part of my brain continued to watch it, with a half expectation of seeing it descend out of its frame. The eyes had begun to move, and the lips trembled; the mouth opened slowly in a yawn which the brown gloved hand was raised languidly to conceal; and then from behind the picture I heard a little mocking laugh. These things bewildered me, but did not startle me; and through them I became conscious that Mrs. Carroll was coming up the stair and that she was speaking to me. I answered her in words which I knew were perfectly idiotic, and which moreover sounded husky and strange, as if some other voice than my own were speaking through my lips. Again I heard the little mocking laugh. This time I thought it came from the top of the picture, and glancing up I saw, sure enough, a black imp, like a small, naked, negro boy, perched cross-legged, on the top of the frame, from which he grinned down at me impudently, raising his fingers to his snub nose, and spreading them out in a derisive and very familiar grimace. I began to talk about the picture, about school, and about Miss McWaters. Then a cloud waved back from my brain; the portrait slid into its place, the imp disappeared, and everything was once more as it should be. But I felt a burning thirst, and when Mrs. Carroll opened the door of a large, bright, sunny room, I was glad to fling myself down on the bed. Almost immediately I was seized by a deadly sickness. I managed to get off the bed in time to avoid making a mess, but the vomiting returned again and again, till I collapsed into a state of exhaustion. Heavy clouds waved across my brain, obscuring my thoughts, and again clearing, leaving consciousness to flicker up, like the flame in a dying lamp, so that I knew I had been undressed and was safe in bed. And all the time I wanted to drink—to drink. . . . . More than one person was in the room with me; Mrs. Carroll was there, and old Doctor O'Brian. In the open doorway Miss Dick hovered. And then suddenly I was alone. I could hear a fire crackling in the grate, and it had grown darker. A lamp was burning on a table some-where over beside the fireplace. I listened to the fire, and presently it seemed to me I could hear the lamp burning too. It burned with a soft low continuous sound that was like the note of a flute, and it occurred to me that everything in the world was only sound—the bed I was lying on, the shadows flickering across the ceiling, the dancing firelight—all were but notes of a tune. This appeared so strikingly obvious that I could not understand why I had never noticed it before. I tried to make out what the tune was, but it eluded me, flickering away from me like a butterfly. I turned round in my bed, for I had heard a slight noise at the door. All seemed now to have grown silent. I could not hear the lamp burning, nor even the fire. This silence was surely unusual, abnormal; it filled me with a vague disquietude. It grew deeper and deeper till I could not hear, even when I strained my ears, the faintest murmur either without or within the house. The silence was like a liquid, luminous atmosphere, through which strange things were floating nearer. It was like a sea, and gradually it darkened into colour—there was a broad, dark, blue sea before me, in a strange, rich light, as if I were

watching it through old stained glass. I saw sirens swimming about
in the warm, swelling waves, appearing and disappearing. They
followed a high-pooped, fantastic ship, just as I had often seen
porpoises following a boat out in the bay. The ship moved along
slowly, and its broad, coloured sails were embroidered with green
dragons that shone like fire, and at its bow was a green, jewelled
serpent's head. Then once more there was nothing but the room,
and I heard a faint noise as of someone moving in a chair. Another
sound immediately followed, and I started, for it was curiously different; it was the sound one hears before something happens. I
watched the handle of the door turn, and the door itself open and
close quickly yet stealthily. Three figures had entered. One was a
tall figure in brown, with a gun in his gloved hand, and he was followed by a great dark brown dog, who at once leaped on to the bed
and sat at the foot, watching me with sombre, burning eyes. The
third figure was Miss McWaters. Her nose was longer and redder
than I had ever seen it before, and it kept twitching from side to
side in a curious way; her big teeth flashed in an unpleasant grin,
and her fringe waved and curled about as if it were alive. For the
third time I heard the strange little mocking laugh that had come
from behind the picture, but I could not discover who had uttered
it. Perhaps it was Miss McWaters, for I knew she was waiting for
me to say something—a verse of poetry—yes, I remembered:

> "Our bugles sang truce, for the night-cloud had lower'd,
>   And the sentinel stars set their watch in the sky."

Then a dense, heavy darkness swept up, blotting out everything.

CHAPTER V

I AWOKE in broad sunlight. The room was full of it, and the scent
of flowers floated in through the open windows and mingled with
the faint smell of drugs. For some time I lay there quietly, too
languid to make a movement or to speak. Then the door softly
opened, and I saw Mrs. Carroll come in and stand beside my bed.

"Is he asleep?" I heard her ask, for I had closed my eyes. I opened them and looked up at her.

"No," I answered, smiling.

She smiled, too. "It's time for you to take your medicine," and the nurse came forward to give it to me. When I had swallowed it, I lay back among the soft pillows deliciously. . . . .

The memory of my convalescence is a strange one, for it came at a time when certain physical changes were taking place within me, and I seemed to myself to be somehow different from what I had been before I fell ill. My voice had altered; my mind was coloured by vague and happy dreams. Sometimes when I turned in bed or stretched myself, the contact of the fine linen sheets against my skin gave me a peculiar thrill, which ran all down my spine. It appeared I had been very ill, that it had been a touch-and-go matter whether I should manage to pull through; yet now I did not feel that I wanted to get well too quickly. The flowers, the fruit, the brightness, the big delightful room—so different from my room at home—the care everybody took of me, the books that were read to me, the sense of being here so securely, with everything just as I liked it, and with Mrs. Carroll to look after me—all that was delicious. The one jarring note was my father's letter, which I read, and then put back in its envelope. It was about my escape, how near to death I had been, and how he hoped the mercy that had been shown me would make me think seriously. I did not want to think seriously: I wanted to bask in the sunshine of these pleasant days while they lasted. If I had died it would have been all over by this time, and since I hadn't, why should I be different? It seemed to me hardly the time to talk of God's mercy, seeing that I had barely scraped through a severe illness. It was like thanking a man, who has just broken your head with a stick, for not killing you outright. My father talked of a miracle, but I had slender faith in miracles, and I regret to say his entire letter struck me as amazingly unintelligent. In a kind of lazy and sublime egotism I began to ponder on the oddity of a man like my father having a son such as I was; and while I was engaged with these speculations Mrs. Carroll sat beside me, playing "patience."

She told me my father could not come to see me for fear of carrying the infection to school, and I received these tidings with an
immense relief, for I had been dreading that he would want to
talk to me about death, and perhaps make me join in returning
thanks for my recovery. I watched her as she sat there, her plump
hands drawing out the cards, her eyes seriously scanning the faces
of those already turned up. She was a large, placid lady, stout and
ruddy. She must always, even in her earliest youth, have been plain,
but her face was filled with an extraordinary kindness that made
it infinitely pleasant. It was not the sort of kindness which can be
simulated; it was something that was a natural part of her, and was
reflected in all she did and said. It had moulded the expression of
her countenance, just as time and weather will alter the features of
a statue. Her eyes were small and gray, and she wore gold-rimmed
spectacles, which, somehow, were becoming to her. I never saw
her dressed in anything but black, and with a light lace cap on her
gray hair. She was extremely fond of me, and I knew it, and I'm
afraid imposed upon it, though I loved her sincerely. At that time it
appeared to me perfectly natural that she should be fond of me; it
was simply a part of the order of things; it had always been so, and
I couldn't have imagined anything else. It never even occurred to
me that I had no claim upon her, except that which she herself had
established; it never occurred to me that I might, in my relation to
her, have been just like any of the other boys in the village. On the
contrary, I looked upon Derryaghy quite as if it were a second, and
certainly much my best-loved, home.

The "patience" failed, and Mrs. Carroll swept up the cards.
"Shall I read to you?" she asked me, and, I having graciously given
my permission, she took up "Huckleberry Finn." It was a book I
rejoiced in, but I don't think Mrs. Carroll cared for it, I don't think
she even found it funny. She spoke rather slowly, and it amused me
infinitely to hear her gentle voice reproduce the talk of Huck, or
Pap, or the King. . . .

That same day, after lunch, the nurse left. I was getting on very
well, and was to be allowed up toward the end of the week. In the
afternoon Mrs. Carroll had gone out, and I found myself alone.
I went on with "Huck," but a chapter or two brought me to the

end. I began another book, "Bevis," but my eyes grew tired, and I let it drop on the bed beside me. As I lay idle I was seized by a desire to get up. I resisted it for a few minutes, and then I slid into a sitting posture, with my legs hanging over the side of the bed. It struck me that they had grown absurdly thin and long, and I felt wretchedly shaky. I stood up, all the same, holding on to the bedpost till I got accustomed to being on my feet, when I put on my dressing-gown, and walked somewhat uncertainly as far as the door. I turned the handle and looked out with a strange curiosity into the passage. It was as if I had been ill for months, it all somehow seemed so queer and new. The long high corridor, off which the rooms opened, was hung with tall portraits that appeared, in the mellow sunlight of high far windows, to watch me stiffly yet furtively. I liked them, I liked everything about the place, I liked to look down the passage with its long row of closed doors, which seemed so mysterious, reaching right on to the head of the staircase. I listened for footsteps, but heard nothing. Miss Dick probably was out, and the servants' quarters were far away. I had a feeling that I was really the son of the house, that everything about it, its pictures, its ghosts, were mine. I went to my favourite picture and stood beneath it. It was a portrait of a lady with dark hair and dark blue eyes, and it was partly this peculiar contrast, I think, this contrast of blue eyes and black hair, that had originally pleased me. She was young and she had a strange quaint name—Prudence Carroll. The artist had painted her as if she were just come in from the garden, for she held still a bunch of flowers in her hand. She was standing by a queer little piano—or was it a spinet?—the spinet I had now in my room? It was open, and in a minute or two she would lay down her flowers and play some air on it, or the accompaniment of some forgotten ballad. Did the painter intend to show that these were the things she was fondest of—music and flowers? Poor Prudence Carroll had been dust these hundred years, the notes of her spinet were either cracked or dumb, and her tardy lover had arrived a century too late, for she had died unmarried, and but a year after this portrait was painted! Why had no one cared for her? Perhaps some day, between twilight and dusk, she would slip into my room and sing to me, "Rose

softly Blooming," or "Voi che sapete!" A rustle of muslin, a ghostly
scent of ghostly flowers, the twangling notes of the spinet, and
a voice singing a song that would sound thin and far off, like the
sound of wind—that is how it would happen.

I was charmed with these fancies, but I stood there only a few
minutes, for there was something odd in that silence of closed
doors and listening portraits, and I returned to the sunshine of
my room. I went to the window and leaned my forehead against
the pane and looked out. Far away I could see a stretch of sand,
streaked with streams and pools of water, for the tide was out:
and beyond the sand, clear in the sunlight, was the sea, blue-green
under the soft blue sky, marked with indigo and purple where the
bottom was formed of rocks and seaweed. At the water's edge
some children—from this distance I could not make out who they
were—were sailing toy boats. With trousers and petticoats well
rolled up from bare brown legs, with their scarlet jerseys and caps
and striped cotton dresses, they formed a bright note of colour,
and brought me into touch again with life out of doors. On the left
horn of the bay's crescent the sand-hills, with their sparse covering
of bleached, wan grass, were pale and iridescent in the sun.

A gardener was mowing the grass just below my window, and
the sleepy sound of the mowing-machine was delightful, and the
smell of the fresh green grass, turned over in bright cool heaps. I
got back into bed again, and took up "Bevis."

I read for half an hour, when my eyes once more grew tired.
The sound of the mowing-machine had ceased, and a deep silence
filled the afternoon. I lay listening to the silence, half-asleep, half-
awake, when all at once I heard a sound of scraping under my
window. It flashed across my mind that I was alone here in this
part of the house, and that burglars were taking the opportunity
to break in, and perhaps they would murder me. The thing was
utterly nonsensical, and would never have occurred to me had I
been in my normal health, but it had hardly entered my head when
I saw a ladder shoot up past the window, and strike with a grating
sound against the wall. My heart began to thump. I heard steps on
the ladder; somebody was mounting it. The next moment Jim's
face, brown and ruddy and grinning, popped in, and I gasped with

relief. Jim was a boy who worked in the garden, and was about the same age as I was. He smiled broadly, and his bright, brown eyes gazed at me with evident pleasure. "How are you, Master Peter?" he grinned. "They're nobody about, so I thought I'd look in."

"Oh, I'm all right," I answered, "but you mustn't stay there, or you'll be catching the infection."

"I wanted to see the skin peeling off you. What like is it underneath?"

I felt disappointed at this callous explanation of what I had imagined to be sympathy. "You can't see it," I answered crossly. "You'd better clear out before somebody catches you."

Jim disappeared, but I called after him, "I say . . . Jim——"

The round, ruddy-brown face bobbed up again.

"Will you do something for me?" I asked.

"Ay."

"Will you play something to me. I'm sick of lying here, doing nothing."

"I darn't. Oul Thomas'd stop me, an' I'd get in a row. I be to red up all the grass, an' rake the walk."

"All right."

I took no further interest in Jim, and he again vanished. There was a further scraping noise, and the ladder, too, disappeared. I lay on in a kind of waking-slumber till Mrs. Carroll came in, bringing me my tea. When I had finished I once more fell into a doze, but opened my eyes in the dusk, when I heard the notes of Jim's flute under my window, in a slow melancholy tune, with an occasional pause, as if the musician was not very certain of his music. I recognised the air—the Lorelei. It had a curious effect in the gathering twilight, as if the music and the fading light were in some subtle way mingled. I knew that the unseen musician was Jim, yet none the less the mournful notes, coming slowly in a minor key, seemed the very soul of the deepening darkness, and called up before me a world of imaginary sorrows, a passionate regret for I knew not what, a kind of homesickness for my dream-land. Tears gathered in my eyes and ran down my cheeks. Fortunately nobody could see them, but I was ashamed of them myself, though I knew they were partly the result of my physical weakness. Still, it was ridicu-

lous that I should cry over Jim's playing. Jim really couldn't play at
all. It was stupid, idiotic; and the other day I had cried just in this
same senseless fashion over a book I had been reading; I had wept
my soul out in an ecstasy of love and misery.

When Jim's serenade was ended I lay on in the darkness, my
tears drying on my cheeks, and thought what a fool I was. Why
should I have cried? What was the matter with me? It was not
that I was unhappy; on the contrary, I was extremely happy. Yet
somehow I felt dimly that there was a greater happiness than any
I had ever experienced or probably ever should experience. The
meaning of my emotions and desires never became quite clear,
though I seemed on the verge of discovery. It was as if there were
something stirring within me to which I could not give freedom,
something which remained unsatisfied even in the midst of my
keenest pleasures. . . . .

On a bright morning early in June I was allowed out for the
first time since my illness, and I insisted on going alone. As I came
out into the warmth of the sun I felt a charm as of a mysterious
new birth. I went straight to the woods. The green alleys winding
in front of me amid tall old trees, in all the vivid richness of early
summer, seemed exquisitely beautiful. It was as if I had never realized before how lovely the world was. I lay down on my back on
the warm, dry moss and listened to a skylark singing as it mounted
up from the fields near the sea into the dark clear sky. No other
music ever gave me the same pleasure as that passionately joyous
singing. It was a kind of leaping, exultant ecstasy, a bright, flame-
like sound, rejoicing in itself. And then a curious experience befell
me. It was as if everything that had seemed to me external and
around me were suddenly within me. The whole world seemed
to be within me. It was within me that the trees waved their green
branches, it was within me that the skylark was singing, it was
within me that the hot sun shone, and that the shade was cool. A
cloud rose in the sky, and passed in a light shower that pattered on
the leaves, and I felt its freshness dropping into my soul, and I felt
in all my being the delicious fragrance of the earth and the grass
and the plants and the rich brown soil. I could have sobbed with
joy, but in the midst of it I heard the sound of footsteps, and looked

behind me quickly, to see the figure of one of the two idiots, who lived in a hovel outside the village, approaching. This was the man; there was a woman also, his sister. He was perfectly harmless, and he drew near now with smiles meant to be ingratiating. He held an empty pipe in his hand, and made guttural noises that I knew were asking me for tobacco. I told him I had none, but he would not go away. He stood right over me, a grin on his deformed face. The big, misshapen head, the horrible, slobbering mouth, the stupid persistence, all filled me with a cold rage. He had spoiled everything; I hated him, and I could have killed him, for it. But he still stood there and jibbered with his ugly, dripping mouth. It was only when I struck at him savagely with my stick that he moved off, glancing back at every step. And when he was gone I felt nothing but a kind of cold disgust and animosity, mingled with shame at my own conduct. All the beauty had gone out of the woods, and I got up and went home.

CHAPTER VI

When, some time in July, Mrs. Carroll told me that she had invited her nephew and niece, Gerald and Katherine Dale, to come on a visit to Derryaghy, I became at once very curious to see them. I had never even heard of them before, and now I learned such interesting items as that they lived in London, were twins, and about my own age, or perhaps a year older. Mrs. Carroll could not remember. They arrived at the end of the month, and that night I went to dinner to meet them. As it happened, I was late. My watch had stopped for half an hour or so in the afternoon, and then gone on again, an annoying and foolish trick it occasionally played me. I was told they were already in the dining-room, but that dinner had only begun. The prospect of meeting strangers always produced in me an unconquerable shyness, and, to-night, partly because I was late, and partly because these particular strangers were so nearly my own age, my shyness was doubled. I did not look at either of them as I entered the room where, though daylight had not yet quite failed, two softly shaded lamps burned, amid a pro-

fusion of flowers, upon the white and silver table. I shook hands
with my hostess and with Miss Dick, mumbling out apologies, and
had begun a lengthy and involved description of the cause of my
delay, when Mrs. Carroll cut me short by introducing me to the
Dales. I shook hands with one and bowed to the other, blushing
and incapable of finding a word. I should never have guessed they
were even brother and sister, let alone twins, for in appearance
they were utterly unlike. Katherine pleased me. She was fresh and
bright and attractive; I even thought her beautiful, for there was
something of the open air about her, something of nature. At any
rate she gave me that impression; her beauty had a kind of grave
simplicity; and, if I had been a poet, and had been describing her,
all my similes would have been taken from nature, from open hill-
sides, from the wind and the sky. As I sat down beside her, her dear,
dark, very blue eyes rested on me frankly, and with that she suddenly set me puzzling over where I had seen her before, or whom
she reminded me of. I kept glancing at her furtively, but, seen in
profile, her face was no longer suggestive, and I decided I had made
a mistake. She appeared to me friendly and candid and unaffected,
but I doubted if she were clever. Her brother, on the other hand,
probably *was* clever. I did not take to him, he was smaller than she,
thin and brown and subtle; also he had a way of looking at you
that made you want to ask him what it was he found amusing.

"Peter will be able to show you everything, and take you
everywhere," Mrs. Carroll explained, comprehensively, and then
Katherine asked me if I played golf.

I answered, "No," and felt ashamed. I went on to prove that it
was not my fault, that my father had refused to allow me to join
the club, but at that point I caught Gerald's eyes watching me with
an expression of interest, and I suddenly blushed. "Do *you* play?" I
asked him aggressively.

He seemed surprised. His glance just brushed mine and rested
on a picture above my head. "No," he answered quietly.

"Gerald is studying music abroad," said Mrs. Carroll, "at Vienna,
where I don't suppose they have ever heard of golf. He is going to
be a musician."

"How interesting!" exclaimed Miss Dick. "Fancy, Vienna!"

Miss Dick was Mrs. Carroll's companion, and was even, in some distant way, related to her. Her family, however, had fallen on evil days, and she was permanently settled at Derryaghy. She was a gushing, fussy, kindly creature, with a minimum allowance of brains, but overflowing with good intentions and amazingly loyal in her affections, though these latter, I must add, had never been bestowed upon me. I took Mrs. Carroll's word for it that she had once been very pretty, but now her thinness, accentuating a peculiar type of feature, gave her an absurd resemblance to a lean and restless fowl. I noticed that she had attired herself to-night as for a striking festival. She was a person liable to these unexpected changes in the degree of her brilliancy, which at present was positively dazzling. She began to ask about Vienna, and expressed a deep regret at never having visited that city.

"We have had the piano specially tuned for you," said Mrs. Carroll to Gerald.

"Oh you shouldn't have bothered," he answered.

"You evidently don't know what it was like before!" I began, and then stopped short. Nobody took any notice.

Miss Dick, who seemed determined, cost what it might, to keep the conversation on the subject of music, mentioned that her mother had heard Patti in "La Sonnambula," and how, when that great prima donna had paused in the middle of the opera to sing "Home Sweet Home," the entire house had risen to its feet with enthusiasm. "It has always seemed to me that music is the most perfect of the arts," she added, fixing her lace collar.

"Painting is the most perfect of the arts," I contradicted. Somehow, when they were uttered, all my remarks sounded unhappy, not to say rude, though I was only trying to be agreeable. Miss Dick accentuated this last one by helping herself to potatoes in significant silence. "You can look at a picture oftener than you can read a book," I went on, addressing Gerald, "and oftener than you can listen to a piece of music."

"I daresay," he answered, and I resented his politeness. "Why can't he stand up for his own business?" I thought.

I glanced at Katherine, and wanted to say something pleasant to her, but that was apparently beyond my power. My solitary "No,"

in answer to her question about golf, had been the one word I had
so far addressed to her. I relapsed into silence and did not speak
again till dinner was over.

When we went to the drawing-room it looked as if we were
going to have a musical evening, for Miss Dick sat down at the
piano with all the air of a person opening a concert. She played an
arrangement of something or other, by Thalberg. All Miss Dick's
pieces were arrangements, except those that were fantasias, and it
was a feature of them that the beginning of the end could be heard
about a couple of pages off, in a series of frantic rushes and arpeg-
gios. She played now with a fierce concentration on the task to be
accomplished; her face getting redder as Thalberg became more
surprising; her mouth screwed up slightly at the right corner,
through which just the tip of her tongue was visible; her eyes
glaring, devouring the sheet of music before her, at which every
now and then she made a frantic grab with her left hand, to turn
the page—she would never allow anybody to turn for her.

When she had struck the last note, to which she indeed gave an
astonishing rap, there was a general sigh, as for a danger evaded.

"My dear, I don't know how you do it!" Mrs. Carroll murmured,
almost as breathless as the performer.

"It does take it out of one," Miss Dick panted complacently.

Gerald sat looking on with a barely perceptible smile. "Won't
you play something now?" Miss Dick said to him.

His eyebrows twitched slightly. "Not just yet, I think. In a little.
I want to smoke a cigarette first." He passed out on to the terrace,
and we all gazed after him. When he thought, I suppose, that the
echoes awakened by Miss Dick had had time to subside, he came
back, and began to fiddle with the music-stool, screwing it up and
down. Yet when he did commence to play, after many preliminar-
ies, it was in a broken fragmentary fashion, beginning things and
suddenly dropping them after a few bars. I was prepared not to like
him, but he had not struck more than a note or two when I knew I
had never heard the piano really played before. In spite of myself I
felt the dislike I had conceived for him slipping away, and then, just
as I was commencing to enjoy myself, he stopped abruptly. He got
up and walked over to the window where I sat.

"You haven't altered, Gerald," said Mrs. Carroll dryly.

"Do you mean my playing, Aunt?" he asked sweetly. "It is supposed to have got rather better, but I am sure you are right."

Mrs. Carroll gave something as nearly resembling a sniff as she could give. I saw she was not in love with her nephew; but Miss Dick's cat jumped on to his knee and he began to stroke it. There was something in his extreme self-possession which, though I knew it to be based on a profound sense of superiority to everybody present, I could not help admiring, just as I could not help admiring his playing, or, for that matter, his personal beauty, which was striking. And I admired the way he was dressed. While remaining quite conventional, it managed to suggest individuality, and its perfect taste, apparent in the slightest details, gave him, as he sat there, something of the finish, of the harmony and tone, of an old portrait. Again his glance met mine. I believe he knew I had been watching him, and perhaps something of what I had been thinking, and I turned away abruptly. Miss Dick, who had taken a great fancy to him, begged him to play again. He refused, yet a moment later he said, speaking so that nobody but I could hear him, "Would you like me to?"

"Not in the least," I answered rudely. Rather ashamed of myself I got up, crossed the room, and boldly took possession of a chair beside his sister. But with that my boldness ended, and I could think of nothing to say. I had not even sufficient courage to look her in the face, and the fact that I had so deliberately come to sit beside her only to maintain a fixed and gloomy silence made me feel ridiculous.

"Do you play golf?" I stammered out at last, the inanity of my remark only striking me after it had left my lips. "She will think I am a fool, and dislike me," I told myself miserably; but Katherine answered as if the subject had never been alluded to before. Her reply only left me to rack my brains anew. It was no use; a malignant spell appeared to have been cast upon me, holding me tongue-tied, my mind a blank. A perspiration broke out all over my body and I could feel my shirt sticking to my back. Every minute was like an hour, yet I could think of nothing but this accursed golf. I described the links and even the Club House, and might have gone on to enumerate the caddies had I remembered their names. I became suddenly conscious that my hands and feet were enormous. I thrust my hands in my trouser pockets, but my feet still remained visible. I knew my thick nose had neither shape nor character, that my coarse, brown hair was more like a kind of tropical plant than like hair, and that my overhanging brows and the shape of my mouth gave me a sullen look. I had tried to alter my appearance by doing my hair in different ways, but it was no use. I remembered having noticed in the morning, when I was tying my tie, that a slight frown made me more thoughtful looking, and I instantly assumed one. I compared the appearance I imagined myself to present with Gerald's, and then I saw him watching me with what I believed to be a kind of veiled mockery in his eyes. My shyness turned to rage. Katherine tried to talk to me, but I answered in monosyllables, and, an hour earlier than I had intended, I got up to say good-night.

"We shall see you to-morrow, Peter," Mrs. Carroll suggested, as I shook hands with her. "What would you like to do to-morrow?" she added, turning to Katherine.

Katherine smiled at me as if we were quite old friends. "I want to climb some of the mountains," she said. "I planned that the minute I saw them."

Again her face awakened in me the memory of another face I had known—but where? when?

"In that case you ought to start early," Mrs. Carroll went on, "and you could take your lunch with you. Peter knows all the different walks for miles round."

I was on the point of declaring that I had an engagement, but I overcame the temptation. I promised to come soon after breakfast, and made my escape.

CHAPTER VII

I WENT home in a state of profound depression. I had made a hopeless fool of myself; probably they were talking about it now. These thoughts were rendered no brighter by being mingled with anticipations of what I was returning to. Above all else in the world, perhaps, I hated, and almost feared, that atmosphere of dullness and joylessness, which hung like a mist over our house. It exasperated me, it seemed to sap my vitality, and with all the strength of my nature I tried to resist it. It was as if the narrowness and dinginess, the gray, colourless, melancholy monotony of my father's existence, had a hateful power of penetrating into my brain, like the fumes of a drug, clouding my mind, subduing it to a kind of cold lethargy: there were times when I had a feeling that I was struggling for life.

My father was in the parlour when I came in. He glanced up at the clock, which meant that he was surprised at my returning so much earlier than usual, but he made no remark. I sat down to take off my boots; then I took up the book I was reading. My father all this time had not spoken a word, and I had returned him silence for silence. Sometimes, after a whole evening of this kind of thing, my feeling of constraint would become so acute that the effort required to say even good-night would appear almost insurmountable, and I would invent all sorts of excuses for slipping out of the room without doing so. My father was correcting exercises. The books were arranged in two piles in front of him—those he had already finished with, and those he had not yet touched. Behind him was the wall, with its cheap, ugly, flowered paper, and illuminated texts. I glanced at him from time to time over the top of my book. There was a perpetual dinginess in his appearance; his linen was not often scrupulously clean, and his nails never were. Just now I wanted to ask him to stop snuffing. How could I read while he kept on making such disgusting noises! He had a peculiar way of breathing through his nose so as to produce a sort of whistling sound, which I could never get accustomed to. Often I had gone upstairs and sat in an ice-cold bedroom merely to be rid of it.

Suddenly he looked up over his spectacles and addressed me across the table. "I intended to ask you about that book you have brought home. Who gave it to you?"

I at once assumed an air of elaborate nonchalance. "Nobody gave it to me. I found it in the book-case."

"What are you reading in it?"

"'Venus and Adonis.'"

"I don't like the books you have been reading lately."

"But this is Shakespeare!" I exclaimed, feigning tremendous astonishment.

"I don't care who it is. Why can't you read what other boys read?"

"I thought he was supposed to be the greatest poet in the world!"

"You know very well what I mean. If you *do* read him, why don't you read the plays—'Julius Cæsar?'"

"I'd rather have poems than plays. What is the harm in this?"

"The harm is that it is not suited to your age. It is full of all kinds of voluptuous images and thoughts. You have been too much at Derryaghy lately."

The train of reasoning which connected voluptuous thoughts with Derryaghy was difficult to follow, yet I was not surprised that my father had come out there. With him all roads led to Derryaghy, and I could never understand what he really felt about my position in relation to Mrs. Carroll. When he spoke face to face with her his manner always expressed something like a carefully repressed disapproval, and at the same time he allowed me to remain under countless obligations to her. For example, she looked after, that is to say, she paid for, my clothing. Also it had been settled recently that she was to pay my school, and later my university, expenses. I believe a struggle was perpetually going on within him between his consciousness of my interests and a desire to tell her to mind her own business and to leave him to look after his son himself. This peculiar combination of natural anti-pathy, a fear to give offence, and a sense that it was his duty to be thankful, was singularly ill adapted to produce a graceful attitude in his personal dealings with her, and I do not think she cared for him.

"Now that Mrs. Carroll has her nephew and niece, there is no need for you to go there so often," he went on. "I was glad to see that you did not stay late to-night." He added the last words in a conciliatory tone, even with approval.

"Why don't you like her?" I asked simply.

He fixed his eyes sternly upon me. "Why don't I like whom?"

"Mrs. Carroll."

"Mrs. Carroll! I don't think I understand you!"

As I gave no further explanation he returned to his exercises, but I could see an irrepressible desire to justify himself working in his mind. It broke out in another minute. "You don't appear to realise that your question accuses me of both ingratitude and hypocrisy! Or, possibly, that is what you intended to do?"

Oh, how well I knew this mood, and how we would go round and round the same little circle, and how he would outwardly be so calm and reasonable and not in the least annoyed, yet inwardly be perfectly furious. "I think I'll go to bed," I murmured, getting up, and pretending to yawn.

My yawn was only meant to convey sleepiness, but my father saw in it impertinence. "Why do you try to vex me?" he asked.

"I don't try to vex you. Why should I?"

"Mrs. Carroll is different from us. Her position in life is different; it alters her view of everything; it is only natural that she should be more worldly."

"Is she very worldly?" I asked, without enthusiasm. Anybody less so, I could hardly imagine, but there was no use arguing.

My father branched off in another direction. "To-night, at dinner, were you offered wine?"

"I had some claret."

"You remembered I had told you I would rather you didn't take anything?"

"No."

"Are you speaking the truth, Peter?"

"I don't know whether I remembered or not," I answered petulantly. "I didn't think it important enough to make a fuss about. You always want me to do everything differently from other people. If I can't do as other people do, I'd rather not go at all."

"I'm not aware that I told you anything except what would please me," he answered coldly. "I left you perfectly free."

"How can you call it 'leaving me free' when you're for ever asking me whether I've done it? You say you don't forbid me to do things, but you always talk about them afterwards."

There was a pause. It was broken by my father who seemed

now deeply offended. "Did you make any arrangement about going back?"

"I promised to go to-morrow, after breakfast."

"What for?"

"I was asked to take the Dales somewhere."

"Can't they find their own way? It isn't very difficult."

"Does that mean I'm not to go?"

"You can't be always going there. You seem to me to live there."

"It's easier than living at home," I muttered.

"It is pleasanter, I daresay; but I don't want you to make yourself a nuisance to strangers."

"Aren't they the best judges of whether I'm a nuisance or not?"

"Well, I don't wish you to go to-morrow."

"You might have said so sooner," I burst out. "What reason have you?"

"I hope you don't intend to be as disrespectful as you are," my father said slowly. "If I had no other reason for not wanting you to go, I should have a very good one in the way it seems to make you behave when you come back. I *have* another reason, however: I don't desire you to grow up with an idea that you have nothing to think of in life but your own pleasures. You are quite sufficiently inclined that way as it is."

He spoke quietly, but there was a concentrated feeling behind his words. "What have I been doing?" I asked, trying to be equally calm, though I knew my eyes were bright, my cheeks flushed, and my lips pouting.

"I wasn't alluding to anything particular so much as to your whole way of looking at things. You appear to wish to be absolutely independent, to go out and in just as you please. You appear to think you have no duty to me or to anybody else. You are becoming utterly selfish."

"Selfish!" I was too indignant to protest more than by simply repeating the word. People always called you selfish, I thought, bitterly, when you only wanted to prevent *them* from being so. I was convinced I was capable of making the most sublime sacrifices, if there were any need for them. Indeed I had often imagined myself making such sacrifices, making them secretly, but to be discovered in the end, when all my unsuspected nobility would suddenly be revealed, in some rather public way, perhaps, but too late to save those who had wilfully misunderstood me from agonies of remorse. It was my father who was selfish, with his idea of making everybody think and act exactly as he did. He was not only selfish, but he was jealous. That was at the back of all these objections to my going to Derryaghy. Only, he never realized his own faults; he found moral justifications for them. One thing was certain, I was going there to-morrow, whether he allowed me to or not. I was so full of these thoughts that I missed a great deal of what he was saying, but the gist of it I gathered—and I had heard it frequently before—that I should have my living to earn, my way to make in the world, that I shouldn't have Mrs. Carroll always, and that the fewer luxurious tastes I acquired, the more chance I should have of being happy in the very obscure and humble path that was apparently all my father saw before me.

If he really wanted to inspire me with feelings of humility, however, he could hardly have wasted his breath on a more thankless task. It was not that I saw myself becoming remarkably successful, but simply that I seemed to have had a glimpse of what an extraordinary youth I was. My interview with my father had made me forget all about my unhappy behaviour at Derryaghy, and as soon as I was in bed I began to compose a passionate drama, of which I was, naturally, the hero, but in which, without any rehearsal, Katherine Dale appeared as heroine. I had braved my father's anger in order to be with her, and now I was no longer shy, the right words rushed from me in a torrent. Sometimes our love story was happy, more often it was a perfect bath of tears. Indeed, I think I must have had some inborn feeling for the stage, so frequently did I lead up to the most telling and lime-lit situations, on the very weakest of which a curtain could only go down to a thunder of applause. In this present drama there was a fathomless well of sentiment, of "love interest" of the most uncompromising type. I had read lately, in bound volumes of *Temple Bar*, one or two novels by Miss Rhoda Broughton, and as I lay there in my small room, with a text above my head, I was far from anxious to "keep innocency." On the contrary, I was one of those bold, dark, rugged, cynical creatures, one of those splendid ugly men, who carry in their breasts a smouldering fire of passion for some girl "with eyes like a shot partridge"; one of those men who gnaw the ends of their moustaches, and have behind them the remembrance of a fearful life. My name was Dare Stamer, or Paul Le Mesurier, and my heart was sombre and volcanic. The plot of our romance did not vary a great deal. We met; we loved; we quarrelled. I married somebody else—a cold, soulless, blonde beauty with magnificent shoulders—and Katherine sometimes went into a consumption, and sometimes did not, but in either case there was a last meeting between us, when the veils of falsehoods were torn aside, and for one wild, mad, delirious moment I held her in my arms, my lips pressed on hers. It was these wild, mad, delirious moments that so appealed to me. They followed one another thick and fast as rain-drops in a thundershower. I was ever at a climax. The room was brimmed up with lovers' tears and lovers' kisses, meetings and partings, yet never perhaps had the text above my head, though I was far from thinking so, been obeyed so literally and so successfully.

CHAPTER VIII

I WAS wakened in the morning by Tony scratching at my door. Still half-asleep, I got up to let him in, and then returned to bed, where he had already taken the most comfortable place. He looked at me for a moment or two and then closed his round, dark, innocent eyes till they showed only as two slits of dim silver, and set up a loud snoring. I was too lazy to get up, and lay idly watching him. He had a curious and expressive beauty, resembling that of some wonderful piece of Chinese porcelain, at once bizarre and attractive. There was something quaint about him, an adorable simplicity. In colour he was white, decorated with brindle patches. Leonardo would have made a drawing of him, would have delighted in the superb limbs and wide deep chest, the big, broad, heavy, wrinkled head, with its massive, low-hanging jaw, its upturned, flat, black nose, its silky ears, like the petals of a rose, and those dark, lovely eyes, in which, when he was at rest, a profound melancholy floated. As a pup, able to walk and no more, he had been a birthday present from Mrs. Carroll: now he weighed about sixty pounds and was three years old.

As I watched him I tried to make up my mind whether I should say anything further about going to Derryaghy. In spite of all last night's bravery I knew well enough that, when it came to the point, it was really rather impossible deliberately to disobey my father; and, what is more, that I shouldn't want to do so. I somehow kept seeing the thing from his point of view, and this irritated me, because it made me powerless to do anything but sit at home and sulk.

"I'll have to go up to the house and say that I can't come," I told him after breakfast. He had risen from the table and was in the act of taking down our Bibles from the book-shelf, preparatory to "worship"—a function which took place every morning and evening, and which consisted in my reading aloud a chapter from the Bible, and in my father making a prayer. Sometimes he commented on what I read, explained a verse, drew a lesson from it—interruptions I secretly resented, as they tended to prolong "worship"—sometimes he listened in silence.

He put my Bible down beside my tea-cup before replying. Then, when he had resumed his seat, and fumbled with his spectacle-case, he said, "You may go with them; I have been thinking it over."

I answered nothing, though I had a sort of uncomfortable feeling that thanks might possibly be expected. I wondered what would happen if I were to say I didn't want to go, that I should never go again, that I would rather stay here with him quite alone, free from all "worldly temptations." It was really the most perfect opportunity imaginable for a thoroughly sentimental scene, like those in the stories he used to read to me. I pictured how it would be wrung out to the last drop of sloppiness, and be promptly followed by my conversion, or even death-bed.

"I think it is the ninth chapter of Isaiah," my father said, interrupting these meditations.

"I read the ninth yesterday," I replied. "It's the tenth."

My father turned another page, and I began:

"'Woe unto them that decree unrighteous decrees—'" I felt my cheeks grow red, because the verse seemed to me so extraordinarily apt to the decree about my not going to Derryaghy. I did not look at my father, but keeping my eyes glued to the page went on. The rest of the chapter, however, was less pertinent.

"'He is come to Aiath, he is passed to Migron; at Michmash he hath laid up his carriages:

'They are gone over the passage: they have taken up their lodging at Geba; Ramah is afraid; Gibeah of Saul is fled.

'Lift up thy voice, O daughter of Gallim; cause it to be heard unto Laish, O poor Anathoth.

'Madmenah is removed; the inhabitants of Gebim gather themselves to flee,'" etc., etc.

It was not wildly exciting in itself, and I cannot say my reading of it made it more so. The only good point about it was that it did not lend itself to exegesis. The kind of thing my father liked was, "Servants, be obedient to them that are your masters." Then he would interrupt me to say, "That means, when their masters tell them to do what is right. If we are told to do something we know to be wrong, we must refuse to obey."

When I had finished we knelt down before our chairs. My father prayed aloud, and I stared out of the window, and tried to decide whither I should take the Dales. Between the sentences my father, as usual, kept crossing and uncrossing his feet, and scraping them together, as if he were trying to remove a tight pair of slippers. It seemed odd to me that he could pray so earnestly and at the same time use such artificial language, crammed with "thees" and "thous," and "hearests" and "doests." Before he had reached "Amen" I was on my feet, dusting the knees of my trousers.

CHAPTER IX

A QUARTER of an hour later, as I walked up to Derryaghy, Willie Breen, the grocer's son, a little boy of ten or eleven, ran out from the shop, and, after gazing carefully up and down the road, slipped a small piece of paper into my hand. One side of this paper was painted black; on the other a single word, "Friday," was printed in red ink. I put it in my pocket and walked on without making any sign or uttering a word, which was the proper etiquette to observe under these peculiar circumstances; and in equal silence Willie returned to the shop.

When I reached the house, though I had been intending all along to ask for Katherine, I suddenly asked for Gerald instead.

"Gerald isn't down yet," Mrs. Carroll informed me, coming into the hall from the dining-room. "Probably he's not even out of bed. Go up and tell him to hurry. He's in the room next yours. Katherine is seeing about your lunch."

Rather reluctantly I went up to Gerald's room and tapped at his door. "Come in," he said, sleepily.

He was indeed still in bed, and, in spite of the fact of our appointment, did not seem in any hurry to get out of it.

"Oh, it's you!" he exclaimed. "Good-morning."

I felt uncomfortable, for I was sure he would think it queer my coming into his room when I hardly knew him. "Good-morning," I answered, trying to imitate the tone he had used. "I was told to tell you to hurry."

He sat up and yawned. "It's late, I suppose," he murmured. "They hadn't sense enough to send me up my breakfast."

"Do you always have breakfast in your room?" I asked.

He looked out of the window as if I did not interest him. "No," he answered, after a perceptible pause, "but I have it when I want to."

I felt snubbed. I didn't know whether to stay or go, but he decided the matter by telling me to wait till he had had his bath, that he shouldn't be long. He put on a dressing-gown, and left me. When he came back I didn't know why he had asked me to stay, for he began to dress without taking the slightest notice of me. I sat on the edge of the bed and watched him. It seemed to me stupid that I should feel slightly in awe of him, but there was no use pretending that I didn't. I had already made up my mind that I disliked him, yet somehow I could not be indifferent to him—I wanted him to think me important, to admire me. He was only a year older than I was, but he was infinitely more a man of the world, and it was this, really, that impressed me. He dressed very quickly, yet I noticed that the result was just as harmonious as it had been last night. His clothes were of a light brown colour, that was exactly the same shade as his hair, and a little darker than his skin. A pale violet tie was loosely knotted over a cambric shirt. His forehead was broad; his yellow-brown eyes were set widely apart, and were neither large nor small; his nose was straight and his mouth extraordinarily delicate. His ears seemed to me, too, to have their own peculiar beauty. His skin was of a golden-brown colour, but clear almost to transparency, and a tiny blue vein was faintly visible on his left temple, running from the delicate eyebrow to the cheekbone. When he listened his brows slightly wrinkled. I would have given a good deal to have looked like him.

Suddenly I caught his eyes in the mirror watching me ironically. "Do you know you were extremely rude to me yesterday?" he said, without turning round.

I blushed and had nothing to reply.

"Well, I forgive you." He patted me on the shoulder. "I'm ready now. Come along."

"Why wouldn't you play properly when you were asked?" I blurted out, as we went downstairs.

"I would have played if there had been anybody to play to. Neither Katherine nor Aunt Clara knows *God save the Queen* from the *Moonlight Sonata*, and that Dick person is too absurd for words. I'll play for you some time when they aren't there. And now I must have breakfast; I won't keep you very long. . . . What do you want all that for?" he asked, as Katherine suddenly appeared with a large basket.

"For lunch; we're not going to starve ourselves."

"Poor Katherine; evidently you're not. We can each take our own lunch; a basket like that is only a nuisance."

"You needn't carry it," said Katherine. "You and I will carry it by turns," she said to me.

"What's the use of talking like that," answered Gerald. "It doesn't mean anything. If that huge thing has to be dragged all the way I shan't go at all."

He departed to the dining-room, while Katherine and I were left standing in the hall, the basket between us.

"We needn't take any drinkables," I began, "there'll be plenty of water."

"I haven't put in any," said Katherine.

We sat down in the porch to wait for Gerald. When he rejoined us, which he did very leisurely, I glanced at his shoes, and suggested that he should change them for something more substantial.

"Why? We're not going through ploughed fields, are we? I haven't any hob-nails even if we were." A panama hat shaded his face and he swung a light cane in his hand. I knew at once we should have difficulty in getting him any distance, and was very nearly proposing he should stay at home.

"Why aren't we driving?" he asked.

"Such nonsense!" exclaimed Katherine. "If Aunt Clara had wanted us to drive she would have said so."

"I don't mind making inquiries," Gerald intimated. "I somehow feel it's the proper thing to drive."

"You're not to say anything about it; Aunt Clara won't like it, I know."

"I'll drive with our young friend Peter, here," he said airily, tapping me on the shoulder with his cane.

I could see Katherine was becoming impatient; Gerald was the only one who was perfectly cool. "About carrying Katherine's lunch," he began. "Hadn't we better get a stick and put it through the handle of this thing?" He kicked the basket lightly. "Then two of us could struggle with it together."

The idea was a good one, and we put it into practice.

Our road kept all the way by the coast: on the right, the mountains; on the left, a strip of waste land, varying in width, and covered with dry, sapless grass upon which, nevertheless, there were goats feeding; below this, the steep drop down to the sea. Shadowless in the strong sun, the road wound on ahead, white with dust, like a pale ribbon on the green and russet landscape. We had gone about a mile when Gerald suddenly announced, "I'm not going any further; it's too hot."

This brought us again to a standstill. "It's so like you to spoil everything," said Katherine.

"What am I spoiling? I suppose I can please myself. Only, since I'm not coming, I'd advise you to chuck some of that grub away." He took his cigarette-case from his pocket and offered me a cigarette, which I refused. He lit one himself.

"You know very well that if you go home Aunt Clara will think I ought to have come with you, or at any rate be back for lunch," said Katherine quietly.

"How should I know such absurd things? And I can't help what she thinks, can I?"

"We could have stayed out all day."

Gerald had begun to whistle an air very softly, and I recognized it as something he had played last night. His eyes were fixed on the distant horizon, and he seemed slightly bored.

"Perhaps if we were to bathe it might make a difference— who knows? Suppose young Peter and I bathe while you watch the basket here in this pleasant sunny spot; or you could walk on slowly with it, and we might in the end even overtake you?"

I turned to Katherine. "Come along," I said brusquely. "What's the use of bothering about him?"

He looked at me and coloured faintly. "Then I'm to say you won't be home till dinner-time?" he asked, speaking directly to his sister.

Katherine hesitated. "Shall he say that?"

"Let him say what he likes," I returned, shortly.

We moved on together, and I did not look back, though Katherine did, more than once. "I'll make no more arrangements with your brother," I remarked.

Katherine was silent. "Perhaps we should come another day instead?" she began presently, and in a hesitating way.

"You mean you are going to give in to him?" I said, making up my mind that there should be no other day, so far as I was concerned.

She was again silent, and meanwhile we continued to walk on. I could see she was uncertain as to what she ought to do, that she did not want to disappoint me, and that, on the other hand, she was not sure about Gerald. "He's offended at something," she began. "He takes offence very easily. . . . He thinks you didn't want him."

"Why should he think that?"

"I don't know. . . . But it is something of that sort, I'm sure."

I was going to say that I did not care a straw what he thought, but checked myself. "He didn't appear to me to be offended," I replied. "It was simply that he thought it too much fag."

"You don't know him," said Katherine.

And we continued to trudge along, our feet white with dust. It really *was* very hot, and I was glad I had so little clothing on—merely a light cotton tennis-shirt under my jacket. When we reached a low grey bridge that spanned a shallow mountain stream we branched inland. This was the Bloody Bridge, I told Katherine, and a religious massacre had once taken place here. I pointed out the remains of an old church, with its fallen tombs, and after resting for a few minutes we began to climb the valley, which was the walk I had proposed to take them. This valley was wonderfully beautiful, widening out gradually, and gradually ascending; on each side of it steep dark mountains, covered with heather, and grass, and gorse, and hidden streams which flowed into the broader, deeper stream we followed. The colouring was rich and splendid—dull gold, bronze, dark green and even black, with the brighter purple of the heather woven through it, and the long, narrow, pale, silver streak of water, glittering and gleaming, far, far up, till in the end it was lost over the edge of a higher valley which crossed ours at right angles.

"These are the Mourne Mountains?" Katherine asked gazing up at them. "I've seen them from the Isle of Man. On a clear day you can make them out quite distinctly."

She began to talk to me about mountains, about Switzerland, where she had been last spring, and I felt ashamed never to have been anywhere. Yet, while she was describing it, I had an instinct that I should not like Switzerland. By some chance I indeed pictured it very much as, later on, I was actually to find it. Katherine's enthusiasm could not remove this conviction: in fact, what she said, secretly strengthened my idea that it must be an odious

country, and, years later, amid all the showy banality of its pic-
turesqueness, I remembered this particular walk, and my own
beautiful dark country rose up before me, with its sombre hills, its
dreamy, changing sky.

But at the time I had nothing to say, I had no comparisons to
make, I had seen nothing. "I should like to go to a big city like
London or Paris," I told her, "not to live there, but to see it."

"I don't believe you'd like it."

"Why?"

"I don't know. . . . You're so much a part of all this." She glanced
up at the hills.

"Do *you* like cities?"

"Oh, I simply love them; but then I'm quite different."

"I'd like the picture galleries any way," I declared.

"Are you fond of pictures?"

"I've not seen many—only reproductions."

"I'm fond of them too. There was a splendid picture in the
Academy this year of a girl skating. She was holding a muff up to
her face so that it covered her mouth and chin, but she was awfully
pretty, and when you came into the room you would just think
she was a real person. And the snow was so nice, with a sort of
pink light on it. If you come over to London I'll take you to see
everything."

But again, just as in the case of Switzerland, my instinct told me
I should detest this picture. For a moment I had a feeling of depression; it seemed to me of infinite importance that Katherine should
like the things that I liked.

"I don't care for pretty pictures," I said. "I hate everything
pretty," I went on almost angrily.

"Would you rather have ugly ones?" asked Katherine, laughing, as if she had caught me in an absurdity. I had no answer to
give, though I knew myself exactly what I meant. I felt lonely and
melancholy. Then I looked at Katherine. She was very beautiful, and in a quite different way from her brother. And suddenly I
knew where I had seen her before—her eyes, at least—they were
the eyes of Prudence Carroll. . . . I gazed at her, seeking some
further resemblance, but could discover none. Her skin was very

white, save where in her cheeks it flushed to a soft radiant glow. Her brown, crisp hair was pulled back straight from her forehead, though one or two little tufts had got loose and waved in the faint wind. Her nose and mouth had the same delicate beauty as Gerald's, but her expression was quite different, and it was there that her greatest beauty lay. . . . Yes, there again was a resemblance to Prudence Carroll—her expression was the same as Prudence Carroll's. She had the same eyes, the same expression. . . . perhaps, then, the same spirit. . . . A sort of daydream had begun to weave itself into my thoughts.

"How far can we go this way?" Katherine interrupted me.

"As far as you can see. There is another valley beyond. We could go along it and home over Slieve Donard, but it is a long distance."

We climbed slowly, not talking very much. It was past noon now, and hotter than ever, and when we reached a deep green pool under a waterfall we stopped to bathe our hands and faces in it. Its cool sweetness was alluring, as if a water-sprite sang up through it into the hot sunlight, and the white spray sparkled in the sun. "It would be splendid for a bathe," I murmured.

"Bathe if you want to; I can walk on and you can overtake me."

I remembered Gerald, however, and refused to do this, being full to the brim just now of unselfishness and chivalry. "We might have our lunch here," I suggested. "Then we could hide the basket somewhere, and not be bothered by it again till we are going home."

We spread a napkin on a broad flat stone, and our lunch on top of that. I now discovered why the basket had been so heavy, but, though it had been a nuisance carrying it, its contents were extremely welcome. We had almost finished when a peculiar feeling rather than a sound made me look up, and I saw a man standing not more than three or four yards from us. It was as if he had risen out of the earth. When you are under the impression that you are miles away from any human being, such a sudden apparition is a little startling, nor was the appearance of this visitor reassuring. He was large and pale, with short brown hair, and at the back of his head he wore a cap, like a boy's cap, which was too small for him. His clothes, without being ragged, were stained and worn, and of a nondescript, brownish colour. He was young, probably between twenty-five and thirty, and strongly built. There was something coldly malevolent in the pale, clean-shaved face, something indescribably corrupt and cruel, which seemed to stare out of the hard brown eyes, and to hover about the smiling lips. He stood before us, looking down in obvious enjoyment of our discomfiture, making no movement to pass on. It was curious that features so perfectly regular, features neither bloated nor disfigured, could give so vivid an impression of ugliness. It was the ugliness of something positively evil, and my first feeling was one of instinctive repugnance and disgust, as if I had been touched by an obscene and noxious creature. I felt, I can't say why, that I was in the presence of something actively dangerous, and not only to my body, but reaching beyond that: I felt as if I were in the presence of some form of spiritual corruption or decay, that I knew nothing about, and that yet I had a horror of, as a young rabbit is afraid of a hawk. That prolonged, impudent stare, passing over me, seemed to leave a trail of filth, of slime, of something that defiled like a loathsome caress. His eyes slid from me to Katherine with the same repulsive scrutiny. What was he doing here? He was no country man. As my first startled feeling passed, my temper began to rise. "What do you want?" I asked. "How much longer are you going to stand there?"

He laughed almost noiselessly, though he still neither moved nor spoke. It was as if the sound of his laugh touched a spring within me, and I lifted a sharp piece of stone lying near my feet. I felt a sudden rage, an extraordinary desire to destroy. I could actually feel my lips draw back ever so little, just like the lips of an angry terrier. I had no longer the faintest sensation of fear: on the contrary, what I wanted was for him to make a movement forward, a gesture that I could take as threatening. And the rough, natural weapon I had picked up must have acquired a sudden appearance of dangerousness, for our visitor drew back and his face altered. Then he laughed more loudly and on a different note as he passed on his way down the valley. I felt elated. Somehow, I was certain my stone would not have missed its mark, and that there would have been no hesitation, no lack of force, on the part of the wielder. Katherine and I watched him as he retreated, now disappearing from our sight, and now again appearing, but always at a point farther down.

"Well, he's gone," I said. "He was horrible looking." I faced her with a proud consciousness of having behaved very well.

"Do you know what *you* looked like?" asked Katherine. And before I could answer: "You looked just like David when he threw the stone."

I blushed. Then, "I never cared much for David," I answered ungraciously, and moreover untruly, for I was, secretly, extremely pleased and flattered.

"Neither did I till a minute ago, but that was because I didn't know what he was like."

My blush deepened. "Well, the beast's gone at any rate," I said to cover my gratification. "I will tell Michael when we get home. He can't be prowling about here for any good."

"Who is Michael?"

"One of our policemen—the decentest."

We hid the basket under the heather. A quiet had fallen upon us, through which the noise of the splashing water seemed to weave itself in patterns and arabesques of sound.

"Shall we go up higher?" I asked, and without answering me Katherine began to climb the hill-side, and I followed her over dry, springy, fragrant heather, and between huge mossy boulders that had lain undisturbed for centuries. We stopped to look at a fly-catching plant, that curious, unpleasant mixture of the animal and the vegetable. Katherine had never seen one before, and she examined the outspread, concave disc, with the skeletons, the grey husks of flies, adhering to its green surface. We found a bee struggling on his back on the purple flower of a thistle, waving his legs in the air, a ridiculous picture of intoxication. But in spite of these interruptions the silence that had crept over us lingered still. When we reached a place where the ground rose steeply for a yard or two I gave Katherine my hand to help her, and when we came to more level ground we still went on hand in hand. And with this light contact there came to me a strange, thrilling pleasure, intense yet dreamy, unlike anything I had ever known before. I did not look at my companion. When I spoke, telling her to avoid a patch of soft ground that had here spread across the path, the sound of my own voice astonished me, so unfamiliar was it, even trembling slightly; and I felt my limbs trembling. But why should it be so? What was there? Why was I nervous? Nothing had happened but this short easy climb hand in hand. I threw my hat from me and flung myself down among the heather, lying with my hands clasped behind my head, and my face turned up to the dark blue sky. Far, far below us, the sea, blue and deep, broad, beautiful and free, lay shimmering in the hot sun. I had a sensation of intense happiness, physical and mental, into which I seemed to be sinking deep and deeper. I felt my eyes grow moist, and I turned away my head that my companion might not see my face.

Presently I looked round. Katherine was sitting beside me, gazing straight out at the distant sea. The broad brim of her black hat shadowed her face. The deep blue of her eyes seemed darker than before; they had the blue now of the eyes Renoir so often painted, and that I have seen nowhere else. I wanted to say something, I hardly knew what. I hovered shyly on the verge of it, like a timid bather on the brink of the sea, but there was no one to push me in, and my plunge was not taken.

"It's jolly nice here!" Those feeble words were all I could find to express the rapid rush of emotion that had shaken my whole being. The vast and complex forces of nature were stirring within me almost as unconsciously as the new leaf germinates in the growing plant. Yet there was something which, without any words at all, I must have expressed, had there been an observer to see it. I mean the helplessness of youth, its pathetic credulity and good faith, its brightness and briefness in the face of those hoary old hills, and of feelings that were almost as ancient.

I sat up and clasped my hands about my knees. "I wonder what it will be like living in town?" I said.

"Yes, you're going away next month, aren't you? Aunt Clara told me."

"My father wanted me to try for a post in a Government office. There is a boy who lives here who is going to do that: he is working for his exam. now." Then I added, I don't know why; "Mrs. Carroll is paying for me, and will be afterwards, when I go to college. I'm to go to one of the English universities—Oxford, I think. Of course my father couldn't afford to send me, and indeed he'd rather I didn't go at all. He let me decide, however, though there was really only one thing that made him give in."

"What?"

"My mother once sent money to be used for my education, and he would not take it."

Katherine was mystified, and, as I saw this, it dawned on me that I should not have spoken. I had taken it for granted that she knew all about me.

"You know, my mother doesn't live at home," I explained; and then, to change the subject, I took the piece of paper Willie Breen had given me that morning from my pocket.

"Can you guess what that is?" I asked.

She turned it over.

"It means that on Friday there will be a meeting of a kind of club we have," I said. "It is a night club. The whole thing is a secret. We have supper round a fire, and talk, and tell yarns, and all that."

"Outside?"

"Yes; over on the golf-links usually."

"But why at night?"

"Oh, I don't know. Pretty late too—about half-past eleven or twelve. I got it up last year with some of the boys who were staying down here. And then, afterwards, I kept it up with two or three of the chaps at school. This year I got sick of it, and I've only been to one meeting."

"At night! It must be rather queer. I love the sea at night. Are you allowed to bring visitors?"

"There is no rule; there are no rules of any kind. Would you like to come?"

Katherine hesitated. Then she laughed. "Yes. Would it matter?"

"There'll be nobody but boys there."

"But you'd take me; and of course, Gerald would come."

"I'll take you if you'll come by yourself," I said.

"Without Gerald? I couldn't. What harm would he do?"

I did not say; but without Gerald I knew I could carry the thing off, with him it would be difficult. "You'd have to promise not to tell anybody," I explained.

"Of course. If I told, I shouldn't be there myself."

"But I mean even afterwards."

"I'll not tell."

For a minute or two we looked down the hill-side, bathed in the afternoon sun; then I made up my mind. "If you can promise that Gerald won't talk about it I'll take you. But won't you find it difficult to get out?" I added immediately afterwards.

"No; we'll simply sit up later than the others. They seem to go to bed about ten."

"But the lodge-gate will be locked."

"I can easily manage about that."

I regretted having mentioned the matter at all, yet I hadn't the courage to draw back. "I'll tell you on Friday morning exactly when to be ready," I said.

We sat silent. Katherine had taken off her hat and it lay on the ground beside her; she was fastening a bunch of heather into her blue and white muslin dress.

"Have you looked at the portraits in the long passage yet?" I asked suddenly.

"Yes; not very particularly, but I noticed there were some."

"Did you see one of a dark lady standing by a spinet, holding a bunch of flowers?"

"I don't remember. Who is she?"

"Prudence Carroll," I answered. "Look at her when you go in."

Katherine had completed her task. "Why?" she inquired, turning to me.

"I think she is very like you—or you are very like her."

"I shall see; but suppose I don't care for her?"

"Then you can say I'm a fool. But you will care for her—at any rate, I do. I don't mean that your features are just the same as hers."

"And I'm not dark, am I?"

"No; at all events not *so* dark. However, you will see what I mean—perhaps you will see."

"You're not sure? It can't be so very striking then."

"That's just what it is—it *is* striking. It mayn't, however, be exactly obvious to everybody. When I first saw you, I kept wondering who you were like. I couldn't get at it for a long time—then I knew."

"Well, I never even heard of her, but I'm shockingly ignorant of my ancestors."

"She wasn't an ancestor: she was never married; the likeness isn't physical."

"Oh, then I shan't see it. Besides, I never *do* see likenesses, even when they're much less mysterious than this."

"I don't know,—perhaps, in a way, it is mysterious. I can see it more clearly sometimes than others. I don't think I should see it at all if you were asleep or dead."

"What a horrid idea!" She laughed, but not quite easily.

"Do you not feel that these hills are familiar to you?" I asked dreamily. "I can imagine a person coming to some house like Derryaghy for the first time, and then finding that he knew this room and that, where this passage led to, what view he should see when he looked out through that little window at the top of the stairs. Or it might be that two people would come there together, and everything they said would sound like an echo from something that had been spoken before, and each, while they waited for it, would know the answer, before it had left the other's lips."

"I'm not sure that I follow you," said Katherine prosaically, "but I imagine you are trying to make out that I may be what-do-you-call-her Carroll come to life again. You're the strangest boy I ever met."

"You told me I was like David. But—but—pretend it for a moment. Say you were Prudence Carroll, then who should I be?"

"I haven't any idea. Perhaps the apprentice of the artist who painted her picture, if he had an apprentice."

I considered this. It had never occurred to me before. But I could not get back, I could not discover even a faint gleam. It was not the time; I was too saturated with my actual surroundings.

I did not pursue the subject, for I saw it had no interest for Katherine. Besides, I wanted to be quiet. I thought if we sat in silence, if I held her hand; above all, if we sat in silence close together, her arms about me, my cheek against her cheek, the past might swim up into the present, and we should know. But instead of that we began to talk, to talk of things that did not matter, until, by and by, we got up to return home.

CHAPTER X

I STAYED in the house all the evening, but I could not read, and so I sat down to write to Katherine. I wrote for more than an hour, though I was very doubtful whether, in the end, I should post my letter. It was the first time in my life I had ever written to anybody. Of course I cannot remember now what I said: I can remember the sense of it, or the nonsense, possibly, but not how I expressed it. Very badly, I suppose, for I tore my first attempt up, and began another, over which I must have spent an even longer time, since, to finish it, I was obliged to get up and light the lamp. When I went out to the post it was quite dark, and immediately after I had dropped my letter in the box I had a strong desire to get it back again. Why had I been in such a hurry? I should have kept it till morning. Then, as I pictured Katherine reading it, a thrill of pleasure swept through my timidity.

I did not go home, but strolled, instead, over the golf-links in the direction of the sea. At such an hour they were absolutely deserted, and the pale sand-hills, stretching away in the moonlight and beside a dark waste of water, wore an unfamiliar, a slightly weird aspect, suggestive of some desolate lunar landscape. I wandered on, utterly oblivious to time, till I found a comfortable spot between two of these hills, on a gentle slope that was almost like a couch. I was filled with a passionate sense of life, and lying there, with the long thin sapless grass about me and above me, and the soft white powdery sand beneath, I could look out over the sea, and feel myself perfectly alone. The water was a dark mass under the moon, darker than the beach, darker than the sky, but not so dark as the Mourne Mountains, which rose away on my left in smooth, bold, black curves.

There was no wind. Down in the hollow where I lay I was as sheltered as I should have been in bed. The night was washed through with the soft sound of the waves as they splashed in a long curving line on the flat strand that stretched on round to Dundrum, three miles away. Moths hovered above me with a beating of pale delicate wings; and all around, like a vast background for the sound of the sea, was the deep, rich, summer silence of the slumbering world, a silence of unending music, as though the great, living earth were breathing softly in its sleep. I lay on my back, and above me was the vast, deep vault of the sky, full of a floating darkness, in which the white moon hovered like a ghost. And I lay there in luxurious enjoyment of the night, and of the life that was running through my own body. It seemed to me at that moment as if my spirit were no longer merely passively receptive of what was borne in upon it, but that it had actually taken wing, had grown lighter, more volatile, were flowing out through the surrounding atmosphere, through the sky and the sea, were moving with the movement of the water. The earth beneath me was living and breathing, and, obedient to some obscure prompting of my body, I turned round and pressed my mouth against the dry grass, closer and closer, in a long silent embrace.

It was very well there was no one to observe this exhibition of primitive and eternal instinct. I felt a passionate happiness and excitement. My head was bare, the salt sharp smell of the sea seemed to have set all my nerves tingling, and I unfastened my shirt that my breast might be bare also. All the past had slipped from me, and I lived in this moment, squeezing out its ecstasy to the last drop, as I might the juice of some ripe fruit. It seemed to me that I was on the brink of finding something for which all my previous existence had been but one long preparation and search. I was fumbling at the door of an enchanted garden: in a moment it would swing open: already the perfume of unknown flowers and fruits was in my nostrils. My feeling was deep and pure and clear as a forest pool. In my mind I went over the story of Shakespeare's "Venus and Adonis." I thought of the shepherd-boy Endymion. I imagined myself Endymion, as I lay there half naked in the moonlight. My eyes dimmed and the blood raced through my veins; it was as if the heart of the summer had suddenly opened out, like a gorgeous flower, and brought me some strange rapture. . . . .

When I awakened to more commonplace things I knew that it was very late indeed. I wondered what had possessed me, and what story I should tell my father standing there in the hall, holding up a candle, looking at me before he turned round to fasten the chain. I raced home to the fulfilment of this vision, but it was already past midnight, and my father would not listen to my excuses. He was very angry indeed, but his anger could not come between me and my happiness. I listened to it in a kind of dream, and as soon as a pause came, slipped away from it and on upstairs. In the dark, as I undressed, the delicate scent of heather still clinging to my clothes filled the small bedroom, and seemed to bring the whole day back to me from the beginning. Comfortably between the cool sheets I went over every incident of it, while the scent of heather still floated about me; and now I had acquired an extraordinary bravery; I gave utterance to every thought arising in my mind; the embrace which had been so impossible was perfectly easy. One by one exquisite pictures drifted in through the windows of my closed eyes; one by one they opened out before me, like flowers, full of delicious sweetness, and in the midst of them I fell asleep.

But my sleep was only a completer realization of my waking thoughts. I was again with Katherine, and again we were alone on the mountain-side. We were coming home and I was a little behind her, when she stooped to gather a handful of heather. But instead of fastening it into her dress she turned and flung it at me, and then ran on down the hill. I followed quickly, and all at once she stopped running and we stood there, hot and panting and laughing. Then she impulsively lifted her face, and I kissed her. I held her close to me and kissed her again and again. . . . . And the scent of heather floated about my bed, the heather of reality mingling with the heather of my dream.

CHAPTER XI

DURING the morning my father kept me working in the garden where he was erecting a kind of arch of trellis-work above the gate, but after our early dinner I went up to Derryaghy. Ever since I had awakened, my mind had been filled with the letter I had written, and with guesses as to how it would affect Katherine. I hurried along, for our dinner was at two, while their lunch was at one, and I had made no appointment, so that when I reached the house, and found they were all gone out, I was not greatly surprised. Katherine and Gerald had gone out riding; they would be back for tea. I left a message to say I would call some time in the evening and went upstairs to choose a book. In the silent library the faint sound of my feet on the thick carpet made little more noise than the rustle of a ghost, and when I had found what I wanted I paused with the book unopened in my hand. Through the window I could look out into the afternoon garden, sunlit and mellow, but in the house itself the silence of those upper rooms struck me, as always, with a suggestion of a faint, bygone life, of spiritual presences, unseen, yet watching and listening. I walked slowly down the passage, looking at the portraits, and trying to picture the lives of those who had sat for them. Were they aware of my scrutiny, of my curiosity, possibly indiscreet? did I disturb the dust of the past, did they welcome or, perchance, resent my intrusion into that delicate dream-life that had fallen upon them? I loved to amuse myself with such fancies, idle enough, not to be communicated to others. The air seemed heavy with a kind of still, intense reverie, through which there came the vibration of a hidden mysterious life. Were I the true son of the house, I told myself, a sign of recognition might have been given to me; but I was a stranger, an intruder, and my robuster, noisier presence could but disturb their ethereal existence. There was something almost vulgar in being physically alive among that shadowy company. I longed to pass the threshold of their world and learn its secrets. Perhaps if I were really to love

that dark, sweet lady, Prudence Carroll, to declare my love, to kiss
her painted lips, I might be admitted to it. Would she be jealous
when I left her? To love a dream, a memory, that was very possible;
but to be faithful to it? Through the door I had left ajar a golden
stream of sunlight, filled with floating specks of dust, swam across
the shadowed passage, and just touched the flowers in her hand.
But my ghosts had never been afraid of sunlight: they were not
afraid to walk in the deserted garden or to pass me on the stairs or
in the hall. Often I had felt them to be there, and some day, I knew,
I should see them. With this thought there came to me a desire
to revisit their own garden, a walled place of dark green graves,
where they wandered undisturbed.

I went out, forgetting after all my book, and took a short cut
across the fields and down a disused, mossy lane, purple with tall
foxgloves, and sleepy with droning bees, which brought me out
abruptly at the old church. Service was still held here, and as I came
up I saw the door was open. I went inside, and an old woman who
was dusting the pews wished me good-day. I talked to her for a
few minutes and then began to wander idly about, trying my Latin
on the inscriptions, peeping behind doors and through windows.
A church on a week-day was for me quite a different thing from
a church on a Sunday. Its quiet appealed to me, a sort of homely,
gentle charm that was at once dissipated by the entrance of a congregation. I went into the pulpit and imagined myself preaching,
while the old woman, Margaret Beattie, leaned on the handle of
her broom and watched me.

"You'd make the queer fine curate, Master Peter," she said, evidently seeing in this exhibition the betrayal of a vocation.

"They'll never get me, Margaret," I replied. "The Church is not
what it was. I believe you are an old witch," I went on, for she was
half-deaf, "and when you have done your mischief here, you will
ride away on that broomstick."

I went out into the sunshine and pottered about among the
graves. All were old, for nobody was ever buried here now. Most
of the head-stones were stained green with age and weather, and
the lettering was so worn that it was often necessary to peer close
to read a name or a date. I lingered in the corner where lay the

bones of some of those fine ladies and gentlemen whose pictures I had been looking at. Well, it was a pleasant place. . . .

Margaret came out, locking the door after her. I heard her shambling feet on the gravel, followed by the clanging of the iron gate that left me to myself. Had my ghosts preceded me here, or did they still linger in the upper rooms at Derryaghy? I threaded my way among the graves to the low, sun-warmed wall, all golden and green and grey with velvet moss on weathered stone. Before me lay the broad open country I must cross to go home, rich and dark in the late afternoon light. The gleam of water, of pool and stream, shone palely amid long grass and darker gorse bushes: and beyond were trees, black and soft against the western sky, as if rubbed in by a dusky thumb. Distant hills stood out from the grey clouds and the softer, deeper background of luminous sky. Everything shimmered and gleamed in a kind of romantic richness and divine softness that I was to see later in dreamy landscapes by Perugino. And over all was a great sea of light and sky—grey, faint green, and deeper, warmer yellow, with clear silver where the water lay.

I turned from it and sat down on the wall, facing the churchyard. It was a quiet spot, designed for contemplation. The faint wind in the trees was like a low pleasant tune, and there was nothing melancholy in its charm. To me it had a kind of happy beauty which I loved. I had fallen into a mood when I seemed close to my dreamland. It lay beyond an enchanted sea, whose shore was that bright cloud there. I could hear the low, continuous sound of surf breaking on the pale glistening sand; I could see deep lagoons, and sleepy rivers winding slowly down through green lawns and meadowlands. I tried to draw nearer, but it swam away from me, leaving only a broken cloud, and beyond that the endless sky. Had it already been, or was it still to come? Was all this world, apparently so solid under my feet, but my dream, and should I presently awaken to that other? I had a sudden temptation to risk everything: the fascination of death stole over me, quickening my curiosity to know what lay beyond. Only *should* I know? Death might not really solve anything! If I tried to force an entrance I might lose my only chance of finding one. A large, splendid but-

terfly, a red admiral, flitted over the wall and perched on one of the
grave-stones, spreading his gorgeous wings, black and crimson,
flat against the grey, sun-baked stone. He remained there with the
stillness of a painted thing, drinking in the heat, knowing nothing
save that.

The afternoon was waning. The sun had crept down the sky
till he was almost hidden, and the violet shadows were blurred on
the tangled grass. Again one of those strange, breathless silences
seemed to wash up as from some depth of Time, and I listened—
listened for a sign, a word, for in the stillness the faintest whisper
would have reached me. What were they, these strange pauses
in life, in everything—these feelings of suspense, of expectation?
A kind of ineffable happiness and peace descended upon me. A
delicate spirit of beauty seemed to be wandering through the
unmown grass, which bent beneath its feet, wandering under the
broad-leaved trees, beside the grey old church. Surely there was
something of which all this was only the reflection! I could feel it;
I knew it. What did it mean? what was I waiting for? what was it I
desired? I thought of my soul as a little candle-flame, hovering at
my lips, ready to take flight. If I blew it from me it might flicker
away over the grass, down into the graves, up into the air, a tiny
tongue of flame, no bigger than a piece of thistledown. I thought
of the old, silent, listening house, darkening now to twilight,
mysterious, haunted, with its closed doors and brown portraits: a
dream-thing that, too, and all the ghosts who lived there.

CHAPTER XII

It was half-past eight when I left home to go to Derryaghy, but at
the corner of the Bryansford Road I met Willie Breen and stopped
to get particulars about our meeting to-morrow night. I did not
mention the Dales because I was almost sure that in the end Katherine would not come, and in the midst of our talk he broke off
abruptly with: "Here's your fine friends," delivered half-contemp-
tuously. At the same time he stuck his hands in his pockets and
strolled off whistling.

I wheeled round to face Miss Dick and Katherine and Gerald coming towards me. I raised my straw hat.

"We're just going as far as the station and back," said Katherine. "We thought we'd meet you."

I dropped with her a little behind the others and walked as slowly as I could.

"I got your letter," she went on, simply. "It was very nice of you to write, but I hope you didn't want an answer. Letters are beyond me."

"You weren't angry?" I asked, timidly.

"No. What was there to be angry about? Of course, I couldn't make out what it all meant: you didn't intend me, I suppose, to take it quite seriously: but it seemed very flattering and poetic. . . . . I was sorry we weren't in when you came for us. Tell me what you did with yourself all afternoon."

"I walked out to the old graveyard and sat there," I replied.

"How cheerful!"

"It was rather: at any rate I liked it. . . . Let us go along here," I added. "We can get home round this way. It is a good deal longer, but— Do you mind?"

"Not if it doesn't keep us too late."

"I have been thinking about the artist's apprentice," I began. "Do you smell the meadow-sweet?"

"The artist's apprentice? Oh, yes! Well, what were you thinking about him?"

"That he must paint your portrait."

"But can he?"

"He can try, like other apprentices."

"When?"

"Any time. To-morrow."

"Really? Do you paint?"

"Only a little in water-colours. I've not had any lessons."

"And you've made pictures?"

"No, just a few sketches. I never finish anything. Just something to remind me of—things."

"You must show them to me."

"If you like; but you won't see anything in them; nobody ever does. They're only meant for myself—and they're no use anyway."

"What did you really mean by your letter, Peter?"

"I don't know—burn it. I meant everything that's there, but I'm not sure now what *is* there. After I had written it I went out and lay down on the golf-links and listened to the sea. . . . . Would you like me to take you to my old graveyard? I expect you'll be going to church there on Sunday."

"Do you mean now?"

"Yes. It's not far away—just across those fields."

We walked on through the scented darkness.

"I don't know that I like graveyards," said Katherine, doubtfully.

"I don't either—new ones—but this is very old."

I helped her across the stile. Out of the shadow of the tall hedge, the grassy country lay grey and unsubstantial under the rising moon. The black spire of the church showed through the trees, and in a little while we reached the low wall where I had sat all the afternoon. But how changed the place was! Flooded with fantastic moonlight, only the shadows now seemed real.

"You do not want to go inside?" Katherine asked, dissuasively.

"No; we can see it from here." And I leaned over the low wall. "It is not like a modern cemetery," I again told her. "There is nothing horrid here. There are no bodies;—nothing but a little dust, and a few spirits, perhaps, that have not gone away."

"Ghosts? Are you not afraid of them?"

"I don't know. Not now, at any rate; these ghosts are friendly; they are so old."

"Have you seen them?"

"No. I saw one at home in my bedroom when I was a little chap, but it was not nice; it was not like these. . . . You are buried here," I added, smiling.

But Katherine turned away quickly. "Don't," she said. "Why do you like to be so morbid? Besides, I don't think it is right."

I could see that I had vexed her, and I changed the subject.

Down by the grave just below us the tiny green light of a glow-worm glimmered, but I did not point it out to Katherine. A fairy tale of Hans Andersen's came into my mind, and I saw Death, like an old gardener, floating over the wall with a soul, like a baby, folded in his arms; and I watched him lay it softly to sleep under the trees. I had forgotten all the details of the story, but I made a story for myself, and the moonlight on the grass and on the weather-worn gravestones, and the black, lurking shadows, and the still, moon-drenched church, wove into it a mysterious beauty. It seemed to me that something might happen now that would make, for me at least, all things different for ever after, that would push the boundaries of life infinitely further back, by bringing a dimmer, vaster world directly into relation with me. In that world, perhaps, they dreamed of this, just as I was now dreaming of it.

I was aroused by Katherine. "We must go, Peter." She laid her hand on my arm.

"All right."

I took a last look, and then stepped out briskly beside her.

"I oughtn't to have brought you here," I said, "out of your way."

"I enjoyed coming. I am not in any hurry myself, but you know how early they go to bed, and it must be getting late."

"Do you like me, Katherine," I asked, pleasantly.

"If I had disliked you I don't suppose I should have tramped all these miles with you."

"You are sure I don't bore you, or anything?"

"Not up to the present. Why do you ask?" she smiled.

"I just wanted to make sure. Girls, as a rule, would rather have older people than I am—wouldn't they—fellows like the curate? I only mention him because you happen to have met him. You're seventeen, which means that you're grown up, and——"

"I can't make up my mind what you are," Katherine interrupted, laughing aloud. "The first night I saw you you were frightened to open your mouth, and now you're saying all kinds of things."

"That shouldn't be said?"

"No; I like them. I dare say in ten years' time I won't care to be told how old I am, but at present it's all right."

"I didn't mean anything except that there's a difference between us. Girls often get married at seventeen."

"I think, you know, you're rather a dear in your own way," she said, thoughtfully.

CHAPTER XIII

IT was late, and the house was quiet. When I leaned out of my window I could hear the sound of the waves, but no other sound; then I opened my bedroom door softly, and crept out into the passage. From my father's room there came a heavy, muffled snoring as I made my way downstairs. The hall-door I unfastened with the same elaborate precautions against noise, but I left it open behind me, only slipping in the door-mat to keep it from slamming. Once outside, I felt safe.

The night was clear and full of moonlight, and my black shadow danced fantastically before me on the white, bare road. Not a soul was abroad, and as I walked I had a curious sense of freedom and exhilaration; old songs of romance and adventure hummed in my ears, and I wanted them to come true. Contrary to my expectation and to my desire, Katherine and Gerald were waiting for me at the lodge-gate, in the shadow of the hawthorn hedge, and Katherine held a parcel in her hand.

We did not talk very much as we went quickly on, following the same road we had taken on the morning of our picnic. I kept a sharp look-out, but could see no sign of any of the other boys. Below us, on our left, the sea murmured and splashed through the warm delicious night; on the right, the Mourne Mountains rose, black against the sky.

"I'm afraid we're rather late," I remarked after a while. Then I added, "You'll have to take an oath of secrecy."

I had already told them all they would have to do, but I was a little nervous, for I had no idea what kind of reception they would get, and to help to tide matters over I had recommended Katherine, if she came, to bring a supply of provisions, which would always be so much in their favour. For myself I didn't care a straw, though I knew what I was doing would make me unpopular.

We had walked for about a quarter of an hour and had left the village well behind us when down towards Maggie's Leap I saw the red glow of a bonfire. We turned to the sea, clambering over the rough ground, till presently, in a hollow, we saw them, seven or eight boys, sitting round a fire. Thirty feet below, the sea looked black and strange; and the mysterious night floated about us, a night of wonderful beauty.

There was an awkward moment when we advanced into the firelight, and before I introduced them. A silence followed my very lame speech, in the chill of which Gerald lit a cigarette, and we took our seats, slightly beyond the main circle. Nobody made room for us, and when Katherine produced her contributions to the supper I feared at first they were going to be refused. We seemed to have dissipated the romantic atmosphere of the gathering, nor was anything said about the Dales taking a vow of secrecy, which was, nevertheless, one of the rules of the club. I could see Sam Geoghegan, a boy whom I had never liked, but who was the biggest boy there, whispering to his right-hand neighbour, and I knew he was talking about us.

However, as supper progressed, the atmosphere thawed somewhat, and I began to hope things would turn out all right. Willie Breen, who had been fumbling in his pocket, now produced a small bottle filled with some bright red liquid and held it up to the light, gazing at it in silence. Suddenly, when everybody's attention was fixed on him, his face stiffened into an expression of suppressed agony, and he gasped for breath, drawing his hand across his forehead.

"What's the matter, Billy? Stomach bad?" asked Sam.

But Willie's eyes were closed. "If I fall down," he sighed in a whisper, "an' a deadly pallor creeps over me, force open my teeth with a knife, and pour a single drop of this blood-red liquid down my throat——"

"How can you pour a drop?" interrupted Sam.

"Unless it is too late," said Willie, "you will see the colour slowly come back to my cheeks and suffuse them with the glow of life, until at last, when you don't expect it, I'll open my eyes and say, 'Where am I?'"

"*Does* he have fits?" Katherine whispered.

"No: it's only 'Monte Cristo,'" I told her.

Katherine looked at him wonderingly, but Willie had already his mouth crammed with bread and sardines, the sardines she herself had brought.

Most of the boys now lit cigarettes, which Gerald had given them. From the darkness below, the sound of the sea rose up, weird and melancholy, full of an inexpressible loneliness. The warm, ruddy light of the fire flitted across fresh young faces. A dim fragrance seemed to be blown down from the woods, and to mingle with the saltness of the sea.

Sam Geoghegan said suddenly, "I'm a socialist."

This announcement fell rather flat. The beauty of the night had cast a vague spell upon the other members of the club, and they were content to be silent.

"Do you mean like the chaps who were round last week with the cart?" somebody asked indifferently, after a long pause.

"They gave one of the wee books they had with them to my father," said Sam.

"What is it?" asked Willie Breen.

"What's what?"

"A socialist."

"It's not an 'it,' it's a man. It means that everybody ought to get the same chance. There should be no privileges nor private property nor anythin'."

"But whenever you've got things they're yours," said Willie Breen, unconvinced.

"You don't have things—isn't that what I'm saying? Everything belongs to the State—they belong to everybody."

"Socialists are always poor," put in Sam's chum, Robbie McCann, unenthusiastically. "Those lads that were round here tried to get up a collection."

"Of course they're poor," said Sam, pityingly. "You can't give up everythin' and be rich, can you? For dear sake have a bit of wit!"

"Would *their* aunt have to give up her place?" asked Willie Breen, jerking his head toward the Dales.

"Why wouldn't she? Does it belong to her?"

This was a bold idea, and Sam accompanied it with a glare of defiance at Gerald, from whom, nevertheless, a minute ago he had accepted a second cigarette.

"Of course it belongs to her," said Willie, wonderingly.

"Not rightly. Man alive, but you're all thick in the head. The point is that nobody has a right to anything—more'n anybody else, I mean."

"You know all about it, don't you?" asked Gerald, gently.

"I know more than you, anyway, stink-pot," said Sam. Two or three of the bigger boys laughed, and I began to foresee trouble.

"We needn't start a row, need we?" I suggested, amicably.

"I'm not startin' a row; it was him. What call has he to put in his jaw. He wasn't asked to come."

"He was asked," I replied.

"Ay—maybe by you—that's nothin'."

"Let's tell stories," Willie Breen proposed. "Do you know how they make castor oil? There's a woman told me she saw it. It was a big round room, and corpses hanging from hooks in the ceiling; and from the ends of their toes yellow drops were falling into a basin. That was castor oil."

"I'm sure. Anybody can blether you up, Billy."

"I'm not saying I believe it."

"It's a wonder."

Suddenly a deep, low boom rose up from the sea, as if coming out of the infinite night, swelling, like the heavy bass note of an organ, and dying away.

Katherine laid her hand on my arm. "What was that?" she said.

"It's nothing," I murmured; but a vague sense of awe had crept over the little group.

"It came last summer for the first time, didn't it?" asked George Edge, a boy who had not spoken before. He had been lying on his back, looking up at the floating stars, but he now raised himself on his elbow and looked out to sea. He was not one of the village boys, but his people came down every summer for two months, and I had known him all my life. "My mother gets frightened when she hears it," he went on.

There was a pause, and then the sound came again, floating up, weird and mysterious, as from somewhere far out on the water.

We drew closer round the fire, and began again to talk, but the conversation had grown darker.

"It was here that the murder was," said another boy, hidden in the shadow of the rock, so that his voice seemed a disembodied sound speaking out of the darkness.

"Just over there," said George Edge.

"What murder?" asked Gerald.

The voice from the shadow spoke again. "It was a man called Dewar. There was two of them comin' home one winter afternoon from Annalong, O'Brian and Dewar. O'Brian had been gettin' money, and they both had their load of drink. It was dirty weather and no one on the road, and maybe they fell out about somethin'. Any way, next day they got O'Brian down below there on the stones, his face bashed in you wouldn't know him. Him and Dewar were seen leavin' Annalong together, and they got Dewar lying drunk in his own house, and he confessed and was hung for it."

"But how did he do it?" Gerald asked.

"He smashed him on the face with a lump of rock, and then threw him down into the sea. They say there are nights when you can hear O'Brian. It's like this." He gave a low wail that shrilled up to a cry.

"I'm goin' home," said Willie Breen, rising to his feet.

"Wee scaldy! You'll have to go by yourself," jeered Sam. "And you'll meet him as sure as death. You'll know him, because he won't have any face on him, only a lock of blood. And Dewar with him, with his neck broke." Sam's head drooped horribly to his shoulder.

Willie Breen sat down.

"When you talk about ghosts or spirits it's supposed to bring them near," said George Edge. "It gives them a kind of power over you."

"For goodness sake stop all that rubbish," cried Katherine, indignantly. "Can't you see you're frightening the child out of his wits!"

"Go to her, baby. Hold her hand," mocked Sam.

Willie turned angrily on his protectress. "I'm not frightened. It's you that's frightened. You shouldn't be here at all. There shouldn't be any women in the club."

"Faith, he's right there!" Sam exclaimed.

But George Edge, sitting up, pointed out to sea. "Listen," he said impressively.

We all sat still, Willie Breen with wide-open eyes. A moment after, with a blade of grass between his thumbs, Sam made an unearthly screech in the little boy's ear. It was too much, and Willie set up a howl.

At the same instant Katherine turned to Sam and he received a resounding slap on his fat face. Instantly there was tumult. Sam was on his feet, red as a turkey-cock, blustering of all he would do if Katherine were not a girl. Then he spied Gerald, and gave him a blow on the chest that almost sent him into the fire. "That's for you, you 'get.'"

Gerald drew back, neither speaking, nor returning the blow: the other boys had surrounded them. I saw Gerald's face, and it was very white; but he did nothing, he was afraid. That he should be disgusted me, and at the same time I was furious with Sam, whom, for that matter, I had always detested. I waited just long enough to give Gerald a chance to face him, if he wanted to; then I gave Sam a slap with my open hand on his cheek. It was the second he had received within two minutes, and somehow, even in the excitement, I couldn't help being amused.

We stripped to our shirts and trousers and moved out into the moonlight. Katherine hovered in the background, but made no attempt either to interfere or to go away. Gerald had disappeared. I looked at Sam's big fists. I knew he was taller and heavier than I was, but I was not afraid of him; instead, I had a cold determination to lick him. I felt elated; I was glad Gerald had drawn back, since it gave me this chance of showing Katherine what a hero I was. We chose seconds, and there was a time-keeper, though no one had a watch, for mine was wound up and safe under my pillow at home. We had little science, but were mortally in earnest.

At the beginning of the second round the nervous tremor of Sam's mouth as he stepped into the ring gave me a cruel pleasure. I did not believe very much in his pluck, and I was now quite con-

fident as to the finish. It was in the middle of the third round, and
we were both panting and bleeding, when Michael, the policeman,
appeared on the scene, springing up as if from the bowels of the
earth. How he came to be out of bed at such an hour, and in this
particular spot, I never discovered, but he stepped in between us
and stopped the fight.

"Well now, this is nice goings on! Will you tell me what it's all
about?"

"You go quietly to hell," said Sam in a low voice.

The others chimed in. "It's none of your business, Michael,
we're not in the town."

"Do you tell me that, now? Well, I'll be troubling you to go
home to your beds every one of yous. This is no place for you,
Miss," he added, having discovered Katherine in the background,
"with a lot of young rapscallions. I'll see you safe home."

But Katherine did not move.

"Let them finish, Michael. Nobody'll ever know you were here.
There'll be no talk."

Michael wavered. The presence of Katherine obviously both
troubled and puzzled him, for of course he knew who she was.
He turned to her again, but she had withdrawn into the shadow of
the rocks, whither he followed her, and they whispered together in
inaudible tones. Then he came back. Katherine had disappeared;
possibly she had followed Gerald, who would hardly have gone
very far without her; at any rate I could not look after her now.

"Well, I suppose you'll be wanting to settle this," said Michael,
doubtfully.

His words were received with an outburst of cheers and laughter. A faint greyness of dawn was already spreading over the
eastern sky. "Time!" called George Edge, and I noticed that he had
actually borrowed Michael's big silver watch.

CHAPTER XIV

NEXT morning I got a rowing up from my father. Indeed, as soon
as I saw my face in the glass, I knew it would be quite useless to

try to hide what had happened, and I told him frankly I had been fighting. Fortunately, it was not necessary for me to say anything about our club, nor did I even mention Sam's name. I simply told him that the fight had taken place at night to prevent its being stopped, and after that held my peace. My main feeling, in spite of my father's lecture, was that I was extraordinarily glad it *had* taken place, for I had come out of it victorious, even though I was pretty sure I had received more punishment than I had given. My state of mind absurdly resembled that of a young cock who gets up on a wall to crow, and nothing my father could say had the least power to damp my spirits. My face—especially all round my forehead and temples—was beautifully and variously marked, yet there was nothing I more ardently desired than that Katherine should see me in this condition. I even felt amicably disposed towards Gerald, who, after all, couldn't help being a coward. Perhaps he would come round this morning to see how I had fared.

But nobody came, and in the afternoon I determined to go up to Derryaghy. Willie Breen, who now regarded me in the light of a hero, accompanied me. When I left him at the lodge-gate, instead of going to the hall-door, I went round to the back of the house, hoping to find Katherine on the terrace. She was not there; nobody was there but Miss Dick, who cried out at once on seeing my battered condition. Her tone was certainly far enough removed from that of Willie Breen to have cooled my conceit had such a thing been possible, but fortunately she was too much occupied with a letter she kept folding and unfolding to bestow any very lengthy attention on my appearance. "My sister, Mrs. Arthur Jenkins," she began, not because I was worthy of her confidence, but because there was nobody else, "wants me to go and stay with her. I don't know what to do. Mrs. Carroll may not be able to spare me; though I haven't been there for a long time."

"Oh, you ought to go," I said easily. "Where is everybody?" I looked round, preparatory to making my escape. Miss Dick regarded me doubtfully.

"The last time I was there the youngest child had croup. They were very anxious about him; indeed the doctor almost gave him up; though he managed to pull through in the end, and is quite strong now. Not that any of them are actually what you would call robust. They really take after Arthur, Mr. Jenkins that is, though Sissie, that's my sister, always says *he's* stronger than he looks. I'm sure I hope so, for he looks wretched. The whole family, you know, the whole Jenkins family I mean, are vegetarians, and vegetarians, whatever they may feel, invariably *look* ill. When I say that to Sissie she always gets cross, as if I could help it! But that's what people are like. Arthur wants to bring up the children in the same way, which is silly, and, to my mind, trifling with their lives. Besides, it's so difficult when you've only one maid who has to do everything: and they only give fourteen, and what can you get for fourteen nowadays, even in the country? You certainly can't expect a girl like that to cook two dinners a day, because, you see, Sissie eats meat." She stopped suddenly, as if she had lost the thread of her discourse. "We're all going to a garden-party at Castlewellan. I'm just waiting for the others. Except Gerald—he won't come. You'll find him over there,"—she waved her left hand. "He's put up a hammock and he's been sleeping in it all day. He's dreadfully lazy. He won't even practise. And though he's so polite and gentlemanly, I must say he's really rather irritable: he got quite cross at lunch. I don't think Katherine understands him. People with very artistic feelings, I'm sure, *are* more easily annoyed than others. It's not as if he were just an ordinary person like you or me."

Whether I was an ordinary person or not, I didn't relish being told so, even by Miss Dick, and I decided, as I had frequently decided before, that she was a stupid creature, and that I didn't like her. I left her referring to the epistle from Mrs. Arthur Jenkins, or Sissie, or whatever she was called, and went to look for Gerald.

He had heard me coming, for when I found him he had swung himself out of his hammock and was standing beside it.

"Are the others gone yet?" he asked.

"They're just starting. I only saw Miss Dick."

"They're going to some party, thank the Lord!"

"Yes; she told me."

A pause followed, for I didn't know what to say, and he himself kept silence. What I had intended to do was to put him at his ease, to let him know that it was all right about last night, but my magnanimity and sympathy were evidently quite superfluous, and I was annoyed at this.

We strolled back slowly to the house. "Wouldn't it be rather a good time to play to me?" I said. "You promised to, and now we have the place to ourselves."

"If you like."

We entered by the open window, and pulling the sofa over beside it, I lay down in supreme laziness among a heap of coloured cushions. Gerald went at once to the piano.

"What sort of music do you care for?" he asked me. "Or shall I just play anything?"

"Yes; whatever you feel in the mood for."

His head was bent a little over the key-board, and he seemed to be thinking of what he should play. I watched a tendril of clematis that waved softly over my head, and every now and again I breathed in the sweet scent of a stalk of mignonette I had gathered in passing. My thoughts floated away through the quiet afternoon, and I began to wonder what things were like when there was no one there to be conscious of them.

I know now that it was the fifteenth Prelude, but at the time I had never even heard the name of Chopin, and all I was aware of was that a soft, very delicate tune, was coming to me across the room, with a curious pallor, suggestive of the whiteness of water. I half closed my lids and lay absolutely still. Even in my ignorance I knew that the beauty of Gerald's playing was extraordinary. It may have had many faults; he may have been incapable of doing all kinds of things that professional pianists can do; he may have been, and probably was, deficient in power: I do not know. He seemed to caress the notes rather than to strike them, he seemed literally to draw the music out, and the whole tone had a kind of liquid, singing quality, such as I have never heard since save in the playing of Pachmann. As I listened, the music gathered force and sombreness, growing louder and darker in a heavily marked crescendo, and then once more it passed into the clear soft tune with which it had begun.

The sound had stopped. I said nothing; I simply waited. The cool, pleasant summer afternoon had become full of lovely voices which flickered, like waves of coloured light, across my senses.

Pensively, a little shyly even, a simple, drooping melody breathed itself out on the air with a strange hesitation and indecision, rising and falling, faltering, repeating itself, resting on the "F" with a kind of desire that gathered intensity as the note swelled and died away, sinking back into "D."

Listening to Gerald playing that sixth Nocturne, listening to him playing all that followed it, you would have thought he was a youth of the deepest feelings, yet I could never find any trace of those feelings at any other time. Somewhere, I suppose, they must have been, somewhere below the surface, but I was never able to discover them. It was as if his soul only came into being when he sat down at a piano. When he played you could see him listening to his own music, you could see him drinking it up as if it were the perfume of my mignonette, as if there were some finer echo audible only to himself. And his playing would alter, would grow gayer, or a kind of weariness would creep into it. I offer these only as the impressions I received at the time; what I should receive now I cannot tell. Yet I find it hard to believe I was utterly mistaken. It was never my fortune to hear him in later years, when I had heard many famous pianists— and I suppose I have heard practically all those of my time—but I cannot help thinking he might have been among the greatest had he not chosen to be something else, something I last saw at a café in Berlin. The puffed, horrible face, the glazed, sodden eyes—no, there was no music there. Or if there was, it was hidden, buried, lost for ever in that desecrated, half-paralysed body, buried alive, like a lamp burning in a tomb. Now, I have nothing to go upon save those first impressions of a boyish, uncultivated taste, and the fact that in after years the playing of Vladimir de Pachmann brought back sharply to me the memory of that afternoon.

He played on for nearly two hours. In the end he stopped abruptly and got up from the piano, while I thanked him. I knew that he knew he had given me a tremendous pleasure, and there was no need to say much. He told me the music I had been listening to was all, or nearly all, by one composer.

"And that last thing?" I asked.

"That was one of the Studies—the one in A flat. I can't play anybody else. I don't mean that other things are more difficult, but they don't suit me." He was silent, until he added, "I may as well tell you that I'm not as good as you think."

"I haven't told you yet what I think," I answered, smiling, for I was still under the glamour of his mood, and indeed at that moment I could have hugged him. I did not want to talk of ordinary things. The music had wakened in me a feeling of melancholy, like a memory of some delicious thing that had happened long ago, and would never happen again.

I tried to explain my very tenuous ideas to Gerald, but they did not interest him. And already I felt our relation altering. When he was at the piano he had seemed to me a kind of angel; now that other element, that element of latent antagonism, was beginning to re-awaken in me.

Tea had meanwhile been laid for us upon the terrace. Tony, who had been asleep outside in the sun, threw off drowsiness like an outworn garment, and sat up beside my chair, with raised head, and beautiful, dark eyes that watched every movement I made, especially those which happened to convey a piece of bread and butter or cake into my mouth. When I looked at him he instantly gave half a dozen quick wags of his tail, and then resumed his former attitude of motionless expectation, to which attention was attracted by a variety of queer little highly expressive noises he produced from somewhere in his throat. Nobody being there to prevent me, I gave him about half the cake, piece by piece, each of which he swallowed almost whole, and with a wag of the tail to show how he appreciated this delicate pastime.

"Did you get much hurt last night?" Gerald asked me suddenly.

The question was unexpected, for I looked upon the whole incident as closed. I glanced up from feeding Tony. "No; not much," I answered.

"And the other—I forget his name—Sam something?"

"Oh, Sam's all right."

"Do you think I should have fought him?"

"One was enough," I said carelessly.

"Did you think I was afraid?"

I looked away. His question seemed somehow to be all wrong. "I didn't think about it," I answered, after a slight pause.

"It must have looked as if I were afraid," he went on. "I thought so afterwards."

I couldn't imagine what he was trying to get at. I wanted to stop him talking like this. It was even less to my taste than his funking Sam last night had been.

"Are you working at anything besides music?" I asked him, jerkily.

He shook his head. "Not very much. I have a tutor. Why won't you talk about last night?"

"What is there to talk about? I'm sorry it turned out that way, but I can't help it, though of course it was my fault for taking you without letting the others know. I should have told them beforehand."

"I'm not afraid of that lout, anyway. If I see him again——"

"Oh, well, what's the use of worrying about it?" I interrupted, disgusted with his persistence.

The pause that followed was an uncomfortable one. If he had deliberately tried to efface the impression his music had made upon me he could not have succeeded better.

He gave a strange little laugh. "I see you don't believe me."

"No: I don't believe you," I answered bluntly, "and I don't know why you should want me to."

"I suppose you think it is pleasant to be taken for a coward?"

"I'm sure it isn't pleasant; but I can't imagine that it matters greatly to you what I think."

"Of course, if I hadn't done what I did, you wouldn't have had *your* particular little swagger!"

"Isn't that rather a rotten sort of thing to say?" I answered as I got up. "I think I'll move on. Come, Tony."

Gerald began to apologize.

"Oh, it's all right," I said, coldly, leaving him there.

CHAPTER XV

KATHERINE, who had promised to sit to me for her portrait, kept putting me off from day to day, and it was nearly a week later when I made my first attempt. By some happy chance on that particular afternoon I had found her alone, for as a rule Gerald was there, and even now it was almost as if he were with us, since she began at once to talk about him.

"You must take off your hat," I said, ignoring her remarks.

She obeyed me, and I began to draw in my outline.

"Gerald likes you," she said. "I wish you would be friends with him."

"But I am friends with him," I answered, abstractedly.

"Not very much. You would rather he was not with us."

"That doesn't mean I'm not friends with him."

"He has so few friends," she went on, still clinging to the subject.

"Has he? I'm afraid, no matter how much I tried, we could never really be chums."

"Why?"

"I don't understand him."

"Why don't you understand him?"

"I suppose because I'm stupid. Besides, what I do understand I don't greatly like."

She was not offended; she simply asked, "What is the matter with him?"

I feared I had been horribly rude, but the words had slipped out before I could check them. "There is nothing the matter with him," I answered hastily. "I wasn't thinking of what I was saying. It is only that—that we're not suited to each other: we're too different. At all events, it is of very little importance, seeing that you're going away in a few days."

"We'll be back again next year, I expect. Aunt Clara wants me to come. *She* isn't very friendly to Gerald either."

"Oh, you only fancy that; of course she is. And there's Miss Dick, who worships the very ground he walks on."

"Miss Dick's too silly for anything."

"There you are! And yet you want me to worship him too!"

"I don't want anything of the kind; and you know that. But of course if you don't like him I can't make you. I think that night— the night we went with you to your meeting—has something to do with it."

"Oh that!" I answered lightly. It seemed to me a long time ago, though there was a yellow bruise still visible above my left eyebrow.

I finished my outline and began to paint. The other picture had been painted indoors, I reflected. I don't know what made me think of it, but I couldn't get it out of my mind. It kept floating between me and my work, and I seemed to see it quite as clearly as I saw Katherine herself. Still I persevered, though my progress was slow and from the beginning unsatisfactory. I talked to Katherine, or rather I replied to her, for what she said penetrated only the fringe of my consciousness. She had brought a book out with her, and by and by she began to read aloud, but I have no idea what it was she read. I painted away most diligently, yet all the time I couldn't get rid of a foolish impression that I was being watched. And this fancy, utterly absurd if you like, took possession of me, grew stronger and stronger, till it seemed to tremble on the verge of reality.

"What are you looking at?" Katherine asked me suddenly, having reached, I suppose, the end of a chapter or a story.

"Nothing," I answered guiltily.

But she wheeled round in her chair, and stared back at the house. I dipped my brush in water, and remarked quite quietly, "It's only that I thought I saw someone at the window—the third window from the left, upstairs."

Katherine shaded her eyes with her hand. "I can't see anybody: the sun catches the glass. It must be one of the maids, for there's nobody else in." She yawned and took up the book again. "If it *is* one of the maids," she added, "she might have had sufficient sense to bring us out tea. I've been simply dying for some for the last half-hour, only I didn't like to disturb you."

"She hasn't been there half an hour," I replied. "I'll go and tell them. Promise you won't look at what I've done while I'm away: it isn't finished."

"All right. I must see it when it *is* though: you're not to tear it up or anything."

"No, of course not."

I walked back to the house, and not till I was quite close did I glance up at the windows above me. Naturally there was nothing. I hesitated in the hall. Had I been really sincere in thinking I had seen anything or not? I couldn't be quite sure, for there was no doubt I often deliberately gave my imagination a kind of push in a certain definite direction, started it off, as it were, and then left it to perform all kinds of antics. Before me lay the broad, low staircase. Should I go up? I leaned against the balusters and listened, gazing aloft into the cool shadow. Suddenly I heard a door open near the kitchen, then the rustle of a dress, and one of the servants appeared. I told her that Miss Dale would like tea brought outside, and went into the morning-room myself for a small folding-table, which I carried back with me.

I looked again at my drawing. "Tea will be here in a minute or two," I said. Then I handed the drawing to Katherine, for it was a failure, and there was no use going on with it.

"Don't hold it so close to you," I cried, and Katherine obediently stretched out her arm full length.

"I think it's quite good, you know, if it wasn't meant to be my portrait,—but it's no more like me than Adam."

"Don't be so rude. Of course it's like you."

A servant appeared with a tea-tray, and as soon as she was gone I seated myself on the grass at Katherine's feet. When I had finished tea and had handed her back my empty cup I still sat there.

"Do you see that strip of yellow sand down below? It always reminds me of a certain poem."

I knew Katherine was not fond of poetry; she had told me so herself; but I repeated the verses aloud for my own pleasure, in a sort of sing-song, laying tremendous stress on the rhymes.

> "It was many and many a year ago,
>   In a kingdom by the sea,
> That a maiden there lived whom you may know
>   By the name of Annabel Lee;
> And this maiden she lived with no other thought
>   Than to love and be loved by me.

"*I* was a child and *she* was a child,
    In this kingdom by the sea;
But we loved with a love that was more than love—
    I and my Annabel Lee;
With a love that the winged seraphs of heaven
    Coveted her and me.

"And this was the reason that, long ago,
    In this kingdom by the sea,
A wind blew out of a cloud, chilling
    My beautiful Annabel Lee;
So that her highborn kinsmen came
    And bore her away from me,
To shut her up in a sepulchre
    In this kingdom by the sea.

"The angels, not half so happy in heaven,
    Went envying her and me—
Yes!—that was the reason (as all men know
    In this kingdom by the sea)
That the wind came out of the cloud by night,
    Chilling and killing my Annabel Lee.

"But our love it was stronger by far than the love
    Of those who were older than we—
    Of many far wiser than we—
And neither the angels in heaven above,
    Nor the demons down under the sea,
Can ever dissever my soul from the soul
    Of the beautiful Annabel Lee:

"For the moon never beams, without bringing me dreams
    Of the beautiful Annabel Lee;
And the stars never rise, but I feel the bright eyes
    Of the beautiful Annabel Lee;
And so all the night-tide, I lie down by the side
Of my darling—my darling—my life and my bride,
    In her sepulchre there by the sea,
    In her tomb by the side of the sea."

I looked up at Katherine and saw that she was smiling. "It was written about this place," I declared, "about just that strip of yellow sand and that blue sea."

"And about just this little boy," said Katherine, stroking my hair back from my forehead.

"Just this little boy," I answered, narrowing my eyes under her touch, "whom you think such a very little boy indeed."

"Such a dear little boy," murmured Katherine, lulling me with her voice, and all the time stroking my hair.

"Is he dear?" I asked eagerly.

"I think so."

"And you like him?"

"I like him very much."

"How much? What do you like about him?"

She laughed. "I like everything about him."

"But what?"

"The way he is: the way he looks: the way he pouts when he is cross: the kind of things he says: the way he asks questions: even the way he hesitates before some letters, so that you can see what he is going to say in his eyes before he can get it out."

I was intensely happy. I leaned back my head, and Katherine's dark blue eyes looked straight down into mine. I could see nothing but that clear dark blue which seemed to shut me out from the world, yet I knew she was smiling. Then she bent lower and her lips lightly touched my forehead.

Almost at the same moment I heard the swish of petticoats rustling over the grass from behind. I sat up straight, but did not look round till the rattle of tea-cups had ceased, and the servant who was bearing them off had almost reached the house.

"Gracious! I hope she didn't see me kissing you!" said Katherine, half-laughing.

"What matter?"

"Of course it matters; and it's your fault too, for pretending to be a little boy and all that nonsense. I'm sure she's telling the cook about it at this moment. *She* doesn't think you're a little boy. Get up at once."

I knew Katherine wasn't really much perturbed, but I got up
and began to put away my colours, and we went back to the
house. I left my painting materials on the windowsill, and, having
made Katherine a present of my drawing, we strolled down to the
shore. As we walked along the hard sand by the edge of the sea I
wanted to tell her how much I cared for her. It was an admirable
opportunity, and, if I could only get the first plunge over, I knew
it would be all right. But I couldn't. White sea-gulls were swoop-
ing and wheeling over the dark blue water, calling their peculiar
lonely cry, and the foam of the waves was white as snow. "I will
tell her: I will tell her," I kept repeating to my soul; and all the time
I maintained a most discreet silence on the subject, and babbled
instead of the regatta that would take place on Saturday, and of
the chance of a fine day. I had entered for two swimming-races and
a diving-competition, and Katherine was coming to see me. I kept
on talking about this, though I knew very well everything would
happen exactly as it had happened last year; that in the swimming-
races George Edge would be first and I should be second, and that
I should win the diving-competition; and moreover I didn't in the
least care just then whether the regatta took place or not.

CHAPTER XVI

As a matter of fact I didn't win the diving-competition; I wasn't
even second; and my defeat was brought about simply by my own
exceeding eagerness to show off.

On that Saturday the village was a holiday village. The men and
boys perspired freely under heavy, ugly, Sunday clothes, and the
women and girls were decked out in all kinds of finery—bright
dresses, trinkets, ribbons, and cheap but brilliant hats. Why was it,
I wondered, that all these fine garments should have been chosen
apparently for a mysterious property they had of bringing out
in the appearance of their wearers a coarseness I never noticed
on ordinary occasions? Sam Geoghegan's salmon-pink tie, Mr.
McCann's fancy waistcoat, the peacock-blue dress of Annie Breen,
with its white lace collar—these were things positively bewilder-

ing, if one realized that they represented the actual taste of the persons they adorned.

Every year the same programme was followed. In the morning the water-races—boat-races and swimming-races—took place; in the afternoon there were sports—foot-races, tugs-of-war, wrestling—held in one of Mrs. Carroll's fields.

I drifted about in the crowd with a group of boys. Our swimming-races came off fairly early, but I was only third in each, and George Edge second, for a youth, whom neither of us had ever seen or heard of before, turned up and carried off both first prizes. This made me anxious about the diving-competition, which he had also entered for. We were to go in off the end of the pier, where a platform with a spring-board had been erected for us. Then, when we had dived, we swam round to the ladder and climbed up to take our turn again. It was the last event but one of the morning's programme, and had always been the most popular. When the hour for it came round, having learned in the meantime from some of the spectators that the victorious stranger was a poor diver, I had regained confidence, and, as the crowd drew in closer to watch us, I was fully prepared to show them what was what. As a matter of fact, my first two dives were all right, but, before my third and last, I caught sight of Katherine standing quite close to me, and the result of this was that I determined to excel anything ever seen. I took a tremendous race the full length of the platform, but, just at the end of the spring-board, my foot slipped and I sprawled in flat on my belly. The shock knocked all the wind out of me, and the smack I gave the water could have been heard half a mile away. It was extremely painful, and it put me out of the competition; yet when I clambered up the iron ladder I was greeted by volleys of laughter and humorous remarks. My accident, indeed, appeared to be by far the most enjoyable event of the morning. It did not seem to occur to anybody, except one of the stewards, that I might be badly hurt, and him, when he came to ask me if I were all right, I sent about his business. I put on my overcoat and went to the dressing-shed in a furious temper.

The field where the sports took place lay about a mile out of the village. Mrs. Carroll and some other ladies were dispensing

refreshments to all comers, and afterwards the prizes would be
given out. I went up to Derryaghy to call for Katherine and Gerald,
to go with them, but found they were going to ride over, and were
all ready to start when I arrived. It was the first time I had seen
Katherine on horseback, and she looked to me more beautiful than
ever. In her dark-blue riding-habit, with her sparkling eyes and rosy
cheeks, her radiant youth and health, she made me think of the
girl in the equestrian portrait by Millais and Landseer, a coloured
reproduction of which I had cut out of a Christmas number and
tacked up on the wall in my bedroom. And straightway I saw in
myself the page-boy who stands by the gateway in that picture,
his eyes fixed in rapt admiration upon his mistress. They rode
away, an amazingly handsome pair, telling me they would see me
later up at the field, and to this I answered, "Yes." Mrs. Carroll and
Miss Dick had already gone on in the carriage, so I was left quite
alone. I decided immediately that I wouldn't go to the sports: if
they chose to leave me like this I wasn't going to run after them.
I mooned about, building a romance on the equestrian portrait
motif. I imagined myself as dying; some accident had happened to
me, and suddenly Katherine rode up and springing down from her
horse threw her arms round me, kneeling in the blood and dust of
the road. She kissed me passionately, careless of all the people who
watched her, repeating again and again, "I love you—I love you—I
love you."

I gloated over this imaginary scene till I had squeezed the last
drop of colour out of it, and it ceased, by dint of much repetition,
to thrill me even faintly: then I went into the house and nosed
about for a book. A dozen had just come down from the library in
town, and, with a couple of volumes of "Two on a Tower" under
my arm, I made my way to the shore.

Gradually, in the warmth of the sunlight, I grew drowsy, and the
beautiful, breaking sea, and the harsh crying of the gulls, soothed
me and seemed to build up an enchanted world about me, where
I was shut in with the romance of the tale I was reading. By and
by, after perhaps two hours, I closed my book, though still keeping
my finger in the place. I reflected that nobody up at the field had
spent such an afternoon as I had spent, and I compared my spiri-

tual pleasure with their rough commonplace pleasures, and the extraordinary superiority of my soul became immediately apparent. Then my thoughts turned to the story I had been reading. My sympathies were entirely enlisted by Lady Constantine and her youthful astronomer, but particularly by Lady Constantine. Even the fact that she was so much older than her lover appealed to me. Her gentleness; her intense femininity; her dark eyes; the softness of her skin; the perfume of her hair; and the delight of her caresses—these were present to me vividly, almost physically, and I rejoiced in the love-scenes in the tower with a frank and innocent sensuality, filling in the picture, where it was blurred or vague, from my own imaginings.

CHAPTER XVII

DURING that last week of August, after the Dales had left, "I wandered lonely as a cloud." Up to the eve of their departure I had been happier than I had ever been in my life, but as soon as they were gone I became a prey to sentimental regret. If Katherine had cared for me as I cared for her I might have found more comfort; but she didn't, and I was perfectly aware of the fact. Mingled with it all was an increasing dread of the new existence I already saw opening out before me. I distrusted it: I had, indeed, that instinctive distrust of life itself, which contemplates anything unknown with uneasiness, and clings with passion to familiar faces and things.

When the day of my departure, a Saturday, came round, and I saw my box all corded and ready in the hall, I felt extremely depressed. Now that I had said good-bye to Mrs. Carroll it was as if I had cut myself completely adrift from the past, and yet I believe I should have been willing to go had I not been going to the McAllisters. The McAllisters were our relations; the only ones I knew of. Aunt Margaret was my father's sister, and her husband kept a shop in a street called Cromac Street. I had never been to their house, but they had been down a good many times to visit us, and I did not care for them. There were four children, and I disliked them all, except George, the eldest; and I disliked Aunt Margaret in particular; while to Uncle George I was indifferent, seeing that he did not very much count one way or the other. But to live with them! . . .

Mrs. Carroll had wanted to send me to a school in England, but my father would not permit this. He had an idea, and nothing would ever shake it, that English public schools were dens of iniquity. This he had gathered from some article that had appeared in a review, and from the story "Eric." I suppose he thought I should fall a particularly easy victim to the temptations I might be submitted to; take, like the boys in "Eric," to drink, "little by little," or even quite rapidly; come home disgraced; at any rate he would not run the risk, when, by sending me to the McAllisters, he could provide me with the "influence of a religious home." For Uncle George was religious, and so was Aunt Margaret; and so, I supposed, were the children—George, at least, I had been told, was a communicant—and it was the thought of all this that now lay heavy on my soul.

I was not to go up to town till the afternoon, and as we sat down to our early dinner I could not, though I knew it was absolutely useless, refrain from again taking up the tabooed subject. I suggested how much better it would be for me to go into lodgings of my own choosing. If they were more expensive, Mrs. Carroll would not mind. "Whether she would mind or not," my father answered, "I should have thought you would not have wanted to put her to any unnecessary expense."

"But she wouldn't mind doing it," I repeated, obstinately. "She told you she wanted to."

"You know very well that is not the question," my father said, more coldly. "I have explained why I think it better that you should be with those who will look after you. You are not old enough to be by yourself."

"I don't like the McAllisters," I answered, sullenly.

My father looked annoyed. "Perhaps you think they are not good enough for you?"

"They certainly aren't," I replied.

It was a pity that our last meal together should have been somewhat embittered by these remarks, but it was not altogether my fault. For my father had been too extreme in his measures. Under the impression that what I needed was to get into surroundings which would more or less counteract the supposed relaxing influence of Mrs. Carroll's indulgence, he had arranged that I was not even to come home for week-ends, but was to submit myself during the entire term to the bracing effect of the McAllister family.

No more was said upon the subject, and my father gave me after dinner a little book, called "Daily Light," which I promised to read every night and morning. He came to the station to see me off, and, as we were far too early, he was obliged to stand for a quarter of an hour at the window of the carriage, while I longed for the train to start, and we both tried hard to find something to say. I was tormented by an uncertainty as to whether he would expect me to kiss him when I said good-bye. At the sound of the guard's whistle I thrust out my hand. We shook hands; that was all; and, with the train beginning to move out of the station, I sat back in the corner of the empty third-class carriage.

I had a sense of leaving everything behind me, as if I had been starting for the world's end; and, curiously enough, as much as, or more than, by any human face, I was haunted by a vision of the house. I had forsaken it, and I felt its low, faint call coming to me through the rain. I could see the silent, closed rooms upstairs, the long passage with its rows of brown portraits and the tall window at the end, and it was as if a dust were dropping down upon these things, covering them to sleep till I should return. The shadowy ghosts slipped back into their picture-frames; gradually the life died out of their eyes; and a cold, unbroken silence, like the chill of death, closed over all that hidden under-world. Outside the apples had begun to redden on the high brick walls of the fruit-garden, but within the house all was frozen and lifeless. They were my spirits, my ghosts, and could live only while I loved them. I loved them still, but I was too far away, and I might not find them when I came back.

The landscape gliding past me showed through a fine, grayish mist. It was cold, and I pulled up the windows, which almost immediately became covered with the same mist that drifted in the air outside. I wondered where Katherine was, and what she

was doing. I had not heard from her, though I had written twice.
Then I lay back in my uncomfortable corner and tried to think of
nothing.

CHAPTER XVIII

AT the other end I was met by my cousin George, a big, red-haired
hobbledehoy of seventeen, with a curiously small face, bright
brown eyes with a reddish light in them, and a freckled skin.
George, I remembered, used to be amusing, and when I saw him
standing on the platform my spirits rose a little. He proposed that
I should send on my luggage, and that we ourselves should walk,
as he wanted to make a call on the way. When we had arranged
this we set out. I had not been so frequently in Belfast that I did not
take an interest in the streets. Just now, it being Saturday afternoon,
they were full of people, and at the end of the Queen's Bridge some
kind of noisy meeting—religious or political—was in full swing,
but we did not stop to listen. Presently we turned to our left into a
long straight street lined with unattractive, unprosperous-looking
shops, and so narrow that in one place there was not room for two
trams to pass. There was a liberal sprinkling of public-houses, of
cheap clothiers and greengrocers, while here and there the gilded
sign of a pawnbroker hung out over the greasy pavement. I was
about to ask why we had chosen such a disagreeable route, when
George touched my arm and said cheerfully, "Here we are."

"Here!" I echoed, with involuntary dismay. "But——"

"We live over the shop," George explained. He had noticed my
surprise, however, and had coloured.

I pretended to have been only astonished that we had reached
our journey's end so quickly, but I don't know that George was
deceived. Inwardly I was furious with my father for arranging for
me to come to live in such a place, with a public lavatory hardly
ten yards away, and facing the windows. The crowded street,
the mean, dingy houses, the mean, dingy people, the noise and
rattle of innumerable trams: it was all disgusting, even beyond my
expectations! And I was to live here! I simply wouldn't do it.

"We haven't been here very long," George continued. "We used to be round in Shaftesbury Square." Then, as I stood motionless on the pavement, "Aren't you coming in?"

I followed him into the shop in silence. As he pushed open the door a bell answered with a clear, decisive ping. There was a shop on either side of the passage—one stocked with pipes, tobacco, cigarettes, and sweets; the other with newspapers, stationery, and cheap editions of books in hideous paper bindings. In the tobacco department there was nobody; in the stationery department a girl was moving about, fixing things. She turned round on our entrance and George introduced me: "My cousin, Mr. Peter Waring, Miss Izzy."

Miss Izzy and I shook hands. She smiled brightly upon me and hoped I was in good health. She evidently knew all about me, and had no need of George's introduction. I observed that she had a lot of glossy, brown hair, which she wore twisted up in a coil on the top of her head in a way I had never seen hair arranged before, and which was kept in its place by long things like skewers, with large coloured balls at their ends. She wore a pince-nez, and was neatly dressed in dark blue, with a white linen collar and white cuffs, rather mannish in type. It was very plain to me that Miss Izzy had a great deal of style. She had also good features, but her femininity had been slightly eclipsed by a tremendous air of business efficiency, and by the severity of her pince-nez. I had never yet seen anybody nearly so business-like as Miss Izzy looked, and if I had been an employer of labour I should have engaged her as manager at a large salary on the spot. Through the open door there came the shrill angry voices of small boys playing football in an alley at the side of the house. There was a squabble in progress, a cross-fire of abusive language suddenly broken by cries of, "Start a new match—Start a new match."

George was standing against the counter, and had begun to pick his teeth with a pin extracted from the bottom of his waistcoat. Miss Izzy went back to her task of arranging a pile of new books, evidently just come in. She was working out an elaborate pattern with their pictured covers, and as she did so she read the titles aloud. "'The Hour of Vengeance,'" she proclaimed. "'In Love's

Sweet Bondage,'" she added, more dreamily. "'The Clue of the
Broken Ruby'; 'Cynthia Cyrilhurst'—it's well for people that have
names like that!"

"I don't think much of it," said George.

Miss Izzy sighed, "It's better than some, any way."

"Don't you like your own name?" I ventured.

"My Christian name's all right. But there's no use being called
Althea, if it isn't going to be backed up by anything! Althea Izzy is
neither one thing nor another."

"You can easily remedy that!" declared George, gallantly, from
the midst of his dental experiments.

Miss Izzy scrutinised him. "It wouldn't be McAllister that would
do it," she said.

But George continued placidly to attend to his teeth. "I hear
Miss Johnson's getting married at eight o'clock next Friday," he
remarked.

Miss Izzy bounced round, knocking over a box of note-paper.
"How do *you* know?" she demanded, glaring at him.

"Oh, I just heard," said George, calmly. He carefully inspected
the pin before returning it to his waistcoat.

"'Just heard!'—through the key-hole, I suppose. It strikes me
you 'just hear' a deal you're not meant to. And they don't want it
talked about—mind that!"

"Why don't they want it talked about," I asked.

"Because they want a quiet wedding. She's in a bakery, and he's
a clerk in Nicholl's, and, if it got out, the church would be full."

The conversation was at this point interrupted by the entrance
of Uncle George, who appeared in the doorway, coming in from
the street. He was a quiet, gray little man, and his movements
always reminded me of those of a small dog in a strange room,
wandering about, sniffing furtively at the legs of chairs and tables.
He was timid, and when he spoke to you he rubbed his hands
together with an affectation of cheerfulness that was directly contradicted by his dark, melancholy eyes. He had always struck me as
being kind in his intentions, and I regretted that they had seemed
to count for so little when opposed to Aunt Margaret's. Uncle
George was afraid of Aunt Margaret. He had an air of assuming

that there was perfect harmony between them, but I had noticed that he rarely made a remark in her presence without glancing at her to see how she would take it. He reminded me of one of those old photographs one discovers at the backs of frames, their features almost obliterated from long exposure. His whole face, indeed, in its pale irregularity, had a suggestion of vagueness, as if it had been softly sponged over. His manner too—there was something in it which seemed to blur, to rub out, the impression of everything he said. His mind was lit by a kind of twilight in which the outlines of things were lost, in which opposites ceased to be contradictory, and impossibilities found a friendly shelter. And this twilight was reflected in his eyes, in their vague credulity, in the mildness of his glance, which peeped out innocently from under ridiculously fierce and bushy eyebrows. I knew Uncle George had failed in his business some years ago, and it was difficult to believe that he could ever be successful. His interest was not primarily in such things, but in the church, where he was a more perpetual figure than the minister, and in the church meetings, which he never missed, and which he sometimes even got up. I rather liked him; there was something about him that made it easy to talk to him; and though he was desperately religious, and held the same severe doctrines as my father, his nature was so little aggressive that in practice he was the most kindly and human creature in the world.

"How are you?" he asked, shaking my hand. "We're very glad to see you. How's your father?" His left eye twitched slightly while he talked, giving him a comical appearance of winking very knowingly.

"Quite well, thank you," I answered.

"Haven't you been upstairs yet? Haven't you seen your Aunt Margaret? Why didn't you take him to see mother, George? Well, come along now, it's time for tea. I think you might leave the shop, Miss Izzy, and come too—a special occasion, you know, a special occasion!" he laughed and patted me on the shoulder.

"Thanks, I've had my tea already," Miss Izzy returned, without enthusiasm. "And you're having yours upstairs to-night," she added, somewhat tartly, seeing him move in the wrong direction.

"Oh! In the parlour; in honour of this young man; a special occasion, a special occasion!" He repeated his pleasantry, chuckling softly and rubbing his hands, while it was all I could do to keep from returning his friendly and unconscious wink.

"I'd rather stay here than run up and down stairs every time the bell rings," Miss Izzy continued, the invitation to tea evidently rankling in her mind. From behind his father's back George blew a kiss to her.

Aunt Margaret welcomed me without effusion. She was an enormous woman, dark, middle-aged, and with a peculiar smile that always made me feel uneasy. Her lips parted and her teeth became visible, but otherwise her face underwent no change, the expression in her hard, shining, black eyes did not alter. It was, somehow, not a smile at all, but a grimace, and disappeared with a startling suddenness, leaving no trace behind it. When her face was at rest, her lips drew in, as if by some mysterious suction. She wore a wig, and it was this I think that helped to make her look peculiar, and even slightly uncanny. I had been told that she suffered from some obscure, internal disease, which at times caused her great pain, but though she was white and fat and puffy, she presented no appearance of being an invalid. As she kissed me, a ceremony I would gladly have dispensed with, I became conscious of a vague, sickly odour, reminding me of the smell of a chemist's shop.

Uncle George asked her if tea would soon be ready, but she gave him no answer; she only smiled in her strange fashion, and began to question me about my father and my journey—one would have thought I had been travelling all day. Two small boys held her by her voluminous skirts, my cousins, Gordon and Thomas. They were about six or seven, I suppose, and singularly unattractive, the kind of children who have perpetual colds and are never provided with an adequate supply of pocket-handkerchiefs.

I shook hands with Gordon and Thomas; I really couldn't do anything more; but their mother noticed my omission, for they had raised damp, red-nosed, little faces to be kissed, and though she only smiled again, I was convinced that already she had taken a dislike to me. Possibly her dislike dated back to an earlier period than our present meeting, but, with a boy's subtle instinct, I was certain of its existence. Just then the door opened and another child entered the room. This was Alice, a little girl of ten. She completed the family, though there had been several others, who had died in infancy. Alice I did not kiss either. Looking up, I saw my aunt's hard black eyes fixed upon me. I gave her back stare for stare, without flinching, and she turned away, with that curious, grimacing smile I now hated.

Alice herself did not appear to resent my coldness; she hung on to my arm and laughed up at me as if we were the oldest friends in the world. She was a strange, elf-like child, with a pale face and big black eyes that were not hard like her mother's. She looked as if she had been allowed all her life to sit up too late. She was small for her age, and extraordinarily fragile; she was like a little figure cut out of a Sime drawing.

Meanwhile Uncle George, who had been out in the rain, and had removed his boots, was sitting before the gas-stove, presenting the soles of two large, gray-socked feet to the red bars. A light steam began to rise from them, and Uncle George declared that his new boots must "let in," and that he had a good mind to take them back to the man he had bought them from, and that it was too bad. I sat down near him and talked to him, while I watched the steam float up from his feet. Aunt Margaret was getting tea ready in another room, and little Alice hovered behind my chair. Every now and again she leaned over the back of it and said something. She brought a book to show me, and while I looked at it she put her arms round my neck and kissed my cheek.

"Run away, Alice, and quit bothering Peter," said Uncle George. "It's queer the way she's taken to you," he added in a gratified whisper. "She's usually that shy you couldn't coax her out of a corner!" Alice retreated, but almost immediately came back, and again put her arms round me. She held her small white face close to mine and looked at me with her great black eyes and smiled. She gave me an impression of a little house haunted by queer and not altogether pleasant ghosts, and yet somehow I felt sorry for her, and I stroked her thin hand that rested on my sleeve, delicate and light as a leaf.

"You're a lovely big boy," she whispered in my ear, rubbing her face up and down against my jacket, as if it had been the fur of an animal.

I couldn't help laughing, and she cuddled close against me, her chin on my shoulder. "She must be awfully nervous," I thought, for the thunderous approach of one of those hideous traction-engines, that I was soon to find were a feature of the town, made her tremble.

When we sat down to tea Alice insisted on sitting beside me. I had an idea, possibly suggested by Miss Izzy's words, that the room we were in was not often used. I hoped it wasn't, for it was stuffy and uncomfortable, and so small that you felt everywhere beneath the table the warm proximity of other people's limbs. I hated being cramped in this way; it seemed to me that all the time I was breathing other people's breaths, and once I got this notion into my head I couldn't forget it. The furniture was cheap, flimsy, and uncomfortable. The curtains, the gaudy vases, the hideous wall-paper, were of the brightest and least accordant colours, and I even preferred our parlour at home, where, if the things were not less ugly, there were fewer of them. Several pictures hung on the walls, and one hung directly in front of me. It was an engraving, and represented a young man in armour visibly torn between a desire for virtue, embodied in a flaxen-haired lady in floating white drapery, and a deplorable weakness for all that another lady might be taken as symbolising. This latter person was a brunette, and rather more scantily, though quite decently, draped. She held a glass of champagne in her hand, waving it triumphantly aloft, like a torch. I confess that the work fascinated me, for it was my first acquaintance with the type of art it represented.

"A fine picture," murmured Uncle George, seeing me gazing at it. "It's a Royal Academy picture that!"

I said nothing. I did not know what a Royal Academy picture was, nor did I admire this example. It was not so much that the figures looked like unsuccessful waxworks, as that the banality of the moral irritated me. It was the first time I had ever seen art of this extremely ethical character, and in its spirit it reminded me of my old friends in the "Golden Ladder Series."

I hoped tea would not last much longer. In the small room, the large yellow slices of an extremely odoriferous cheese made the atmosphere heavy and unpleasant. Moreover, when this cheese was offered to me with hard, pink, sugared biscuits, I didn't quite know what to do. I had refused several things already, and I knew Aunt Margaret thought I was turning up my nose at the food provided for me, and provided specially, I could guess, from the behaviour of the others, because it was my first night. So I accepted the cheese and sugared biscuits, and struggled through them.

After tea George asked if we were going to have "worship" now or later? We had it "now," and as soon as we rose from our knees he suggested that we should "go out for a bit."

"Where are you going to?" Aunt Margaret inquired.

"Oh, I don't know: up the street just. We can't sit in the house all the evenin'. It's quite fine now."

I was nothing loath, and clattered down the stairs after him. As soon as we were outside George's uncertainty as to our destination appeared to vanish. "Did you ever see a boxing match?" he asked.

"A boxing match?"

"A fight—a prize-fight—whatever you like to call it. Come on an' we'll go to the Comet, only for the Lord's sake don't say anythin' about it at home!"

"Are you not allowed to go?"

"Allowed! Wait till you know them a bit better. The boss's idea of an enjoyable evenin' is some Sankey and Moody touch."

We turned down a side street, and then another and another, till I completely lost my bearings; but very soon George said, "There it is, Coxy. You're goin' to see a bit of life, eh?" and pointed to a small theatre at the opposite side of the road. Above the entrance, a round purplish globe threw down a pool of light on the dirty pavement. A number of men and youths in caps, and with mufflers round their necks, hung about the door, talking and spitting, and at the corner some small boys looked on. George pushed boldly in and I followed. We took tickets for the front seats from an extremely friendly and pock-marked person, who wore a black patch over one eye. When we got inside we found there were not many spectators in our part of the house, but the pit, at the back, was already crowded.

"That's the thunder and lightning over there," said George, jocosely, "in other words, the nuts. How would you like to be in among them?" But the stragglers who kept dropping in and taking seats all round us did not seem to me to be very different.

A branch of lights hung from the ceiling, and other lights fell from the flies on to the curtainless stage. A kind of gray mist, doubtless the accumulated smoke of many nights, floated in the air, and a sickly-looking youth was hammering out music-hall tunes on a worn-out, toneless piano. The stage was quite bare, save for three double rows of yellow wooden chairs, that composed three sides of a parallelogram, and within which was a space marked off by a thick rope stretched about four stout posts clamped to the floor. Over this rope, at two diagonally opposite corners, hung towels, and in each corner was a chair, a heap of sawdust, a basin, a sponge, and a water-bottle. There was no person on the stage, and these bare accessories, possibly because I saw them now for the first time, had to my eyes a most suggestive appearance. I began to feel excited: this unadorned stage appeared to me to be distinctly thrilling.

By degrees the house filled up. The audience, though mixed, was on the whole a very rough one, and there were no women.

"Twig the peelers," said George, and I noticed half a dozen policemen lounge in and take up positions in different parts of the auditorium.

At about five minutes to eight even the chairs on the stage were filled, and, at eight sharp, an important person with a cigar stepped into the ring, and made a short speech introducing the first pair of boxers. He retired amid loud applause, but the boxers, to my surprise, turned out to be a couple of half-grown, ill-nourished, ill-washed lads, no older than myself. They were naked except for short linen drawers, and it seemed to me that it would have been no harm had they been put into a bath prior to their appearance. They grinned sheepishly at the audience, amongst whom they evidently recognised "pals"; and these "pals," in turn, greeted them with cries of "Go it, Bob," "Go on, the wee lad," "Go on, the stripes"—this last in allusion to Bob's unambitious costume, which had all the appearance of being simply a pair of bathing-drawers. They shook hands in a nerveless way, without looking at each other, and began to spar feebly. Bob was so thin you could count his ribs, and the big gloves at the ends of his long skinny arms looked like gigantic puff-balls. The "wee lad" was sturdier, but he seemed to me to be slightly deformed. Even to my inexperienced eye it was perfectly obvious that the main concern of both was not to get hurt, and they hadn't finished the first round before the audience was shouting, "Take them off them! Take them off them!" This was in allusion to the gloves, but they also shouted other things, most of which I daresay I had heard before, though never so many at one time, and I reflected that George had managed to steer fairly clear of the "Sankey and Moody touch."

The referee cautioned the unfortunate combatants, but the second round was no better than the first, and in the middle of the third round the fight was stopped. The sleek, well-fed persons occupying the chairs, and the more impatient persons occupying the auditorium, had not paid their money for stuff of that sort. There followed a fresh pair of boxers, older, more experienced, and this time things were sufficiently brisk. The battle was a hard, ding-dong struggle, and it was at least exciting. At the sight of the first dark ugly streak of blood on one of those white faces I felt a little queer, in fact my impulse was to go away; but as round after round passed, and I watched the blood from the same wound burst out afresh in each, it began to quicken a sort of unsuspected lust of cruelty in me, and I took pleasure in it, I wanted the fight to be a real one, the thud of a blow that got home thrilled me. It was as if I had undergone some transformation. The dirty theatre, the low faces, the foul language, ceased to matter. I was carried out of myself. I longed at the same time for the fight to continue, and for its climax. There would be only three more rounds, and I wanted, before the last, to see somebody knocked out. The man whose face was bleeding was the heavier of the two, but I thought he had little chance. He was out-matched, he must have known it himself, and yet he continued to come up with a kind of dogged stupidity. His seconds spat water into his face, sponged him, rubbed him and fanned him, slapped him with towels and massaged his muscles; but the artificial invigoration this produced lasted only a few moments after the beginning of each round, and, as I watched him weakening, I could feel myself delivering the blows that dazed him, my muscles tightened and slackened, I could hardly sit in my seat. "Now he's got him," I said aloud, as he staggered into the ring for the last time. There was a blow and a crash on the boards. The referee was counting over him, one—two—three—four—five—six—seven—eight; and then this helpless creature, out of whose swollen, hideous face all humanity had been battered, staggered up almost blindly. He did not even lift his hands to protect himself from the blow that smashed him down again, and with that dull thud on the floor the fight came to an end. He lay on after the counting had stopped, and as I watched him being supported, almost carried, out of the ring, while the victor received congratulations, a pang of misgiving assailed me. There was no doubt the whole thing was absolutely brutal, and there was equally no doubt that when it had been most brutal I had been most pleased.

I should like to be able to add that I got up and left the theatre. I did not. I reflected that *the* fight was still to come: I even waited for it eagerly, and when it took place, I was disappointed because nobody bled, and because the decision was given on points at the end of the twelfth round.

As we walked home I proved to George that boxing matches were really all right; that they were infinitely less dangerous than football matches. Every one of my arguments convinced George, and after I had finished he found some for himself, which I accepted as equally incontrovertible. Considering that there was nobody to take up an opposite point of view, our apologies might have appeared hardly necessary, but George was able to give me, in addition, a list of all the good qualities fighting brought out, or even brought into existence. Most of these did not exactly fit in with my more superficial impression of the audience, and there were others I could not help feeling many of them would be better without—courage, for instance. I had a dim idea that a little extra courage might result in a majority of them figuring at the next Assizes.

But when we were three-quarters way home I said to George, "It was all pretty beastly, and that's why we liked it—eh?"

He got quite offended, telling me that if *he* had thought it beastly he wouldn't have waited on to the end, as I did.

This was just possible, yet my opinion of George sank. "If you admire it so much," I said, "I'll give you a turn any time you like."

George was silent, and flushed slightly.

"Well?" I kept on, pugnaciously.

George mumbled something, I don't know what, and I saw that I had actually frightened him. We walked the rest of the way home in silence. George was angry with me, but when we were in the house and had sat down to supper he became friendly again. As I discovered later, company was the one thing absolutely indispensable to him; he could have kept on being angry with me, and, indeed, would have enjoyed doing so, had he had anybody else to talk to, but solitude he could not bear. And I, on my side, forgot his having sulked on the way home, just as, later on, I was to forget more than one unpleasant thing, simply because he amused me, because he could always make me laugh.

After supper I said good-night to the others, and George and I went upstairs. George went in front of me and lit the gas in the bed-room. "Is this my room?" I asked, noticing that there were two beds in it.

"Yours an' mine," George answered.

His reply was unexpected. I had never slept with anybody in my life, and it had not occurred to me that I should not have a room to myself. I said nothing, but George, who was far from stupid, saw I did not like the arrangement. "There is no other room," he admitted frankly. "I thought you knew. I thought ma put it in her letter."

"I didn't see her letter," I murmured.

"Oh, we'll be all right together, won't we?" George went on, pacifically. "You can have your bed moved wherever you would like it best." He had already begun to undress, and, after hanging up his jacket, he took a photograph from an inside pocket and handed it to me. It was the photograph of a lady extremely lightly clad. "I've better ones than that," said George, with a peculiar smile. He went to a corner near the window and raised a loose board. From the hollow beneath he drew out a large fat envelope, but, as he looked at me, he hesitated. "I'll show them to you some other time," he suddenly said, and returned the envelope to its hiding-place. He undressed rapidly, and got into bed.

I took longer, and all the time I felt George's eyes fixed on me curiously. I hated this lack of privacy. It wasn't that I hadn't undressed hundreds of times before other boys, when we were going to bathe; but this was different. I disliked the feeling of not being alone. I hated to have somebody watch me all the time I was taking off my clothes, or folding them. I determined to write to my father in the morning.

When I was in bed and in the dark I wanted to think of Katherine. I did this every night; I looked forward to it, because it seemed to me that this was the hour when everything became clearer; besides, there was always the chance that if I thought of her I might dream of her. But now George began to talk.

"Do you know any girls?" he asked.

"No," I answered, shortly.

"Don't you like them?" George persisted.

"No."

"What do you think of Miss Izzy? Not bad—eh?"

"I don't know anything about her."

George was silent a few minutes. Then, just as I was beginning to think my own thoughts, he began again.

"She's nothin' compared to Miss Johnson—the girl we were talkin' about to-day—who's gettin' married. Miss Johnson was in the shop before Miss Izzy came. Ma sacked her for givin' lip. Ma sacks them all."

George continued to talk until he grew sleepy, and I had no choice but to listen.

CHAPTER XIX

NEXT morning I was awakened by somebody singing, and opening my eyes I saw George, in his shirt and trousers, strutting up and down the middle of the floor, a hair-brush in his hand. It took me half a minute to realise where I was, but George, when he saw I was awake, proceeded to give me imitations of various music-hall artists, until there was a sharp rap at our door, and Aunt Margaret's voice told him to remember what day it was. With that I remembered myself, and simultaneously made up my mind that I wasn't going to church. I determined that now I was away from home I would be my own master, and do just what seemed good in my own eyes, and that I would begin this policy at once.

Our room was at the back of the house, and from where I lay I could see through the window a strip of gray, desolate sky, broken here and there by a chimney, and across which the dark branch of an unhealthy tree waved. As I watched it, my mind strayed to a book of Japanese decorations, and to the library at Derryaghy, and to other things I cared for. I had already guessed from the little I had seen of the McAllisters that their fortunes were drooping. It was not so much that everything in the house was worn out and patched and on its last legs, that the children were ill-clad and looked ill-nourished, as that I seemed to scent that mysterious atmosphere of anxiety, worry, and struggle, which invariably accompanies a decreasing ability to pay one's way. I hated it. I hated all that it implied—sordid economies and cheap pleasures, a degrading and enchaining struggle to keep things going. It did not awaken pity in me, but only disgust. It was like a horrible monster that clung and squeezed with a thousand slimy tentacles, sapping your strength, and sucking out your life-blood. I could even sympathise with those who had freed themselves from it by some bold decisive action, that might lie well outside the laws of morality and society.

In the midst of these reflections George informed me that I had better get up. He was tying his tie. His red hair was carefully plastered down with water, and he was examining his small, freckled face in the looking-glass. George had not yet begun to shave, but he had long, silly-looking hairs growing out of his chin, and I thought he looked extremely ugly and horribly common as he stood there.

When we went downstairs the others were just beginning breakfast. The whole family was terribly *endimanchée*. Aunt Margaret was redolent of cheap scent. Gordon and Thomas were dressed in green plush with white mother-of-pearl buttons. Their little, damp, red, snub noses seemed to have been set that very morning accidentally in the middle of their round faces, which were of the complexion of fresh putty, and their eyes were exactly like blue glass marbles. Uncle George, who was breakfasting in his gray shirt sleeves, suggested that I might like to go with George to the Bible-class, but I refused. I added, to prevent all future trouble, that I preferred to take a walk on Sunday morning.

"Do you go for walks when you are at home?" Aunt Margaret asked me, with her strange smile.

"No," I answered.

"Doesn't your father expect you to go to church?"

"I don't know what he expects, I'm sure."

"And don't you think yourself you ought to go?"

"No." I was quite certain about this at all events, and I added that, once you were familiar with any particular ideas, no matter how valuable, I couldn't see that you gained very much by listening to them being repeated ad infinitum.

This explanation, far from convincing, evidently annoyed Aunt Margaret, though she only said, "I would rather you didn't talk like that before the children. They have been brought up to look upon religion with respect."

I did not reply.

"I think I'll go for a walk too," George announced, with a wink at me.

"You'll do nothing of the sort," cried Aunt Margaret, flaring up into a shrill rage. "You see what comes of such talk! I'll have no Sabbath-breaking in this house."

"Ssh—ssh," Uncle George mildly intervened. "To force people to do things against their will isn't the proper way to take."

"You want your children to give up going to church, then?"

"Nobody is giving up going to church. George is coming of course. Young people very often say things without meaning them. If Peter is for taking a walk this morning, I expect he will come out with us this evening to hear Dr. Russell, won't you, Peter?"

But, altogether apart from Dr. Russell, that Sunday was a dreary day. In the afternoon I accompanied George, and we loafed about in the Ormeau Park, where he was evidently accustomed to meet his friends. These friends of George's were all in business, and all looked upon themselves as young men. They smoked cheap cigarettes, wore their handkerchiefs in their sleeves, and were tremendously knowing and rakish, while the larger part of their conversation appeared to be concerned with the merits of professional football players. I could get on all right with George when he was by himself, but his friends, among whom he was remarkably popular, did not improve him. It took no great perspicacity to discover that they on their side regarded my company as a very questionable acquisition. This feeling, far from diminishing, obviously increased as the afternoon advanced. George described our adventure of the night before with immense gusto, and gave a burlesque imitation of the knock-out. To have an appreciative audience was his greatest delight, and the others, for that matter, left him a fairly free stage. Now that he had them he ignored me utterly, so that, in the end, I was left practically alone. I fulfilled a sort of highly disagreeable rôle of silent hanger-on. I did it most reluctantly, yet I could not summon up sufficient moral courage to go away.

CHAPTER XX

On Monday morning I went to school. I arrived half an hour before the proper time, and as my classes had already been arranged, I had nothing to do but loiter about and take stock of the place. It stood, a long, low, unlovely building of soot-darkened brick, in its own grounds, not far from the centre of the town. Just now, on this gray autumn morning, it presented an appearance of singular, of almost jail-like dullness, though in summer, as I was to learn, when the grass was green, and the tall dusty elms waved against a blue sky, and the sun shone through narrow, small-paned windows, and splashed on wooden floors, on hacked wooden desks and forms, on faded maps, and bare, discoloured walls, it could be pleasant enough, in spite of the complete absence of anything save the sunlight and the trees that might appeal to a sense of beauty. Beside the main building was a Preparatory School, and at the back, separated from it by a yard, where a score or so of boys were at present kicking about a football, were the Mathematical Schools, and beyond these, the larger playing-field. It was really a day-school, only two masters living on the premises, with about a couple of dozen boarders: the rest of the scholars, numbering between a hundred and fifty and two hundred, were day-boys.

As I hung about uneasily, not venturing to join the others, I was painfully conscious of my isolation. Not one of those faces had I ever seen before, nor had I the slightest knowledge of the school itself, for George, who had been at a National School, could tell me nothing about it. Nobody took any notice of me. Several masters passed, and disappeared through mysterious doors, and when, at ten o'clock, a white-haired, white-bearded patriarch rang a huge hand-bell in the porch, and I watched the boys scattering with extraordinary rapidity in various directions, it looked to me as if I might very easily spend my whole day in the yard. I had no idea which door to try, yet at the same time I was anxious not to be late. I was still hovering uncertainly about the porch, like a soul strayed into the wrong Paradise, when a boy, running past, glanced at me, stopped, and asked me where I wanted to go to.

I told him I wanted to go to Mr. Lowden's class.

"It's the end door on the left over there," he said, good-humouredly, and I thanked him and hurried off.

Coming in, I found the whole class already in their places, but a boy at the end of the third form moved up to make room for me, and I sat down. Mr. Lowden, who was standing, with a piece of chalk in one hand and a duster in the other, close by the black-board, asked me my name, and then informed me I was late and that he objected to lateness. I said nothing, but took down on the slate in front of me the sum he had just written out.

I worked at it, and was struck by the animated conversations that were going on all over the room, in spite of Mr. Lowden's efforts to check them.

"Has anybody finished yet?" Mr. Lowden asked, and the boy who had moved up to make room for me held up his hand, cracking his fingers. I glanced at him. He had a round, merry face, rosy cheeks, bright eyes and dimples.

"How often have I told you not to crack your fingers, Knox?" asked Mr. Lowden, discontentedly. "Well, what answer do you get?"

"Ten bob, a deuce an' a make."

"Come in to-day, Knox, at recess."

He wrote down another sum, and I had begun to copy it, when something went off with a sharp report under my feet. Mr. Lowden was gazing straight at me, and he instantly told me to stay in at recess.

I knew well enough what had happened, that I had trodden on a wax match softened and rolled up with the head inside. I told Mr. Lowden that I hadn't done it on purpose.

"I can't help that: you must stay in."

"But it wasn't my fault if I didn't know it was there," I argued.

"You must stay in," repeated Mr. Lowden, in a silly, obstinate kind of voice, horribly irritating, "and, Knox, you stay in after school as well as at recess."

"I don't see what *he* has to do with it, any way," I muttered.

The boy beside me laughed.

"Oh, yes: Knox put it there," Mr. Lowden said monotonously.

I had taken a dislike to Mr. Lowden, and at the same time I thought him a fool. A few days later something happened to make me dislike him even more. He had read aloud a problem which we were to work out mentally, putting down our answers when he gave us the word. My answer was right, but, unfortunately, when he asked me how I got it, the problem itself had gone out of my head. For the life of me I couldn't remember it; yet I was ashamed to say so, and simply sat silent while he repeated two or three times, as if it were some kind of refrain, "Well, now, how did you work the sum, Waring?"

As I was unable to tell him, he said, "You must have copied the answer from Knox."

"I didn't," I protested, angrily.

"Then why can't you tell me how you got it?"

Again silence.

"You must be telling a lie, I'm afraid," said Mr. Lowden, in his apathetic voice, "and the silliest kind of lie, because it's obvious to everybody."

"I'm not telling a lie."

Mr. Lowden shrugged his shoulders; he never seemed to get angry, or even moderately interested, no matter what the circumstances. "If you're not, then why can't you tell me how you worked the sum? If you had done it once, you could do it again."

"I did do it."

"Well, how?"

Renewed silence.

"You'd better stay in at recess."

And I stayed in.

Yet Mr. Lowden was really only a mild and inoffensive young man, who had been inspired with the unlucky idea that he could earn his living by teaching boys, when he had neither the desire nor the capacity to understand them. The aversion I felt for him was really founded primarily upon grounds less rational than those I have mentioned. The secret of the matter was that physically he was repulsive to me. He suffered, I imagine, from some affection of the lungs or throat, for he wore, winter and summer, a thick white muffler, fastened by an opal pin. His face was pale, cadaverous, and hollow-cheeked; his moustache scanty; his hair lank and damp; but what I disliked most was his peculiar odour. Whether this emanated from his person, or from the pastilles he was perpetually sucking, I don't know. It was something sickly and persistent, and for no reason that I know of I associated it with death. When he sat down on the form beside me to work out a sum, I used to edge gradually away from him, until he would notice it, and ask me in a querulous voice what I was doing, and perhaps keep me in. This physical repulsion I could never have conquered, even had it not been backed up by that kind of mental sickliness which characterized him, and which had made him punish me once at least unjustly. He left six months later, and nobody among the boys ever knew or cared what became of him. Perhaps he went to another school, perhaps the mysterious odour which had sickened me had been really the odour of death. . . .

When I think now of those who were in charge of my education, upon my word I cannot help but be filled with wonder. What
did they teach me? What did I ever get from them that I could not
have got, with less trouble, for myself? Never once did any of my
masters show the faintest interest in me, or make even the most
perfunctory attempt to get to know me, to get to know what I was
capable of, if I had any definite tastes, if I were good or bad, moral
or immoral, intelligent or a fool. What they did instead was to ask
me a couple of questions from a book, and, if I failed to answer
either of these satisfactorily, keep me in to sit for twenty minutes
with my lesson-book open on the desk before me and my thoughts
miles away. Of my masters only one, Mr. Johnson, had any distinction, and he, unfortunately, was a mathematician. He had written
a "Euclid" so perfect in its expression that he had managed to get
a kind of æsthetic charm into the dry bones of geometry. He was
an Englishman, but was slightly Jewish in type. He wore a long,
flowing beard and moustache, like an early northern chief, and he
had small, sleepy, gray eyes, which during school hours were usually
closed. Most of his time he passed, either in reverie or slumber,
in his chair on a daïs at the end of the room; but when aroused
he had, for the unmathematical, a richly terrifying voice, and a
disheartening manner of slashing down a long black cane on the
desk, within a few inches of your nose. His classes were models of
order. Never a faintest sound. In dead silence you played your game
of noughts and crosses, or did your Latin composition, or wrote
out cricket teams—but you never spoke, and rarely moved. Of all
those whose business it was to mould my mind his figure remains
the least spoiled by time. I remember the shock I received when,
some years after I left school, I came upon Dr. Melling, the head
English master, in the Campo Santo at Pisa, sucking an orange,
and dressed in garments that Moses or Ikey would have bid for but
languidly. When I spoke to him he seemed so narrow, so unimagi-
native, so unintelligent, that I felt half-ashamed, as one might who
has learned by accident a secret he ought never to have known.
Even in stature he was curiously shrunken, though he neither
stooped nor showed signs of decrepitude or age. But Johnson I can
see now, as I saw him so often then, coming up the path between

the two front cricket-fields, a large black bag in his hand, which one
had been told contained his lunch. I can see him leaning back in his
chair, his eyes closed, like one of those beautiful owls that ignore
from their cage in the Zoo the staring stranger, his beard spread
out over his waistcoat, his hands folded on his stomach. Johnson
was a gentleman, and, though he knew nothing of, and cared little
for, boys, if chance brought him into temporary relation with one,
even a very small and idle one, he took it for granted that he was
a gentleman too, and in his deep, slow, musical voice, and in his
sleepy eyes, there would come a curious charm.

CHAPTER XXI

I HAD formed no definite conception of what my new school
would be like, but there was a flatness about the reality for which
I was unprepared. I seemed to slip into my place at once, without
attracting the slightest attention either of boys or masters, and at a
week's end any strangeness there might have been had completely
worn off. I did not play football, which was the only game played
this term. I got to know a good many boys, but I formed no friend-
ships. I found my new companions to be, on the whole, little, if at
all, more congenial than the boys at Newcastle, in spite of there
being so many more to choose from. I liked them well enough,
and they were, with one exception, perfectly decent to me, but it
all ended there: that is to say, in my relation with them I had invariably to approach them on their own ground, I had to enter into
their world, they were incapable of entering into mine, or even
of meeting me half-way. There was a boy I had felt attracted to,
purely on account of his good-looks, and as our ways home lay
in the same direction I joined him one afternoon just as he was
going out at the gate. But the first words he uttered shattered my
illusions. He had a harsh, loud voice and spoke through his nose.
Almost at once he began to tell me what he imagined to be a funny
story, and before I had been with him five minutes I said good-bye
abruptly, and left him standing on the pavement, staring after me,
nor did I ever speak to him again.

Day by day I went to school, neither liking it nor disliking it. Yet it was all rather dismal, for life without any kind of human sympathy, either given or received, is a dreadful, almost an impossible, thing. I thought a good deal of Katherine, and wrote to her, but got only an occasional scrappy note in reply. I did not see much of George, for he was kept in his business till nearly seven o'clock, and in the evenings I had to prepare my work for the next day. George, moreover, had his own circle of friends, none of whom, as I have said, were particularly eager for my company, while George himself, when he was among them, was the least eager of all. Sometimes when I was with him alone I would remember this and resent it, but he could always make me forgive him when he wanted to: he could be extraordinarily pleasant when he wanted to, and it was impossible to be bored in his company.

We still shared the same bedroom, and at night he liked to talk before going to sleep. He had obtained a considerable influence over me, more than anybody else ever did or was to do, yet it is difficult to describe what it consisted in, or why it should have come about. I had an extremely poor opinion of him: I knew he had not even a rudimentary conscience: frequently he repelled, and even disgusted, me: but always, by some instinct, he seemed to know when he had done so, and he had a special gift for recovering lost ground. His influence was bad—absolutely—and yet what was so harmful to me did not, so far as I know, have any particularly disastrous effect upon George himself. He had an amazingly licentious imagination, and, in this direction, a power of vivid suggestion. As I became more accustomed to him, things that had at first jarred upon me ceased to do so; but it was doubly unfortunate that I should have been thrown so intimately into his society just at this particular time. Had I been either older or younger, or had I had any other friends, the effect would not have been so injurious. It was not that I had not heard my share of Rabelaisian talk before. This was, somehow, different. At all events, the other had passed off me easily, awakening no after-thoughts, leaving my senses untroubled. It was not so now. My mind became disturbed, and, above all, my dreams were coloured by certain obsessions which George took a delight in evoking. In my dreams his suggestions

became realities, and his imagination seemed to brood over them
like an evil angel. I do not think he was himself conscious of it,
conscious, that is, that what for him appeared to be no more than
a sort of intellectual pastime, which he could shake from him as
easily as one might turn off a tap, assumed with me a darker form.
His words appeared to touch me physically, and with an appalling directness and persistency. He had a trick of re-telling stories
he had read, twisting them and altering them with an astonishing ingenuity, so as to introduce the element he revelled in, and
he never became crude or brutal till he had carefully prepared his
ground. And it was all transformed by a curious gift of humour,
which was in itself something quite inimitable, consisting, as it did,
largely in his personality and manner, in an unquenchable liveli-
ness, and a faculty of mimicry.

CHAPTER XXII

Two months went by in this fashion, and I had begun to look
forward to Christmas and to count the weeks that separated me
from the holidays, when an incident occurred which was the
means of my forming an acquaintance that was to develop into
the most intimate friendship of my life. It befell in this way.

A series of thefts had been committed, thefts of school-books.
A boy would leave his books down on a window-sill, or even in
a class-room, and when he came to get them again, one would
perhaps be missing. I had never lost anything myself, and knew
nothing of what was going on till the afternoon when the matter
was divulged to the entire school.

It was not far from three o'clock, I remember, the hour when we
broke up for the day, and I was in one of the English class-rooms,
where, every Monday, if you liked to pay half-a-crown a term extra,
you had the advantage of a lesson in elocution from Mr. (or was it
Professor?) Lennox. Professor Lennox was a fat, pale, absurd little
man, with a high-pitched tenor voice that struck against the drum
of your ear like the blow of a stick. He waxed his moustache, and
greased his hair into carefully arranged, solid-looking locks, while

his skin, by some natural process, greased itself. Professor Lennox was an amateur of fancy trousers, of coloured waistcoats, of large breast-pins, of spats with pearl buttons, and of rings more striking than precious. To-day the whole class—some fifty or sixty boys—was reading after him, line by line, a poem from Bell's "Elocution."

> "In arms, / the Aust / rian phal / anx stood,
> A liv / ing wall /, a hum / an wood.
> Impreg / nable / their front / appears,
> All hor / rent with / project / ing spears."

Or, as it sounded according to local pronunciation, shared impartially by the professor and the majority of his pupils:

> "In arms, / the Orst / rian phah / lanx stude,
> Ah liv / ing wall, / ah hue / man wude.
> Imprag / nable / their front / appears,
> All hoar / rent with / projact / ing spears."

We had just reached "projacting spears," when Dr. Melling, better known by the name of Limpet, came in, followed by an old woman, who paused on the threshold. Limpet turned round and waved her forward impatiently, but a couple of yards from the door she stopped again, and all the time she stared hard at us with small, sharp, gray eyes. Her bright little eyes and hooked nose, taken with her air of timidity, gave her the appearance of an innocent and frightened witch who has been dragged out of her lair very much against her will. I wondered who she was, but Limpet did not leave us long in doubt. It appeared that some boy had stolen a number of school-books, the property of various other boys, and had sold them to this woman, who was now here to identify him. Limpet explained the situation with an air of wishing to get a disagreeable duty over as quickly as possible, but to us it was quite exciting. Each of us in turn stood up to undergo the witch's scrutiny. She had already, as I afterwards learned, been round the other classes, and Limpet, who had accompanied her on this voyage of discovery, was by now in rather a bad temper. Evidently he found the

whole business singularly distasteful, and as one boy after another
received her head-shake, he fidgeted and frowned nervously. She
herself looked frightened and bewildered; I expect she was secretly
worried about her own share in the matter, and considering how
she could make the best of it. As for me, I felt for the first time
as if school-life really bore some faint resemblance to the tales of
the *Boy's Own Paper.* Here was one of the pet adventures actually
taking place, except that the old woman should have been a man
with a small fur cap. When it came to my turn to stand up, I had an
extraordinary wish that she would pick me out as the culprit. Sure
of my innocence, I had a mind to be the hero of this adventure,
and I stood so long, waiting to be identified, that Limpet told me
sharply to sit down, and I could see had it on the tip of his tongue
to give me an imposition. My neighbour tugged me by the jacket,
and I resumed my seat abruptly amid suppressed laughter. One by
one each boy rose in his place and sat down again, and then, in the
back row of all, a boy stood up who *was* identified. This boy I did
not know except by name, though he was in all my classes. He was
called Gill, and I had always looked upon him as rather odd and
unapproachable. When his turn came, he stood up indifferently,
glancing out through the window at the clock, which could only
be seen when you were on your feet. But next moment I saw the
old woman say something to Limpet, and the latter instantly told
Gill to stand out.

Gill stood out, his indifference gone, his face flushed and angry.

"Is that the boy?" Limpet asked, as if daring her to say "Yes," but
the old woman mumbled out an affirmative.

"Do you know anything of this, Gill?"

"No."

I was somehow pleased that he had not added the customary
"Sir." He stood with his head up and gazed straight at Limpet and
the old woman, with a kind of contemptuous wrath, his gray eyes
dark and very bright, a frown on his face.

The old woman was so obviously uncertain and uncomfortable
that the whole thing appeared to me ridiculous, and I impulsively
gave voice to this impression. "She doesn't know anything about
it," I called out. "Anybody could see she's only trying it on."

Limpet on the spot gave me two hundred of Sir Walter Scott's bad verses to write out. My remark had the effect, nevertheless, of drawing a wavering expression of uncertainty from the old woman herself, which, in his now undisguised irritability, Limpet pounced on, as a cat pounces on a mouse. "Why did you point to him, if you don't know?" he whipped out, frightening her nearly out of her wits. "Don't you understand that it's a serious thing to bring an accusation of theft against a boy? Sit down, Gill. I want to see you after school."

He was so angry that he forgot all about the half-dozen remaining boys, and conducted his companion unceremoniously from the room.

Gill sat staring straight in front of him. Certainly he did not look guilty. He had a dark, narrow face, with a bright complexion. His thick, rough, black hair grew low on an oval, narrow forehead, and between his clear gray eyes there started a high-bridged, somewhat aggressive-looking nose, the most striking feature of his rather striking face. He had the reputation of being a peculiar kind of chap, and he was sometimes made fun of—mildly, for he was extremely quick-tempered and very strong—but anybody could see that he was a fine fellow, and that an accusation such as had just been brought against him would require a great deal of proof.

When the bell rang he remained on in his seat while the rest of us went out. I hung about the porch watching two little fellows playing chestnuts, and when they stopped playing I still hung about with nothing to watch, and with, indeed, no very definite purpose in view. Presently Gill emerged, but whether he saw me or not, he took no notice, as he walked on swiftly down toward the gate.

Since I had flung about him the mantle of my protection, however, I had begun to take a lively interest in him, and before he had gone fifty yards I made up my mind and hurried in pursuit. He looked round at the sound of my footsteps and waited, but without smiling. I had an idea he had passed me deliberately in the porch, and now he received me coldly enough. As we walked along together he made no attempt to defend himself against the

charge that had been brought against him; he did not even refer
to it, nor to what had taken place during his subsequent interview
with Limpet, from whom, nevertheless, he received next morning
a public apology. Though I was simply dying to hear what had happened I couldn't very well ask, and as we proceeded I had to talk
about other things. Then, quite suddenly, some change seemed to
take place within him, and he inquired abruptly if I had read any
of the writings of Count Tolstoy. I had never even heard of Count
Tolstoy, but I was not to remain much longer in ignorance. I like
enthusiasm, and I got it now. Gill had just finished "Anna Karénine," and offered to lend it to me, adding that it was in French.
I had been learning French in the way one did in those days, and
perhaps does still; that is to say, I had been learning it for six or
seven years, and was now obliged to confess I couldn't read it.

"Aren't you coming out of your way?" he demanded with the
queer abruptness that characterized him.

"Oh, no."

"Do you live up the Malone way?"

"No; I live in the town."

"Then why isn't it out of your way?"

"That is only my fashion of telling you I want to come with
you," I answered meekly. "Pure politeness."

He did not smile. "You haven't been at school long?" he asked.
His manner was the oddest mixture of stiffness and shyness, and
sometimes he frowned portentously, while at the slightest thing he
blushed.

"No," I answered. "Have you?"

"Yes—all my life—ever since I was a kid." He spoke quickly, one
would have imagined impatiently.

"Have you? I thought, somehow, you hadn't."

I don't know why I should have made this wise remark, nor,
apparently, did Gill.

"Why?" he asked me at once.

I laughed. "You don't seem to have very many friends."

He coloured, and I realized that my remark had been lacking in
tact.

"I have as many friends as I want," he answered shortly.

I saw I had touched him on a tender spot. "Does that mean you don't want any new ones?" I ventured, half-laughing, though I was serious enough.

His answer was startling. "Perhaps you think you are doing me a favour by walking home with me?"

I did not say anything, but I looked at him with some astonishment. He was so odd that his manner had the effect of divesting me of all the shyness I usually suffered from myself on making a new acquaintance, nor did I even feel angry at his rebuff.

"I came with you," I said at length, "to please myself."

He turned crimson, began to speak, was silent, and then apologized.

At the garden gate I would have left him, but he insisted on my coming up to the door. "I will get you 'Anna Karénine'; then we can talk about it together—if we're going to be friends." He spoke the last words shyly, and I knew that he had found a difficulty in saying them at all.

"But I told you I couldn't read French."

"You can if you like. Don't try to translate it; read straight ahead."

He came back with two books bound in gray blue paper, which he handed to me. "It doesn't matter if the covers get torn or the books come to pieces. My father gets them all rebound in any case. By the way," once more he blushed, "you needn't bother about those lines Limpet gave you."

"Why?"

"Because I'll be doing them."

"Oh, rot."

He frowned. "You can do them if you like, but it will be a waste of time."

"I know that."

"I mean, I'm going to do them in any case, whether you do or not."

I laughed. "Couldn't we each do half?"

"I'm going to do them all."

"All right."

He strolled back down the garden path with me. "What's your name?" he asked.

"Waring."

"I know that. I mean your first name."

"Peter."

"Mine is Owen. I'll come part of the way back with you: I told them inside."

"Shall I call you Owen?"

"I don't care," he answered quickly, without looking at me. But before we had gone another hundred yards he said: "That isn't the truth. I told you my name because I wanted you to call me by it."

"All right," I said, smiling.

CHAPTER XXIII

THAT night, for the first time, I felt George's fascination falter, and it is a fact rather melancholy in its significance that this consciousness came to me in the form of a sense of freedom, of relief. He began to talk to me, just as usual, as soon as he had turned out the light, but I told him brusquely to shut up, that I wanted to go to sleep, and when he tried to begin again I let him see I was in earnest.

As I lay there I determined that at Christmas I would make another effort to get into rooms of my own choosing. If I wanted to ask Owen Gill, for instance, to come to see me, how could I do so? For one thing, his people would not like him to come here; for another, I should not myself care to ask him. I was by this time firmly convinced that my aunt was frequently more or less under the influence of drugs. It may have been on account of her illness; I could not say; but there were times when she seemed hardly to know what she was doing, and at such moments her dislike for me, which she usually more or less successfully concealed, jumped to the surface. I had no idea how long she had been in this condition; I was quite sure my father knew nothing about it; yet she appeared to me to have already lost something of her hold upon reality. I had heard her make statements so obviously untrue that they could have deceived nobody but Uncle George. I had heard her repeat a harmless remark made by Miss Izzy, and, by altering it ever so slightly, give it a quite new and highly disagreeable meaning. But Uncle George never dreamed of contradicting her, whether it was that he was afraid of her, or whether he was simply blind, I could not tell.

On the Sunday after my becoming acquainted with Owen I was alone in the house with little Alice, who had been unwell and had not gone out with the others to morning church. As usual, she had climbed up on my knee, and was sitting with her thin brown arms round my neck, and her queer little face close to mine.

"Ma looked through all your pockets yesterday morning, when you were at school," she said.

"What pockets?" I asked quietly.

"The pockets of your clothes—every one."

"Well, did she find anything?" I murmured, in as indifferent a tone as I could manage.

"She found a letter—and some other things."

"And did she read the letter?"

"Yes."

"How do you know? Where were you?"

"I saw her."

"How did you see her?"

"I saw her through the key-hole."

"Oh; I didn't think you would look through key-holes."

"Didn't you? I do—often."

"You shouldn't. It isn't nice, you know. You must never do it again."

"Why?"

"Because it's not a nice thing to do. It's spying."

"I've often done it," said Alice, with perfect detachment. "I've looked at you through the key-hole."

"You must never do it again. Promise, or I won't be friends with you any more."

"If I promise, will you be friends?"

"Yes. But you must keep your promise, remember."

I returned to "Anna Karénine." "I must buy a desk," I thought, "or some kind of box I can lock up." Presently little Alice began again. "I've got a secret."

I had lugubrious forebodings in regard to this secret. "Have you?" I answered dismally.

"Don't take any soup to-day," the child said, softly.

I laid down my book. There was something arresting about this injunction, something even startling. I looked into the strange dark eyes that seemed almost to fill the small elf-like face, and I knew that a confidence of a highly unpleasant character was imminent.

"I put a dead mouse into the soup," little Alice whispered.

"Oh;" I exclaimed feebly. I felt inclined to put her down very abruptly from my knee, and it was with difficulty that I controlled this impulse. "What made you do such a thing? Now it will all be wasted."

"Nobody knows about it," the child continued artlessly, rubbing her cheek against mine. "Once I put something in before, when people were coming for dinner. It was fun to watch them all looking so stiff and solemn, and eating away, and not knowing what was there all the time. I laughed so much that ma sent me out of the room. But I wouldn't do that with you, because I love you."

Her strange little face turned to mine, and her eyes were fixed on me. She must have seen the disgust I felt, for she began to tremble and her eyes filled with tears. Then she hid her face against my shoulder and clung to me. I was frightened to scold her. Even without my having said anything she seemed to shrivel up like some bruised and broken plant. I patted her head gently, and at once she brightened. She got down from my knee and began to dance about the floor.

Meanwhile I was left with the problem of the soup. If the soup were strained the mouse, I supposed, would be discovered; but if it were, as it was practically certain to be, simply turned out into a tureen, the revelation might come too late. On the other hand, were I to turn informer, little Alice would most surely be whipped, and, whether she deserved it or not, the idea of that was as revolting to me as would be the ill-treatment of a sick monkey. There was a young girl in the kitchen who looked after the rougher work, and I thought of explaining the matter to her, after swearing her to secrecy, but before I had made up my mind I heard the others downstairs.

They had evidently got back from church, and now I didn't know what to do. Uncle George, preceded by Gordon and Thomas in their green plush suits, came into the parlour. Uncle George began to warm himself before the gas-stove. "You should have come out this morning, Peter," he said, in his gentle voice. "You missed a treat."

I listened to his comments on the sermon, feeling all the time most uncomfortable. Gordon and Thomas tried to climb about my chair, but I kept them off with a firm hand. The parlour door was open, probably the kitchen door too, for all at once there came a scream from that department, not very loud, yet distinctly audible. I glanced at Alice. The others hadn't heard it. Uncle George was still in the midst of his mild enthusiasm, and Gordon and Thomas, flattening their little round red noses with a finger, were practising squinting with remarkable success. Alice had become perfectly still, her big black eyes fixed on mine: and, as for me, I knew the mouse had been discovered and felt vastly relieved. Conceive of my amazement, therefore, when the soup after all appeared at table. Alice and I did not take any, and Aunt Margaret did not either, so that there was enough left to do Monday's dinner; but of the mouse I never heard again.

CHAPTER XXIV

My friendship with Owen was at present the one quite satisfactory thing in my life. Neither at school nor at home was I particularly successful. I worked very little, merely sufficiently to prevent myself from getting into trouble; I did not play games. I had gone to the School of Art for a few weeks, but as I was never put to draw anything except curves and squares and geometrical flowers, I got sick of this and gave it up.

I saw a good deal of Owen, though not so much as I should have liked. Of course I saw him every day at school, but I had never been inside his house, and I could not ask him to mine. I did not want to let him see the kind of people I had sprung from. I was ashamed of them. On Saturdays and Sundays we usually went for long walks together, during which we threshed out the affairs of the universe, and built it over again. It was all quite new to me, just as was the peculiar type of Owen's mind, its extraordinary eagerness in the pursuit of ideas. My head already swarmed with an amazing mass of unsettled notions which buzzed in it like bees in a shaken hive. It seemed to me we never discussed anything less serious than the immortality of the soul. Owen was not sure of the existence of God, and I, so far as Christianity was concerned, was an Agnostic also. But to Owen it appeared to make an enormous difference, he was positively unhappy about it; while to me, though I did not let him suspect this, it was a matter of supreme indifference. Levine's acceptance of Christianity, at the end of "Anna Karénine," was for Owen an endless source of dissatisfaction and query. We discussed it by the hour. Yet, when actually reading the book, I had been far more struck by the appearance in Wronsky's and Anna's dreams of the strange little man, who seems to pass out of vision into reality just before the suicide. What did *that* mean? Why was he there? Had he, like some added flick of colour in the work of a master, been put in, not because he was there in Nature, but because he was needed for the picture? For me, at any rate, he had the effect of making all the rest more convincing, and, while he appeared to be purely fantastic, of corresponding to some esoteric reality. Or was the apparition at the railway station also only a vision, in that case the vision of a vision? To Owen such a question was of no interest whatever, and it was Owen's questions that we principally discussed.

Very often I walked home with him and hung swinging on the iron gate while we finished an argument. At such moments he exhibited an exhilarating eagerness, and he was never anxious to get the better of me in merely verbal dispute, as I frequently was of him. It was the thing in itself he saw, and he went at it like a terrier at a rabbit-hole, sending up showers of sand into the air, but never getting to the bottom. Sometimes, when we were talking, he would catch me by my arms and swing me slowly back and forward. Sometimes he would draw me close up to him till my face almost touched his, and his eyes seemed to look straight into my spirit, and then he would suddenly release me. He had a very quick and passionate temper, and was ridiculously sensitive, so that, though I employed infinitely more tact with him than I had ever done with anybody else, I occasionally offended him. Then he would leave me, his face as red as a turkey-cock, and his grey eyes dark and bright. Possibly for the rest of that day he would ignore me utterly; indeed, the first time it happened, I was sure we had quarrelled for ever. But the next morning he came up to me with a shy and shame-faced smile, saying he was sorry. At such times there would come into his voice so charming a gentleness that it was impossible to remain angry with him.

"Will you come to the opera to-night?" he asked me one morning, looking up from an old, ink-stained Virgil. We were sitting in the window-seat, where we always sat together, and which just held two. As Dr. Gwynn, the head Classical-master, was very old, very blind, and rather deaf, it was possible to pass the time quite pleasantly in this retreat.

I had not yet been inside a theatre, and Owen had been but seldom. "What is on?" I asked.

" 'Faust.' "

" 'Faust'? All right."

"I'll meet you outside the theatre at a quarter to seven."

"Very well; I'll be there."

I went home straight from school, in order to get my work done for the next day, but when I pushed open the door I became conscious that an altercation between Aunt Margaret and Miss Izzy was in progress in the other shop. They were so busy that they did not even hear me enter, though the shop-bell had rung, and, as I lingered on the threshold, I gathered that the dispute was about a young man, and I guessed who he was. I had seen him; his name was Moore; he travelled in the stationery line, and he admired Miss Izzy.

I heard Aunt Margaret's familiar *"some* people," with an accent on the "some." It was in this indirect manner that she invariably produced her most disagreeable remarks, and it was very much in the air just now. Miss Izzy displayed an icy dignity by stiff elbows, an erect head, and an elaborate preoccupation with the business of the shop. She seemed all collar and cuffs and freezing silence, which she could not quite keep up, for every now and again she threw out a retort. Aunt Margaret's ponderous black form filled up the inner doorway. Her large face, her drawn-in mouth, her black, shining eyes, her wig, gave her an alarming and bizarre appearance, but Miss Izzy was not in the least alarmed.

I came in, not wishing to be caught listening. Miss Izzy just cast a glance at me, and tossed her head.

I brushed past Aunt Margaret and went upstairs to my dinner, leaving the parlour door open, however, so that I might still hear the conflict going on below. When the shop-bell rang Aunt Margaret's voice would cease; then, when the customer had departed, it would begin again. Presently I heard Uncle George shuffling downstairs, and his entrance on the scene was followed by an outburst of both feminine voices together. The noise was becoming exciting, but I could no longer make out the words, though I hung over the balusters to listen. Then I heard Aunt Margaret coming upstairs, and Uncle George following her. She was in a violent passion. "Fool—fool—fool," she screamed at him all along the passage. Then came confused remonstrances in Uncle George's quiet voice, but they were interrupted by the banging of a door that shook the whole house. I came out into the lobby once more. I heard Uncle George trying to get into the room, but the door must have been locked from the inside, and through it came a shrill torrent of abuse. Uncle George's face was white and strange as he turned round and caught me staring at him. He told me to go away, but almost immediately he came after me into the parlour, where I had sat down again to my dinner. He told me Aunt Margaret was not well, that she had had a very bad attack last night, and been kept awake and in pain all night long. I could see that he would have liked to know if I had grasped the nature of several of those words that had come out to him through the closed door, but I continued stolidly to eat my dinner, without giving any sign. When I had finished, I got out my books, but as soon as the coast was clear I slipped downstairs to the shop. Miss Izzy was there alone, and affected not to see me.

"What's the matter with Aunt Margaret?" I asked; at which

ingenuous question Miss Izzy gave a short contemptuous laugh.

A blowzy girl, sucking a sweet, came in to buy a novelette, and when she had gone I informed Miss Izzy that I was going that night to hear "Faust." Miss Izzy expressed not the faintest interest in this project.

I turned over a book of views in melancholy silence—views of the Linen Hall Library, and of Donegall Place; of the Cave Hill, and the Albert Memorial; and I wondered if it would please Katherine were I to send her a complete set. I looked at the price, written in Miss Izzy's secret code, on the back, and could not make up my mind.

"When people can't control themselves there are places where they can have people to look after them," Miss Izzy announced to a bundle of "Horner's Penny Stories," which she next moment swept viciously into a corner.

This cryptic remark I took as referring to Aunt Margaret, but, seeing my expectant face, Miss Izzy unkindly refused to follow it up.

I was disheartened, and began to read aloud advertisements of art books from the back of a magazine I had bought on my way home. The third of these bore the simple title "Michael Angelo," and Miss Izzy astonished me by saying, "That's one of Marie Corelli's."

I ventured to tell her that Michael Angelo was a great painter and sculptor, but the information was lost on Miss Izzy, who in the midst of it said sharply, "Oh, don't bother."

I waited for a while, digesting this snub. Then, "Was she talking about Mr. Moore?" I asked, indiscreetly.

Miss Izzy regarded me at first mildly and absently, but as the sense of my question slowly forced its way through the meshes of her cogitations, suddenly in extreme wrath: "If you'd mind your own business," she snapped, "you'd hear fewer lies. I don't know what you're doing down here at all!"

"I'm doing nothing," I answered, crestfallen.

"People talk about girls being curious and gossiping," Miss Izzy went on, scornfully, "but if other boys are like you——"

I retired upstairs without waiting for the conclusion of the parallel. I worked for an hour and a half, and by then it was tea-time. Aunt Margaret did not appear, and we were told she was lying down. George, who had come home earlier than usual, inquired where I was going to, and when I informed him, asked if he might come too. I did not like to refuse, though I did not want him, and knew he and Owen would not get on together. I told him I was going with Owen.

"Is that the chap you're so thick with? I don't suppose he'll mind me, will he?"

I introduced them to each other at the theatre door. We were early, and had nearly three-quarters of an hour to wait. Owen and I began to talk, but our conversation evidently bored George, who, in the midst of it, introduced a characteristic remark of his own, at which I laughed, though I did not want to. Owen, who did not always see a joke, and who would have detested the best joke in the world of the particular kind George most affected, instantly relapsed into silence. He looked at George for a moment; then he took a copy of the "Golden Treasury" translation of Plato's "Republic" from his pocket and began to read. I had known well enough something of this sort was bound to happen, and I made no attempt to bridge it over. George nudged me with his elbow and closed his left eye. Owen's disapproval did not put him about in the least, and he continued to chatter quite unabashed.

Presently the fire-proof curtain went up, the lights were raised, and the band straggled in and began to tune their fiddles. The conductor followed, a fat little German with a bald head which shone like a large ostrich egg. He faced the audience and bowed two or three times to their applause; then, turning round, he tapped the music stand sharply with his baton, and the first phrase was drawn slowly out on the 'cellos.

With the end of the overture the lights were turned down, and the curtain rose on the lonely Faust, seated before a skull, an hourglass, and a large book, in his study. I had already forgotten Owen, George, and everything but what I saw before me. I was surprised to find that this old, grey-bearded man, who looked, in the dimness, like an Albert Durer print, had a fresh, strong, tenor voice. Outside I heard the singing of the peasants; then followed the rage and

despair of Faust, and, in a flaming red light, the apparition of
Mephistopheles. Faust pleaded for his lost youth, and Mephistopheles tempted him; the wall of the study suddenly dissolved like
a mist, and the vision of Margaret, seated at her spinning-wheel,
rose before the unhappy philosopher; and the swinging, sensual
phrase, repeated again and again in the orchestra, lulled me to a
dreamy languor.

    Faust.—"Heavenly vision!"

    Mephistopheles.—"Shall she love thee?"

There could be but one answer, and I saw Faust yield to the
tempter; I saw his rejuvenescence; and a triumphant duet between
them brought the act to a close.

    I had become lost in this appealing melodrama, and though my
mood was broken in the next act, in the third act, in the celebrated
garden scene, it was revived and intensified. The sugary sweetness of the music had an almost hypnotic effect upon me, for I
had never heard it till now, and the ecstatic sensuality of the duet
rapt me into a world of love, where everything else was forgotten. It was all utterly new to me; it thrilled me; it drowned me in
erotic dreams that swept me onward like the waves of the sea; and
through all, subconsciously, as I listened and watched, I was carrying on another love-making of my own, with which Faust and
Margaret had nothing to do. Through the next two acts I followed
more closely the fortunes of the unhappy heroine, not without
a naïve wonder why so much tragedy, so much remorse, should
attend on what appeared to me—but for the intervention of the
devil—a quite natural and straightforward courtship. For some
reason, possibly the fault of the libretto, more probably because
I could only catch about half the words, I could not discover
wherein lay the secret of the trouble, nor why the lovers did not
get married. I accepted the situation however: I accepted, I think,
everything but the absurd "Soldiers' Chorus," and the death-scene
of Valentine. This latter nearly made me sick at the time, though
I forgot all about it when the curtain rose to reveal the wretched
Margaret in prison. With enthusiasm I watched her reject her lover
and the demon, and fling herself on her knees to pour out her soul
in a prayer which finished on the high B. At last I saw her released

from all the ills of life, her body stretched on the miserable straw bed. And with that the walls of the prison rolled back, and I had a vision of her soul being borne to heaven by angels. It is true those white-clad, flaxen-haired creatures, with glistening wings and golden crowns, bore a not remote resemblance to several of the livelier persons I had seen mingling with the soldiers and students at an earlier stage of the drama; nevertheless I beheld them, in this pause on their way to heaven, with respect, if not exactly veneration.

"I doubt they're as near it now as they'll ever be," said George, cynically, pulling his cap from his jacket pocket.

And out in the street, under the gas-lamp at the corner, I had to submit to a deluge of criticism from both my companions. I don't know which I liked least, the scorn of Owen, who revealed the tangible source of Margaret's woes, and would have had it adopted by the State, or, after Owen had left, the ribald jibes of George, who found Faust a poor creature, requiring a moon, a garden, a casket of jewels, a devil, and several incantations, before he could beguile an innocent rustic maiden who was already in love with him. I resolved that I would go to the opera every night that week, but that I would go alone. Between the acts I had eagerly studied my programme, and the delightful, unfamiliar, romantic names, "Tannhäuser," "Il Trovatore," "Aida," "Lohengrin," were like syrens singing to me through the darkness, with an irresistible and passionate sweetness.

CHAPTER XXV

I went to the opera every night that week, as I had planned to do, but the edge of my appetite was blunted, and, save in the case of "Tannhäuser," and of "Lohengrin," I was disappointed. I had already become more critical, and I now doubted if "Faust" were the admirable work I had fancied it.

One evening there came a letter for me, and, when I opened the envelope, I found inside a card which told me that Miss L. Gill and Master E. Gill would be "at home" on Friday, the 23rd of

December. My own name was written at the top of the card. In the bottom left-hand corner was the word "Dancing," followed by the numerals 8-12; and in the corner opposite were four mysterious letters—"R.S.V.P."

I knew it to be an invitation to a party, but "R.S.V.P." was puzzling. Neither Uncle George nor Aunt Margaret could throw any light upon these symbols, though Uncle George pondered over the card half the evening, as if it had been a kind of magazine competition. Miss Izzy probably would have known, but Miss Izzy had gone, and would not be back till to-morrow morning, whereas I had a keen conviction that action should be taken to-night.

"Who are they?" Uncle George asked, referring to the Gills.

"Mr. Gill is a solicitor. Owen Gill is in my classes at school."

Uncle George examined the card anew, bringing this fresh light to bear on it. He held it at arm's length, and then put on his glasses and peered at it through them. "Miss L. Gill and Master E. Gill," he read aloud slowly and solemnly.

I laughed. "They're Owen's young sister and brother," I explained.

"A solicitor. I suppose he will have some letters after his name," said Uncle George, weakly.

"Oh, they're not those," I answered, impatiently. It seemed to me that everybody was very stupid.

"R.S.V.P." Uncle George threw out thoughtfully. He turned the card round and examined the back.

"Reply soon: very pressing," suggested George.

His father looked at him doubtfully, and laid the card on the table. "It can't be so pressing," he said, glancing at the calendar, "when it's a fortnight off."

"You see they have to make sure he's coming before they ask anybody else," George explained. "Rippin' spread: veal pie."

"I suppose you think that funny," I broke in; whereupon George, seeing I was inclined to be cross, kept it up.

"Royal spree: von't you partake? Refined soirée: veather permittin'. That's it, da, right enough; you can leave the card by."

But Uncle George continued to regard it searchingly, glancing at me every now and again over his spectacles.

Nothing was done that night, and in the morning, before school, I approached Miss Izzy on the subject; though when I saw her examine the card almost as carefully as the others had done, my faith in her sank.

"You'll have to answer on a card," said Miss Izzy, loftily, having at any rate settled the first point, and waving aside the sheet of note paper I held in my hand.

"I haven't got one."

"There's a box of them in the shop somewhere. They've been there since the dear knows when. Nobody ever asks for cards." She hunted about in a drawer under the counter, and at length succeeded in finding the box. Without breaking the pink paper band that held the cards together she carefully extracted one from the bundle. I took it and dipped my pen in the ink and waited.

"Just answer it in the usual way," said Miss Izzy, off-handedly, with the air of one who dashes off at least half a dozen such communications every day.

"I don't know the usual way," I confessed.

Miss Izzy aggravatingly paused to shake out a paper lamp-shade. Then she attended to a little boy who came in to buy a "Deadwood Dick" tale.

"Tell me what to say," I begged, humbly.

"Mr. Peter Waring," dictated Miss Izzy, with much dignity; and I wrote "Mr. Peter Waring" in terror all the time of making a blot.

Miss Izzy glanced over my shoulder. "You've begun too high up," she said, reassuringly. Then, as I made a movement to tear the card, "Oh, it'll do."

"Mr. Peter Waring begs to thank Miss L. Gill and Master E. Gill for their very kind invitation."

The shop-bell had rung again. It was the little boy back to change his story for another he had discovered in the window, and which it took Miss Izzy hours to extract. "Corduroy Charlie," she murmured, as she handed it across the counter. It was the title of the work.

"Yes?" I said, trying not to appear impatient.

Miss Izzy came back to my affairs. "Oh! what have you got?"

"Mr. Peter Waring begs to thank Miss L. Gill and Master E. Gill for their very kind invitation——"

"Invitation. . . . And will be very pleased to accept same for the date mentioned."

"Yes?"

"That's all. Don't be signing your name, stupid!"

I hastily checked myself.

"What do those letters in the corner mean?" I asked timidly. "I suppose I oughtn't to put them on mine?"

"Of course not. They're French, and mean they want an answer."

I read over what I had written and thanked Miss Izzy, but secretly I was not satisfied. I felt sure there was something wrong somewhere. It did not read well. I put it in an envelope, however, and posted it, though immediately afterwards I became more unhappy about it than ever. I made a mental note to ask Mrs. Carroll for information when I was at home at Christmas.

CHAPTER XXVI

I HAD been asked to the Gills' for eight o'clock, and at half-past six I began to dress. After posting my acceptance my next care had been in regard to the clothes I should wear. There is no doubt greatly increased opportunities had tended to develop in me a latent dandyism. At all events I took the matter of my dress quite seriously, and had very definite ideas in regard to it. I went to the best tailor in town, my bills were sent on to Mrs. Carroll, and that was all I knew about them. I tried to get the soft greys and blacks and whites I admired in old Spanish and Dutch portraits, with perhaps a colour-note of olive green in my neck-tie, but always with the tones kept low and harmonious. Dandyism certainly, but it was in its way merely an expression of those same sensibilities that enabled me to see the charm of the pictures I have mentioned; that is to say, it was not based on any feeling of personal vanity, for I had no illusions in regard to my beauty. So, in this particular instance, I took immense pains to see that everything should be exactly right, and at the same time pleasing to myself. The cloth I had chosen was of the very blackest and finest and softest. Each garment had to be fitted on me till I could find no fault in it. The broad braid down the sides of my trousers seemed to me perfectly decorative. It was really in its use of linen that modern dress most conspicuously failed; what would Franz Hals or Velasquez have thought of the stiff, glazed collar convention obliged me to wear?

When I had finished dressing I looked at myself critically in the inadequate glass, beside which I had set two or three candles, standing in pools of their own grease. It seemed to me that the peculiar, sullen expression of my face, caused by the formation of my forehead and the shape of my mouth, must always create an unfavourable impression. If I could recognise it myself, it would probably be a great deal more striking to other people. It disappeared when I smiled, but as soon as I stopped smiling it came back again.

I went downstairs and strutted about before Miss Izzy and little Alice, that they might admire my fine feathers, and it was only when I reached the Gills that every other feeling was swallowed up in a horrible shyness.

The whole house was brilliantly lit up, and I was shown to a room already half-filled with boys, who were removing their overcoats, putting on their dancing shoes, talking and laughing perfectly easily, just as if the most frightful ordeal were not staring them in the face. Evidently they all knew each other quite well, whereas I knew nobody. Owen came up, indeed, and spoke to me, but forsook me almost immediately, as people were arriving every minute, two or three of them, I observed, quite grown-up. I wished Owen would come back. When I saw a boy I knew slightly and heartily disliked, I was ready to welcome him as the oldest and dearest of friends, but, not being in my solitary condition, he merely nodded to me, and went over to join a group at the other side of the room. I was left standing by myself, not knowing what to do; and all the time fresh guests were arriving, and I felt I was in the way, but could not summon up courage to make a movement. I now bitterly regretted having been such a fool as to come. I noticed several other boys with whom I had a casual acquaintance at school, but beyond nodding they paid no attention to me, and I became filled with rage against them and against Owen himself. Then I heard a voice saying over my shoulder, "If you're ready you may as well come upstairs."

It was Owen, and I followed him obediently. I passed a group of boys loitering outside an open door, and found myself all at once in a large room. The light at first half-dazzled me. With a heart furiously beating I was led up to a tall, slight lady in black, who was standing near the fireplace. This was Owen's mother. I shook hands with her, and with his father, and with one of his elder sisters. But when this was accomplished I was again in that horrible position of not knowing what to do and being afraid to move. Owen had once more deserted me. All about me were a crowd of brightly-dressed girls, chattering and laughing among themselves, and pretending not to look at me. The boys, with whom I would have liked now to be back again, were hovering near the door, and I tried to screw up my courage to the point of crossing the room. Then somebody—I think it was Owen's sister—gave me a programme. I stood clasping it tightly in my hand. It seemed to me now unthinkably idiotic that I should voluntarily have placed myself in this position of torture, when all I had had to do was to refuse the invitation and stay at home. At that moment a lady to whom I had not been introduced spoke to me, though I was too much upset to hear what she said. She had a pleasant smile, a voice soft and attractive, and she asked me my name, and told me I must get some partners. Many of the other boys, I noticed, had begun to ask for dances, and were scribbling down names in their programmes. My new friend bore me off to a fair-haired, fair-skinned, demure-looking maiden in a pink, fleecy dress, and introduced me. Unfortunately, at this point, one of the grown-up persons, a tall young man, called out, "Annie, half a mo," and my protectress turned away, leaving me to make my own advances. I could do nothing. How could I ask this wretched girl to dance with me when I had never danced in my life? For an agonizing moment I stood there; then I stammered out something, turned on my heel abruptly, and walked away.

It was dreadful. Before me I saw a conservatory, the door of which was open, and I escaped into it as my only refuge. I felt utterly miserable. It occurred to me to slip out quietly and go home, but to do that I should have to cross the room, and somebody would be sure to pounce upon me. Besides, what would the McAllisters think? The first dance had commenced, and I saw that my golden-haired maiden had found another partner. He happened to be one of the boys I knew, and I was certain she would tell him what I had done, and that everybody at school would get to know about it.

In the midst of the dance the lady called Annie bore straight down upon me, having detected my hiding-place. But she did not seem angry; on the contrary, she was laughing. She threaded her way among the palms, while I felt my face becoming purple.

"What do you mean by running away like that from the partners I choose for you?" she asked gaily. "Elsie told me you wouldn't ask her to dance, and she says it's my fault, that I made you come when you didn't want to."

"I can't dance," I answered huskily. Nevertheless, Elsie's explanation of my conduct, in spite of the fact that it redoubled its rudeness, gave me relief.

The "Annie" lady looked at me, still laughing. Then she said very kindly, "Oh, don't mind; it really doesn't matter in the least. Come and dance with me."

"But I can't," I muttered, "I never tried in my life."

"Well, come and talk to me then, and we can watch the others."

She led me back into the room. She asked me all kinds of questions about myself, and very soon I was chattering away as if I had known her all my life. I had forgotten what an extremely small boy I had been only ten minutes ago, as I looked about me boldly, and gave "Annie" my opinion on all kinds of things.

We talked of the opera, and when she told me she preferred the "Trovatore" to "Lohengrin" I thought her taste very crude. All the same I liked her. She laughed in a nice way, and was interested in everything you said to her. I pulled up my trousers a little so that my delicate silk socks should be more visible. As I glanced round the room I decided that I was much better dressed than anybody there, and this conviction increased my confidence. I would have liked to ask "Annie" what she thought of me from this point of view, but instead, she inquired if I was fond of reading. I replied in the affirmative, and she asked me if I had read "Tom Brown's School-days." I again said, "Yes," and asked her if she had read "Anna Karénine."

"What a curious book for you to get hold of! I should have thought you would have preferred 'The Coral Island,' or 'Midshipman Easy.' Those are the kind of books *my* brothers like. That is one of my brothers there, that fat ugly boy with red hair, dancing with the little girl in white."

I inspected the brother. "'Anna Karénine' is a fine book," I answered. "Why didn't she ask for the divorce at once, do you think? I mean as soon as she went away with Wronsky?"

Out of the tail of my eye I saw the young man who had before interfered between us again approaching. She saw him too, and immediately called out, "Bertie, we're discussing 'Anna Karénine.' I'm sure you haven't read it."

We didn't really discuss it, for she changed the subject directly afterwards, without even having answered my question, and Bertie, who I heard later was a football player of great renown, asked me if my school was going to win the cup this year. The first square dance "Annie" insisted on my dancing with her, and, so far as I could judge, I shuffled through it all right. After that she left me to my own resources, and I returned to Bertie. There was something between Bertie and her, I believed. I was sure he had only come because she had told him she was going to be there to help to look after the kids. Bertie had danced all the dances up to this one, but he now told me that if he didn't have a smoke he should die, and asked me to come to the billiard-room with him. We played a hundred up, Bertie going two to my one, but I beat him, for I had often knocked the balls about on the table at Derryaghy, though there was rarely anybody to have a game with. Bertie said I should make a good player if I practised, and he showed me a lot of strokes. He was very jolly and I liked him. Presently he asked me if I didn't want some supper, and we went downstairs. Refreshments had been going on all the evening, but the room happened to be empty when we came in. There was a great deal of lemonade and stuff, but Bertie secured some champagne, and by the time I had had two glasses I began to feel extremely comfortable and jolly. Bertie's jokes were twice as good as they had been before, and my own conversation suddenly acquired an interest and brilliancy that made me want to talk as much as possible. After my third glass Bertie suggested I should try Apollinaris, but I refused. The room had somehow by this time got full of people. Bertie told me to keep quiet, but just then he was called away, and I was left to finish my supper alone.

CHAPTER XXVII

WHEN I got to my feet to go back to the dancing-room, everything swayed before my eyes, and I held on to the back of my chair till I had steadied myself. I felt now as bold as a lion, and as soon as I clapped eyes on Elsie, my golden-haired maiden whom I had insulted earlier in the evening, I determined to apologize. I went up to her, looking neither to right nor left, and placing myself in front of her asked her to give me the next dance.

She looked at me somewhat timidly, and said she was engaged already, showing me her programme. I at once stroked the name out.

"Now," I said, "let's go and sit down somewhere. He'll never find us."

She hesitated, but only for a second or two. Then she rose and put her hand lightly on my arm.

"Don't you think it's awfully hot in here?" I went on, with amazing aplomb. "Besides, we have to hide any way, haven't we?"

But outside, the landing was full of people. I glanced at the staircase before us, seeming to lead up into regions of dim coolness and solitude, and proposed we should try to find some place on the next floor.

There was indeed a seat there, in the dusk, but Elsie looked at it with misgiving. "I don't think we should have come so high up," she said. "I'm sure we're not meant to. I think we'd better go down: nobody else is coming up here."

"But isn't that just the reason we came? It's all right. If anybody else does come we won't be the only ones, and if they don't who's to know anything about us?"

I don't know whether Elsie was convinced by this sophistry, but at any rate she sat down. "I want to apologize to you," I began softly. "Are you very angry with me?" I was surprised at the amount of expression I was able to throw into my voice, and I had a delightful feeling of not caring a straw what I said or did. It was fairly evident that Elsie rather admired the mood I was displaying, though I could see she was slightly puzzled by it.

"No," she answered simply. "I knew you were shy." She lifted her innocent grey eyes to mine, and it came over me, very intensely, that she was extremely pretty. She looked very soft and demure in her fleecy pink dress, and with her hands folded in her lap.

"Do you think I'm shy now?" I asked, smiling.

"No," she answered sweetly.

I couldn't help laughing. At the same time I felt a sudden tenderness for her, which it seemed most essential that I should put into words.

"You've forgiven me then?" I went on.

She laughed. "What nonsense you talk. As if it mattered."

"It matters to me. Say you forgive me."

"I won't. There's nothing to forgive." She blushed and looked down.

"Say it," I persisted, bending towards her. "If you don't I'll think you dislike me."

She kept her eyes downcast, and I drew closer still.

"Well?"

"I don't dislike you," she whispered.

I kissed her. She blushed a deep delightful blush, but did not move away. The swinging melody of a waltz rose up to us through the dim cool light.

"Are you angry now?" I asked.

She shook her head. I put my arms round her, and as I felt her yielding I had a strong strange pleasure. I held her close to me, kissing her again and again, while she closed her eyes like a cat that is being stroked. For a moment I felt her lips touch mine, then she struggled away from me, and without looking back hurried downstairs.

I followed, but before I could rejoin her Owen caught me by the arm. "I've been looking for you everywhere. I've hardly seen you all the evening. What have you been up to?"

I laughed.

He looked at me, slightly perplexed. "What is there so amusing?" he inquired.

But I didn't try to explain.

"What is the matter?" Owen went on, gazing at me.

"Nothing," I answered.

"Come on upstairs: it's cooler there. There's a seat on the next lobby."

"Is there?" I replied, as I followed him.

CHAPTER XXVIII

"I hope you haven't been awfully bored?" was Owen's first remark after we sat down.

"No; I think it's a lovely party."

There was a silence.

"What *is* the matter, Peter?" Owen asked again.

"Nothing, Owen, except natural excitement. Don't be suspicious."

Owen looked unconvinced, but he decided to change the subject. "Do you know the part of the book that I really like best? It is where Levine mows the meadows with the peasants."

I knew we were back again at "Anna Karénine," but I couldn't bring my mind to bear upon it.

"That is the real kind of life," Owen pursued, "where all is simple, and natural; where there are no balls and clubs and lies and all the rest. I hate towns. I shall always live somewhere in the country."

"It doesn't suit everybody," I brilliantly observed.

"It doesn't suit people like Anna and Wronsky."

"You're always down on poor Anna."

"She's not poor. She had every chance to be happy. Why couldn't she have been content to be friends with Wronsky? All the rest was pure selfishness."

"You don't understand," I replied.

Owen hated to be told this. "Understand what?" he demanded, impatiently.

"The kind of love Anna and Wronsky had for each other."

"Why, then, as soon as she goes to live with Wronsky, does she begin to talk so much of her love for her son? I don't like her. It seems to me that she deliberately spoiled the lives of her husband and her son for her own gratification."

"She didn't spoil her son's life. He was only a little boy."

"But she forsook him."

"You don't understand," I was obliged to repeat. "You never *will* understand."

"Do you want to stick up for that sort of thing?"

"I'm not sticking up for it; but I don't think it's the kind of thing a person can accept or refuse just as if it were an invitation to a party. If you knew anything about it you wouldn't say they might have been content to be friends."

"And do you like the way she makes fun of her husband to her lover?"

"What has that to do with it?"

"Even when she is making her confession to her husband she thinks only of herself. She tells him that she hates him. It does not occur to her that he can have any feelings, because his manner is stiff and he has a habit of cracking his finger-joints."

"It didn't much matter how she made her confession."

"It did. She needn't have been brutal."

"Oh, she wasn't brutal."

"And all the lies?"

"But you never seem to think of her situation!"

"I do. She deliberately brought about her own situation, after having been warned by her husband. You admire her simply because she loves Wronsky; but there is nothing very wonderful about that kind of love."

"I never said I admired her; I said I understood her. If she sacrificed her husband, she sacrificed herself too."

"Yes—and her lover, and her friend Kitty, and her son, and every-thing. Levine's brother, who drinks himself to death, also sacrifices himself. And Yavshine, who gambles away all his fortune."

"You don't see any difference?"

"I don't see anything fine in the kind of love Anna felt. And when she says she won't have any more children, it seems to me that it becomes simply disgusting. Have you thought what it means?"

"Oh, I know what it means," I answered sulkily. Owen had managed to completely alter my mood, and I no longer felt pleased with myself or pleased with him. I was irritated because he seemed, now as always, to try to judge what was a matter of emotion by reasoning about it.

"If you had ever loved anybody," I said, "it would make you look at such things differently."

"Perhaps I mightn't see them any clearer for that."

"Perhaps not. But to judge human beings you require first of all to understand something about human nature."

"Understand! You're always harping on that! It's a very cheap way of arguing. Why should I think *you* understand?"

"Because I have felt what we are talking about, and you haven't." I suddenly grew violently excited. "You don't know what it is to care for a person so that nothing else in the world matters, so that it is like a kind of sickness, preventing you even from sleeping. You know nothing, have felt nothing, and yet you bring out your miserable little catechism arguments and pretend to pronounce judgment. I'd rather have a man who had committed all the crimes on the earth than one of those cold, fishy, reasonable creatures you admire, who never did anything wrong, and never made anybody happy."

Owen looked at me in amazement, which is indeed hardly surprising. But suddenly my excitement passed, and I felt only a passion of home-sickness and regret. It swept over me like a heavy, resistless rush of water. All that was here around me grew black as night. I longed to get away from everything that could even remind me of my life of the past few months. I seemed to have a sudden bright light in which I saw myself clearly. In these few months I had deteriorated, the quality even of my love for Katherine had deteriorated; it had become less of the spirit, more of an obsession. And now, as I stood there before Owen, I seemed to hear the soft breaking of waves, infinitely peaceful, and I had a vision of my own bedroom, where I went to sleep, and wakened up, with the low sound of the sea in my ears. I said good-night hurriedly to the astonished Owen. I told him I was sorry for speaking as I had done, but that I would explain it all to him another time; only now I must go. I ran downstairs to the cloak-room, and a few minutes later left the house, without having said good-night to Mrs. Gill.

When I reached home I let myself in quietly with a latch-key, but as I was undressing George wakened up and began to ask me about the party. I did not feel in the least like going to sleep, and after I had got into bed we lay talking. Presently George got up and lit the gas, which I had turned out. I saw him go to the hiding-place he had shown me on the night of my arrival, and again take from it that mysterious bundle of photographs. He came over and sat down on the side of my bed.

"I don't want to see them," I said, pushing him away; but he may have detected a note of weakness in my voice, for he only laughed.

"Don't be a fool," he answered brutally. "I'm not going to do you any harm."

He drew them from the envelope and showed them to me, one by one, while the gas flamed and flared above our heads.

CHAPTER XXIX

OWEN stepped back off the foot-board on to the platform.

"Good-bye," I said, leaning out of the carriage window. "There's no use your waiting till the train starts. I hope you'll have decent holidays."

He smiled. "I'm sure I will. I wish, all the same, you were going to be with me. I thought of it, but then I thought you would rather go home."

"Yes," I said.

"Wouldn't you really? Don't you want to go home?"

"Yes, of course. Why do you ask?"

"I don't know. You don't seem, perhaps, quite so keen as you were——"

Owen still waited, but I had taken my seat.

"Well, I'll see you again in a fortnight," he went on, cheerfully. "Write to me, won't you, if you aren't too busy?"

"Yes."

Another pause followed, while Owen looked up and down the platform. He seemed to me extraordinarily happy.

"Well, good-bye again," he said.

"Good-bye."

And this time the guard's whistle blew, the train jolted forward with a clatter of coupling-irons, and then glided steadily on. I waved my hand to Owen, catching a last glimpse of his bright, animated face before I settled down to the indifferent contemplation of the staler, and coarser-looking persons who shared my compartment. What I had been looking forward to for many weeks had come to pass; I was on my way home; outwardly nothing was wanting; yet not even the thought of seeing Mrs. Carroll again seemed to have power to awaken that joy I had anticipated, though she had written to ask me to spend part of my holidays with her, and I tried now to think of some scheme by which to make this part as large as possible.

I looked at the people opposite; I looked out of the window; I turned the pages of *Punch's Almanac*, which Owen had bought for me at the bookstall. Then I shut my eyes and tried to doze.

When the train drew in at the station I saw my father standing on the platform. Somehow, I had not expected him to be there, and he upset my calculations. I opened the carriage door, and as I shook hands with him I realized how much easier it is to make plans than to carry them out, and hoped Mrs. Carroll herself had approached him on the matter of my going to Derryaghy. His careworn, anxious face was lit by a smile as he asked me how I was. A porter meanwhile had secured my box and was wheeling it on a truck along the platform. But, as we walked behind him, that old stupid feeling of constraint had already begun to take possession of me, and my replies to my father's questions sounded, for all I could do to the contrary, stiff, and even reluctant.

It was after one o'clock and dinner was ready when we reached the house.

"The train must have been late," I remarked, indifferently, as we sat down; and then I could think of nothing further to say.

It struck me that my father was older and dimmer and shabbier than I had remembered him. He presented the picture, drab and dreary, of perfectly achieved failure, and I found myself looking out for all his old habits, the peculiar noises he made with his nose, his fashion of smacking his lips. I noticed that his hands were not very clean, and that his coat looked as if he had brushed his hair over it. These things struck me all the more forcibly, somehow, because I tried to think how superficial and unimportant they were. I had a vision of the solitary meals he must have taken for the past four months, and I was sorry for him, though subconsciously, at the same time, I was considering how soon it would do for me to mention my proposed visit to Derryaghy.

After dinner he asked me what I wanted to do. "It is nice and dry for walking," he said. "We have had quite a hard frost."

It sounded as if he intended coming with me, a thing he seldom or never did.

"I was thinking of going up to Derryaghy," I answered, with an assumption of carelessness that did not prevent my noting the immediate change that came into his face.

"Had you planned anything?" I asked hastily.

"No, no."

"Perhaps you would like to go for a walk?"

"No, no. Please yourself," he replied.

So I went up to Derryaghy, with a guilty sense that I had hurt his feelings. It was a pity that I should have begun in this fashion; that I could not, for once, have been cheerfully and spontaneously unselfish, but my longing to get back to my old haunts was intense, and I yielded to it.

After all, when I reached Derryaghy, Mrs. Carroll was not there. She had left a message for me to say that she had been obliged to go up to town, but that she hoped I should be able to dine with her at the usual hour. I wandered out into the winter woods, beautiful with the strange and delicate beauty of naked trees. I loved this place really with a kind of passion, and I was glad my father was not here, glad that I was alone. Dark slender branches traced fantastic arabesques against the grey sky above my head. The black- and sil-ver-stemmed birches gave the note that was carried out through all the colouring. Only the fir-trees, laurels, and an occasional holly-tree, were green. I loved the woods in winter; they seemed to me to have then a peculiar grace they did not possess at any other season. And the wind whistled so hollowly in the leafless trees, and the darting birds were so black against the sky, and all was so silent and solitary, with a sort of frozen loveliness, that I could conceive of nothing more beautiful even in the green pomp and splendour of summer. And behind everything was a vision of long, lamp-lit, fire-lit evenings, with dreamy, delicious books. The leaves of the laurels and holly were coated with frost; the dead fronds of the bracken were a dull brown; here and there the sombre colouring was splashed with the red leaves of brambles. There was a hint of approaching snow in the air, there was almost a silence of snow, and I seemed to feel it drawing closer to me through the cold, remote sky. The ground was hard as iron. Sometimes a single leaf, pallid and faded, trembled still at the end of a twig, but almost all the leaves that were going to fall had fallen long ago. I saw the flash of fur, brown and white, in the frozen grass, but Tony, who followed at my heels, was indifferent to rabbits.

It was dusk when I returned. A servant preceded me into the drawing-room, and lit the lamps, and made up the fire, throwing on another log or two. I sat down in one of the big, soft armchairs and began to turn over Christmas numbers—the *Graphic*, the *London News, Holly Leaves*—looking at Caldecott's, Sambourne's, and Fred Barnard's drawings. I began to read a story by Bret Harte. It was extraordinarily nice to be here again. This dear old house, how I loved it! The huge wood fire, the roomy depth of my arm-chair, the soft, thick carpet, all the surroundings of pleasantness and comfort, appealed to me after my prolonged and reluctant experience of the McAllisters. The fragrant China tea that was brought in to me tasted more deliciously than anything I had ever tasted before, and when I had finished my story ("The Chatelaine of Burnt Ridge," I think it was called) and the servant had cleared away the tea-things, I sat and dozed.

I had asked after Miss Dick, but of course she had gone home for Christmas. I was really to be alone this time—just myself and Mrs. Carroll.

As I sat there, looking into the fire, I felt that it would have been nicer of me to have gone home on this, the evening of my arrival, but six o'clock, our tea hour, had struck ten minutes ago, and still I had not budged from my chair. Curious thoughts, thoughts I should have been ashamed to tell anybody, came to me unbidden, and for the first time. It made a tremendous difference just who happened to be one's father, I reflected; and I thought of how the Dales were Mrs. Carroll's nearest relatives. "She likes me better than anybody else," I said to myself. "If I were by myself she would adopt me. All this—the house—everything will belong one day to somebody else; but to whom? . . . . The house?". . . . And I remembered she did not care for Gerald, and that Gerald did not in the least try to make her alter her opinion. Probably he had only come over last summer because his people had insisted on it. All at once I realized that these speculations were not particularly charming, and tried to put them from me. At the same time I heard the sharp sound of a horse's hoofs on the frozen ground, then the crunch of gravel under carriage wheels, and I knew Mrs. Carroll had returned.

She opened the door and came straight to me, smiling and holding out her hand. "You've grown so big," she said, lifting her thick veil, "I don't know whether you want to be kissed or not, but I think I'll risk it." She kissed me, and then held me at arm's length to look at me. She moved me a little so that the lamp-light fell on my face. "My dear child," she asked, with a sudden anxiety, "aren't you well? How did you get those black lines under your eyes? You can't be getting enough sleep. Have you been working too hard?"

"No," I answered, "but I was up late last night."

"You must be more careful: your health is infinitely more important than any wretched examination. Well, at all events, I'm very glad to see you."

A couple of hours later, after dinner, she again took up the subject of my appearance, which evidently did not satisfy her, though I assured her there was nothing the matter.

"You've altered," she said, thoughtfully. "It isn't only that you've grown, but you, somehow, look older. Do you get your meals properly? I expect you stop to play after school instead of coming home to your dinner!"

I changed the subject as soon as I could by asking after the Dales. "Will they be here next summer?"

"If you would like it I daresay we can manage it. In fact I invited Katherine for Christmas, but she couldn't come."

"I hope they will come in the summer."

I inquired after all the other people I could think of: I felt interested in everything that had happened since I had gone away. Then I sat quiet, and quite suddenly, when I thought she had forgotten all about it, Mrs. Carroll said, "I wish you would tell me, Peter, just what is troubling you."

"But there is nothing," I answered, smiling. "I was only thinking how nice it was to be back here again."

"Remember you are to come to stay for a few days, before the end of your holidays. You must stay at least a week. When have you to go back?"

"On the eighth."

"And those people you are with—the What-do-you-call-ems— how do you like them?"

"The McAllisters?" I hesitated. "Not very much."

"Do they look after you properly?"

"Oh yes."

"I think I'll come and see you there. I would have gone before this, only your father didn't want it."

"I'd rather you didn't," I said.

"Why?"

I had no answer and she went on: "I must call and have a talk with your father before you go back."

"It won't do any good so far as that is concerned. He wants me to be there. Aunt Margaret is his sister."

"I know that, but you'd rather be by yourself, wouldn't you? I can see there is something you don't like."

"My father wouldn't let me. He has some idea about a home influence—but I told you before, and of course he told you himself."

"Home fiddlesticks! You'd have been far better at a good boarding-school. This, it seems to me, is neither one thing nor another. I must speak to him."

"There is no use really," I said, for I knew that if she were to take the matter up again it might end in my not even being allowed to come to stay at Derryaghy next week.

"Your father is far too anxious about you. If there had been two or three more of you it would have been much better."

"It isn't that." I waited a while before I brought it out: "He doesn't trust me."

"Doesn't trust you? In what way doesn't he trust you?"

"In every way. He thinks I'm inclined naturally to—to do things—"

"To do things? What sort of things?"

"To be bad," I said abruptly.

Mrs. Carroll stared at me. "Nonsense, child," she answered. "I don't know what can have put such an idea into your head!"

"*He* did," I muttered. "There are times when I think he may be right," I went on dejectedly, "that he must surely have some reason. I don't know. . . . . He is always thinking about my mother."

Mrs. Carroll had been on the point of speaking, but at this she paused.

"I know nothing about her," I pursued. "I can't remember her at all, and there is not even a photograph at home. What *is* there? Do *you* know nothing?"

Mrs. Carroll hesitated. "Nothing," she then said. "Nothing more than you know yourself, Peter dear," she added.

"You have never heard? I should like to go to see her."

"Yes?" There was a note of doubt in this monosyllable which made me look up.

"I should like to judge for myself," I continued, impetuously. But the question was, or to Mrs. Carroll appeared to be, an impossible one for us to discuss together, and she made no reply.

"And how do you like your school?" she asked presently, holding up a magazine between her face and the blazing fire. "Tell me all about it—about all your friends and everything you do."

I began to tell her, giving, as I went along a kind of rough, rambling account of my ordinary day. I told of how I had come to know Owen; how the real thief had never been discovered. I described Owen to her; I said he was the only friend I had made. I told her of the party last night, leaving out the episode of Elsie.

"It makes such a difference when you find somebody who is more or less like yourself."

"I don't think he is very like me," I answered. "I don't think we're a bit alike, but—" I tried to puzzle it out: "I suppose we must have some things in common."

"Tell me about him," she encouraged me.

"He's a very good chap," I said lamely. Then, as this didn't in the least express my meaning: "I mean he's very straight, and decent, and all that. He's not like anybody else."

"What is the difference?"

"Well, for one thing, he's awfully serious. I don't mean dull—but serious about what things really mean and that sort of thing."

"Is he clever?"

"I don't know. He's very simple."

"And George—isn't that his name? the name of your cousin?—what is *he* like? Are you friends with him?"

"Oh, yes."

"Tell me about George too."

"There's nothing to tell. He's in business. You wouldn't much care for him."

"Why not? Don't you?"

"Yes, very well." And it suddenly struck me as strange that I did so, that I did not positively detest him.

"You do not seem enthusiastic. Is he not nice?"

"Oh, he's all right. He's nice enough, I daresay—just as nice as I am."

"Why won't you tell me what is the matter, Peter?"

"There is nothing."

"You haven't done anything wrong, have you?"

"I don't know."

I closed my eyes for a minute as I leaned back in my chair. A silence had fallen on the room with my last words. Then suddenly my self-control deserted me, and I hid my face against the arm of the chair, just as if I had been a child.

CHAPTER XXX

It was a beautiful, clear, winter night when I walked home. Over the low wall I looked out at the dark, smooth sea, stretching away, almost black, save where the moonlight touched it. I trailed my right hand on the wall as I walked, heedless of the cold, though it was freezing keenly. The tide was in, and the chill, listless splash of the small waves, running through my thoughts, seemed to increase their sadness. On the verge of the distant golf-links a ruddy light from the big hotel shone out into the night.

As I turned up the Bryansford Road, I saw, in the moonlight, my father standing leaning over the garden gate, and behind him the house door was open. Unconsciously I slackened my pace. He was looking for me, perhaps. He must have already heard me, for the sound of my footsteps rang out sharply on the hard road.

"Where have you been all this time?" he asked abruptly, as I came up.

There was a hardness in his voice that, in my present mood, I shrank from more than I should have from physical violence. I knew he knew where I had been, and I thought he might have let the matter pass. "I didn't intend to stay so late," I said, apologetically, "but Mrs. Carroll had gone up to town and left a message for me, asking me to wait. After dinner she wanted me to tell her all I had been doing since I left home."

"I hope you were more communicative than you were to me. You hadn't time, I suppose, to come back and say you were staying. I waited tea for you for nearly an hour."

"I didn't think it mattered," I mumbled. "I'm very sorry. I thought you would understand."

I had already climbed half a dozen stairs on my way to bed, when my father called me back.

"Why are you rushing off like that, now?"

I hastily returned. "I was going to bed: I didn't know you wanted to sit up." I went on into the parlour, where there was a smoky fire in the grate, just large enough to make you realize how cold it was, and on the table some bread and butter, a jug of milk and a tumbler. I sat down beside the fire.

"I'm not going to sit up; but I don't want you to treat your home as if it were an hotel, a place where you come merely to sleep. I've no doubt things are more to your taste at Derryaghy, but while this *is* your home, you must try to make the best of it."

I looked at my father helplessly, but I said nothing. I had an uncomfortable vision of his sitting here all evening by himself. If he would only make friends with somebody! I wondered if he had been happy before mamma went away.

"Seeing that it was your first day at home," he went on, putting down my silence to sulkiness, "you might at least have been content to be out all the afternoon. Now that we are on the subject, I had better let you know that Mrs. Carroll asked me to allow you to spend part of your holidays at Derryaghy, but I told her you must decide that for yourself." He paused, with the intention of letting me say I didn't want to go.

"She told me to-night," I murmured.

"Well?"

"I think I'd like to go."

There was a silence, and I wondered how long we were going to sit shivering here.

"I had a letter to-night from your Aunt Margaret. She says you have made friends with some people called Gill, and have been to a party at their house."

"Yes: it was last night."

"Why do you never tell me of any of these things yourself? One would think I was a total stranger to you!"

"I didn't know it would interest you."

All at once I remembered my visits to the opera, and I couldn't understand how my father had not heard of them. He had not mentioned my laxity in regard to church either, and both these omissions puzzled me greatly, seeing Aunt Margaret had made such a fuss about them at the time.

CHAPTER XXXI

AFTER breakfast I screwed up my courage to the point of broaching the subject I had most on my mind. "There is something I want to say to you," I began, and my father instantly adopted an attitude of motionless attention, so excessively attentive that it had the effect of putting me out, and I forgot the phrases I had prepared beforehand, and could only stammer awkwardly that it was my desire to leave the McAllisters and choose some lodging for myself.

A return to this question I saw was not pleasing to him, and I had hardly expected it to be so.

"You are very self-willed," he said, slowly.

I knew from the tone in which this opinion was uttered that he had already made up his mind about my request, yet some obscure instinct of self-preservation still kept me from giving in. I don't suppose I could have satisfactorily explained that instinct to my father, even had I become perfectly confidential, and certainly no such thought ever crossed my mind. The result was that he looked upon my wish as a mere caprice.

"It seems to me we have already fully discussed the question," he remarked unsympathetically.

"I didn't know then. . . . I mean I don't like sleeping with George."

"Why? You have your own bed, haven't you?"

"Yes."

"George is your cousin."

"I know he is my cousin," I answered wearily. "What difference does that make?" Already I felt the whole thing was hopeless.

"It is just this sort of nonsense which makes me object to your going to stay at Derryaghy," my father began impatiently. "You are pampered with every luxury there, till you begin to dislike and look down upon everybody who hasn't had your advantages."

"I'm not thinking of advantages," I muttered, with a sort of irony.

"I didn't know when I arranged for you to stay with them that they would not be able to give you a room to yourself. On the other hand, I don't see that it is at all a sufficient reason for your leaving now you are there. I told you so when I wrote to you. It is only an excuse to get your own way. You have always been like that; though I should have thought you would hardly have considered it worth while to bring the matter up again after all these months."

I accepted my father's decision without further protest. As a matter of fact, a kind of listlessness had come upon me, an apathetic indifference to whatever might happen.

It was Christmas Eve. A heavy fall of snow had occurred during the night, and on the hard, frozen ground it lay unmelted to the dark border of the sea. All the morning I spent beside the fire reading "Richard Feverel," but about half-past three I went out for a walk over the golf-links. The snow was several inches deep, but being perfectly hard was not unpleasant for walking. I had slept badly last night, a sleep broken by wretched dreams, and I had a mind to go for a really long walk and tire myself out. In spite of being at home again, in spite of this beautiful, bright, exhilarating weather, in spite of the fact that I would be getting a Christmas-box from Mrs. Carroll to-morrow, and a letter from Katherine, and another from Owen, my spirits were of the gloomiest. Never before had I looked so closely into my own soul, and never before had I found so little there to comfort me. I knew that for months past my mind had been gradually submitted to a poisonous influence that had filtered through my blood, like a vapour from some fever-breeding marsh. Yet certain seeds, I thought, could perhaps only have taken root within me, could perhaps only so quickly have sprung to tall dark flower, because they had found a soil already apt to receive them: and I remembered my father's suspicions in the past. I thought of a book I had been reading lately—a book written for boys, and all about boys—and I compared myself with its heroes. I compared the gloom that weighed upon me now with the troubles they had experienced, and it seemed to me I must be

alone in a dead world

different, not in degree but in kind, from every boy in that book, from the bad just as much as from the good. I remembered hours, whole days, when I had been like them, like the decent ones I mean, for with the others I had nothing in common—I had never wanted to shirk games; and bullying, gambling, dishonesty, and "pubs," had no attraction for me. But it was just because there were bits of the book in which I could see a part of myself that I was troubled by the absence of other parts, of so many other feelings that none of these boys shared. I wondered if I were quite abnormal, but how could I ever find out even that; for just as nobody knew what I was, I knew nothing really of anybody else, save what they cared to show me or took no trouble to hide. I was hopelessly shut in to the little circle of my own sensations, desires, and emotions. Owen, whom I knew better than any other boy,—what, after all, did I know of him? I know no one but myself, and of myself I knew much that filled me with shame.

A deep silence overshadowed all things, the silence of the fallen snow. I had come to a stand-still. Around me was an infinite stretch of whiteness, almost unbroken, save where the sea was dark and restless under the whip of the rising wind. Dusk had crept up imperceptibly, and more light now rose from the ground than fell from the leaden sky overhead. Snow had again begun to fall. A few flakes turned and fluttered down out of the darkness, but I knew this was only the beginning. I walked to the edge of the black, desolate sea, and watched the waves rolling in to break at my feet, and at that moment I felt infinitely alone, and indeed for miles round there was probably no other human being. But it was as if I were alone in a dead world. The whirling flakes of snow fell ever faster out of the winter sky; the barren, frozen land was wrapped in a stillness that was more like the stillness of death than of sleep; the only sounds there were came from the waves breaking at my feet, and from an occasional sweep of wind forlorn as though no ears were there to listen. The creeping on of night seemed to be the shutting out for ever of all life, and one could imagine there would never be anything more, that the end had at last been reached.

And the thought of death came to me, without terror, came, rather, as a solution. All that bound me to existence seemed now

attenuated to the thinnest cobweb. If I just lay down here and
waited. . . . .

Tony, who had grown restless at my long delay, suddenly broke
into my consciousness. He began to urge me to come on, with a
peculiar, eager, discontented note in his voice. He jumped up with
his large paws against me. I knelt in the snow and hugged him in
my arms, while his warm red tongue passed rapidly over my face.
I held him close, and his black nose was pressed into my cheek, and
he wagged his tail and nibbled at my ears.

CHAPTER XXXII

Two or three days before, I had sent off a small picture to Katherine as a Christmas-box. It had taken me a long time to choose
something I thought she might care for, and which at the same
time pleased myself. In the end I had got her a photograph of
Francia's portrait of the boy Federigo Gonzaga, the son of Isa-
bella d'Este—the Miserden Park picture. I had had it framed in a
flat, dull, dark frame, and very carefully packed; and over and over
again I had pictured her opening the parcel, her surprise. It was
two days after Christmas when the postman brought me a letter
from her, but instead of reading it, I put it in my pocket. It was a
fairly thick packet, so, though her writing was very large, I knew it
must be a long letter. I could feel it as it lay in the inner pocket of
my jacket, and a dozen times that day I drew it out and inspected
it, but no more than that, for I had determined not to read it till I
went to bed. All day long I thought of the pleasure I should have,
and in the end I became so impatient that I went to bed about nine
o'clock.

I put the letter on my pillow, and placed a lighted candle on the
painted, deal chest-of-drawers beside my bed. I undressed, got into
bed, and only then, with eager fingers, tore open the envelope and
drew out its contents.

I looked at them as they lay upon the bright, patch-work coun-
terpane, a single sheet of note-paper, and a New Year card in the
form of a pocket calendar. My disappointment was so great that

for a little I did not even read the letter, but lay on my back and stared dismally at the iron rail at the foot of my bed. My thoughts were bitter. I recalled the many letters I had written to her, undiscouraged by her brief replies. Some of these had been pages long; the one I had sent with my present, for instance, I had given a whole evening to. I glanced at what she had written—three sides of a sheet of note-paper hastily scrawled over in huge characters, about two words to a line. She thanked me for my picture, which was very pretty. She would have liked to write me a really long letter, but there were some people staying in the house, and she had to look after them, and had only been able to snatch a moment to wish me a happy New Year. That was all.

I blew out the candle and lay with my eyes wide open staring into the darkness. The few, conventional phrases of her letter were vivid in my mind. To begin with, the picture was not pretty; if it had been, I shouldn't have bought it. If she had wanted me to have a happy New Year it would have been very easy for her to make it so. But it had been too much trouble. I thought of how I had sat up far into the night to finish my Christmas letter to her. I heard my father's step on the stairs, the shutting of his bedroom door. I pulled the bed-clothes up to my chin, and as I did so my hand touched something—the pocket-calendar. I tore it in two and flung the pieces at the opposite wall.

My mind was divided between despondency and anger. I pictured her enjoying herself with a houseful of her own and Gerald's friends, while I was forgotten. Of course there was no particular reason why she should remember me. Still, the irony of those foolish New Year's wishes might almost have been intentional had the whole letter not been so thoughtless. She knew well enough how happy I must be now, stuck in this wretched hole by myself; and I asked myself how anybody could be so completely devoid of imagination, of sympathy, even of tact? I began to compose a letter to be written to-morrow, a letter expressing what I felt. I imagined her reading it in the midst of her friends, and realizing how she had wounded me. I tossed and turned till I was almost in a fever. Sleep was out of the question, for I knew it must be nearly morning already, and I had half a mind to get up and dress. . . . .

When I opened my eyes it was broad daylight. I sprang out of bed and hurried into my clothes. The first thing after breakfast I sat down to write my letter of reproach, and wrote it at furious speed, a fire burning in my soul. Yet when I came to read it over, it seemed childish and stilted, and in my haste I had left out so many words and mis-spelt so many others that I was obliged to make a fair copy of the whole. This I posted, but had two days more of impatience before a reply reached me. When it came, it had the effect of turning away my anger. Katherine seemed really sorry; at any rate she said she was. She told me that she cared far more for me than for any of the people I imagined she found so delightful, and that I might have known this by now, even if her letters *had* been short. She said it had been horrid of her to write such a miserable scrawl, but that, if she had guessed I should mind it so much, she would have written me a whole book.

I sat down to reply at once, but I cannot account for the unfortunate tone my letter took. It was morbid and self-conscious, without being in the least frank. I begged her forgiveness; I made a parade of a melancholy that bore no resemblance to the kind of melancholy I really felt; I talked vaguely about not being as good as she believed me to be, and the whole production was a little sickening. I don't know, or rather I do know, what she made of it. She replied that she had never for a moment thought me good, and that she should prefer not to hear from me at all to getting letters like the last I had written.

It was not, perhaps, extremely sympathetic, but I knew well enough myself I had done the wrong thing. My letter had been odiously self-conscious. I had accused myself of not being good, but what on earth did that mean? It might mean that I went into the pantry at night and stole the jam!

CHAPTER XXXIII

ABOUT this time, influenced by Amiel, whom I had come across in Mrs. Humphry Ward's translation, I had begun to keep a diary, or journal, of my "sensations and ideas." I unearthed it the other day, with the paper time-staled as the sensations, and the ink faded as the ideas. On reading it over I found it so unbalanced, so one-sided, that I can scarce quote a passage as really expressive of what I actually was. It expresses only what I was when I sat down to write my journal, and I never appear to have done this except when I was in a particularly unhealthy mood. Some of this journal is descriptive, some of it merely notes certain thoughts that came to me and that I evidently, the Lord knows why, imagined worthy of preservation. A single entry, the description of a dream, will, I fancy, give an idea of the whole.

"Last night I went out and wandered about the streets for a while, and when I came home I went straight to bed. I did not go to sleep for a long time. I remember hearing the clock strike two, and when I awoke it was just four, but of course I cannot really tell how long my dream lasted.

"I was in a room with some people I knew very well. My father was there, and Aunt Margaret and Uncle George. I was laughing at something, I cannot remember what, only that it had to do with a question of religion, when suddenly the figure of Christ appeared, in a long, purple, velvet robe—a slight figure, with narrow effeminate face, pointed beard, and a soft treacherous expression in the slanting eyes. Everybody in the room except myself fell on their knees in fear, but I stood still. He watched me and then came closer, holding out his pierced hands and making the sign of the cross. He did not speak, but I knew what he meant, and I detested him. He drew still nearer and still I would not kneel. My defiance filled me with a mingled fear and exultation, and, as he was about to touch me, I cried out, invoking Satan, offering myself to him. A horrible look of baffled rage and malice distorted the face of the Christ. Outside a storm was raging and the wide window was a black square. With a shrill scream the Christ vanished, and a man, naked, superb, the colour of dark, greenish bronze, shot through the window as though propelled by some invisible force. (From this on, an undertone of strange music floated through my dream, rising and falling with the rise and fall of my emotions.)

"The face of this dark angel was beautiful and proud. His forehead was broad and low and slightly overhanging, giving him a stern and brooding expression, but although I was afraid of him I loved him, and felt an irresistible longing to put myself in his power. We were now alone together in the room, which had suddenly grown dark, and he seized me. I struggled, but in his grasp I was helpless as a young bird in the clutches of a boy. He stripped me naked and rubbed my body over with some kind of ointment that left no mark. And somehow I knew he was going to send me down into hell, and that after a while I should return again to earth, but that I should be his for ever.

"'I shall not be tortured?' I asked him, and he answered in a deep voice, 'There are no tortures such as you are thinking of.'"

"'When I come back,' I said, 'I shall have forgotten all I saw there; I shall think I have been only dreaming. Can you not mark me in some way?'

"He placed me in front of the mirror that was at one end of the room, and which seemed to shine in the dark as with fire. And in the glass I saw over my right breast a red flush, and upon this a white streak, broad and long as his fore-finger. He took my hand, and suddenly the room I was in seemed to be dropping. Down and down it rushed, so rapidly that the walls glowed red hot, but because of the ointment with which I had been covered I felt nothing. And we seemed to be sinking down through a bottomless sea that hissed in steam against the walls. Then the speed increased a thousandfold and I lost consciousness.

"I do not know what interval had elapsed, but it was evening and I was back again in the room, our parlour at home. My father was kneeling down and calling upon me in desperation to pray to God before it was too late—to pray—to pray. But I would not pray. Mrs. Carroll was there and she was crying. Then a voice said aloud above our heads, 'It was all only a dream,' and for a little we believed this; and then all at once I knew the voice was lying. My father read in my face what was passing in my mind, and his own face grew white as paper. But I knew; and I exulted and wept at the same moment. I tore away my shirt from my breast. 'Look—look! It is his mark!'

"A loud cry rang through the room, and I awoke, bathed in perspiration, to the silence and darkness of night. I could hear George breathing quietly in his sleep. Then I got up and lit the gas and looked to see if the mark were indeed there upon my breast, but there was nothing."

Could I have been mentally, morally, even physically, well when I had this dream? Childish and foolish, perhaps, it had at the time an intensity the effect of which lingered on long after I had awakened. There is something disquieting in the thought that so slender a veil should separate the world of order and sanity from a world of disorder and delirium such as my eyes were opened to then. Yet that other world is always there, waiting, and the veil may be torn at any moment, letting tongues of the dreadful, flaming light shoot through. The Christ of my dream was not a blasphemous creation of my own mind, but a sort of distorted memory of one or two pictures in a book about Byzantine wall-paintings I had looked at years before. The main fact, however, psychologically, is, I suppose, the fact that I kept a journal at all. Probably what was at the bottom of it was an idea of confession which now haunted me. It came to me in several relations. I thought of Owen, thought it was my duty to tell him everything about myself, and that in this way we might make our friendship perfect. At other times I feared that instead of doing this it might do just the opposite. I was not sure, either, what my motive really was—whether it really proceeded from a sense of duty, or only from a desire of personal relief. It was strange that while in many respects I continued to have an exaggerated opinion of myself, I should yet have been so frequently visited just now by hours of despondency, when I imagined my life as already irretrievably doomed to failure. I did not look upon myself as an ordinary person, or the crisis through which I was passing as an ordinary crisis. I began to ponder over the meaning of sin and damnation, and I figured this latter quality as a condition of mind which attracts evil, and from which no evil can be hidden. When I was with Owen my troubles grew fainter, and even disappeared. Mentally, morally, he had upon me much the same effect as, physically, a draught of fresh air would have had, after long confinement in a stifling atmosphere. I admired him; I envied him his freedom from all that made my own life just now so difficult. I discussed the question of free will with him, but I no more believed in it than did my Arabian Nights heroes. I was as closely imprisoned in my own physical temperament as a rat in a trap. And if I were to die? For the first time it dawned upon me that one might pass into a spiritual world as dark and dreadful as any I had ever seen in a dream. With this appalling thought it occurred to me that a priest might be the best person to confess to, and I began to consider to whom I could go.

CHAPTER XXXIV

THE matter, as I soon perceived, was not at all so simple as in the first flush of discovery it appeared to be. But one excellent effect it had, and that was to make Sunday, which had been the dullest, the most interesting, day of the week, while I went from church to church in search of my confessor. In almost every case I could tell at once that I had not found him, and I was on the point of giving up the whole idea as hopeless, when one Sunday evening I went to St. Mary Magdalene's. The clergyman who took the service was already well past middle-age. He was delicate and ascetic-looking, with a peculiar expression on his worn face, as of one who had had to make a fight against something—possibly it had only been ill-health—and who had come out of the struggle victorious if not unscarred. He preached a sermon which may have been slightly vague, but which appealed to my imagination. Even the weakness of his voice and the almost colourlessness of his manner had the curious effect of making what he said to me more real. Listening to him was like listening to a spirit, to a disembodied voice; and through all there flickered a kind of nervous exaltation, like a tremulous, uncertain flame. There were no signs of that mental and imaginative poverty which had so frequently discouraged me. But he struck me, above all, as a man who had been unhappy, and therefore, if he had found peace, there must be some reason for it. I returned to hear him several times, and although my first impression was not strengthened, it was not effaced. I persuaded Owen to come with me to hear him, but Owen did not like him at all.

Far from shaking me in my view, this unfavourable opinion helped to confirm me. Not through any perversity, but simply because I knew the person I was in search of would not particularly appeal to Owen. I did not want a purely reasonable being, I did not perhaps even want one whom Owen would consider quite healthy—I wanted one who would understand. That night I wrote a letter to Henry Applin, asking if I might come to him, and, if I might, would he tell me when.

CHAPTER XXXV

As I walked home with Owen next day after school I wanted to tell him what I had done, but it was somehow difficult to do so quite abruptly. I turned the conversation to Roman Catholicism, and from that to the general subject of confession to a priest, but to Owen this idea appeared to be so distasteful that I did not attempt to introduce my own particular case.

On our way we met his mother, who told me to go on in and get something to eat now, and to stay and dine with them at seven. I refused, having an idea Owen didn't particularly want me. I knew it was only because he wished to finish an epitome he was making of Herbert Spencer's "First Principles" (he had told me he had reached the last chapter) and as I had a strong desire to stay I felt annoyed. I came to the door with him.

"You'd better come in," he said.

"What's the use of my coming in when you don't want me?" I replied.

He laughed. "Of course I want you; don't be an ass."

I came in. While we were having tea I looked over the epitome. It represented a good deal of work, and I remembered having asked him to read Blake's "Songs," and his refusing because he hadn't time. It was the same with nearly everything I recommended to him, though I was always reading books to please him. He offered now to lend me the "First Principles" as soon as he should have finished it.

"I don't want it," I answered, discontentedly. "I'm sick of all that stodgy stuff. You're always complaining about not being able to be religious, yet you're never happy unless you're reading something against religion."

"I'm not anxious for a religion that won't bear examination," replied Owen, coldly.

"No religion *will* bear it," I said, and both speeches had that infinite priggishness which not infrequently characterized our conversation.

"People who have read a hundred times more philosophy than I have have been able to remain Christians," Owen continued, with a naïveté that was quite lost on me. He was particularly fond just now of talking about people who had or had not read philosophy.

"You're thinking of Levine in 'A.K.,'" I answered disrespectfully, a decreasing enthusiasm having led me to abbreviate the title of this work.

"I'm not," said Owen.

"You are. And Levine doesn't remain a Christian. He drops it and then takes it up again, and, as he hasn't any more reason for doing one than the other, I don't see what it proves."

"Why do you say he has no reason?"

"I don't call half a dozen words spoken by an ignorant peasant a reason. If you claim religion to be the most valuable thing in life, it oughtn't to be at the mercy of a chance phrase. At any rate the words that affected Levine seem far from wonderful to me."

"I don't know that they aren't wonderful," Owen declared.

"'One man lives for his stomach,'" I jeeringly quoted, "'another for his soul, for God, in truth.' You'd find the same thing in any tract. And why should it turn you to Christianity particularly? A man who believed in Pan could live just as much for his soul as a Christian."

"I don't believe anybody ever believed in Pan," said Owen, "any more than they believe in Father Christmas. Because certain words happened to help Levine, Tolstoy does not mean that they will help everyone."

"He does. Only you're nearly as bad as Levine yourself."

Owen was not listening; he was working out an argument he

would produce as soon as I had done; but I was beginning to be tired of Tolstoy, and I wanted to express my own point of view. "If one were to see a ghost, it would make an enormous difference," I admitted. "It would open your eyes to a new world, to a deeper, finer world."

"Isn't this one deep enough for you? And I don't see that it would necessarily be any finer. It might very well be extremely objectionable. All that would happen if you saw a ghost is that it would frighten you very much at the time, and afterwards you wouldn't believe in it."

"I don't think it would frighten me. I don't think it would frighten anybody, if it were the ghost of somebody they had cared for a great deal."

Owen considered this. "I don't suppose the ghost of your mother would frighten you. *Your* mother is dead, isn't she?" he added, and then stopped short. "I'm awfully sorry," he stammered, "I wasn't thinking of what I was saying."

I laughed. "It's all right. My mother isn't dead. Shall we go out before dinner?"

Owen got up.

We walked by the road as far as Shaw's Bridge, where we branched off on to the river bank. It was already well on in April. The brilliant tender green of the opening leaves had spread like a delicate green flame over the black branches of the trees. The sky was clear, and there was a sharpness in the air that made us walk quickly. Owen's dogs, two rough-haired Irish terriers, ran along the bank, sniffing among the coarse grass, alert, eager to hunt anything, whether a rat or a stick.

Owen's remark about my mother had reminded me that I had told him singularly little about myself, or rather, about my people. He did not know anything beyond the fact that we lived at Newcastle, and, from the way I had spoken of it, he might easily have imagined that Derryaghy was my home. I'm afraid an unconscious snobbery had kept me from revealing the obscurity of my origin, and I was suddenly struck by the stupidity and odiousness of this, especially with Owen, for whom such things meant nothing.

"Why did you think my mother was dead?" I asked him.

"I don't know. I suppose because you never—I don't know, I'm sure."

"I want to tell you about my people."

Curiously enough, though I had been so reluctant to mention that my father was a National schoolmaster, it did not trouble me in the least to talk about my mother. I even had some dim notion that it made me rather interesting; so I told him all I knew. "I have not seen her since," I wound up, "and perhaps my father is not my real father." Why I should have thrown in this after-touch I cannot conceive, as I had never in my life had the faintest doubts concerning my legitimacy; but I suppose it was to heighten the romance.

"Do you think I ought to try to find out something more?" I asked.

"You never did try!" exclaimed Owen.

"Never very much. I don't know who to ask. I can't very well ask my father."

"Why?"

"I can't."

"There must be somebody else who knows. Your friend, Mrs. Carroll."

"She won't tell me."

"Have you asked her?"

"I asked her the last time I was at home."

"And what did she say?"

"She doesn't like her."

"She said she didn't like her?"

"No, of course not; but I know it all the same."

"The whole thing," Owen began, but tailed off abruptly, "—it seems rather queer."

We walked on for a long time in silence. I was determined to tell him about Mr. Applin, but it was not till we were coming home that I began my explanation.

"And you're really going to him!" Owen marvelled.

"I'll have to go now. That is, if he does not tell me not to."

"He can hardly do that. You're not making fun?"

"Fun?"

Owen was silent.

"I didn't know whether you meant it," he said. "What are you going *for?*" he suddenly asked. "Just to talk to him?"

"Yes, I suppose so."

"But what about?"

"About? . . . . Do you remember talking of confession?"

"But it's not that, is it?" said Owen, very seriously. "You're not——"

"Why not?" I smiled dimly.

"But what is the matter? Why should you? What have you done? And if you have done anything, what is it to him?"

We had come to a standstill on the lonely river bank. Owen's eyes were fixed upon me questioningly. I had nothing to say, or, rather, I could not say it. I stood before him, looking on the ground, my hands in my trouser pockets.

Owen hesitated. He put his hands on my shoulders, but I did not look up.

Presently I raised my head, but I looked away from him, and across the fields. "Come along," I said, quietly. "It's getting late, and we must hurry."

When I reached home at about half-past nine little Alice came running to meet me. Her white face, her bright black eyes, and long straight black hair, brushed back from her forehead and spreading out on either side of her face in the shape of a fan, were vivid in the gas-light, under which she stood looking up at me while I opened the letter she had brought me. It was from Mr. Applin, asking me to call on Wednesday evening between nine and ten, or on Friday between the same hours, if Wednesday did not suit me.

CHAPTER XXXVI

SINCE Christmas I had been working harder than I had ever done in my life. The Intermediate examinations would be coming on in June, but it was not any particular anxiety to shine in them that had goaded me to this unprecedented industry; merely I had discovered that on the plea of work I could sit in my bedroom in the evenings, and that the work itself kept me from thinking of other things. To-night I went straight upstairs as usual, but after writing to Mr. Applin to say I would come on Wednesday, I sat idle. So it was all the next day, and the next night: I had an open book in front of me, but I read without comprehending what I read: I was intensely excited: a kind of emotional cloud had descended upon my mind, and I could think of nothing but my approaching interview.

Ideas, words, shot across this mental haze like meteors, but I could not follow them in their swift flight. On Wednesday afternoon when I got home from school and had had my dinner I went out into the streets and wandered aimlessly about. I had said to myself that I would not think about the matter any more, but, needless to say, I thought of nothing else, and so it was that when I came to a Roman Catholic church and saw the door was open, I could not help going inside and sitting down before one of the confessionals. The name of the priest, Father Dempsey, was printed in large letters above it. I had a faint hope of seeing somebody come out or go in, but in this I was disappointed. Three little girls were busy with their beads, but they suspended their acts of devotion to cast glances at me, and whisper, and even giggle. A woman was kneeling before an altar that shone with ornaments suggestive of decorations from a Christmas tree. Her eyes were fixed on a bright oleograph of the Virgin, and her lips never ceased moving. A couple of lighted candles seemed to sweat ugly yellow tears, which ran down over dirty candlesticks. And then I saw a fat little sallow priest, his chin, upper lip, and cheeks, blue from much shaving, come waddling down the aisle, and I wondered if this were Father Dempsey. As he passed he stared at me, and I saw in his dull little eyes that expression of invulnerable stupidity I had noticed in the faces of so many of his brothers when I met them in the street.

The fascination that had drawn me into the church had disappeared. Everything—the smell of stale incense, the cheap decorations, the bad pictures, the kneeling woman, the girls with their beads—had become almost nauseating. The appalling unintelligence of it all shocked me, much as the display of a diseased body had now and then shocked me. It was wrong, it was gross, anything less spiritual I could not imagine. And my idea of confessing to a priest was wrong. I got up and left the church, the last thing I saw being the thick sediment of dirt at the bottom of the stoup.

After tea I went up to my bedroom, George's and mine, and got out my books to do some work. At first I thought I would not go to Mr. Applin, but as time passed this decision grew weaker, and presently, instead of reading, I tried to make up my mind on the point. Then when it drew near to nine o'clock I was no longer even uncertain. What had my impressions of this afternoon to do with the step I was about to take? Besides, they had been very superficial, and to be influenced by them would be as stupid as to refuse to read a book because its binding happened to be soiled.

I walked quickly to Mr. Applin's house and knocked boldly at the door. It opened with a startling promptitude; evidently the servant had been in the hall.

"Is Mr. Applin at home?" I asked, my stammer suddenly beginning to manifest itself.

"He is. Who shall I say wants him?"

"It doesn't matter. He expects me." I felt reluctant to give my name.

The servant did not press me to, but disappeared upstairs. She came back very soon and asked me to "step this way," and I obeyed her nervously.

I entered a room and heard the door close behind me, as a man rose from a table near the window, removing a green shade from his forehead. I was conscious of tired eyes that looked at me out of a pale, dim, emaciated face, but the flickering light that had seemed to shine through them when he was preaching was not there, and his manner of greeting me struck me as a little distant, a little chilly. I sat down on the extreme edge of a chair and my impressions grew clearer.

"You are Peter Waring, are you not?"

"Yes," I answered.

He had taken the chair opposite mine, and he leaned a little forward, the tips of his fingers joined, and blue veins showing under the loose yellow skin of his hands. He was much older than I had imagined. He was wearing a threadbare jacket which I did not like, and I noticed that one of the buttons near the top was not the same as the others. My confidence had suddenly drooped. I glanced round at the unfamiliar room, at the book-shelves which made but a poor show, and maintained an idiotic silence. It struck me that he might think I had come for a subscription towards a cricket club.

"I got your letter," he said. "You want to speak to me? You are not a member of my congregation, I think?"

"No—I come sometimes in the evening."

I was glad I had said nothing in my letter but that I wanted to speak to him, and he evidently hadn't the least suspicion of the truth.

"Yes—yes—I understand. Well, don't be afraid. If I can do anything for you I shall be very glad, very glad."

I thanked him and again became silent. It would have been absolutely impossible for me to have said what I had come to say. He was too old, too far away. It would have been like stretching out one's hands to warm them at the ashes in an early morning grate. I knew he wanted to be kind, but I felt, somehow, that if I sat very still he would, in a minute or two, forget I was in the room.

"I think I had better write," I murmured.

"Write? But why? What is it about?" he spoke almost testily.

There was a tap at the door, and a thin, middle-aged lady, possibly a daughter, came in with a little tray on which were some biscuits and a tumbler of hot milk. She bowed to me and wished me good-evening. I wanted nothing now but to get away as quickly as possible, and I envied her as she went out, closing the door softly behind her. Suppose I had been in the middle of my confession when the hot milk came in, I thought. The whole thing was somehow becoming lugubriously comic.

"Are you in business or at school?" Mr. Applin asked, between two sips of milk. "I hope you'll excuse me taking this while it is hot, but I had a funeral this afternoon, and I'm afraid I caught a slight chill."

"Certainly," I answered hastily. "I'm sorry for disturbing you. I have really nothing to say. It is only that I liked your sermons so much, and that I wanted to tell you so. I hope you'll forgive me." I got up.

"Sit down—sit down," he murmured. "It was a very kind and charming impulse, and I'm glad you yielded to it."

I resumed my seat and he continued to drink his milk. He was quite pleased with me. He asked me to what church I belonged; where I went to school; all kinds of questions. I told him that I thought he must be lonely sitting here by himself, and that he should have a dog, or even a cat. I told him about Tony, and all the wonderful things he could do. Before I came away he made me promise I would come to see him again. Yet just as I was going out a sort of vague suspicion of other things appeared to float into his consciousness. He detained me, with his hand on my shoulder. "When you first came in," he said, "I thought something perhaps was worrying you, that you had something on your mind." He paused. For an instant I had seen in him what I had seen when I had listened to him preach; for an instant I was on the point of resuming my seat, and telling him all I had come to tell him, but he himself broke the charm next moment by saying good-night. "And when you come again you won't be shy?" he added, smiling wanly.

He did not accompany me downstairs, but stood on the landing till I had opened the hall-door. And as I pulled it after me, and ran down the steps, I knew I should never go back.

CHAPTER XXXVII

SPRING gave place to summer, and still I kept studiously to my books. I saw less of Owen, for in the afternoons I played cricket, and Owen did not. On the thirteenth of June my examination commenced, and from the first I did well, having good luck with the papers. On Tuesday evening when I went home I had only one more exam. in front of me, and it would take place the following afternoon. After that I should be free for the summer.

It was a hot, breathless kind of night, and I did not intend to work too much. I loafed about the shop after tea, talking to Miss

Izzy. She had asked me to go to the Free Library to get her a book, but nothing on the list she had given me, though it was a fairly long one, was in, and I had come back with a tale of my own selecting.

"You might have got one of Annie Swan's," Miss Izzy said, eyeing the work I had chosen, dubiously. "but of course you couldn't tell what ones I'd read."

"Annie Swan's?"

"Yes; they're all good. Mr. Spicer mentioned 'Carlowrie' from the pulpit on Sunday, and you don't often hear *him* praise a novel."

"When he does it's a spicy one," said George, who was going out.

Miss Izzy took no notice.

"I've got to meet the girl at a quarter-to-eight, so I can't stop," George threw back gaily from the door, which next moment swung after him, as he stepped into the street, fixing a flower in his button-hole.

"You get 'Aldersyde' and read it," said Miss Izzy, "or 'Across Her Path.'"

"I thought you said Carl-something-or-other."

"You'll maybe like the others better. If George McAllister would join the literary society instead of running about the streets at nights it would answer him better. Who's this girl he's going to meet?"

"I don't know."

"It's only talk, I suppose. Girls have more sense than to bother with the likes of him."

"Do you think so?" I murmured sceptically. "The kind that George cares for I don't imagine have very much."

"You know nothing about them. If you'd any sisters you'd know more."

"I'm very glad I haven't," I replied.

Miss Izzy bounced round. "Why?" she demanded sharply. "Girls can do everything as well as men can; only they never get the chance."

"That's all rot," I said ungallantly. "They're quite different. You might as well compare cats and dogs."

"And we're the cats, I suppose? It's well you're still a puppy."

"I didn't mean you, Miss Izzy. I know there are exceptions. But most girls don't think; or if they do, it's only about who's going to marry them."

"Don't think! Well, of all!—And you and George McAllister and the others—you think a lot, don't you?"

"George doesn't," I admitted.

"But *you* do—especially about yourself. Do you know this, Peter Waring, you're about as conceited and full of yourself as a monkey that's been taught a few tricks!"

"Well, I'm going away to-morrow, and you'll not see me again for a long time."

This was not fair, as I knew it would soften Miss Izzy, and it had indeed this result. "I don't mind seeing you," she confessed, with a sigh, "if that's all. It's hearing you talk. You may give me your photograph if you like."

I had had my photograph taken quite recently for Mrs. Carroll's birthday, and I ran upstairs and brought one down. Miss Izzy examined it critically. "I've got a red plush frame at home that's about your mark."

"Don't put me in red plush," I begged.

Miss Izzy looked up from the photograph to the original. "Is red plush not good enough for you? You'd like a gold frame, maybe?"

"It's not that," I said hastily. "It's only that I don't care much for red plush. Can't you get a plain frame? I will get one for you."

"No, thanks. I always put a plain person in an ornamental frame: it gives them a better chance."

"All right."

There was never any use trying to get an advantage over Miss Izzy in verbal skirmishes, so I gave in, and, as the shop appeared to be comparatively deserted to-night, I sat down on an empty wooden box, and read aloud to her the first two chapters of the novel I had brought from the library. It was Hardy's "Two on a Tower," and as I turned the pages, the circumstances, so different, under which I had read them before, kept floating into my mind. When I had finished the second chapter, and drummed for a while with my heels against the box, I went upstairs, and got out my notes on French composition to look them over before

to-morrow's examination. The room, although the window was
wide open, seemed to me unbearably stuffy, and moreover I had a
slight headache and felt tired and irritable. I put up with the heat
for half an hour, and then undressed and sat down in my night-
shirt close to the window, which looked out on to a dirty strip of
back garden, threaded with clothes-lines, and forming, after dark,
a kind of debased Paradise for dissipated cats.

At half-past ten or so George stepped jauntily in. "Hello! Not
done yet?" He took the now withered flower from his button-hole
and flung it out among the cats; then he began to turn over some
papers I had laid down on the table in the exact order I required
them.

"You'll mix those up," I said crossly. "Leave them alone."

George threw the papers down. "All right. Keep your wool on!"
Two or three of the sheets fluttered to the floor.

I picked them up in a very bad temper, and George began to
whistle—the same few bars over and over again. "Oh, shut up," I
cried. "Can't you see I'm working?"

"Temper! Temper!" said George, cheerfully. "I'll have to tell
Katherine about this!"

He was standing before the looking-glass, and had begun to
remove his dickey; but at the very moment of speaking he knew
he had made a mistake. He looked round with a sort of foolish,
apologetic grin. I, too, knew that his words had slipped out unin-
tentionally, for I had never mentioned Katherine's name to him.
There were, in fact, only two ways in which he could have come
by his information: either Aunt Margaret had managed to get
hold of some of my letters again, or else he had read one of them
himself.

"What do you mean?" I asked coldly, looking steadily into his
eyes as they were reflected in the glass.

George tried to laugh it off. "I was only joking," he said,
nervously.

But I wanted a better explanation than this.

"Who told you about Katherine?" I asked, getting up from my
chair deliberately, and walking over to him, while he spun round
to meet me with bright eyes and a forced smile.

"What's the matter? What are you losin' your rag about? I don't want to annoy you."

"The matter is this: I want to know if you have been reading my letters? If you have, you must have unlocked the box I keep them in."

"I never unlocked any box." George backed away from me, his eyes not leaving mine.

"You'd better tell me," I said, but George would say nothing further. He stood with his back now against the wall. I struck him on the cheek with my open hand. "Answer," I said.

I saw his eyes turn to the door, and anticipated the spring he made to get past me. The next moment I had him by the throat and we were struggling together. Suddenly I released my hold, flinging him from me. He struck out at me as I came toward him again, but it was the feeble, half-hearted blow of a coward, and I felt my fist in contact with his face, almost as if he had run up against it. He staggered back, and a crimson stream poured down over his chin and on to his shirt, making a horrible mess, while he stood blubbering like a baby. I did not hit him again, but simply watched him. I knew he was really more frightened than hurt, for though his nose was bleeding profusely, I had seen it do that on several occasions before, quite spontaneously. We must, all the same, have kicked up a considerable racket, for I heard the sound of quick footsteps in the passage, and then our door was flung open and a wild figure rushed in. It was Aunt Margaret, in a stained, red dressing-gown, her black eyes blazing in her big, puffy face. Her huge loose body shook and panted with rage as she turned from George to me. I stepped quickly out of her way, for there was something rather fearful in the great white mask of hate she turned on me. She said not a word, but shooting out an arm, like a shoulder of mutton, gripped me by the collar of my nightshirt, and began to rain down a torrent of heavy blows on my head and uplifted arms. I protected myself as well as I could, and at last, with a violent wrench, tore myself out of her grasp, my nightshirt ripping down to the hem, a considerable portion of it remaining in Aunt Margaret's hand. "Stop that!" I shouted furiously, but she came at me again, her fat body panting yet displaying an incredible activity, her eyes shining with madness.

I knew there would be mischief done, for I saw her catch up an iron rod that was part of George's trouser-stretcher. I was really frightened now, and made a dive to get past her and out of the door. I felt her nails tear my naked shoulder; at the same moment I flung up my arm and, it may be, saved my life, for something crashed down over my elbow, striking on the back of my head with a sickening jar that I seemed to hear as the floor swept up to meet me.

CHAPTER XXXVIII

WHEN I opened my eyes I was lying in bed, with a hot jar at my feet, and the pungent irritation of smelling-salts in my nostrils. Uncle George was in the room, and there was a stranger there also. I knew what had taken place, and, if I hadn't remembered, there was an atrocious pain in my head to remind me. I put up my hand and discovered my head was bandaged.

"Well," said the stranger, drawing closer. "How do you feel now?"

"My head's pretty sore," I answered.

He mixed me something in a glass and I drank it. Uncle George came over and began to ask questions, but the doctor pulled him away. "Leave him to go to sleep now: he'll be better able to talk in the morning. It might have been a nasty thing. I'll look in to-morrow."

I had closed my eyes, and when I opened them again I was alone and in the dark. A ray of moonlight floated through the window and lay across the floor where George's bed had been, but the bed itself was gone, and I wondered languidly how they had been able to take it away without my hearing anything. In spite of an abominable headache I felt drowsy—perhaps it was the effect of whatever drug I had taken—and I must very soon have lost consciousness.

The first person I saw in the morning was Uncle George, who carried me in my breakfast. My head still ached, though not nearly so violently. While I drank a cup of tea Uncle George sat in silence, his eyes fixed on me, with an expression of anxiety that was almost comic. As for me, I felt better, and, when Uncle George had removed the tray, I allowed him to tell me how sorry he was, but without replying or giving him any encouragement. I could see he was dying for me to say something, but I thought a little suspense would not do him any harm, so I maintained a discreet quiet. Secretly I was glad, for this disagreeable adventure gave me just what I had needed, but I was far from letting Uncle George know that.

"She wasn't responsible," said Uncle George, dejectedly, and plunging straight to the heart of the subject. "You know she has to take drugs sometimes on account of the pain she suffers, and they have an effect upon her. I tell you this in confidence, and that last night she had taken more than she intended to, and didn't really know what she was doin'. But you must forgive her, Peter. And then she is jealous of you—I may as well tell you everything— she is jealous when she thinks of the difference between you and George, and that you will be a gentleman, while George and the others'll have to get along as best they can—and times are so bad, and there's so few openings for lads nowadays. This drug she had taken——" He stopped and his eyes fastened on mine appealingly.

"What do you want me to do?" I asked, smoothing down the sheet.

Uncle George moved nervously in his chair, but did not reply.

"I'm going home to-day," I went on.

"Home? You'll be waiting for a day or two—till you get quit of this pain in your head, won't you? And then there's your examination! Will they take marks off if you get a doctor's certificate?"

"A certificate for what?"

"That you can't go in for the examination."

"I'm going in for the exam. And I'm certainly going home."

Uncle George, who had never ventured to remonstrate with me on any subject whatever since my arrival, and who treated me as, if anything, slightly older than himself, did not begin now. "And what will you tell them?" was all he asked.

"Would you like me to say I fell downstairs?" I suggested innocently.

Uncle George fidgeted. "I don't want you to tell a lie," he made answer, which was a pretty big one for him.

"Oh, I don't mind," I observed, pleasantly.

Uncle George considered this. "I suppose there's times, maybe, when it's best not to tell all the truth," he brought out lamely.

"This is one when I should think it would be best not to tell any of it," I replied.

Uncle George was silent. I was not letting him off particularly easily.

"There must, however, be two lies told," I pursued. "The first by me, and the second by you, in a letter saying you can't take me back after the holidays—that you haven't room—any reason you like."

"But won't you come back?" asked Uncle George, dolefully. "You were always quite comfortable, quite happy till—till this accident. And it wouldn't have happened if you hadn't been knocking George about. I don't know what he had done on you."

"I was never happy," I said impatiently. "Either you or Aunt Margaret will have to write as I say, or I'll tell my father exactly what happened. This accident, as you call it, very nearly did for me: and it's only one thing out of a lot."

"Your poor aunt wants to come and tell you how sorry she is."

"My poor aunt needn't bother. I know exactly how sorry she is. If it had been the ceiling that had fallen on me and killed me outright, I don't fancy she'd have minded much—except for the mess."

Uncle George regarded me mournfully. "You're very unforgiving," he said. "I know you've a right to say hard things, but——"

It seemed to me that this was going a bit too far. "What do you mean by unforgiving?" I asked. "Haven't I promised not to tell?"

"It's not that," said Uncle George.

"What is it then? Do you want me to sacrifice myself simply that you may make so much a week out of me? Don't you know that Aunt Margaret has always hated me like poison? Don't you know she is pretty constantly under the influence of whatever it is she takes, though you speak as if this were the first time? I'm not such a fool that I can't see what's going on. She's always prying about my things and reading my letters. Besides, in the very beginning, you know as well as I do that I came to live here expecting to have a room to myself and not to be stuck with George."

Uncle George did not reply, but he looked as he sat there, with his gray head bent, the picture of dejection.

"I'm sorry if I've hurt your feelings, Uncle George, for you've been always very kind and decent to me, and if there was no one here but you and Alice I would come back certainly. But as it is, I can't; I really can't. I wanted to leave at Christmas, only my father wouldn't let me."

As I watched him lift his mild, sheep-like face, and go out, I pitied him—almost enough to have promised to do what he wanted, which would have been idiotic. "If he'd had any sense," I told myself, "he'd have clapped Aunt Margaret into a 'home' or an asylum, or whatever it is, long ago. But he's too soft-hearted to do anything but make himself miserable."

During the morning little Alice came in several times to see me. The doctor also called and examined my head, into which he had put a couple of stitches last night. It was only a scalp wound, he said, and thought I might go back to Newcastle that afternoon if I felt up to it.

At dinner-time George appeared, looking very sheepish, and shuffling his feet. "How are you?" he asked. "Ma says you're goin' home this afternoon, so I thought I'd drop in an' say good-bye. I'm sorry about this. It's my fault, an' it's rotten for your exam. I only read one letter. I went to ma's work-basket for the scissors, an' I saw it there lying open, an' I read it without thinking. That's the God's truth, whether you believe it or not, an' there was nothin' in it you need mind."

"Oh, it's all right," I answered.

"All the same it's damned putrid luck about the exam."

"It can't be helped. Besides, I'm going to have a shot at it."

"Well, I'll have to cut on. So long, Peter." He grinned as he held out a big hand, which, like his face, was covered with freckles.

CHAPTER XXXIX

My examination was at three, and at two o'clock I got up. If I hadn't done so well on the other papers, probably I should have let it go, but it seemed, in the circumstances, a pity to spoil my results if I could possibly avoid it. Yet when I lifted my head from the pillow it throbbed so violently that I thought I should have to lie down again. I steadied myself, holding on to the bed-post, but presently I was able to finish dressing and go downstairs. Miss Izzy was in the shop, alone, and she gazed at me with keen curiosity. I smiled, though I was really feeling fairly bad.

"Are you better?" Miss Izzy asked, for some reason speaking in a kind of hoarse whisper.

"I've a beastly headache, that's all."

"Not much wonder. *She* did it, didn't she?" Miss Izzy was all eyes and secrecy.

I nodded.

"She's getting worse," Miss Izzy announced in an awed tone. "She's really not in her right senses. I don't know what she'll be doing next. You're going to-day, aren't you?"

"Yes—after the exam. I wish you would ask Alice to pack my things for me; she can do it all right."

"I'll help her. I'll tell you this, I've been looking out for another job this while back, and I think I've got one. That's between ourselves; but I can't put up with her any longer. I'll drop you a postcard; give me your address."

I scribbled it on a bit of paper she handed me.

Miss Izzy glanced at it and stuffed it in her pocket. "Right oh! Here's somebody coming in; they never give you a minute's peace—— Are you away?"

"Yes. I think I'll take a cab."

The customer had entered, but Miss Izzy only glared at her. "I'm sure you shouldn't be going at all. It may just give you brain fever or something!"

"Oh, I don't think so," I smiled.

Miss Izzy nodded at me as she advanced reluctantly to her duty. "I'll see you later."

"Yes. You'll not forget to tell Alice?"

"No; that'll be all right."

At the stand by the gas-works I got into a hansom and drove off. I kept my cap on the seat beside me, for any pressure on my head was painful. Fortunately I had only a short distance to go, and once in the cool airy hall I felt better. But my bandaged appearance created quite a sensation. Everybody stared at me, and one of the superintendents came to ask me if I had met with an accident. I told him I had fallen downstairs, at which he indulged in a somewhat obvious jest.

The paper suited me and did not require any great effort, but when I had finished I was glad. Outside, I had to repeat my fiction of falling downstairs, and listen to various versions of the superintendent's joke, before I was able to get Owen by himself. We went into the Botanic Gardens and sat down on the first vacant bench, where I told him what had actually happened. He did not appear to realize that I might have been killed, and, in spite of his sympathy and the questions he asked, I knew his thoughts were really hovering round the examination, and that he was weighing the chances of his having retained his last year's exhibition. We talked of my adventure, but, as we did so, unconsciously, he drew the examination paper from his pocket and unfolded it. Owen had not been doing so well as I had, and a good deal depended on the marks he got this afternoon. "I wouldn't mind," he said, "only there's something I'm doing which the pater will make me give up if I don't keep my 'ex.'"

"If I'd been killed," I said, "I wonder if you'd have gone over the questions with Grimshaw or O'Brian!"

Owen glanced at me to see if I were serious. He had by this time spread out the blue sheet on his knees. "What did you put for 'cane-bottomed chair?'" he asked, anxiously.

But my interest in the exam. had vanished. "Oh, I don't know—'chaise cannée,' or something. Look here, Owen, will you come and see me off at the station? I have to go back to the house, of course, to get my things, but I'd rather have somebody with me."

"'Chaise cannée?' How did you think of it? I wonder if it's right? I put 'au fond de jonc,' but I'm sure that's rot. 'Chaise cannée.' You know, it's not fair giving things like that! What do you think?"

"Of 'au fond de jonc'? I don't think much of it."

Owen was depressed. "It doesn't sound right, does it? What did you put for 'fire-dogs?' O'Brian put 'chiens de feu.'"

"O'Brian's a fool," I answered, truthfully.

Owen laughed, but without merriment, and I was pretty sure he had put 'chiens de feu' himself. "You might drop that beastly paper," I said, "and tell me if you'll come or not."

"Of course I'll come. But tell me just this one thing."

"What? 'Fire-dogs?'—'chenets.'"

"'Chenets?' Are you sure? You're awfully clever at those out-of-the-way words!"

"It's not an out-of-the-way word. 'Chiens de feu' are the sort of things that'll be chasing you and O'Brian in the next world."

Owen laughed ruefully, but another question, in spite of his promise, was already hovering on his lips.

"Come along," I said, getting up. "What good does it do worrying over the rotten thing now?" And I tore my paper in two, and let the pieces go fluttering down the path on the wind.

CHAPTER XL

In the morning Tony's familiar scratching at my door reminded me that I was home again, and this time for two long, idle months. I was very sleepy, but I struggled out of bed with half-open eyes, and let him in. As I closed the door again, I trod on one of his paws. He gave a sharp yelp, and then a great wagging of his tail to show that he knew it had been an accident. Jumping on to the bed he scrambled between the sheets, and I followed, taking what room he would give me. I lay trying to go to sleep, while he sprawled over me. Then when he had thoroughly wakened me up he went to sleep himself.

I lay listening to the sea and thinking of what I should do that day. I would bathe after breakfast; I would take Tony with me, which would mean bathing off the sand, for Tony could not dive, and had a foolish habit, when on the rocks, of trying to lap the sea up to the level he wanted it at. But I had forgotten my plastered head; bathing, I supposed, would be out of the question for at least a week. So, when breakfast was over, I stuffed a book into my jacket pocket, and strolled in the direction of Derryaghy woods. I had the long June day before me, and perfect freedom to do just as I pleased with it. The book I had chosen was "Twelfth Night," the influence of Count Tolstoy, so far as I was concerned, having suffered an eclipse. I had read no second work by him, and the questionings stirred up by "Anna Karénine" had sunk quietly to sleep. Owen, a day or two ago, had got hold of "Katia," and "The Kreutzer Sonata," but I, I regret to say, had not a line of the master's in my possession.

In truth, I was but a degenerate disciple, and moreover unfaithful. For Owen and I had sent the great man a letter for the New Year, protesting allegiance, and had actually received a reply, which, considering it had almost moved Owen to tears, I had allowed him to keep. He regarded it with the kind of veneration that, in earlier days, a devout pilgrim may have regarded some relic of a saint. I shouldn't have been surprised to learn that he wore it, tied up in a little bag, somewhere beneath his clothes. Really it had been quite decent; though that a man of world-wide fame, who must have been besieged by communications of all kinds and from all sorts of persons, should have found time to understand and reply kindly to the epistle of a couple of youngsters, far away in a benighted island, I'm afraid did not strike me then as quite the wonderful thing it was. The letter, however, was not to me, and Owen, at all events, had found it wonderful enough. In spite of my share in the matter, the spirit of our enterprise had been Owen's. The epistle we had concocted had expressed Owen, and Owen alone, and it was delightfully intelligent of the master to have seen behind its crudity something worth encouraging. He had actually asked us—that is Owen—to write again—not at once and under the immediate influence of his letter, but in a month or two. And Owen had written again. By that time I had had the sense to recognize that I was only a shadow in this matter, and to give him a free field. He had waited the full two months, which I, had I felt his enthusiasm, could never have done, and had then written the second letter. This letter I had insisted must be private. I had refused to take any part in its composition, or even to read it when it was finished, though Owen had told me all that was in it—a complete account of himself, of his father's position, of his own acquirements and abilities, his prospects, his ideals, ending up with a petition for advice as to the direction his studies ought to take, and as to what career lay open to him. The reply to this effusion had not yet come or I should have heard of it, but I hadn't the slightest doubt that when it did turn up Owen would follow its instructions minutely, down to the smallest particulars, even were that to entail the wearing of peas in his shoes. It was the sort of thing that was completely beyond me. I could not have borne to admit, even to myself, that anybody was so much my superior as all that. And then, very softly, at the bottom of my soul, I preferred "A Midsummer Night's Dream" to "Anna Karénine." I not only preferred it, but I was sure it was a work of far finer genius. Of course I was always sure that the things I happened to prefer were far finer, but in this particular instance I have not altered my opinion.

As I wandered up into the woods, followed by the lagging Tony, I knew it was going to be a very hot day, though it was not nearly so hot at present as Tony pretended. I hunted about till I had found a pleasant place—where the rising ground formed a kind of natural couch, covered with golden moss and bracken, and where the sun at noon would not be too strong as it dropped down through thick green beech branches. I took my book from my pocket, but it was only to make myself more comfortable, not with any intention of reading. I lay there and let the green summer morning steal into my soul, staining my mind to its own deep cool colour, while Tony gnawed at the trunk of a fallen tree, stripping off the bark in sheets, till he was tired and hot, when he came over beside me and stretched himself on the bracken, with his red tongue hanging out and his eyes nearly closed. And I lay on in the enchanted morning,

my hands under my head, gazing up through the flat, shady
branches, and thinking "long, long thoughts." Already I seemed to
have cast from me, as a snake his old skin, the weight and grime of
a year of town life; already I felt better, cleaner, felt the sap of my
youth fresh and strong within me.

After an hour or two I opened my book and began to read:—

> "If music be the food of love, play on;
> Give me excess of it, that, surfeiting,
> The appetite may sicken, and so die.
> That strain again! it had a dying fall;
> O! it came o'er my ear like the sweet sound
> That breathes upon a bank of violets,
> Stealing and giving odour. . . . ."

I was lost in that world of poetry and music, of lingering melo-
dies and songs, dreamy and happy and sad. Romance! romance! I
felt it stirring in my blood, singing within me! This play of passion,
where passion is never stormy, but a kind of dreaming of love,
exactly suited my present mood. Love was the world I lived in, love
was in the rustling of the beech-leaves, love was in the breaking of
the invisible sea, love was even in the snores of Tony.

I closed the book, my mind filled with laughter and love and
poetry. Beautiful figures glided before me through the sun-washed,
leaf-green air—Viola in her boy's clothes—Olivia—moving in an
atmosphere of sensuous sweetness. I imagined myself a page, vis-
iting Olivia in her palace; I imagined her falling in love with me; I
began to weave a romance of my own, in which scenes from other
romances lingered, the music of their words. . . . .

The sunlight splashed through the beech-leaves on to the green
moss, and where it fell the green took a hue of gold. Green arcades
opened out into the heart of the summer woods. Rarely came the
note of a bird, but the woods were full of life; the flashing whites
and grays of rabbits appeared on the clearing nearer the house;
there were mysterious movements in the brushwood. I roused
reluctant Tony and we went down to the stream. We were out in
the broad sunshine here, and the rocks were quite hot. The dark

green silky waterweed spread out, seeming to flow with the rapid, shallow water, and sleepy summer noon held me spell-bound. In the shadow of the rocks were deep pools, where the water looked almost black. Tony waded out into mid-stream and began to lap up the water. Then he lifted his head, his red, dripping tongue still hanging out, his dark, beautiful eyes half-closed, and looked at me while he panted. The woods on either side were full of green shadow and mystery. We walked home over soft turf and across a blazing field dotted with fly-tormented cows. Tony was too hot even to give them a passing bark. On the right the ground sloped down gently, forming a vast meadow, with scattered trees and flaming gorse-bushes; and beyond, under the deep blue sky, the great glorious sea danced and gleamed, blue also, with a long white line where the surf curled up over the flat, sun-drenched sand.

I felt lazy and contented, conscious only of the warmth of the sun and the beauty of this world, wrapped in a kind of sleepy happiness. In the afternoon I would go in search of some of my old friends; go out, perhaps, with Willie Breen in his boat, though as a rule boating in any form bored me to death. Trivial and bizarre thoughts passed through my mind. I wished the world was the way it is in old romances and fairy-tales. I was sure that this was the very day on which some wonderful thing would happen; when one might find a magic door leading into a strange world that was yet quite close at hand; for all my life long I had had the feeling that such a world was there.

CHAPTER XLI

DURING the next three weeks I led a solitary enough life, in the woods and by the sea. I read a good deal, and dreamed still more. In the mornings, and often in the afternoons as well, I went for long swims, and, coming back, lay in the sun on the rocks, sometimes for hours at a time, so that the skin all over my body had been tanned to a deep golden brown. And I was growing stronger. I could feel it; I could even see it in my limbs, which were becoming more muscular. And with my increasing physical strength I suppose other alterations took place—alterations in my outward appearance, marking the passage from boyhood to adolescence. Annie Breen, for instance, had spoken to me several times of late in a way that betokened a consciousness of this change; and more than one girl whom I met on the road in the evenings, when wishing me good-night, had put something into her greetings which made it quite different from what it would have been last year. Several of the village boys, no older than I, had already sweethearts, and I knew I had but to give a sign to any of these girls to have a sweetheart also; and while I held myself aloof, and responded with the barest politeness, I none the less felt flattered.

I received news of my examination. I had done better than I had expected, getting first place in the school and third in Ireland. Owen, too, had not done badly; at all events he had retained his exhibition.

CHAPTER XLII

I MET Owen at the station, and, as he jumped out of the carriage, he cried, "I've got the letter. It was waiting for me when I reached home." He waved it triumphantly in my face, beaming with the delight of it and with the pleasure of showing it to me.

"I can't possibly read it here," I said, grasping his bag.

"And I say, you know, you did rippingly in the exams. I knew you would."

He had come down by the first train, and I wanted to take him for a bathe, but he was so excited that he could hardly listen to me. I had brought our towels, and I delivered Owen's bag to a carman outside to take up to the house.

"Where are we going now? It was jolly decent of him writing, wasn't it?"

"Who? Tolstoy? Not bad. But we're going to bathe: I waited for you. It's some distance away, unless you would rather wade in off the shore; there's plenty of time, however."

"I'll do whatever you like."

"Then I think we'll go round to Maggie's Leap."

As we went we talked of his precious letter. "You won't like it, I daresay," he said. "It's not much in your line."

"I wish you would tell me what my line is. I've been trying to discover during the last fortnight."

"I know very well. . . . There's one thing he says that I can't quite——"

"Well?"

"Well, it's this: He says everything is in the Gospels. What people have got to do is to read over the words of Christ, and mark with a red pencil everything that is perfectly clear to them."

"A red pencil?"

Owen was too eager to notice anything. "Yes. What are you amused at? Then you cut those bits out, and never bother about the rest. In what you cut out you'll find everything that it is necessary to know in order to map out your life and your work. The whole teaching of Christ, all that is essential, will be in those bits. Later on you may read over the other things, that were obscure, and perhaps some of them will by then be plain. I am to consider what kind of work I have a taste for, and at the same time the work I devote myself to must fulfil certain tests or I am to have nothing to do with it. Work you do with your hands is best of all. I haven't shown the letter at home yet. I thought I'd think it quietly over down here and talk about it with you. We'll read the Gospels together. My father wants me to be a solicitor and go into his place, but I don't want that. On the other hand, I must make up my mind soon, I suppose. I'm seventeen, you know."

I took the letter from him, and read it slowly and with some difficulty as we walked along. After that, I thought over it for a while.

"Will you have to earn your living?"

"Yes, naturally. There are a good many of us, you know."

"Then I don't see how the Gospels are going to help you, no matter what way you mark them."

"Why not?"

"Because you'll have to live as other people do, unless you can afford to be different; and other people don't live according to the Gospels."

Owen was silent.

"A carpenter, a gardener, for instance," he began, "couldn't they live in accordance with the teaching of Christ? Tolstoy says I will never be happy unless I do."

"It's all very well for Tolstoy talking: he is his own master and has plenty of money. But how can you be a carpenter or a gardener? Your father would never allow you to, and the first thing would be a quarrel with him. We go down here, over this wall."

Owen scrambled after me.

"A man must leave his father and his mother."

"Yes, Owen dear, but you're not a bit the kind of man who does, to say nothing of leaving your brother and your sisters. At any rate, while you are learning to be a gardener your father will have to keep you."

"I only mentioned those trades because they happened to occur to me; there are plenty of others."

"There are not plenty: that's just the difficulty I've been finding."

We clambered down on to the rocks, from which the sea stretched away, deep and clear and blue, glittering in the hot sunshine, moving with a low, smooth swell, like some huge, splendid, living creature.

"You will require a profession in which you can be your own master from the very beginning. It wouldn't do to be subordinate to anybody who hadn't had a letter from Tolstoy, or perhaps even read 'Anna Karénine.' If you go in for the Church, for example, you will have to do what you are told until you get a church of your own, when you'll be always having rows with your parishioners and elders, for, of course, you'll have to preach the Tolstoy gospel or the tests will get in the way. If you become a doctor you won't make a living, because you will want to doctor the widows and the fatherless, who are no use in the matter of fees. I admit the lawyer idea is absurd—even without Tolstoy and the Gospels it wouldn't have done—and no doubt your father only thought of it because he's a solicitor himself. You'll have to be content with something that fulfils perhaps one or two of the tests. Then, when you get married and have a swarm of children, your wife will rise in revolt against them *all*."

"I can choose a suitable wife, and there's no need to have a swarm of children. I shall have just as many as I can afford to bring up properly. . . . . That reminds me, I brought you down the 'Kreutzer Sonata.' It's in my bag."

"That's all right; but it's always people like you, frightfully earnest and moral and all the rest of it, who have families of twelve or thirteen."

"I tell you I won't have them," said Owen, impatiently.

"But Tolstoy himself——"

"I don't care a hang about Tolstoy."

"Oh—h! Owen!"

"Tolstoy could give his children a decent start in life; and if he can do that, the more such a man has the better."

During the latter part of this conversation, all of which Owen was taking in dead seriousness, we were undressing, and I now dived into the deep, green, glittering water. I turned on my back and lay watching Owen, distinctly uneasy, stand hesitating on the edge of the rock.

"Is it cold?" he asked.

"No; come along."

He pulled his shirt slowly off. "I brought you down some of the short stories too."

I laughed. "All right; I'll read them when I come out."

But Owen was really anxious now only about the temperature of the water. He floundered in and came up spluttering. I was a much better swimmer than he, and circled about him, showing off, delighting in the power I felt. We swam out for fifty yards or so, and I timed my stroke with Owen's. He looked very funny. His eyes stared straight before him as if he were set on some desperate adventure. On our way back I splashed him a little and he got angry, swallowing a lot of water. I told him how contrary to the teaching of the Gospels this was; when I asked him to drink a pint of salt water he should swallow a quart; etc., etc.

When we got to the rocks and he had scrambled out, scraping his knees and one of his elbows in doing so, for it was not easy to get out unless you knew the way, he was quite offended, and would hardly speak to me. I was shaking with laughter, but I said

I was sorry and gave him some sticking-plaster. He took the sticking-plaster, but would have none of my sympathy, and on the way
home I had to soothe him into a better temper. Then, as usual, the
cloud passed quite suddenly, and he was all right. As we drew near
the house I wondered, uneasily, what he would think of my father,
and what he would think of my home. Before coming to us he had
been staying in Scotland with people who had evidently possessed
yachts and motor-cars and all kinds of things, whereas we could
not even boast a spare bed, and he would have to sleep with me.

When we came in, I introduced him to my father, who was
working in the garden, and before dinner was over I was delighted
to see that they were going to get on well together. Owen seemed
to notice none of his peculiar habits, or, if he did, he was perfectly
indifferent to them. He displayed an extraordinary interest in the
school, asking all kinds of questions, and bringing out his own the-
ories of education, which may or may not have emanated from the
sage in Russia. I let them talk together without interfering much.
I could see that my father was very favourably impressed, though
the fact that such an admirable youth happened to be a particular friend of mine was naturally perplexing. Owen was frightfully
polite. He called my father "Sir," and listened deferentially to
everything he had to say, never offering his own opinion as of
any particular value. They talked almost exclusively of education.
Owen told how he was teaching a boy at home in the evenings,
the son of their coachman, and how clever this boy was, and how
he had got Mr. Gill senior to promise to pay his college fees if he
did well at school during the next year or two. It was the first time
I had heard of the matter, but I supposed it was the mysterious
something which had interfered with his own work, and had made
him so anxious about retaining his exhibition. "Didn't *he* do splen-
didly?" Owen said suddenly, nodding his head in my direction.

"Peter can be clever enough when he chooses," my father
answered dryly.

This was to prevent me from exaggerating the merit of my
achievement, but I did not care, for in my own mind my perfor-
mance was somewhat stale already, and I did not give a fig for such
distinctions. It occurred to me, as I watched them and listened to

them, that Owen and my father were perhaps more alike, mentally and spiritually, than Owen and I, though my father had but a fraction of Owen's fineness, and none of his generosity. They were related as a coarse weed and a delicate flower might be, but I was of a different genus. And then I thought that, though I cared little for Gerald, and loved Owen, perhaps it was Gerald with whom I had really most in common.

CHAPTER XLIII

OWEN and I were standing by the low sea-wall, looking out across the wet brown sands, when I saw her. It was a gray, cloudy day, and the air was full of mist and damp, which hung in heavy, livid-coloured veils over the black mountain-tops, and sometimes dropped half way down the slopes. The tide was out and the noise of the waves sounded remote and musical. The broad stretch of wet sand and shingle reached out to the cold, gray-green sea, with its white curling line of foam; and at the water's edge, a little bent forward, her light dress floating out behind her in the fresh wind, one hand raised, holding the brim of her big black hat, she moved along, a solitary figure against the broad line of sea and sky. It was Katherine, and as I watched her it struck me that the whole picture, from her presence in it, became curiously like a Whistler water-colour. The next thing I noticed was that Katherine was quite grown-up, which had the effect of producing in me a sudden shyness, so that I made no attempt to go to meet her. Yet here was the meeting I had lain awake half the night imagining! I had an almost overpowering impulse to turn tail and slink away, and perhaps I might have done so had I been alone.

Owen, who took no more interest in girls than in octogenarians, asked me what I was staring at.

"At Miss Dale," I answered.

"Who's Miss Dale?"

"Katherine."

"And who is Katherine?"

"Mrs. Carroll's niece."

Then Owen looked at me in surprise. "Aren't you going to speak to her? I thought you knew her very well?"

"So I do."

We clambered over the wall and crossed the beach to intercept her path. My idiotic nervousness was increased by Owen's presence. She had noticed our approach now, and altered her own course to meet us. As she came up she smiled with her bright frank smile and held out her hand. She was perfectly natural and easy in her greeting, while I began to stammer and splutter. I managed to introduce Owen, saying he had come down yesterday, and we all three walked on together.

"I wondered if I should see you," she said. "We arrived this morning. Gerald is up at the house, but I had to come out and get some fresh air after our travels."

"There's p—plenty of it at all events," I stuttered.

"I like it. I like wind," she added, turning her smile upon Owen. "Don't you? It's very nice to be back here again. I always love coming back to any place I know."

"When the tide is out it looks like a Whistler watercolour," I went on, thinking it a pity that this should be lost.

But probably neither Katherine nor Owen had ever heard of Whistler. "It looks to me very like rain," said the former, glancing at the heavy clouds over Slieve Donard. Owen took no notice at all of my remark. "Conversation means nothing to Owen," I reflected, impatiently, "unless it takes the form of argument. Anything merely suggestive or decorative is lost upon him." And I felt annoyed because they had both begun to chatter commonplaces about Katherine's journey—what kind of passage she had had; as if it mattered!

Then I became lost in contemplation of her. A year had certainly made a tremendous difference! "Last winter she probably came out," I said to myself, with vague memories of Miss Broughton's novels. At all events, in twelve months she had managed to put at least five years between us. It was quite conceivable that she was already engaged to be married, while I was but a timid school-boy, who could only envy from afar the happiness of her lover. And the thought that perhaps there *was* a lover cast a vivid

illumination on my own feeling for her, made plainer than ever
the difference, how carefully veiled soever, between friendship and
love. I loved her with that love which, idealize it as I might, was
really the expression of a simple law of nature.

Meanwhile she was talking to Owen, who was explaining to
her some theory of the influence of the tides upon the earth,
and of the moon on the tides. How, in the first five minutes, he
had contrived to get on to such a subject I could not guess. It was
fearfully like him, nevertheless, and Katherine appeared to be
interested.

No matter in what company he found himself Owen never
talked about anything except the things he was interested in.
Last night it had been a little delicious to hear him discuss Plato's
"Republic" with Miss Dick, who, though immensely pleased, was
always at her silliest when taken seriously. To converse with Miss
Dick was like trying to get a definite impression from a kaleido-
scope; you no sooner fixed your attention on one particular idea
than it dissolved into something quite different. And yet Miss Dick
had views—political, religious, social,—derived from a deceased
parent, who had been an apostle of free thought. Only she would
interrupt her expression of the profoundest of these to wonder if
Sissie McIldowie was really engaged to young Stevenson.

And now Owen was talking to Katherine about the tides. I
watched her and knew she liked him. She liked his rough brown
mane, his clear eyes, with their kindness and innocence, for Owen,
in spite of the "Kreutzer Sonata" and the rest, was as innocent as
a child. There was something fine about Owen, and it was very
visible in his face.

At present he quite monopolized the conversation, turning it
into a sort of scientific discourse; and I knew so well that he had
been reading some little book about tides—probably in the train
on his way down. I yawned two or three times when he looked
in my direction, but I might have spared myself the rudeness, for
it had not the slightest effect upon him while Katherine kept on
asking questions as if she found what he said absorbing. My apparent indifference simply had the result of producing a *tête-à-tête*
between them.

"You ought to become a University Extension lecturer," I said, maliciously. "You should write and ask Tolstoy about it."

It was a highly disagreeable remark to make, and as soon as I had said it I was filled with shame. Owen coloured and stopped talking at once. I was very sorry. Inwardly I went down on my knees to him and begged his pardon, but outwardly I showed only a sullen stolidity. I said something to Katherine, but she answered coldly, and turned again to Owen as if to make up to him for my bad manners. And at this my remorse degenerated into sulkiness.

Nevertheless, as we walked home together, I had the grace to apologize. "I'm sorry for what I said," I muttered. "It was a most beastly thing to say. It's not so much because it was rude as because it was rotten."

This distinction I cannot undertake here to explain; let it suffice that in my mind it was a very clearly defined one.

"Oh, it doesn't matter," said Owen. "I always do talk either too much or too little."

After tea we went for a long walk and discussed all our old subjects. But in my present mood they bored me, though I was determined not to show it. What I really wanted just then was to be alone, that I might recall the past and make plans for the future. We went to bed when we came in, but long after Owen had dropped asleep I lay awake, wrapped in beautiful, desolating dreams. I gave Owen a gentle kick, for he had begun to snore, which troubled the quiet that was necessary for the perfect enjoyment of my visions. It woke him up, which was not what I had intended, but it couldn't be helped, and, before he had dropped asleep again, I was myself lost in slumber.

CHAPTER XLIV

I HAPPENED on the thing by the merest accident. My father had been going through the papers in his desk the night before, tying up old letters in bundles, and burning many in the grate. He had been quite absorbed in this dusty task when Owen and I had come in from our walk, and he had been still absorbed in it when we had left him and gone up to bed. This afternoon we were to call for the Dales, and Owen was waiting for me now in the garden, sitting on the wall, nibbling nasturtium leaves, whistling, and swinging his legs to and fro, while I, having broken my shoe-lace, was in the parlour replacing it. And as I bent down, through the tail of my eye I caught a glimpse of something white between the desk and the wall. I laced up my shoe, and then, pushing the desk further to one side, with the help of the poker I fished out an envelope. There was no writing on this envelope, and the flap was loose, but inside I felt something stiff and flat, like a card or a photograph. I pulled it out. It was a photograph, considerably faded, and certainly most astonishing if it had fallen from my father's desk, as I supposed it must have. For it represented a person very much like the ladies in the chorus at the Christmas pantomime I had gone to see with George—better looking, possibly, than most of them, but similarly clad, in doublet and tights, and with a velvet cap, with a cock's feather stuck in it, set rakishly at the side of a curly head. The face wore the conventional simper such faces seem naturally to assume in the presence of photographers, displaying an admirable set of teeth. A sword dangled from the waist, a short cloak hung from the shoulders, and the right hand was raised to the cap in a dashing and coquettish salute. There was something so comical in the idea of my father, of all persons in the world, having treasured up this souvenir of what I took to be a youthful flight of fancy, that I laughed aloud, and was on the point of calling in Owen to show it to him, when I turned the photograph round and on the back read, in a sprawling feminine hand, "From Milly."

I stopped short. Owen was still kicking his heels against the whitewashed wall, still whistling, but I did not disturb him. I heard my father coming downstairs, and my first impulse was to cram both envelope and photograph into my pocket. I heard him in the hall, I heard him turn the handle of the parlour door, and then I went to meet him.

"I found this," I said, "on the floor." And I held it out to him.

My father glanced at it indifferently, but when he saw what it was a faint flush crept into his face. It was the first time I had ever seen him change colour. He took it from me without a word, and,

putting it back in its envelope, unlocked the desk. He opened a
drawer somewhere, and I saw him, still without speaking, slip in
the envelope. Then he pulled down the lid of the desk, which shut
with a sharp click, and turned to me.

"Do you know who it was?" he asked, abruptly.

I stammered and blushed. "I'm not sure—I think—Wasn't it
mamma?"

He turned away without answering. "Owen is waiting for you,"
he said, as I still hung about nervously. "I suppose you won't be in
for tea?"

"No," I replied, and went out to my friend.

"I'm sorry for keeping you," I apologized; and as we walked
round to Derryaghy I half thought of telling him of the incident.

And my mother? I had known vaguely that she had been on the
stage in some not particularly brilliant capacity, but somehow the
real thing, in all its callous actuality, to have that suddenly thrust
upon one, was very different. I did not like it.

Visions of the girls I had seen in the pantomime kept rising
before me with a disagreeable relevancy. They strutted before my
mind's eye just as they had strutted, jaunty and assured, about the
stage, their eyes boldly seeking the male occupants of boxes. They
swaggered by me with a peculiar movement of the hips, a perfect
self-confidence; one of them even winked as she passed. And I saw
their fat legs, their bold eyes; I heard them laugh, and sing idiotic
songs, in shrill falsetto, about Bertie, and Charlie, and latch-keys,
and staying out till three.

I wished I had never found my mother's portrait, though I tried
to persuade myself that she only looked like that because she was
dressed up for the theatre, and that in ordinary dress she must
have been quite different. But my attempts to *see* her as different
failed. I had nothing to go upon, no memories, no other portrait;
for me tights and doublet would remain her perpetual garb. I was
not disillusioned, for I had had no illusions—that is to say, I had
thought very little about the matter—but I was certainly shocked.
I remembered Mrs. Carroll's reserve on the few occasions when I
had questioned her. Mrs. Carroll must have known, and so must
Miss Dick.

It was, doubtless, fortunate that I had never built up any imaginary and sentimental picture of my mother, as I might easily have done. Mrs. Carroll's presence in my life probably had prevented this.

"Here we are," cried Owen, catching me by the arm. "Wake up. I suppose you don't know that you've been fast asleep all the way!"

We found Katherine at the lodge, talking to the gardener's wife, a stout, ruddy young woman, with a flaxen-headed little fellow clutching her by the skirts, one of my father's youthful scholars, or, more likely, one of Miss McWaters', since he was still at the age when problems connected with "twice times" awaken bewildering difficulties.

We stopped and joined in the conversation.

"Isn't your brother coming?" Owen asked, after a minute or two.

"He said he was. He's up at the house; he's got some new music." Katherine smiled at me. "Do you mind hurrying him up? It's a shame to bother you, but if nobody fetches him he'll never come."

I complied with an extremely bad grace. It seemed to me I was always chosen for these messages. If Gerald didn't like to come himself, why couldn't he be left behind? I knew the others wouldn't even wait for us; in fact, when I turned round, they had already begun to walk on slowly.

I found Gerald busy with his music, and not looking in the least as if he intended to be anything else but busy with it all the afternoon. "The others are waiting," I said, with sulky abruptness. "Are you ready?"

He raised his head and his brown eyes rested on mine curiously. "They won't wait very long," he replied. "Do you really want to climb that ridiculous mountain?"

I looked down sullenly. "Why not? We arranged to do so, didn't we? Owen wants to."

"Let them go alone, then. They've begun to study botany. Katherine was examining things through a little lens all yesterday evening."

His drawling irony made me furious. "We must go," I said,

shortly. I knew well enough that he knew what was passing in my mind, and that I had been fighting against it for the last fortnight. He was the only one, I fondly imagined, who *did* know, and I had begun to think that the spectacle of my jealousy was pleasing to him, and that he had his own delicate ways of encouraging it. He did not like Owen, yet, for some reason I could not fathom, he appeared to regard favourably his friendship with Katherine. That friendship had made astonishing strides in the past week or two. When we went anywhere together now, it was invariably Owen who was Katherine's escort. Things seemed to arrange themselves naturally in that way, and this afternoon was no exception.

It was not till I told him I would follow the others, and was leaving the room, that Gerald made up his mind to accompany me, and even then, about a quarter way up Slieve Donard, he announced that he had gone far enough and would wait here till they came down. Owen and Katherine were not in sight, for Gerald had made the ascent at the pace of the pilgrims in "Tannhäuser," and I had had to keep with him. He stretched himself full length on the grass, and, as if it were an amusing question, asked me what I proposed doing. I did not know myself whether to wait with him here or to finish the climb. I stood hesitating, with a face like a thunder-cloud.

"I suppose they're at the top by this time," said Gerald, casually, and his supposition decided me.

I climbed up alone and full of bitter thoughts. Presently I saw Owen and Katherine far above me, but they never once looked back. I remembered that day, long ago it now seemed when Katherine and I had climbed the hill from the Bloody Bridge Valley, and how I had helped her over rough places, as I supposed Owen was helping her now, and walked hand in hand with her.

When I reached the summit I saw them standing together under the lee of a huge gray rock, gazing seaward. They heard my approach and turned round.

"Where did you leave Gerald?" Katherine asked, amused. "I didn't think he would get very far!"

"You might have waited for me then," I answered gruffly. "You were in a mighty hurry to start."

It gave me a sort of stupid pleasure to think I was showing by my manner that I considered myself neglected, so I proceeded deliberately to be as unpleasant as possible. That I had joined them had obviously not annoyed them in the least—Katherine had certainly shown no annoyance when she had greeted me—yet I told myself that this was only pretence, and that they wished me away. And then, as I thought how there might have been some secret understanding between them, and that perhaps Katherine had arranged to be down at the lodge when we arrived so that she might send me back to the house for Gerald, I felt—though I really did not believe in any such scheming—a violent anger against them both. When she saw the kind of humour I was in, Katherine ceased to take any notice of me, and this made me worse. I had not sense enough to leave them. A kind of perversity seemed to force me to do everything I could to make myself objectionable. I had an insane desire to quarrel with Owen, and presently I contradicted him flatly when he said something I knew to be perfectly true. He flushed and his eyes brightened angrily, but he controlled himself. "What is the matter with you, Peter?" he asked.

"Nothing," I muttered.

I bounded away from them. I ran down the mountainside at the risk of breaking an ankle, leaping from one point to another. I did not pause when I came to where Gerald lay in the grass, but continued my headlong descent till I reached the woods. I had come down in an incredibly short time, and the violence of my flight had relieved me. I walked now at an ordinary pace, wondering what the others would think, conscious that I had made a fool of myself, yet laying all the blame on Katherine.

The woods were silent save for the occasional note of a robin or the low twitter of a swallow. I stopped by a marshy hollow to look at a vivid splash of yellow irises, and I gathered an armful of them for Mrs. Carroll.

CHAPTER XLV

Owen and I dined at Derryaghy that night, but all through dinner I sat very quiet. No allusion was made by the others to my having left them, which showed, I thought, that they had discussed it among themselves and had agreed not to take any notice.

After dinner Gerald stayed behind to smoke a cigarette, and I stayed with him. When we followed the others to the drawing-room, he went to the piano and began to play. Owen sat by the window looking out. He had not once spoken to me since I had left him and Katherine at the top of Slieve Donard; I thought he had even avoided meeting my glance, but I was not sure. Katherine and Miss Dick had each some needlework. Mrs. Carroll was not with us. From my corner of the room I watched Katherine as she worked, her beautiful head bowed in the lamp-light, and secretly, in my soul, I knew Owen was more fitted to be her mate than I. It is true, I did not believe he could love her so intensely, but the love he gave her would be more unselfish. I became lost in gloomy thoughts. I knew they both belonged to a world where I was a stranger, an outcast. In that hour I recognized my moral inferiority to Owen, and suddenly I felt how peaceful and quiet it would be in the thick darkness, with the grass over my head, and everything finished and forgotten.

Gerald had begun to play the "Moonlight Sonata," Chopinizing it, as he did everything, and perhaps this unhappy vision came to me from his music. At all events, it hovered before me in an intensity of sadness beneath which I shut my eyes. I got up by-and-by and crossed the room to where Katherine sat at her work. I pulled forward a chair and sat down near to her, and with my back to the others, so that what I said should be heard by her alone.

"Will you come out with me?" I asked, in a low voice.

"Out? *Now*, do you mean?" She looked up in surprise, but she also spoke in lowered tones, and with, I thought, a certain coldness. At this my anger was stirred afresh.

"Now," I answered.

She seemed on the point of refusing. "Are you afraid?" I sneered.

She appeared not to understand me. "Afraid! What is there to be afraid of?" After a moment she decided. "I will come in a minute or two; I want to finish this flower."

She returned perfectly calmly to her work. She was embroidering a table-cloth for her mother's birthday, and was always saying she should never have it finished in time. I, with a burning heart, got up and strolled out on to the terrace, my hands in my pockets, and whistling below my breath, which I imagined lent an air of off-handedness to my exit. Once beyond the windows, however, my whistling ceased abruptly, and I hurried round to the other side of the house, where I waited in a fever till she should come.

She did not keep me long. She had not put on a hat, nor even a loose wrap about her shoulders; evidently she intended our interview to be a short one. I hastened from the shadow to meet her.

"Do you know what I want?" I began gloomily.

"You want to speak to me about something, I suppose?" Again I was conscious of a coldness in her voice.

"Yes. I have so few opportunities now."

"I think you have plenty of opportunities, considering you see me every day."

We walked on slowly, side by side. "Are you angry with me?" I asked, trying to speak penitently.

"About what?"

There was something in her air of calm deliberation that held me at a distance.

"Everything—this afternoon, for instance."

"I thought you weren't very nice to your friend."

"I wasn't. Nor to you."

"Oh, it doesn't matter about me."

"Why?" I asked miserably.

"Well, it doesn't matter so much. I'm not your guest—and—I don't suppose I'm as fond of you as he is."

There was something cruel in those last words, though their cruelty may have been unconscious. For a minute or two I could not speak.

"Why have you changed, Katherine?" I said at length, my voice still not very secure.

"It is you who have changed."

"Have I?"

"You were not like this last summer."

"I think I was."

"I don't know what it is, but there is a difference. I suppose it may be only that you are growing up. I like people to be either men or boys. Why can't you be natural? Why can't you be content to be as you were?"

"I don't think you have treated me fairly."

"I can't help it. Why should you be so jealous? It's horrid. Everything is changed, as you say. It is not nearly so nice. I first began to notice it in your letters, but I thought when I saw you it would be all right. If I had known you were going to be like this I wouldn't have come at all."

There was something in her manner I couldn't understand, something mysterious, as if her words hid a regret, though whether it was for our old friendship or not I could not say.

"Tell me what it is you don't like," I said, thickly.

Katherine's dark blue eyes rested on me while she hesitated. "I can't. I'm stupid. Perhaps I don't really know myself." Then suddenly she broke out, "Don't speak to me or I shall cry or do something idiotic. Let us go back." Without waiting for me she began to walk hastily in the direction of the house. I ran after her; I was lost in wonderment; but I made no attempt to detain her or to question her.

CHAPTER XLVI

No allusion was made to our absence when we returned to the others. Gerald was still playing, but he got up as soon as we entered, and strolled over to the window, where he stood beside Owen, looking out.

"There should be white peacocks here," he murmured idly. "I've always longed to live in a house where there were white peacocks. They are the most poetic creatures in the world. They come over the lawn in the moonlight, delightful fowls, and knock with their beaks against the windows to be fed. They love moonlight. They're extraordinarily morbid and decadent. Their only quite healthy taste is that they want to be fed. Shouldn't you like them, Miss Dick?"

Miss Dick, to whom all Gerald's words were pearls of wisdom, listened to these with close attention. "I'll speak to Mrs. Carroll about them," she said. "It *would* be nice to have them."

Gerald smiled sweetly, and Owen moved away from him, an expression on his face of mingled contempt and disgust, which, had I not been so miserable, I should have found highly comic. There was nothing, I knew, irritated him more than this kind of talk, which Gerald manufactured with extreme ingenuity, principally for Owen's benefit. For Owen's sake he would talk in a world-weary fashion of the "colour" of life, and ever since he had discovered that the word "Philistine" was peculiarly exasperating, it had figured more frequently than any other in his conversation. He dragged it in at every turn, nearly always with absolute irrelevancy. He began to talk of Philistines now, à propos of some concert at which he declared he had been asked to play—a concert he had probably invented for the occasion.

Owen stood with his back against the chimney-piece, his eyes bright, his cheeks red. "There is one class, at any rate, that is a good deal more disgusting than your Philistines—the people who imagine themselves superior to them."

But Gerald could keep perfectly cool. "These people you mention," he began in his most elaborate manner, "I strongly suspect to be only the commanders of the Philistine hosts—their Tolstoys, their chief-priests and scribes. It is the Philistine who imagines himself superior to other Philistines. This is the one flight his imagination is capable of. The artist may *be* superior, but that, I think, is not what you mean?"

"You're right," said Owen, fiercely, "it's not what I mean. And I suppose *you* are an artist?"

"My dear Gill, it is apparent."

"I'm not your dear Gill," said Owen, who had lost his temper.

"Shut up, Owen," I interrupted. "What's the use of taking everything so seriously?"

"Because everything *is* serious. You may say a lot of chatter about white peacocks and Philistines doesn't mean anything if you like, but it does. It is a mask for other things that are real enough—for selfishness, and immorality."

We all gazed at him in silence, almost open-mouthed, Gerald with a faint smile on his handsome face. Miss Dick alone found it incumbent upon her to say something, and she remarked that the Charity Organization Committee to which she belonged had been able to do a great deal, and that the lecture with lime-light views had brought in over three pounds—she meant even after all expenses had been paid.

These observations could not fill up the breach. Nobody, indeed, took any notice of them. Katherine had laid down her work, and her eyes were fixed on Owen's angry face, with, I thought, an expression of admiration and sympathy.

"What has morality to do with art?" Gerald asked calmly. "Peter supports you because he is not an artist, but only a person of taste, who likes to listen to my playing. I *am* an artist, and I know. You not being even a person of—I beg your pardon—you being a person of different tastes from Peter, and uninterested in art, naturally are at a disadvantage when you discuss it. I do not mean that rudely; I say it merely in self-defence. Is anyone coming down in the direction of the station?"

He went out, but nobody offered to accompany him.

CHAPTER XLVII

OWEN and I left shortly afterwards. He was very quiet as we walked home, but when we were in bed he said to me, "I've decided to go back to town to-morrow."

I heard the words with a thrill of mingled pleasure and misgiving. "To-morrow? Why?" I asked. "You must stay till the end of the week in any case." Then something made me add, "Is it because I was rude to you this afternoon?"

"No."

I thought for a little. "Has that nothing to do with it?" I persisted.

"No; at least, not directly. I may as well be quite frank about it. I know you would rather I went; that is my reason. I ought to have seen it before, but I didn't, though I had a kind of feeling several times that there was something wrong. It is partly your own fault that I didn't guess sooner. You always mentioned Katherine as if you were quite indifferent to her; and that first day you seemed even to hesitate about going to speak to her. I remember now what you told me on the night of our party, but until to-day I never connected it with her."

"You think I'm jealous?" I said in a low voice.

"I know you are, but I didn't know it until this afternoon. Don't imagine I'm offended or any silly rot of that kind. There is no reason why I should be. Of course I should have liked it better if you had told me openly—but—well, it doesn't matter. I don't understand your feeling, but that doesn't matter, either; if you have it, it is enough. I like Katherine, I like her very much, but, after all, it is you who are my friend."

"She won't want you to go," I said miserably. At that moment I certainly preferred Owen to Katherine.

"She won't mind very much, and I really can't knock about with her brother. I hate the very sight of him."

"Couldn't we knock about by ourselves?"

"I'm afraid it would hardly do to drop them now."

There was a silence.

"Owen?"

"Yes."

"I don't know what to do."

"About what?"

"About anything. About your going away. About Katherine."

"But when I'm away won't it be all right?"

"No; it will be all wrong. I've been beastly to you as it is. And she doesn't like me—I mean she only likes me middling—not even as much as she did—she told me so, this evening."

"But you will have plenty of time to make it up."

"It isn't that—it isn't that we've quarrelled. And the other—it is no use—it only irritates me. I wish I could explain. Things—things come into my mind."

Owen was silent.

"And I've been beastly to you," I went on.

"Oh, nonsense."

He was silent again till he said, "There's one way, but I know you won't take it."

"What is it?"

"Come back with me, and spend the rest of your holidays with me."

I lay quiet.

"Will you?"

In the dark I shook my head. Then, remembering he could not see me, I answered, "No: I can't."

"Why not? It is only a matter of will."

"But I haven't any will, except to get what I want."

"You could try it for a few days."

"No. There are not a great many days altogether. They will be leaving before the end of the month."

"Well, if you should change your mind, come at any time—I mean without bothering to write."

"Very well."

Owen was silent so long that I thought he had dropped asleep, when suddenly he spoke again.

"Peter?"

"Yes."

"I didn't know if you were asleep or not. It is this. I wrote to my people about you—about your having to go to lodgings when you come up to town after summer; and they want you to come to live with us."

I felt myself grow hot with shame.

"You see there are plenty of bedrooms," Owen went on, "and my study, I daresay, would do for both of us to work in. I hope you'll come: they all want you to. If you think of it I'll speak to your father; but of course if you'd rather be in 'digs' by yourself, it would be better for me not to mention it to him."

"Do you really want me to come?" I asked.

"Of course I want you."

"I mean, do you really and truly want me?"

He laughed pleasantly. "Of course I really and truly want you."

"You're not doing it out of kindness or anything like that?"

"The kindness will be all on your side."

"No: but I mean it. You must tell me."

"I suggested it because I'd like to have you. I wasn't a bit sure whether you'd come or not. My reason for asking you is exactly the same as my reason for asking you every Sunday to come for a walk with me."

"I'll come," I said. "Thanks awfully." But my pleasure was spoiled by the remorse I felt for my own conduct as host. It seemed to me I was a fairly second-rate specimen of humanity, hardly good enough to be taken out and drowned.

CHAPTER XLVIII

I DO not know whether Katherine attributed Owen's sudden departure to me or not, but I think it extremely probable that she did, although she never mentioned it. Yet we sometimes spoke of Owen himself during the days that followed. In those days we slipped back more or less into our former friendship, and I tried to feel that it was just the same. Yet something of the old freedom had gone, and I could not forget what Katherine had said to me the night before Owen's departure. After a few days, indeed, it came into my romantic mind that there might be another interpretation of her behaviour on that occasion, one I hardly dared even to dream of, so much was it what I desired. But it influenced me nevertheless. I longed to have another day alone with her—a day such as we had had last year, and I determined to ask her to come somewhere with me alone, to come, that is, without Gerald.

I went up to Derryaghy one afternoon with this intention, and was shown into the morning-room, where I found Mrs. Carroll and Miss Dick. Mrs. Carroll informed me that Katherine had been washing her hair, and was now drying it at the kitchen fire. She told me to go on in if I wanted to speak to her, but I hung back bashfully. In the end I went, all the same, and discovered Katherine sitting on a stool, a book open on her knee, and her long, thick, dark brown hair hanging loose in the red glow of the kitchen range.

"It's well for you you haven't to undergo torments of this kind!" she exclaimed. "I was baked nearly ten minutes ago. My hair was simply full of salt. I don't know how it gets in under my bathing-cap."

The situation may seem more homely than romantic, but I thought she looked extremely lovely, and gazed at her in silent admiration. Perhaps she noticed it, for she coloured as she laughed.

"My dear Peter, aren't you going to say good-morning to me? I'm not the Sleeping Beauty, you know?"

"What beautiful hair you have," I said, in an awed tone, and involuntarily I touched it with my hand.

She laughed again, but drew back. "Did you come in just to admire it? It's very nice of you."

"I came to ask you to go for a walk with me this afternoon, round by the Hilltown Road—by the road under the mountains— just you by yourself."

"'Me by myself!' When do you want to go?"

"After lunch."

"Very well—if it's not too hot."

The readiness with which she consented made me consider myself a fool for not having asked her sooner, and I began to regret all my lost opportunities.

On my way home I met Gerald, who wanted to know if I had bathed yet.

"I bathed before breakfast. Where have you been?"

"Oh, just down to the Club House."

I turned back with him. I had made up my mind to say something he might possibly resent, but I plunged into my subject without beating about the bush. "Don't you think you are rather a fool to go down there so often?"

"Down where?" asked Gerald. "To the Club House?"

"Yes; though I was thinking more of the hotel. It seems to me you go to the hotel nearly every evening now."

He smiled, indifferently. "There's nothing else to do."

"It seems stupid to chum up with people about twice your age," I persisted.

"They're not twice my age. Some of them aren't very much older than I am. What harm does it do?"

"Well, I was only with you once, but I didn't like what I saw there, especially towards the end of the evening."

"What didn't you like, Peter?" he asked, good-humouredly.

"I thought it looked silly—and a little disgusting. There were you, a chap barely eighteen, calling Captain Denby, who's about fifty, by his Christian name. You must know well enough that he's as gross as a pig. What does he care about your playing? And what pleasure, anyway, can it give you to play a lot of waltzes and popular songs?"

"He cares as much for my playing as you do."

"My dear Gerald, if you think that you're a fool."

"You sat quiet enough at the time. You were afraid to open your mouth."

"That may be so, but it doesn't alter the fact that I was infinitely superior to anyone in that room except yourself."

"I daresay you were, Peter. I never doubt your superiority. There's one thing you forget, however, and that is that any friendship there may be between you and me is a pretty one-sided affair."

"What do you mean?" I asked, uncomfortably.

"Only that you've never given it much encouragement."

"Why?"

"I don't know, I'm sure. Partly, I should think, because you rather dislike me. That always stands in the way of such things."

His irony rang unpleasantly true. "Why should you think I dislike you?" I said, very weakly.

"It would take too long to explain. It never gave me any particular pleasure to think so—at first, just the reverse—and I mention it now merely at your request."

I didn't quite know what to say. "Isn't my speaking to you about this matter a proof of my not disliking you?" I risked. "I thought we had always been friends."

"No, Peter, your friend is a prig called Owen Gill."

"Owen isn't a prig," I said warmly, glad to have a chance to put him in the wrong, but my chance did not last.

"I beg your pardon," said Gerald, "even if he was, I shouldn't have called him one to you."

"Better say it to me, if you're going to say it at all. I can defend him."

"I daresay there is no harm in being a prig."

"Owen is a good deal finer chap than either you or I."

"And yet neither of us would change with him! But the point is hardly worth discussing."

"I don't want to discuss it."

"You want to give me good advice? Well, fire ahead."

"Oh, there's no use in my saying anything. You know it all well enough yourself, and if you think it better to go on as you are doing, I can't interfere. But it seems to me stupid to get into bad habits."

"Have you no bad habits, Peter?"

"I'm not talking about myself."

"That's true."

"You said the other night you were an artist; but you know as well as I do, that if you are going to do anything in that way you will have to work, and that you won't work if you begin to loaf about, taking drinks with this person and that. I can't even understand why you should want to. If I had any particular gift I would cultivate it for all it was worth."

"Have you no gift?"

"No. As you also remarked, I am a person of taste."

"I'm sorry if I offended you. I didn't mean anything."

"You believed it all the same."

"I'm not sure that I did. You're clever enough."

"Thank you. I'll not come any further."

"Won't you? It was good of you bothering about me, and I took it very well, didn't I?" He smiled.

"You didn't take it at all; but that's not my fault."

CHAPTER XLIX

It was a cloudless afternoon when I went back to Derryaghy. Katherine was quite ready and we set out immediately. As I walked beside her, in her simple cotton dress, and with her gay parasol, I thought her adorable.

"Do you remember our picnic?" I asked, for I was for ever harking back to it in my mind.

"Which? There have been so many!"

"I mean our own—the one we went together—the first of all."

"It seems centuries ago. I wonder if Bryansford isn't too far for this afternoon? The others were saying something about driving. That would be better."

"It was a day very like this," I went on, "a perfect summer day." And a strange thrill passed through me as I recalled its incidents.

The air was as soft as velvet. The August sun streamed over the fields. We followed a lane which led us past a long, low house, where an immense cherry-tree, with a trunk nine or ten feet in circumference, spread its branches in a small green orchard. I repeated aloud some lines of a poem I remembered:

> "I know a little garden-close
> Set thick with lily and red rose,
> Where I would wander if I might
> From dewy dawn to dewy night,
> And have one with me wandering."

Two friendly dogs wagged their tails, and a cat lounging on the gray stone wall unclosed its eyes in sleepy yellow slits.

"Can't we be friends, Katherine, as we were then?" I pleaded.

"But aren't we friends?" she asked, with a shade of impatience in her voice.

"You know what I mean."

"I'm afraid I *don't* know what you mean, Peter." Then she unexpectedly added: "You're a very queer mixture. I often wonder how you'll come out in the end."

"I haven't an idea," I replied, somewhat taken aback. The remark appeared to me peculiar, and I felt as if she had pushed me farther away; and with this my self-confidence began to evaporate.

We walked on in silence. There was, at the particular point we had now reached, a certain grandeur in the landscape, which even at that agitated moment impressed me with a sense of solemnity. From childhood I had imagined it—quite without historical foundation—as the scene of ancient Druidical worship. I thought of the dark soil as having drunk up the hot, sweet blood of human sacrifice, while the "pale-eyed priest" lifted his gaze to the clear autumn sky, and watched against it, just that same dark curving line of quiet hills that I was watching now.

Yet, when we began to speak again it was of things about which we were both profoundly indifferent, and I had a sickening feeling that I was failing to interest my companion, and that while she was talking to me her thoughts were elsewhere. Somehow it appeared to be impossible to raise our conversation out of the rut of deadly commonplace into which it had fallen. It seemed to me almost as if Katherine were keeping it there on purpose, and before we came to Bryansford, I proposed trying to get tea at one of the cottages, for I felt that any interruption would be a relief.

When we had finished, and paid for, our refreshment, instead of continuing our way round under the mountains, as I had intended, Katherine decided that we ought to start for home.

"Let us at least go back through the woods," I begged. "We don't want to tramp along that dusty road again."

She yielded to my persuasion, and we entered the estate that lay beyond Derryaghy. It was strangely still in the late afternoon. Not a leaf stirred. On and on we walked, hardly speaking, and suddenly the dead silence, and our complete solitude, became, as it were, visible to me; and with that there rose in my mind, with intense vividness, a memory—the memory of Elsie at Owen's party. The whole thing came back to me almost with the strength of hallucination: her lips on mine, my own kisses, her yielding body as she closed her eyes under my embrace. I was horribly nervous. I felt myself trembling and a faint mist swam before my eyes. I put out my hand and tried to take Katherine's, but she drew away from me at once. I stopped short, facing her, on the narrow path. "I want to speak to you," I said. "What have I done?"

She made as if to pass me, but I barred the way. I was conscious once more, through other things, of a smouldering anger against her. "Why do you draw back when I touch you? You once told me you cared for me. You wrote to me that you did."

"So I do," she answered quietly, though her face had altered. "I don't know what you want, nor why you aren't satisfied."

And, all the time, that other vision was acting like an hypnotic suggestion upon my mind. "You know that I love you," I persisted, hoarsely, my voice sounding queer, though I tried to speak naturally. "Tell me, would you rather have Owen?"

"I don't think you should speak to me like this. I wish you would allow me to pass, please."

Her dark blue eyes were fixed on me; she was very near. I was passionately conscious of her attraction for me; my heart was thumping, and the blood began to drum in my temples, while a sort of shadow veiled my sight. I threw my arms round her; I could feel her body straining away from me, her breath on my face. For a moment she seemed to submit as I kissed her, but the next instant she struggled from me, and I felt a blow across my face. She had struck me with her parasol, which now hung broken in her hand.

Her eyes flashed on me like a withering fire. She was furiously angry. "How dare you touch me! Let me pass at once, you—you beast."

My arms dropped to my sides. A sudden, bitter shame overcame me. I saw her pass me with head erect and flaming cheeks, and then I dropped on my face on the ground.

When I got up she was out of sight. I did not know how long I had lain there, but I made no attempt to follow her. As I brushed mechanically the earth and bits of grass and twigs from my clothes, I felt almost dazed. It had all passed, and I did not want to think. I heard the drowsy prattle of a stream, and became aware that I was hot and thirsty. I went down to it and followed the bank till I reached a deep green pool, from which, lying flat on my belly,

I drank greedily. As I raised my head I saw my own image in the water—my bright eyes, my dark, flushed face, my coarse, ruffled hair.

CHAPTER L

I HAD told my father I should be dining at Derryaghy, yet he made no remark when, instead, I came in an hour late for tea. Fresh tea simply was prepared for me, and again, while I sat at table, I was conscious of something peculiar in the way he watched me, so that for an instant it even flashed upon me that he might have heard of what had happened in the wood.

It was only when I had finished eating that he spoke. "I had a letter from your Uncle George this afternoon," he said, and I knew at once, not so much from his voice as from the face he turned to me, that something serious had happened.

My thoughts darted straightway to Aunt Margaret, to vague, gruesome tragedies, murder or suicide. "What's the matter?" I asked, uneasily. Perhaps it had to do with little Alice? Why couldn't he tell me at once? Then I noticed that he had pushed a bundle of photographs to me across the table.

"Do you know anything of these?" he asked, in a strange voice.

I started. A glance at the top one had been sufficient. I recognized the photographs George had kept hidden in his room, or others like them. I looked at my father watching me, not angrily, but in a kind of hopeless way; I looked into his gray, still face while he went on speaking. "They were found in your bedroom hidden under the floor. Uncle George says that George knows nothing about them, and, that being the case, he felt it his duty to tell me. He does not mention your name. I don't know what to do. I have been trying to think." He looked at the wretched things, as they lay there, with a kind of horror.

I sat silent for a moment. "They're not mine," I then said. "I have nothing to do with them."

A gleam of relief came into his face, but it faded quickly. "You never saw them before?"

I lifted the top one, but immediately put it back again. "I don't know whether I saw them before or not," I answered. "If I didn't see these particular ones I saw others like them." My father winced. "But they never belonged to me. Even if I had wanted them I wouldn't have known where to get them."

"Did you know of this hiding place?"

"Yes."

"And of what was there?"

"Yes."

"Only you and George occupied that room."

"And George says they aren't his." I looked towards the window.

My father hesitated. Then he said solemnly, "Will you give me your word of honour, Peter, that you had nothing to do with their being there?"

"I had nothing to do with it." I answered quietly. "I knew they were there, because George showed them to me. If he was here he would not say they were mine. I knew what he was like from the first day I went there. Those things were there then, and on the very first night he wanted to show them to me, but he was frightened to. I did not see them till a long time afterwards. I would never have seen them at all, if you had let me leave when I first wrote to ask you to."

"You gave me no reason," said my father, sadly. "Do you think I should have allowed you to stay an hour in the place if I had known?"

"You might have guessed there was *some* reason. And at the time I couldn't give any—I didn't know myself."

"Had that anything to do with your not wanting to go back there after Christmas?"

"In a way—more or less," I answered. "Not exactly that, but other things——"

My father sighed. He tore the photographs in two, and placed them in the empty grate, where he set fire to them. It was like an act of purification, and when it was concluded he turned round and said gloomily, "I'm sorry if I misjudged you. I accept your word."

But he didn't accept it—he couldn't. Secretly, and underneath

everything, and, without admitting it even to himself, he couldn't
help being doubtful, and I knew he was doubtful. If I had suddenly
told him the photographs were mine, and expressed appropriate remorse, I believe it would have made him happier than my
denial did. As I saw the wretchedness of his face the injustice of
the whole thing became intolerable. "Do you believe me, or do
you not?" I asked brusquely.

"I have told you I believe you."

"You don't look as if you did."

"I can't pretend to treat the matter as of no importance. My
believing you means that I must disbelieve George."

"Why should you trouble about George? And, at any rate,
though he did have those things, he's decent enough in some ways.
I'm pretty sure he would have burnt them himself after a while."

I'm afraid this speech did neither George nor myself any good.
It simply made my father think me callous.

I went out on the golf-links with Tony, and sat looking at the
sea. I began to think of my father and of the failure of his life. This
last incident seemed but to fit with all the others into its tragic
grayness. And I reflected how for him I must compose a large part
of that failure. Thinking of me could bring him little consolation,
probably just the reverse. It was a pity. I doubtless was not, particularly from his point of view, much to boast of, but I was better than
he thought me. I might be below the average in most things, but I
was not below it in all. . . . .

And then my natural egotism rose once more to the surface.
My mind turned to Katherine, and it seemed to me I was making
a horrible mess of my whole existence. I got up and walked slowly
back to the town. A wandering troupe of open-air entertainers had
arrived during the day, and were busy erecting tents and hobby-
horse machines in a large field not far from our house. Most of the
natives, both young and old, were superintending these prepara-
tions with an unflagging interest which had already stretched over
hours, but I was in no mood to join them. I determined to walk as
far as the pier and then go home. I had not gone above a hundred
yards when I felt my face burning. Before me, coming in my direction, were Katherine and Gerald. Nothing but a straight stretch

of road and footpath lay between us, and it was certain that they must have already seen me. I would have liked to turn back, but my pride prevented such a step, and I walked on, my head up, a flaming blush on my face. Gerald and I raised our caps. My eyes sought Katherine's, but her glance just brushed mine to rest on some distant point beyond me. The next moment we had passed. Hot tears rose to my eyes, but I walked as far as I had intended to. On the pier steps I sat down and put my arms round Tony's broad back and kissed him. If I had committed the greatest crime on earth, I thought, he would have licked my cheek and pretended to bite my ear just as he did now.

CHAPTER LI

"I want to go up to Belfast to-day," I said to my father next morning at breakfast.

His reply was exactly the one I had anticipated. "What do you want to go to Belfast for?"

"I want to see Owen about something."

"Hadn't you a whole fortnight when you saw him every day?"

"I want to speak to him," I answered, very low-spiritedly. I knew he was thinking of the railway-fare, and if I had had any money myself I should never have asked him.

"Can't you write?" he demanded, querulously.

"I want to speak to him."

"Don't go on repeating the same thing like a child."

"But why can't I go?" I asked helplessly.

"Because it is a waste of money."

"It will only cost five shillings."

"Five shillings is a great deal too much to spend upon nothing."

"It isn't nothing. I want to speak to him. I never asked to go before."

"You'll be seeing him very soon—in another fortnight—and you will have plenty of time to talk to him then."

"I want to speak to him now," I persisted. "Can't I go?"

"Peter, you are dreadfully obstinate. What do you want to see him about that won't keep for a few days?"

"I sent him a telegram before breakfast, asking him to meet me, and I can't very well not go."

"It is your own fault if you do things without consulting me."

Nevertheless, in the end, he allowed me to go, and I caught the first train.

I had asked Owen to meet me in the Botanic Gardens, for I did not want to call at his house, and, as I arrived some few minutes before the appointed time, I began to pace disconsolately up and down one of the paths, my head filled with dreary thoughts. Two or three gardeners with long rakes were raking the walks, and a man with a pair of clippers was trimming the edges of the grass. As they pottered over their work they carried on a disjointed conversation, principally about religion, or rather about the evils of Roman Catholicism. I listened to their idiotic remarks, which at another time might have amused me. The man with the clippers was describing some form of service which he called "High Rosary," and the rakers from time to time interpolated words and grunts. A few little boys were playing hide-and-seek, and now and then a nurse passed, wheeling a perambulator. An old pensioner, sucking an empty pipe, hobbled up to the seat I had taken a corner of, though all the others were vacant, and began with much fumbling to unfold a greasy-looking newspaper. The sight of his futile senility somehow irritated me, and I stared at him fiercely, but he sat on. I began to think that perhaps Owen would not come: for all I knew he might be away from home. Two or three untidy, vulgar, little girls, with smaller brothers and sisters in tow, came up to inquire "the right time." After I had satisfied their curiosity they still hovered near me, gazing at me in a silence that it was difficult to construe as flattering. At a distance of three or four yards they then settled down stolidly to some obscure game, in which a great deal of monotonous, rhymed dialogue was the principal feature. They intoned this in shrill, unmodulated voices, but all the time keeping a sharp look-out on my movements. The old pensioner turned his watery eyes on me and made a remark about the weather. I pretended not to hear him, but he only made it again, and I had to answer. He began to talk politics. His fumbling hands, his foolish, empty pipe, his bleared and rheumy eyes, depressed me, and I wondered why he couldn't be put into a lethal chamber. Then I saw Owen turn the corner and sprang up to meet him.

"Why didn't you come to the house? Where are your things?" he asked. The little girls had suspended their game to watch us with breathless interest.

"I'm not going to stay, Owen. I came up just because I wanted to speak to you about something—— Get away!" This last remark was addressed to a child who had drawn nearer, so as not to miss what we were saying. She stared at me with an expression of solemn idiocy, but without budging an inch from the position she had taken up.

"That's all right," said Owen, "but of course you'll stay now you're here. I can lend you everything you need, and I've told them at home to expect you."

"I can't. My father would hardly let me come, even as it was."

"Get yer hair cut," suggested the polite child, putting out her tongue.

"Owen, I want to tell you something: I want your advice."

He at once became serious. He took my arm and we strolled down toward the pond, followed by the whole band of children, who, captained by the same odious little girl, screamed now in chorus, "Get yer hair cut! Get yer hair cut!"

The din they made was terrific. I waited till we had turned the corner and were out of sight of the gardeners and the pensioner. Then I swung round quickly and made a grab at the ringleader. In about two seconds, kicking and screaming, she was across my knee, and I was administering as sound a spanking as she had ever received in her life.

"I say," cried Owen, "what on earth are you doing?"

I released my captive, who with crimson, tear-drenched face, and open mouth, went bawling back in the direction she had come from.

"That's all right, any way," I said to the astonished Owen. "There's nothing like taking these things in time."

The rest of the children had retreated, moving backwards, with round eyes fixed on me, but perfectly callous to the woes of their comrade.

"You'll be having someone coming and kicking up the mischief of a row," said Owen, uneasily.

"I don't care. Can't we find a quiet place?"

Owen considered. "Come down the Lagan walk: there's never anybody there."

I let him take me, and we walked till we were stopped by a low parapet, over which we had a charming view of the black mud-banks of the river, for the tide was out, and beyond this a strip of waste land, dotted with mill chimneys and the backs of dirty houses. It was neither a cheerful nor a beautiful outlook, but we both stood gazing over the wall, as if beyond it lay the New Jerusalem.

"It's horribly smelly," I discovered at length.

"I thought you wanted somewhere quiet," Owen apologized.

"I didn't mean this sort of thing. I'm sure there's a dead cat or dog in that sack down there. Come away."

"I didn't know the tide was out," said Owen patiently.

But I found it difficult now to begin my story. Those wretched children had upset everything. I was quite unreasonably cross, too, with Owen; for bringing me to these hideous mud-banks, with their litter of old boots, of empty tins and broken bottles. I even had it on the tip of my tongue to tell him it was just like him, but refrained.

We retraced our steps and found a seat near the pond. Here we sat in silence, Owen waiting for me to begin my tale.

"Something very unpleasant happened yesterday," I murmured, branching off to a secondary subject.

"Happened to you?"

"Not to me only—— It was a letter my father got from Uncle George—the people I was living with in town here, you know."

"I know."

"You remember the chap who came with us to 'Faust?'"

"Your cousin?"

I nodded. "He had some photographs which he kept hidden under the floor in our bedroom."

"Why?"

"So that nobody would get hold of them. They were—that kind. I don't know where he got them from."

"Bad?"

I nodded again. "And they were found a few days ago, and he denied that they were his, so Uncle George wrote to my father."

"Saying they must be yours?"

"It came to that, though he didn't actually say it."

"But you denied it too?"

"Yes—only—I don't know that my father believes me."

"Even now?"

"He says he does, but I'm not sure. At any rate it has upset him a lot."

"He must be an awfully low cad."

"George? He's not up to much. But I expect it never occurred to him that his people would write, and I suppose he thought, now I was out of the way, it wouldn't much matter to me whether they blamed me or not. Neither would it have mattered, if Uncle George hadn't written."

"Of course it would have. What is your father going to do?"

"I don't know. There is nothing he *can* do, except tell them what I say." I felt suddenly sad and doubtful—doubtful of the quality of my own innocence, which had seemed perfectly clear before. "I'm not sure that I'm giving you a right impression," I went on, after a short silence. "I knew George had these things: I had looked at them: I knew where he kept them."

"It all seems to me very rotten," said Owen, disgustedly.

"It is, rather. Aunt Margaret may write to Mrs. Carroll, for instance, just out of spite."

"She can hardly do that now."

"I don't know. She hates me. And it would be horrible if she did, though Mrs. Carroll wouldn't believe her."

I was silent a while. "But that isn't really what I came up to tell you," I suddenly began. Then I related what had happened yesterday in the wood.

Owen stared in front of him at the drab, seedy-looking, little ducks, who were paddling about on the dirty sheet of water. A rat stole out, and seeing us scuttled back again.

"Why did you behave like that? It was most extraordinary!"

I made no answer.

"It wasn't very gentlemanly, you know," Owen continued, "to say the least of it."

"I never said I was a gentleman," I interrupted. "I'm not one, in the ordinary sense of the word, nor even in the other, according to you."

"Oh, that's rot." He sat trying to puzzle it out. He looked at me and unexpectedly smiled.

I smiled too, but my heart was heavy as lead. "Well, that's all I came up to tell you," I muttered, "—not very much!"

He saw I was not happy. "I know I'm not very experienced in matters of this kind," he confessed, "but if I were you, Peter, I should go to Derryaghy and ask to see her. Would you like me to do anything?"

"There's nothing you could do. Would it not be better for me to write?"

"I don't think so. It might be easier."

"It would be. And suppose she won't see me?"

"You can only try."

"Well, I'll go back and think it over."

"But won't you stay, really?"

"No. I must go."

"Before this happened she liked you very much—she told me so herself."

I shook my head. "It is all over. She will never speak to me again."

"If she doesn't——" He stopped.

"What?" I asked.

"She isn't worth bothering about," Owen concluded.

"Oh, you don't know."

"What was there, after all, so very dreadful? It's not as if you were in any way repulsive!"

He tried to persuade me to change my mind about going home as we walked toward the park gate, but I was firm. "Good-bye, Owen," I said. "Thank you for coming. I will write to you if there is anything to write about."

I got on a tram, and he stood on the footpath, looking after me.

CHAPTER LII

OWEN had cheered me up a little; I was glad I had come; and during my return journey I pondered the advice he had given me and decided that I must follow it. I waited till nine o'clock, by which hour I thought Gerald would probably have gone out, for I wanted to avoid him: then I went up to Derryaghy. So far as I could see, the only way was to call just as usual, and trust to luck to get a few minutes with Katherine alone.

But at the door my courage failed me, and I stepped softly round to the terrace, and, standing hidden in the deep shadow of the house, looked to see who was in the room. The curtain was as usual undrawn and the room was full of lamplight. They were all there. Gerald was sprawling on his back on the sofa; Katherine was working at her table-cloth, her head bent over it so that I could not see her face; Miss Dick was writing; Mrs. Carroll was playing "Patience." Presently Katherine looked up, and, for a moment or two, before she returned to her work, I saw her gaze out into the darkness. The others, except Mrs. Carroll, had their backs to me; a small fire was burning in the grate. I stood there under a kind of fascination. The impression was strange, and even slightly weird. Looking in upon them, all so silent and so unconscious of my presence, I had a peculiar feeling that, if I came right into their line of vision, they would still not see me. I had a strange feeling that I was actually invisible, and, moreover, that I was not the only watcher there, and, that if we were invisible to the inmates of the room, we might not be invisible to each other. Other faces, pale and dim, peered in at other windows; the house was surrounded by shadowy presences—shadowy forms that hovered outside here on the terrace, that glided up and down the wide, dark, creaking staircase, or stood motionless in the upper rooms. I stepped back and looked up at the long line of black, unlit windows, with just here and there a glimmering light. And I felt as if I no longer belonged to the same world as the occupants of the room I watched. I was but a memory, a ghost; my place was upstairs; in dim passages; by trembling blinds, pulled aside for just a moment that we might peep out; in shadowy rooms; behind doors whose handles the timid maid, hurrying by in her glimmer of unsteady candlelight, feared to turn. I was the breath that set the curtains at the bed's head trembling; the faint sound as of a chair pushed back on the upper floor; the draught—was it a draught?—that made the lamp-flame flicker; the pale reflection passing across the looking-glass and gone before there was time to strike a match. I was that mysterious something one turned one's head quickly to see, and did not see; the cold touch that awakened just before dawn; the gray, ghostly figure sitting by the window in the first wan light, and that was no longer there when one rubbed one's eyes; the tapping on the window-pane as of a leaf—the tapping that must surely be only a leaf moved by the wind.

I do not know how long I stood there: it may have been but a few minutes, yet it was long enough for me to realize that the simple act of entering the room was become an impossibility. It would have required too violent an effort, too sharp and brutal a wrench, an effort I shrank from as from physical pain. I must write to Katherine. How could I go in there as if nothing had happened? If she came out on to the terrace I might find courage to speak to her, but she would not come. Gerald, on the other hand, almost certainly would; and if he discovered me prowling about like this what would he think? I slipped away, then, like a veritable ghost, my footsteps making no noise upon the faded grass.

CHAPTER LIII

I wrote that night to Katherine, but she did not reply to my letter, and I had no heart to send a second. Two days passed, during which I did not go near Derryaghy, but took to gardening, and when Gerald came down on the second afternoon I offered this as my excuse for not going with him. The fact was that I felt uncomfortable in his society, not knowing how much he knew. He had witnessed my discomfiture on the night Katherine had cut me, and of course he must have questioned her afterwards.

During these days I made one or two attempts to come to a more cordial relation with my father; yet it seemed to me that he suspected the genuineness of my timid advances, and at all events his unresponsiveness discouraged me from repeating them.

On the evening of the third day, having nothing else to do, I strolled listlessly in the direction of the field occupied by the booths of the steam-circus proprietors. It was recognizable from afar by a luminous cloud that hung above it like a curtain of fire against the night. The wind was blowing from that direction, and, as I advanced, my ears were filled with the rough music blared out by a couple of steam-organs, a music broken every now and again by short convulsive shrieks as of demoniac laughter. Swings, shooting-galleries, throwing-competitions—all were in the full energy of life when I approached; but the chief centres of attraction were the two hobby-horse machines, brightly painted and flashing with mirrors and gilding. I mingled in the outer ring of spectators about the larger of these two wheeling monsters, and stood gazing at it, as it turned round swiftly and rhythmically to the throbbing din of brazen pipes. White puffs of steam shot up against the black sky in the coloured glare of naphtha lamps. Girls with flushed, excited faces, tossed hair and shining eyes, leaned sideways from the horses' backs, laughed, swayed in a kind of innocent abandon toward their accompanying sweethearts. Arms were round waists, the pops of guns mingled with the blare of the music, the shrieks of the steam-whistle, the shrillness of feminine voices. Standing there, in lonely contemplation of all this Dionysian revelry, I felt as hopelessly out of touch with it, as if I had wandered thither from another planet. Suddenly I felt a hand laid lightly on my arm, and looking round saw the laughing face of Annie Breen.

She asked me if I had seen their Willie, but without waiting for an answer went on to chatter about all the people who were here to-night. A whole crowd had come over from Castlewellan; and there were a lot of excursionists from Belfast, who had missed the last train, and nobody knew where they were going to sleep, for there wasn't a room to be had in the hotels. Wasn't it fun? They would have to stay out all night; and if it rained wouldn't it be awful?

"There's room for two there," she cried, "those white horses. Ellen Gibson and Brian Seery are getting off."

I made a half-hearted movement forward, but in my lack of enthusiasm was ousted by a more eager couple whose eyes had been as quick as Annie's. There was no hint of reproach, however, in the smile the girl turned on me.

"We'll get them next time, and I'd just as soon watch, anyway. Wouldn't you?"

"There's Willie over there," I suggested. "Perhaps you would like——"

But she interrupted me. "I don't care about the horses. Only maybe I'm keeping you: maybe you're waiting for somebody?"

"No," I answered, hurriedly.

"Let's go round the tents then. Will you?"

We moved over to the one which appeared to have attracted the largest crowd. In the foreground, just beyond the barrier, was a long counter or table covered with cheap ornaments, artificial jewelry, and boxes of unhealthy-looking cigars; and behind this, set in tiers against the canvas back of the tent itself, were three rows of grotesque, painted, wooden busts, waiting to be knocked down. Surrounded by a group of encouraging spectators, George Edge was stolidly bombarding these figures with a good deal of success, though what he intended to do with his prizes it was difficult to imagine. We stood and watched him, and every now and again a loud smack was instantly followed by the disappearance of one of the dolls.

"Have a throw you," said Annie. "Go on. I'm sure you can do it better than him."

An obliging lady handed me three wooden balls, about the size of tennis balls, in exchange for two pence; but in absence of mind I came within an ace of sending the first of these at the head of the proprietor himself, which just then bobbed up close to the dolls, and in features, colouring, and expression, startlingly resembled them. At my third shot I was successful, and Annie chose a gold and turquoise cross. We passed on to the next booth, leaving

George still pegging away, with a perseverance that must have
cost him about half-a-crown already. Annie herself now won a
walking-stick, by throwing a wooden ring over it, and this trophy
was presented to me.

"Let's get out of the glare for a minute," she said unexpectedly.
"It's that hot with all the lights and things I can't hardly breathe."

We passed behind the tents, and a few steps brought us into
shadow, and a few steps more to a bank under a hawthorn-hedge,
where we sat down. I had nothing to say to her, and, as it did not
seem to matter to Annie whether we talked or not, I pursued my
own thoughts. She leaned up against me confidingly, but I was
hardly more conscious of her presence than of the bank upon
which I sat. I was thinking, and presently I put a question to her,
put it perfectly seriously. "Suppose, Annie," I began very deliberately,—"suppose you were friends with somebody—somebody
like me, say. Suppose you knew he was very fond of you, and,
one day, when you were alone together, without asking you if he
might, he put his arms round you and kissed you—would you be
very angry with him, so angry that you would never speak to him
nor look at him again?"

I kept my eyes fixed upon the ground as I awaited her reply,
and I awaited it with some anxiety. It seemed to me a long while
coming. All at once I felt two warm lips pressed against my cheek.
I was so taken aback by the unexpected nature of this answer that
I'm afraid I drew away from it. I understood that poor Annie had
seen in my question only a somewhat timid method of courtship.
It was distinctly awkward. She leaned her head sentimentally on
my shoulder, and we sat in this absurd position for several minutes,
while I had time to reflect on the hopeless inconsistency of feminine nature. As soon as I could, without hurting her feelings, I
got up. "We must try the hobby-horses now," I said, with feeble
sprightliness, seizing on the only pretext I could think of to escape
from a disagreeable situation.

Annie rose too, but with no great alacrity: in fact, she remarked
that she was sick of the hobby-horses. I pretended not to believe
her. We went back to the spot where she had first spoken to me,
and, when the machine came to a standstill, secured two rider-

less steeds. Mine was on the outside and Annie's of course next to it, but we were no sooner in possession of them than I became aware of Katherine and Gerald among the spectators quite close to us. I looked the other way, and I felt my face grow crimson. It seemed to me that the engine-man would never set us in motion. Already we appeared to have been waiting for an eternity. Annie was laughing and chattering, and I answered at random, though, indeed, to the kind of remarks she was making, any sort of answer served. Had she, too, seen the Dales? for her vivacity had suddenly become much more noisy and familiar, with something about it that smacked rather of town than of country? I noticed that all the other riders were obviously in couples, and that most of the youths were supporting their partners in a strikingly gallant fashion. Annie had already given me permission to follow their example by telling me half a dozen times she was sure she'd fall off. I didn't care very much whether she did or not. At last, with a shrill and frivolous scream, the huge construction began to revolve slowly, and our horses to move up and down on their polished brass rods. We swept by within a yard or two of Katherine and Gerald, but I looked straight before me, my face burning. I would have liked to pretend that I was there for a solitary ride, quite independent of Annie, but her manner made any such hypocrisy perfectly futile. Round we came a second time, and a third, gathering velocity at every moment. Annie had taken off her hat and put it on my horse's head, and her skirts streamed out behind, and flapped against my right leg.

"Peter!"

It was Katherine's voice. She had called my name. It came to me through the night, and an indescribable emotion shook me. I could not have spoken: my eyes were blinded with tears: and again the huge machine swept round. But in the place where Katherine and Gerald had been I could no longer see them. Where were they gone? The organ belched its coarse music, the steam throbbed, the whistle hooted, we rushed on faster and faster. Where were they? She had called me. Perhaps they had gone home. I could not wait any longer, but slipped from my horse's back. Annie screamed; the man who was going round collecting the fares while the ride was in progress made a grab at me; but I jumped—jumped and fell headlong, rolling over and knocking all the breath out of my body, though luckily not breaking any bones. Instantly there was commotion. A crowd gathered about me, and everybody seemed to think I had either gone mad or been seized with a fit. I scrambled to my feet as soon as I had pumped a little wind into myself, and, without waiting to brush the dust from my clothes, without answering any of the questions that poured in upon me from all sides, pushed my way through the people, who appeared inclined to detain me by force, and hurried, as fast as my still rather breathless condition would allow, in pursuit of Katherine and Gerald. Alas, I could see no sign of them. They had vanished as completely and mysteriously as Persephone on that summer morning in the meadows. I clambered through the hedge out on to the road, but there was no one there. I ran on till I reached the turning, but there was no one there either, and I knew I had missed them, for the road here lay straight and bare in both directions. I stood still by the sea-wall. I could not go back. The glare and din were now become impossible, to say nothing of Annie, whom I had flouted in so unscrupulous a fashion.

I took my old path over the golf-links till I reached the hollow where I always came when I wanted to be quite alone. I flung myself down on the soft, white, powdery sand, among the thin gray grasses, in the pallid starlight. My heart was surging with emotions, at once happy and desolating. I could not understand what had occurred; only I heard again and again the sound of my name, as it had come to me in that loved voice through the night.

I lay there for a long time. I was crying, I think, but I did not know I was crying, though I kept wiping my tears away. I was unconscious of everything around me, I was blind and deaf, and it was only when I felt a hand on my shoulder that I looked up, startled, and saw Katherine bending over me.

"Peter, what is the matter? Is it my fault?"

Her voice was all gentleness; in her face a beautiful tenderness; but I could not speak.

"It is nothing," I stammered out at last. "Only I thought—you were never going to speak to me again, and—"

"I was horrid. I can't think now why I was so horrid. Forget about it, Peter dear, won't you? Tell me you will."

"It was my fault," I muttered. "It was all my fault."

"Never mind whose fault it was. Let us forget about it."

"I can't forget," I said. "It was my fault."

"But why—when I want you to? Can't you forget, even if you know I love you?"

I scrambled to my feet and stood facing her. "Do you really?" I faltered. "Don't say it if—if it is not true."

"It is true."

"How is it true?" I asked. "How much? Do you love me as much as you love Gerald?"

She hesitated, and it seemed to me that it was because she feared to wound me. "Yes," she said at last, in a low voice. There was something that touched me, through all my longing and pain, in her desire to be perfectly honest. "Better than Gerald. Better than anybody," she pursued, doubtfully, "better than anybody, I think, except mother."

I sighed; I could not help it.

She looked at me sadly. "Why aren't you content, Peter? Why do you always want more than I can give, when I have given you so much?"

"And Owen?" I asked, though I was ashamed of myself for doing so.

"I like Owen very much. I think he is very nice, but that is all. And now tell me you are content. I must go, and I shan't be happy unless I know you are."

"I am happy," I lied most dismally. I saw indeed that it was all hopeless, and that she would never understand.

"I will see you to-morrow. I can't stay now; Gerald is waiting for me over at the Club House."

"Where were you when I looked for you?" I asked. "I heard you call my name, and I jumped off, but when I went to look for you, you were gone."

"Miss Dick was with us, and she wanted to go home; but we went round the other way—not by the sea. We had to go all the way back with Miss Dick, but I got Gerald to come out again, for

I thought, I don't know why, I might find you here. And I'm very glad I came. I couldn't go on any longer without making it up. But I mustn't really wait now. I told Gerald I should only be five minutes. Good-night, Peter. Come to-morrow morning."

"Good-night."

She was gone, and I was left alone to whatever felicity I might be able to discover.

CHAPTER LIV

OF the days that followed our reconciliation I tried to make the most. Too much time already had been wasted and spoiled by clouds of jealousy and other troubles. I knew the kind of love Katherine offered me was very different from the kind of love I had desired, and in the old days dreamed of, but more than this I did not know, and some instinct kept me from trying to find out. We had become again such friends as we had been last year, and I lent myself to a certain protective quality in her affection for me, because I felt that it was in this way she could care for me most. From her point of view I knew that if I could have dropped back two or three years nearer to my childhood it would really have been preferable. She would have liked to pet me and tell me stories.

What her brother thought of our quarrel, and of our making up again, I never heard. He gave no sign of having noticed anything. I had ceased, indeed, to see very much of him, for he had taken to knocking about the Club House and the hotel more and more. This left Katherine and me almost wholly to each other's company. I saw her each morning, afternoon, and evening, and I moved through day after day in a kind of dream, as if this ideal life were to last for ever.

One afternoon I went up to Derryaghy as usual, but the servant who answered the door told me Mrs. Carroll wished to see me, and when I was shown into the morning-room I found her there alone.

"Oh, I wanted to speak to you, Peter," she said. "Katherine is out with her mother, who arrived an hour ago. They went out after lunch."

I stared my surprise. "I didn't know she was coming!" I murmured.

"Neither did anybody else. She didn't even send a telegram."

From her tone I gathered that Mrs. Carroll was not altogether pleased by this unexpected visit. "What has she come *for*?" I asked.

"That's just what I want you to tell me. The woman is raging with me, and now we're alone we'd better have the whole matter out."

"But what matter?" I inquired innocently. "What have *I* to do with it?"

"Goodness knows! Sit down, child; I want to talk to you seriously. . . . . Miss Dick said something to me more than once, but Miss Dick is a perfect fool when it comes to questions of this kind, and I paid no attention to her." She looked at me. "Don't you understand? It is about Katherine—about you and Katherine. Mrs. Dale's visit is the result of some letter which Katherine sent to her, and which I haven't seen. How was I to imagine such things? I had always looked upon you as children, and now she arrives, simply furious, and accuses me of not looking after her daughter."

I had begun to blush.

"Tell me exactly how much there is in it all?" Mrs. Carroll continued. "You are the only person who appears to have any common-sense."

"What does she say?" I asked ingenuously.

"She says— Oh! what doesn't she say? She says she's going to take Katherine home with her to-morrow, and that she thought she should have been able to trust me!"

I looked at her helplessly, but made no reply.

"I knew you liked Katherine," Mrs. Carroll went on, "but it never occurred to me there was any particular reason why you shouldn't like her—nor, indeed, do I see any now. They didn't expect, I suppose, that she was going to spend all her time with a couple of old women like me and Miss Dick!" She paused. "You *are* very fond of her, aren't you?"

"Yes," I replied, as if I were repeating my catechism.

"And apparently she is fond of you."

I shook my head. Then, as she looked at me interrogatively, "Not like that—not in the same way," I murmured.

Mrs. Carroll continued to regard me. "Not like what? What do you mean?"

"She doesn't even understand," I pursued.

Mrs. Carroll's face altered, grew graver, though not less kind. "Then there *is* something in it? You really care—very much?"

"Yes."

"But——" her perplexity seemed to increase.

I waited, twirling my straw-hat on my knee, and only now and then glancing up. She eyed me thoughtfully. "You know it is all quite impossible," she brought out slowly. "And you're so ridiculously young!" For a moment she smiled. Then she put her hand sympathetically upon mine, which rested on the arm of my chair. Yet I could see she still more or less regarded the affair in the light of a sentimental fancy that would dissolve as quickly as dew under the sun.

I got up. "I think I'll go now," I said, plucking at the ribbon of my hat.

"I'll not keep you, Peter, if you want to go. Remember, I'm not scolding you, or angry with you in any way," she added. "As I told you, I see no reason why you shouldn't be fond of Katherine. I can perfectly trust you. It is just that you are a boy, and of course such things can come to nothing so far as you are concerned; whereas, in Katherine's case, and especially since she is a year older than you, it is quite different. Her mother probably has her eye on a husband for her already. That, I am afraid, is the secret of all this indignation. However, I've taken your part. I told her exactly what you are—that you are a gentleman, and would never do anything dishonourable; that a word would be enough; and that it was perfectly ridiculous to talk of taking Katherine home before the natural end of her visit, which will be on Friday or Saturday of this week. If she *does* take her, not one of them shall ever enter this house again. That, at least, is certain. I'm not going to have any nonsense about it. Will you dine here to-night?"

I shook my head.

"Where are you going now?"

"Out into the woods just."

She kissed me. "Well, whatever happens, I'll promise that Katherine shan't go without saying good-bye to you. Be a good boy, and come to see me to-morrow."

CHAPTER LV

WHEN I left Mrs. Carroll I did not go out at once, but scribbled first a note to Katherine, telling her I had gone to the summer-house, and should wait for her there all afternoon. I then went in search of Jim, who had always been my friend, and whom I could rely upon absolutely. I found him working with Thomas in the greenhouses, and, as soon as I could attract his attention, I beckoned him outside. He was a very different Jim from the one who had climbed a ladder to see my skin peeling off, though he had the same round rosy candid face, like a ripe russet apple, and though he still played doleful tunes on his flute. But he had developed amazingly: he had grown into a strapping big fellow, with limbs like a youthful Hercules. When I explained to him that I wanted him to give a note to Miss Dale, but that nobody must see him do it, he promised to try his best.

I went on to the summer-house and lay down among the bracken close by. I had been there fully two hours before I saw Katherine coming. She smiled brightly as I rose from my ferny bed to greet her.

"Why did I come without an umbrella?" she exclaimed gaily. "It's just going to pour!" And she turned to look at the heavy clouds that were gliding up rapidly against the wind.

"You can shelter in the summer-house," I said, laconically.

"I loathe summer-houses, especially when they're like this old thing, crammed with earwigs and spiders."

"The rain is going to be heavy: you'd better come in now," I went on, without attempting to emulate her lightness of manner. I dusted the rough seat for her with my pocket-handkerchief, in silence, just as the first big drops came pattering down on the leaves.

She sat down, and I stood near the door, looking at her. "Mrs. Carroll told me your mother arrived to-day, because of some letter of yours about me."

Katherine coloured a little. "I know," she answered, eagerly. "It's awfully silly of mamma. I've been talking to her about it."

"And you are to go home at once—to-morrow—perhaps this evening."

She laughed. "Certainly not this evening. How could we? And at any rate, we should have been going in a few days. But I told mamma she was taking it all absurdly seriously, and behaving exactly like a furious parent in a novel."

"It is serious to me," I said, quietly, "though to you it may be amusing." That she should laugh in this way hurt me deeply.

It had grown rapidly dark, and now a heavy rain began, cold and sad, sweeping through the trees, very soon making it plain that the summer-house was in need of repair. From the distance there came the crying of a sea-gull, a mournful, solitary note.

"Don't be angry with me, Peter," said Katherine, coming to the door and looking out. "I know it was stupid of me to write, but I never dreamt of mamma coming over like this. . . . . Why has it got so dark?"

Before I could answer there came a blinding flash of lightning, accompanied, nearly instantaneously, by a hideous din of thunder, which seemed to burst out just over us. A blank silence succeeded this ear-splitting crash, and Katherine said, "Some tree must have gone!"

"I wish it had been this summer-house," I muttered bitterly.

She looked at me, her face grown graver. The flash was followed by no other, but the rain continued in a fierce downpour, beating through our flimsy shelter, and streaming down the paths in brown muddy rivulets.

"I can't understand why mamma should have made such a fuss," Katherine went on, but no longer in the same tone, though I knew well enough the alteration in it was due merely to what I had said. "She is usually very sensible."

"How can you be so indifferent?" I asked, in a rough voice, for her calmness exasperated me.

"I'm not indifferent. I'm sorry I wrote. But we should have been going in three or four days, at any rate. You know that." Her manner was tinged with a faint reproach.

I answered nothing, and she went on. "It is getting lighter—the rain will soon be over."

"Do you want to go?" I asked furiously. "Don't let me keep you if you do!"

"Why do you speak like that, Peter? I told you I was sorry."

"This is the last time I shall see you alone."

"Nonsense."

"If you are going to-morrow, will you promise to meet me to-night somewhere—here—or on the golf-links?"

"I can't possibly. There are people coming to dinner. Won't *you* come—or come in afterwards, at least?"

"Shall I see you by yourself if I do?"

"By myself?"

"Will you come out here with me?"

She sighed at my unreasonableness. "How can I? You know mamma and the others will be there, and how can I leave them? But say you'll come."

"I certainly won't," I answered sullenly. "What does it matter to you whether I do or not?"

I felt her lips touch my cheek. Her face was wet and cold with the rain. I put my arms round her very gently, and kissed her hair and her cheek, but no more than that, for I knew her own embrace had been given merely to console me, and because it was for the last time. Her dark eyes caressed me, and she smiled a little. She laid her hand on my shoulder. "Will you walk back to the house with me now, Peter? You are not angry with me?"

"No," I answered.

"I can't stay any longer, because mamma knows I came out, and she will suspect it was to meet you. She is not so bad about it as she was when she first arrived. I managed to convince her that she had been alarming herself unnecessarily."

"Very unnecessarily," I thought, but I said nothing.

I walked back with her, and then on down the drive and home.

CHAPTER LVI

I was writing to Owen when my father brought me Katherine's letter. It was to say good-bye to me, and there was a veiled reproach at my not having come to the station to see them off. She had looked out for me up to the last moment; so that in the end it was really I who had failed! I smiled dimly.

As I write it now, in this quiet, gray, autumn morning, it appears to me that the thought then hovering at the back of my mind was, after all, not so very foolish. Death, coming without disease, without weakness, before life has grown stale, before illusions have been shattered and innocence marred;—simply upon the bright, fresh comedy of life, the dropping of a dark, rapid curtain.

I finished my letter to Owen, and addressed it; but when that was done I still sat on at the table, holding my pen, on which the ink had long since dried. Then I bent down and leaned my forehead upon Katherine's open letter. When I looked up the sun was shining in the garden, and shining in on me through the window; nothing had changed. . . . .

In the afternoon I went up to Derryaghy, where Mrs. Carroll received me. I spoke quite quietly to her, just as usual; but all I remember now is that there were some red dahlias in a bowl on the table, and that Mrs. Carroll proposed taking me to Paris for my Christmas holidays.

It was when I had left her and had gone out to walk in the woods, that I suddenly felt the full reality of what had happened. It meant that everything was finished, that I should never see Katherine again. I was filled with desolation, with a kind of sick feeling that my love had been superfluous, wasted, and perhaps distasteful. Last year I had been sorry to say good-bye to her; I had dreaded the new life opening out before me; but I had had the prospect of meeting her again at a year's end, and the belief that she cared for me and would remember me. Now there was nothing—nothing.

My grief was mingled with a kind of bitter, impotent rage

against I knew not what. I kicked a stick that lay in my path savagely out of the way, cursing it under my breath. I flung myself down among the bracken. Sometimes a kind of blank would come into my mind, and I would find myself staring stupidly at the trees, while for a few moments an altogether different thought would slip into my brain; then my grief would overwhelm me once more, and blot out the world.

But was this grief I felt? I do not know. It was different from what I felt later. It was something violent and maddening, sweeping over me in paroxysms, leaving me intervals of cold insensibility. And late that night, when, thoroughly wearied out, I went to bed, and from sheer exhaustion would be dropping off to sleep, from time to time it would pierce through my numbing senses, and waken me sharply, as if some one had violently pulled me, so that I would start up, yet for a moment not realize what it was that had wakened me.

I did not go back to Derryaghy on the next day or the next. I took long walks, and it was during these solitary rambles that the thought of death came irresistibly to me. I felt that my life was become an intolerable burden, and in my inexperience I imagined that the pain I felt now I should feel always. I thought of shooting myself, of taking poison, only I disliked the idea of other people knowing. Was there not a better way? I thought of swimming out so far that it would be impossible to return, but I dreaded the pain of suffocation. Then, two days before my time for leaving home, and when Owen had written saying that they expected me and that he would be at the station to meet me, there came a night of wind and rain, and it seemed to me I had found the solution to my problem.

Shortly before midnight, when my father's snores had become deep and regular, I stole out of the house, as I had so often done in the old days of our club. I had put on my overcoat, but under it I wore only my night-shirt, and I hurried down the road and across the golf-links in the cold, driving rain. When I reached an exposed spot, I took off my coat and lay down on the soaking ground, letting the wind and rain sweep over me. I lay there till morning. It did not matter if I were seen returning to the house then; it would simply be thought that I had gone out for an early bathe. As I staggered to my feet my limbs were so stiff and cramped that at first I could hardly hobble along, but after I had gone a little way it became easier.

I got into bed in my wet night-shirt, but I could not go to sleep. My head ached and I was shivering; yet a few minutes later I no longer felt cold; on the contrary, a burning heat seemed like a fire under my skin. I could not lie for two minutes without altering my position; and when I got up to dress I knew I was really ill. At breakfast I only pretended to eat. My father noticed there was something the matter and questioned me, when I answered that I was all right, and presently he left me to go to the school, which was being whitewashed and made ready for the re-opening next week. As for me, I was glad I should not have to repeat my experiment twice, and I had even a naïve curiosity as to the precise nature of my illness.

Before night I began to feel much worse. My father went out to a meeting in connection with church matters, and I was left alone. I should have gone to bed, had not the task of climbing two flights of stairs and undressing appeared almost insurmountable; so I half sat, half lay, in a chair, with my eyes shut and my head leaning back. I was extremely thirsty, and at every breath I drew my side hurt me, the pain being increased by the fact that I had begun to cough a little. It had all come on so quickly that I wondered if I should die that night.

When my father came in he immediately saw I was worse, and sent me to bed, giving me something hot to drink; but all that night I hardly slept, and in the morning he went for Doctor O'Brian. By that time I had almost forgotten the cause of my illness; what had led me to seek it; whether I desired it to be fatal or not. I was examined, stethoscoped, asked questions, gazed at. "Acute pneumonia." I caught the words through a kind of lethargy into which I had fallen. They were talking together, my father and the doctor, but neither could understand how the disease had developed so rapidly. . . . .

CHAPTER LVII

AND, after all, I failed! I did not die. I got better, though not quite well, for my lungs remained delicate, and in October Mrs. Carroll took me to be examined by a specialist. I was examined, sounded, tapped, a sample of my blood taken, and other odious things done to me, before it was finally decided that I must go abroad. I listened to the discussion that followed, taking no part in it myself, but simply sitting on the sofa in the consulting-room.

"For the winter, I suppose?"

"For the winter certainly."

"And afterwards?"

"Afterwards? I'm afraid it is impossible to say. There is no use making promises which may never be fulfilled. Would there be anything to prevent his living abroad always, supposing it should be the best thing for him?"

"There is only the difficulty of his future—that is, of a profession. He was to have gone to Oxford next year."

"I see. It is certainly unfortunate. But apart from that, there is nothing?"

"To prevent his living abroad? Not that I know of."

There were such things as tutors, it then appeared; young gentlemen of excellent scholastic attainments, just fresh from one or other of the Universities, who could be induced to combine the roles of travelling-companion, mentor, and pedagogue.

And on this hopeful note we came away. We had lunch in town, and caught the next train home. When we arrived at Newcastle we took one of the station cars. I was staying at Derryaghy to complete my convalescence; so Mrs. Carroll stopped at our house to give my father the news, telling me to drive on by myself. The October sunlight, still with a little of the warmth of summer in it, slanted through the trees, as I drove in at the lodge-gate. There was a charming autumnal languor in the still air—a kind of dreamy, happy beauty, which made me think of some verses of La Fontaine's:—

"J'étais libre et vivais seul et sans amour;
L'innocente beauté des jardins et des jours
Allait faire à jamais le charme de ma vie."

And, far out on the dark sea, a white sail gleamed in the sun.

The thought of leaving it all behind me, and of passing the rest of my life in exile, was too painful to dwell upon; yet I knew that, once I went away, I might very easily never be back. It had struck me that the doctor had been anything but optimistic, and I knew this meant that my chance must be a pretty poor one.

I went upstairs to my own room. I sat down in my old window-seat and began a letter to Owen, which I did not finish, for it occurred to me that, later on, I might have more definite news to give him; and, at any rate, if I were going away, he must come down first to stay with me. With my incomplete letter before me I sat dreaming. I wondered if, in years to come, another boy would have this room as his own, and sit in this window-seat; and if his thoughts would for a moment perhaps touch mine? All *my* thoughts would be dead then; my dreams vanished; the life that had unfolded here be gone out. A feeling of sadness stole over me. I had been a very little chap when I had first taken possession of this room. If the ghost of that little boy, who had been me, could only come back, how I should have hugged him! For I loved him: he seemed quite different from the "me" who was thinking about him now. Only he was gone, and just one person in the world knew anything about him, and he, too, I supposed, as years passed would forget. . . . .

"Why are you sitting up here in the cold, child?"

Mrs. Carroll had opened the door and was speaking to me. "How long have you been here? Come down to tea."

I looked round and saw that the room had filled with dusk. "Oh, not very long." I smiled. "I'm not cold." But I shivered slightly as I spoke.

"That means you have been here ever since you came in. It is really very wrong of you, Peter. The fire is laid, and all you had to do was to put a match to it."

I followed her downstairs. There was no one in the drawing-room, and I was glad we were going to be by ourselves. I sat on the hearth-rug, hugging my knees, gazing into the red, glowing grate.

"Is Miss Dick out?" I asked.

"She went out to tea."

I waited till the servant had come in and cleared away the tea-things. Then I said, "I have something to tell you."

Mrs. Carroll, her plump, rather large hands moving swiftly and deftly amid soft, fleecy wool, was knitting what looked remarkably like an under-garment for me. "Yes, dear," she replied.

But instead of proceeding I asked a question; "Won't it cost a great deal, my going away—with a tutor, and all that?"

"Not very much. It is of no importance."

"But you will be paying for it, won't you?" I urged.

"My dear child, why do you want to discuss such things now?"

"I have a reason."

"I don't think it can be a good one."

"If I were related to you—if I were your nephew—it would be different."

"What would be different?"

"If I were worth it it would be different too. But I'm not."

"Aren't you?" Her needles clicked placidly.

"Why should you think me so?"

"Because, I suppose, from the days when you were quite a little boy, you have been the principal thing I have had to think about. There was a time when I tried very hard, and very selfishly, I'm afraid, to be allowed to look after you altogether, when I wanted this house to be your home."

"Suppose I told you that all this—all my illness—was not accidental?"

Mrs. Carroll displayed no alarm. "I don't know what you mean, Peter, I'm sure," she said, gently, disengaging her ball of wool from Miss Dick's cat, who had stretched out a tentative paw.

"I mean that I did it myself," I answered, bringing it all out at last. "I did it on purpose. . . . I wanted to die, to kill myself, and I thought of this way. I went out and lay on the golf-links one whole night, in the rain, with nothing on but my night-shirt; and next morning I took ill."

Mrs. Carroll said nothing, but she had stopped knitting. I felt her hand rest on my head.

"Is that true, Peter?" she asked at last, after a long pause, and in a low voice.

"It's true." I stared into the fire.

She was again silent, but she did not draw away her hand. "Why did you do this?" she asked presently.

"Because I felt miserable."

"But—but it was a dreadful thing to do! Don't you know that?" Her voice trembled slightly.

I got on my knees. I put my arms round her neck and pressed my cheek against hers. "I have spoiled everything, I have made a mess of everything," I muttered quickly. "I am not very old; but I have made a mess of any life I have had."

She drew my head down on her breast and held me close. For some time she did not speak.

"It will all come right, if you try," she said at last. "The beginning is not everything."

"It is not for myself I care. It is for you."

"For me, then." She paused. "But for me you are what you have always been and always will be, since I have no boy of my own. You are my son, the one being whom I love. Your future is what I think of and make plans for; and whenever I pray it is that you may be happy."

THE END

ALSO AVAILABLE FROM VALANCOURT BOOKS

MARTYN GOFF	The Plaster Fabric
	The Youngest Director
	Indecent Assault
STEPHEN GREGORY	The Cormorant
THOMAS HINDE	Mr. Nicholas
	The Day the Call Came
CLAUDE HOUGHTON	I Am Jonathan Scrivener
	This Was Ivor Trent
STANLEY KAUFFMANN	The Tightrope (The Philanderer)
CYRIL KERSH	The Aggravations of Minnie Ashe
GERALD KERSH	Fowlers End
	Nightshade and Damnations
FRANCIS KING	To the Dark Tower
	Never Again
	An Air That Kills
	The Dividing Stream
	The Dark Glasses
	The Man on the Rock
C.H.B. KITCHIN	The Sensitive One
	Birthday Party
	Ten Pollitt Place
	The Book of Life
	A Short Walk in Williams Park
HILDA LEWIS	The Witch and the Priest
JOHN LODWICK	Brother Death
KENNETH MARTIN	Aubade
	Waiting for the Sky to Fall
MICHAEL MCDOWELL	The Amulet
	The Elementals
MICHAEL NELSON	Knock or Ring
	A Room in Chelsea Square
BEVERLEY NICHOLS	Crazy Pavements
OLIVER ONIONS	The Hand of Kornelius Voyt
J.B. PRIESTLEY	Benighted
	The Doomsday Men
	The Other Place
	The Magicians
	Saturn Over the Water
	The Thirty-First of June
	The Shapes of Sleep
	Salt Is Leaving

PETER PRINCE	Play Things
PIERS PAUL READ	Monk Dawson
FORREST REID	Following Darkness
	The Spring Song
	Brian Westby
	The Tom Barber Trilogy
	Denis Bracknel
GEORGE SIMS	Sleep No More
	The Last Best Friend
ANDREW SINCLAIR	The Facts in the Case of E.A. Poe
	The Raker
COLIN SPENCER	Panic
DAVID STOREY	Radcliffe
	Pasmore
	Saville
MICHAEL TALBOT	The Delicate Dependency
RUSSELL THORNDIKE	The Slype
	The Master of the Macabre
JOHN TREVENA	Sleeping Waters
JOHN WAIN	Hurry on Down
	The Smaller Sky
	Strike the Father Dead
	A Winter in the Hills
KEITH WATERHOUSE	There is a Happy Land
	Billy Liar
COLIN WILSON	Ritual in the Dark
	Man Without a Shadow
	The World of Violence
	The Philosopher's Stone
	The God of the Labyrinth

FOR MORE INFORMATION AND A COMPLETE LIST OF TITLES, PLEASE VISIT
OUR WEBSITE AT WWW.VALANCOURTBOOKS.COM